Dear Reader,

Thank you for taking a chance on my book. If you're currently holding it in your hand, that means you're into (or thinking of exploring): dark romance, angst, intense groveling, a highly questionable, morally grey hero, and an enemies-to-lovers with push and pull and A LOT of spice.

You've come to the right place. Please make yourself comfortable.

Vicious isn't the first enemies-to-lovers romance I've written (that title is saved for *Sparrow*), but it is certainly one of the more memorable ones.

There's a red flag... and then there's an entire carnival. Baron "Vicious" Spencer definitely fits into the latter category.

So buckle up, take a deep breath, and step into the world of the Sinners of Saint, and the origin of the LJverse.

Enjoy,

ABOUT THE AUTHOR

L.J. Shen is a *USA Today, Wall Street Journal, Washington Post* and #1 Amazon Kindle Store bestselling author of contemporary romance books. She writes angsty books, unredeemable antiheroes who are in Elon Musk's tax bracket, and sassy heroines who bring them to their knees (for more reasons than one). HEAs and groveling are guaranteed. She lives in Florida with her husband, her three sons, and a disturb-ingly active imagination.

Website: authorljshen.com
Facebook: authorljshen
Instagram: @authorljshen
TikTok: @authorljshen
Pinterest: @authorljshen

VICIOUS

L.J. SHEN

HODDER &
STOUGHTON

First published in 2016 by L.J. Shen
This edition published in Great Britain in 2025 by Hodder & Stoughton Limited
An Hachette UK company

The authorised representative in the EEA is Hachette Ireland, 8 Castlecourt Centre,
Dublin 15, D15 XTP3, Ireland (email: info@hbgi.ie)

1

Copyright © L.J. Shen 2016

The right of L.J. Shen to be identified as the Author of the Work has been asserted
by her in accordance with the Copyright, Designs and Patents Act 1988.

Cover and internal design © 2024 by Sourcebooks

All rights reserved. No part of this publication may be reproduced, stored
in a retrieval system, or transmitted, in any form or by any means without
the prior written permission of the publisher, nor be otherwise circulated
in any form of binding or cover other than that in which it is published and
without a similar condition being imposed on the subsequent purchaser.

All characters in this publication are fictitious and any resemblance to real persons,
living or dead, is purely coincidental.

A CIP catalogue record for this title is available from the British Library

Paperback ISBN 978 1 399 74348 8

Typeset in Adobe Caslon Pro

Printed and bound in Great Britain by Clays Ltd, Elcograf S.p.A.

Hodder & Stoughton policy is to use papers that are natural, renewable
and recyclable products and made from wood grown in sustainable forests.
The logging and manufacturing processes are expected to conform
to the environmental regulations of the country of origin.

Hodder & Stoughton Limited
Carmelite House
50 Victoria Embankment
London EC4Y 0DZ

www.hodder.co.uk

To Karen O'Hara and Josephine McDonnell.

PLAYLIST

"Bad Things"—Machine Gun Kelly & Camila Cabello
"With or Without You"—U2
"Unsteady"—X Ambassadors
"Fell in Love with a Girl"—The White Stripes
"Baby It's You"—Smith
"Nightcall"—Kravinsky
"Last Nite"—The Strokes
"Teardrop"—Massive Attack
"Superstar"—Sonic Youth
"Vienna"—Billy Joel

NOTE

In Japanese culture, the significance of the cherry blossom tree dates back hundreds of years. The cherry blossom represents the fragility and magnificence of life. It's a reminder of how beautiful life is, almost overwhelmingly so, but that it is also heartbreakingly short.

As are relationships.

Be wise. Let your heart lead the way. And when you find someone who's worth it—never let them go.

CHAPTER ONE
EMILIA

My grandmama once told me that love and hate are the same feelings experienced under different circumstances. The passion is the same. The pain is the same. That weird thing that bubbles in your chest? Same. I didn't believe her until I met Baron Spencer and he became my nightmare.

Then my nightmare became my reality.

I thought I'd escaped him. I was even stupid enough to think he'd forgotten I ever existed.

But when he came back, he hit harder than I ever thought possible.

And just like a domino—I fell.

TEN YEARS AGO

I'd only been inside the mansion once before, when my family first came to Todos Santos. That was two months ago. That day, I stood rooted in place on the same ironwood flooring that never creaked.

That first time, Mama had elbowed my ribs. "You know this is the toughest floor in the world?"

She failed to mention it belonged to the man with the toughest heart in the world.

I couldn't for the life of me understand why people with so much money would spend it on such a depressing house. Ten bedrooms. Thirteen bathrooms. An indoor gym and a dramatic staircase. The best amenities money could buy...and except for the tennis court and sixty-five-foot pool, they were all in black.

Black choked out every pleasant feeling you might possibly have as soon as you walked through the big iron-studded doors. The interior designer must've been a medieval vampire, judging from the cold, lifeless colors and the giant iron chandeliers hanging from the ceilings. Even the floor was so dark that it looked like I was hovering over an abyss, a fraction of a second from falling into nothingness.

A ten-bedroom house, three people living in it—two of them barely ever there—and the Spencers had decided to house my family in the servants' apartment near the garage. It was bigger than our clapboard rental in Richmond, Virginia, but until that moment, it had still rubbed me the wrong way.

Not anymore.

Everything about the Spencer mansion was designed to intimidate. Rich and wealthy yet poor in so many ways. *These are not happy people*, I thought.

I stared at my shoes—the tattered white Vans lookalikes I doodled colorful flowers on to hide the fact that they were knockoffs—and swallowed, feeling insignificant even before *he* had belittled me. Before I even knew *him*.

"I wonder where he is?" Mama whispered.

As we stood in the hallway, I shivered at the echo that bounced off the bare walls. She wanted to ask if we could get paid two days early because we needed to buy medicine for my younger sister, Rosie.

"I hear something coming from that room." Mama pointed to a

door on the opposite side of the vaulted foyer. "You go knock. I'll go back to the kitchen to wait."

"*Me?* Why me?"

"Because," she said, pinning me with a stare that stabbed at my conscience, "Rosie's sick, and his parents are out of town. You're his age. He'll listen to you."

I did as I was told—not for Mama, for Rosie—without understanding the consequences. The next few minutes cost me my whole senior year and were the reason why I was ripped from my family at the age of eighteen.

Vicious thought I knew his secret.

I didn't.

All I remember was trudging toward the threshold of another dark door, my fist hovering inches from it before I heard the deep rasp of an old man.

"You know the drill, Baron."

A man. A smoker, probably.

"My sister told me you're giving her trouble again." The man slurred his words before raising his voice and slapping his palm against a hard surface. "I've had enough of you disrespecting her."

"Fuck you." I heard the composed voice of a younger man. He sounded…amused? "And fuck her too. Wait, is that why you're here, Daryl? You want a piece of your sister too? The good news is that she's open for business, if you have the buck to pay."

"Look at the mouth on you, you little cunt." *Slap*. "Your mother would've been proud."

Silence, and then, "Say another word about my mother, and I'll give you a real reason to get those dental implants you were talking about with my dad." The younger man's voice dripped venom, which made me think he might not be as young as Mama thought.

"Stay away," the younger voice warned. "I can beat the shit out of you now. As a matter of fact, I'm pretty tempted to do so. All. The. fucking. Time. I'm done with your shit."

"And what the hell makes you think you have a choice?" The older man chuckled darkly.

I felt his voice in my bones, like poison eating at my skeleton.

"Haven't you heard?" the younger man gritted out. "I like to fight. I like the pain. Maybe because it makes it so much easier for me to come to terms with the fact that I'm going to kill you one day. And I will, Daryl. One day, I will kill you."

I gasped, too stunned to move. I heard a loud smack, then someone tumbling down, dragging some items with him as he fell to the floor.

I was about to run—this conversation obviously wasn't meant for me to hear—but he caught me off guard. Before I knew what was happening, the door swung open, and I came face-to-face with a boy around my age. I say *a boy*, but there was nothing boyish about him.

The older man stood behind him, panting hard, hunched with his hands flat against a desk. Books were scattered around his feet, and his lip was cut and bleeding.

The room was a library. Soaring floor-to-ceiling walnut shelves full of hardbacks lined the walls. I felt a pang in my chest because I somehow knew there wasn't any way I'd ever be allowed in there again.

"What the fuck?" the teenage boy seethed. His eyes narrowed. They felt like the sights of a rifle aimed at me.

Seventeen? Eighteen? The fact that we were about the same age somehow made everything about the situation worse. I ducked my head, my cheeks flaming with enough heat to burn down the whole house.

"Have you been listening?" His jaw twitched.

I frantically shook my head no, but that was a lie. I'd always been a terrible liar.

"I didn't hear a thing, I swear." I choked on my words. "My mama works here. I was looking for her." Another lie.

I'd never been a scaredy-cat. I was always the brave one. But I didn't feel so brave at that moment. After all, I wasn't supposed to be there, in his house, and I definitely wasn't supposed to be listening to their argument.

The young man took a step closer, and I took a step back. His eyes were dead, but his lips were red, full, and very much alive. *This guy is going to break my heart if I let him.* The voice came from somewhere inside my head, and the thought stunned me because it made no sense at all. I'd never fallen in love before, and I was too anxious to even register his eye color or hairstyle, let alone the notion of ever having any feelings for the guy.

"What's your name?" he demanded. He smelled delicious—a masculine spice of boy-man, sweet sweat, sour hormones, and the faint trace of clean laundry, one of my mama's many chores.

"Emilia." I cleared my throat and extended my hand. "My friends call me Millie. Y'all can too."

His expression revealed zero emotion. "You're fucking done, *Emilia*." He drawled my name, mocking my Southern accent and not even acknowledging my hand with a glance.

I withdrew it quickly, embarrassment flaming my cheeks again.

"Wrong fucking place and wrong fucking time. Next time I find you anywhere inside my house, bring a body bag because you won't be leaving alive." He thundered past me, his muscular arm brushing my shoulder.

I choked on my breath. My gaze bolted to the older man, and our eyes locked. He shook his head and grinned in a way that made me want to fold into myself and disappear. Blood dripped from his lip onto his leather boot—black like his worn MC jacket. What was he doing in a place like this, anyway? He just stared at me, making no move to clean up the blood.

I turned around and ran, feeling the bile burning in my throat, threatening to spill over.

Needless to say, Rosie had to make do without her medicine that week, and my parents were paid not a minute earlier than when they were scheduled to be.

That was two months ago.

Today, when I walked through the kitchen and climbed the stairs, I had no choice.

I knocked on Vicious's bedroom door. His room was on the second floor at the end of the wide curved hallway, the door facing the floating stone staircase of the cave-like mansion.

I'd never been near Vicious's room, and I wished I could keep it that way. Unfortunately, my calculus book had been stolen. Whoever broke into my locker had wiped it clean of my stuff and left garbage inside. Empty soda cans, cleaning supplies, and condom wrappers spilled out the moment I opened the locker door.

Just another not-so-clever yet effective way for the students at All Saints High to remind me that I was nothing but the cheap help around here. By that point, I was so used to it I barely reddened at all. When all eyes in the hallway darted to me, snickers and chuckles rising out of every throat, I tilted my chin up and marched straight to my next class.

All Saints High was a school full of spoiled, overprivileged sinners. A school where if you failed to dress or act a certain way, you didn't belong. Rosie blended in better than I did, thank the Lord. But with a Southern drawl, offbeat style, and one of the most popular guys at school—that being Vicious Spencer—hating my guts, I didn't fit in.

What made it worse was that I didn't *want* to fit in. These kids didn't impress me. They weren't kind or welcoming or even very smart. They didn't possess any of the qualities I looked for in friends.

But I needed my textbook badly if I ever wanted to escape this place.

I knocked three times on the mahogany door of Vicious's bedroom. Rolling my lower lip between my fingers, I tried to suck in as much oxygen as I could, but it did nothing to calm the throbbing pulse in my neck.

Please don't be there…

Please don't be an ass...
Please...

A soft noise seeped from the crack under the door, and my body tensed.

Giggling.

Vicious never giggled. Heck, he hardly ever chuckled. Even his smiles were few and far between. No. The sound was undoubtedly female.

I heard him whisper in his raspy tone something inaudible that made her moan. My ears seared, and I anxiously rubbed my hands on the yellow cutoff denim shorts covering my thighs. Out of all the scenarios I could have imagined, this was by far the worst.

Him.

With another girl.

Who I hated before I even knew her name.

It didn't make any sense, yet I felt ridiculously angry.

But he was clearly there, and I was a girl on a mission.

"Vicious?" I called out, trying to steady my voice. I straightened my spine, even though he couldn't see me. "It's Millie. Sorry to interrupt y'all. I just wanted to borrow your calc book. Mine's lost, and I really need to get ready for that exam we have tomorrow." *God forbid you ever study for our exam yourself.* I took a silent breath.

He didn't answer, but I heard a sharp intake of breath—*the girl*—and the rustle of fabric and the noise of a zipper rolling. Down, I had no doubt.

I squeezed my eyes shut and pressed my forehead against the cool wood of his door.

Bite the bullet. Swallow your pride. This wouldn't matter in a few years. Vicious and his stupid antics would be a distant memory, the snooty town of Todos Santos just a dust-covered part of my past.

My parents had jumped at the chance when Josephine Spencer offered them jobs. They'd dragged us across the country to California because the health care was better and we didn't even need to pay rent. Mama was the Spencers' cook/housekeeper, and Daddy was part gardener and handyman. The previous live-in couple had quit, and it was no wonder. Pretty sure my parents weren't so keen on the jobs either. But opportunities like these were rare, and Josephine Spencer's mama was friends with my great-aunt, which was how they'd gotten the job.

I was planning on getting out of here soon. As soon as I got accepted to the first out-of-state college I'd applied to, to be exact. In order to do so, though, I needed a scholarship.

For a scholarship, I needed kick-ass grades.

And for kick-ass grades, I needed this textbook.

"Vicious," I ground out his stupid nickname. I knew he hated his real name, and for reasons beyond my grasp, I didn't want to upset him. "I'll grab the book and copy the formulas I need real quick. I won't borrow it long. Please." I gulped down the ball of frustration twisting in my throat. It was bad enough I'd had my stuff stolen—*again*—without having to ask Vicious for favors.

The giggling escalated. The high, screechy pitch sawed through my ears. My fingers tingled to push the door open and launch at him with my fists.

I heard his groan of pleasure and knew it had nothing to do with the girl he was with. He loved taunting me. Ever since our first encounter outside his library two months ago, he'd been hell-bent on reminding me that I wasn't good enough.

Not good enough for his mansion.

Not good enough for his school.

Not good enough for *his town*.

Worst part? It wasn't a figure of speech. It really *was* his town. Baron Spencer Jr.—dubbed Vicious for his cold, ruthless behavior—was the heir to one of the biggest family-owned fortunes in California. The Spencers owned a pipeline company, half of downtown Todos Santos—including the mall—and three corporate office parks. Vicious had enough money to take care of the next ten generations of his family.

But I didn't.

My parents were servants. We had to work for every penny. I didn't expect him to understand. Trust-fund kids never did. But I presumed he'd at least pretend, like the rest of them.

Education mattered to me, and at that moment, I felt robbed of it.

Because rich people had stolen my books.

Because this particular rich kid wouldn't even open the door to his room so I could borrow his textbook really quickly.

"Vicious!" My frustration got the better of me, and I slammed my palm flat against his door. Ignoring the throb it sent up my wrist, I continued, exasperated, "C'mon!"

I was close to turning around and walking away. Even if it meant I had to take my bike and ride all the way across town to borrow Sydney's books. Sydney was my only friend at All Saints High and the one person I liked in class.

But then I heard Vicious chuckling, and I knew the joke was on me. "I love to see you crawl. Beg for it, baby, and I'll give it to you," he said.

Not to the girl in his room.

To me.

I lost it. Even though I knew it was wrong. That he was winning.

I thrust the door open and barged into his room, strangling the handle with my fist, my knuckles white and burning.

My eyes darted to his king-size bed, barely stopping to take in the gorgeous mural above it—four white horses galloping into the darkness—or the elegant dark furniture. His bed looked like a throne, sitting in the middle of the room, big and high and draped in soft black satin. He was perched on the edge of his mattress, a girl who was in my PE class in his lap. Her name was Georgia, and her grandparents owned half the vineyards upstate in Carmel Valley. Georgia's long blond hair veiled one of his broad shoulders, and her Caribbean tan looked perfect and smooth against Vicious's pale complexion.

His dark-blue eyes—so dark they were almost black—locked on mine as he continued to kiss her ravenously—his tongue making several appearances—like she was made of cotton candy. I needed to look away but couldn't. I was trapped in his gaze, completely immobilized from the eyes down, so I arched an eyebrow, showing him that I didn't care.

Only I did. I cared a lot.

I cared so much, in fact, that I continued to stare at them shamelessly. At his hollowed cheeks as he inserted his tongue deep into her mouth, his burning, taunting glare never leaving mine, gauging me for a reaction. I felt my body buzzing in an unfamiliar way, falling under his spell. A sweet, pungent fog. It was sexual, unwelcome, yet completely inescapable. I wanted to break free, but for the life of me, I couldn't.

My grip on the door handle tightened, and I swallowed, my eyes dropping to his hand as he grabbed her waist and squeezed playfully. I squeezed my own waist through the fabric of my yellow-and-white sunflower top.

What the hell was wrong with me? Watching him kiss another girl was unbearable but also weirdly fascinating.

I wanted to see it.

I didn't want to see it.

Either way, I couldn't *unsee* it.

Admitting defeat, I blinked, shifting my gaze to a black Raiders cap hung over the headrest of his desk chair.

"Your textbook, Vicious. I need it," I repeated. "I'm not leaving your room without it."

"Get the fuck out, Help," he said into Georgia's giggling mouth.

A thorn twisted in my heart, jealousy filling my chest. I couldn't wrap my head around this physical reaction. The pain. The shame. The *lust*. I hated Vicious. He was hard, heartless, and hateful. I'd heard his mother had died when he was nine, but he was eighteen now and had a nice stepmother who let him do whatever he wanted. Josephine seemed sweet and caring.

He had no reason to be so cruel, yet he was to everyone. Especially to me.

"Nope." Inside, rage pounded through me, but outside, I remained unaffected. "*Calc. Textbook*." I spoke slowly, treating him like the idiot he thought I was. "Just tell me where it is. I'll leave it at your door when I'm done. Easiest way to get rid of me and get back to your…activities."

Georgia, who was fiddling with his zipper, her white sheath dress already unzipped from behind, growled, pushing away from his chest momentarily and rolling her eyes.

She squeezed her lips into a disapproving pout. "Really? Mindy?" My name was Millie, and she knew it. "Can't you find anything better to do with your time? He's a little out of your league, don't you think?"

Vicious took a moment to examine me, a cocky smirk plastered on his face. He was so damn handsome. Unfortunately. Black hair, shiny and trimmed fashionably, buzzed at the sides and longer on top. Indigo eyes, bottomless in their depth, sparkling and hardened. By what, I didn't know. Skin so pale he looked like a stunning ghost.

As a painter, I often spent time admiring Vicious's form. The angles of his face and sharp bone structure. All smooth edges. Defined and clear-cut. He was made to be painted. A masterpiece of nature.

Georgia knew it too. I'd heard her not too long ago talking about him in the locker room after PE. Her friend had said, "Beautiful guy."

"Dude, but *ugly* personality," Georgia was quick to add. A moment of silence passed before they'd both snorted out a laugh.

"Who cares?" Georgia's friend had concluded. "I'd still do him."

The worst part was I couldn't blame them.

He was both a baller and filthy rich—a popular guy who dressed and talked the right way. A perfect All Saints hero. He drove the right kind of car—Mercedes—and possessed that mystifying aura of a true alpha. He always had the room. Even when he was completely silent.

Feigning boredom, I crossed my arms and leaned one hip on his doorframe. I stared out his window, knowing tears would appear in my eyes if I looked directly at him or Georgia.

"His *league*?" I mocked. "I'm not even playing the same game. I don't play dirty."

"You will, once I push you far enough," Vicious snapped, his tone curt. It felt like he clawed my guts out and threw them on his pristine ironwood floor.

I blinked slowly, trying to look blasé. "Textbook?" I asked for the two-hundredth time.

He must've concluded he'd tortured me enough for one day. He cocked his head to a backpack sitting under his desk. The window above it overlooked the servants' apartment where I lived, allowing him a perfect view directly into my room. So far, I'd caught him staring at me twice through the window, and I always wondered why.

Why, why, why?

He hated me so much. The intensity of his glare burned my face every time he looked at me, which wasn't as often as I would've liked him to. But being the sensible girl I was, I never allowed myself to dwell on it.

I marched to the Givenchy rubber-coated backpack he took to school every day and blew out air as I flipped it open, rummaging noisily through his things. I was glad my back was to them, and I tried to block out the moans and sucking noises.

The second my hand touched the familiar white-and-blue calc book, I stilled. I stared at the cherry blossom I'd doodled on the cover. Rage tingled up my spine, coursing through my veins, making my fists clench and unclench. Blood whooshed in my ears, and my breathing quickened.

He broke into my friggin' locker.

With shaking fingers, I pulled the book out of Vicious's backpack.

"You stole my textbook?" I turned to face him, every muscle in my face tense.

This was an escalation. Blunt aggression. Vicious always taunted me, but he'd never humiliated me like this before. He'd stolen my things and stuffed my locker full of condoms and used toilet paper, for Christ's sake.

Our eyes met and tangled. He pushed Georgia off his lap, like she was an eager puppy he was done playing with, and stood up. I took a step forward. We were nose to nose now.

"Why are you doing this to me?" I hissed out, searching his blank, stony face.

"Because I can," he offered with a smirk to hide all the pain in his eyes.

What's eating you, Baron Spencer?

"Because it's fun?" he added, chuckling while throwing Georgia's jacket at her. Without a glance her way, he motioned for her to leave.

She was clearly nothing more than a prop. A means to an end. He'd wanted to hurt me.

And he'd succeeded.

I shouldn't care about why he acted this way. It made no difference at all. The bottom line was I hated him. I hated him so much it made me sick to my stomach that I loved the way he looked, on and off the football field. Hated my shallowness, my foolishness, at loving the way his square, hard jaw twitched when he fought a smile. I hated that I loved the smart, witty things that came out of his mouth when he spoke in class. Hated that he was a cynical realist while I was a hopeless idealist, and still I loved every thought he uttered aloud. And I hated that once a week, every week, my heart did crazy things in my chest because I suspected he might be *him*.

I hated him, and it was clear that he hated me back.

I hated him, but I hated Georgia more because she was the one he'd kissed.

Knowing full well I couldn't fight him—my parents worked here—I bit my tongue and stormed toward the door. I only made it to the threshold before his callused hand wrapped around my elbow, spinning me in place and throwing my body into his steel-like chest. I swallowed back a whimper.

"Fight me, Help," he snarled into my face, his nostrils flaring like a wild beast. His lips were close, so close. Still swollen from kissing another girl, red against his fair skin. "For once in your life, stand your fucking ground."

I shook out of his touch, clutching my textbook to my chest like it was my shield. I rushed out of his room and didn't stop to take a breath until I reached the servants' apartment. Swinging the door open, I bolted to my room and locked the door, plopping down on the bed with a heavy sigh.

I didn't cry. He didn't deserve my tears. But I was angry, upset, and yes, a little broken.

In the distance, I heard music blasting from his room, getting louder by the second as he turned the volume up to the max. It took me a few beats to recognize the song. "Stop Crying Your Heart Out" by Oasis.

A few minutes later, I heard Georgia's red automatic Camaro—the one Vicious constantly made fun of because *Who the fuck buys an automatic Camaro?*—gun down the tree-lined driveway of the estate. She sounded angry too.

Vicious was vicious. It was too bad that my hate for him was dipped in a thin shell of something that felt like love. But I promised myself I'd crack it, break it, and unleash pure hatred in its place before he got to me. *He*, I promised myself, *will never break me.*

CHAPTER TWO
VICIOUS

TEN YEARS AGO

It was the same old shit, different weekend, at my house. I was throwing another balls-out party and didn't even bother to leave the media/gaming room to hang out with the assholes I'd invited.

I knew what kind of chaos was teeming outside the room. The snickering and screaming girls in the kidney-shaped pool at the back of the house. The gurgles of the artificial waterfalls pouring out of the Greek arches into the water and the slap of inflated rubber mattresses against bare wet skin. The groans of couples fucking in nearby rooms. The mean-ass gossip of cliques crashing on the plush love seats and sofas downstairs.

I heard music—Limp Bizkit—and who the fuck had the balls to play *Lame* Bizkit at my party?

I could've heard all the rest too if I wanted to, but I didn't *listen*. Sprawled out on my wing lounge chair in front of the TV, thighs open wide, I smoked a blunt and watched some Japanese anime porno.

There was a beer to my right, but I didn't touch it.

There was a chick on her knees below my seat, on the carpet, massaging my thighs, but I didn't touch her either.

"Vicious," she purred, inching closer to my groin. She slowly climbed up, straddling my lap.

A tan, nameless brunette in a come-fuck-me dress. She looked like an Alicia or Lucia, maybe. Tried to get onto the cheerleading squad last spring. Failed. My guess was this party was her first taste of popularity. Hooking up with me, or anyone else in this room, was her shortcut to celebrity status at school.

For that reason alone, she was of no interest to me.

"Your media room is rad. Think we can go somewhere quieter, though?"

I tapped the head of my blunt, the ash falling to an ashtray on the arm of my chair like a flake of dirty snow. My jaw twitched. "No."

"But I like you."

Bullshit. Nobody liked me, and for good reason.

"I don't do relationships," I said on autopilot.

"Like, duh. I know that, silly. No harm in having some fun, though." She snorted, an unattractive laugh that made me hate her for trying so hard.

Self-respect went a long way in my book.

My eyes narrowed as I mulled over her offer. Sure, I could let her suck my dick, but I knew better than to believe her indifferent act. They all wanted something more.

"You should get out of here," I said, for the first and last time. I wasn't her dad. It wasn't my responsibility to warn her about guys like me.

She pouted, linking her arms behind my neck and scooting up my thigh. Her exposed cleavage pressed against my chest, and her eyes burned with determination. "I'm not leaving here without one of you HotHoles."

I arched one eyebrow, exhaling smoke through my nose, my eyes hooded with boredom. "Then you'd better try Trent or Dean 'cause I ain't fucking you tonight, sweetheart."

Alicia-Lucia pulled away, finally getting the hint. She sashayed to the bar with a fake smile that crumpled with every step she took in those high heels and fixed herself a bullshit cocktail without checking what liquor she poured into the tall glass. Her eyes were shiny as she scanned the room, trying to figure out which one of my friends—we were the Four HotHoles of All Saints High—was willing to be her ticket to popularity.

Trent was slouched on the couch to my right, half sitting, half lying as a random chick grinded on his cock, straddling him with her shirt pulled down to her waist and her bare tits bouncing almost comically. He put the beer bottle to his mouth and dicked around on his phone, jaded. Dean and Jaime sat on a love seat on the other side, arguing about next week's football game. Neither of them had touched the girls we'd summoned into the room.

Jaime, I understood. He was obsessing over our English teacher, Ms. Greene. I didn't approve of his new fucked-up fascination, but I'd never say a word about it to him. Dean, on the other hand? I had no idea what his problem was. Why hadn't he grabbed an ass and sprung into action like he normally did?

"Dean, dude, where's your piece of pussy for the night?" Trent echoed my thoughts, scrolling his thumb over his phone, surfing his playlist, looking desperately uninterested in the chick he was fucking.

Before Dean could answer him, Trent pushed the girl on top of him away mid-thrust, patting her head gently as she tumbled onto the sofa. Her mouth was still open, half in pleasure, half in shock.

"Sorry. It ain't happening for me tonight. It's the cast." He pointed his beer bottle to his broken ankle, smiling apologetically at his fuck buddy.

Out of the four of us, Trent was the nicest.

That said all anyone needed to know about the HotHoles.

The ironic thing was, Trent had the most reason to be spiteful. He was screwed, and he knew it. There was no way he was getting a full ride to college without football. His grades sucked ass, and his parents didn't have the money to pay for their rent, let alone his education. His injury meant he was staying in SoCal and picking up some blue-collar work if he was lucky, slumming it up with the rest of his neighborhood after spending four years with us rich Todos Santos kids.

"I'm all right, man." Dean's smile was easy, but the continuous tapping of his foot was not. "Actually, I don't want you to be blindsided by something. You listening up?" He grinned nervously, straightening his posture.

Just then, the door opened behind me. Whoever came in didn't bother to knock. Everyone knew this room was off-limits. This was the HotHoles' private party space. The rules were clear. Unless invited, you didn't come in.

The girls in the room all stared in the direction of the door, but I continued smoking weed and wishing Alicia-Lucia would move the fuck away from the bar. I needed a fresh beer and wasn't in the mood for talking.

"Whoa, hi." Dean waved to the person at the door, and I swear his whole stupid body smiled.

Jaime nodded a curt hello, tensing up in his seat and sending me a look I was too stoned to decode. Trent swiveled his head, grunting in greeting too.

"Whoever's at the door better have a fucking pizza and a pussy made of gold if they wanna stay." I clenched my teeth, finally throwing a glance over my shoulder.

"Hey, y'all."

When I heard her voice, something weird happened in my chest.

Emilia. The help's daughter. *Why is she here?* She never left the servants' apartment when I threw my parties. Plus she hadn't glanced in my direction since she ran out of my room with her calc book last week.

"Who gave you permission to come here, Help?" I sucked my blunt, inhaled deeply, and poured a cloud of rancid, sweet smoke into the air, swiveling my chair to face her.

Her azure eyes glided over me briefly before landing on

someone behind me. Her lips broke into a timid grin at the sight of that person. The raucous noise of the party faded, and all I saw was her face.

"Hey, Dean." Her gaze dropped to her fake Vans.

Her long caramel hair was braided and flung over one of her shoulders. She had on boyfriend jeans and a *Daria* shirt deliberately mismatched with an orange-wool jacket. Her sense of style was juvenile and horrid, and the back of her hand was still inked with a cherry blossom tree she'd drawn in English Lit, so why the fuck was she still hot as shit? Didn't matter. I hated her anyway. But her apparent devotion to trying not to be sexy, paired with the fact that she actually *was* sexy, always made me hard as stone.

I tore my gaze from her to Dean. He smiled back at her. A goofy smirk that begged for me to break all of his teeth.

What. The. Fuck?

"You two bumping uglies?" Jaime popped his gum, asking the question I never would've, tousling his long blond surfer hair with his fist. He didn't give two shits but knew it was something that'd interest me.

"Jesus, man." Dean got up from his seat, slapping the back of Jaime's neck and suddenly acting like some kind of a decent guy.

I knew him too well not to recognize that he wasn't one. He'd fucked so many girls on the very sofa he'd just sat on that it was permanently imprinted with his DNA.

This—and only this—made me dislike the whole Dean-and-Help idea. I had enough fucking drama to deal with. I didn't want to be there when her heart broke, in my house. Shattering on *my floor*. Besides, as much as I disliked Help…she wasn't for us to destroy. She was just a country girl from Virginia with a huge smile and an annoying accent. Her personality was like a fucking Michael Bublé song. So easy and un-fucking-assuming. I mean, the girl even smiled at me when she caught me staring into her bedroom in the servants' apartment like a creep.

How stupid could a person be?

It wasn't her fault I hated her. For eavesdropping on Daryl and me all those weeks ago. For looking and sounding exactly like my stepmom, Jo.

"I'm glad you could make it. Sorry you had to come here. I didn't realize I was late. This is no place for a lady," Dean joked, grabbing his jacket from the arm of the black-leather sofa and jogging to the door.

He flung his arm over her shoulder, and my left eyelid twitched.

He brushed a strand of hair that fell from her braid behind her ear, and my jaw clenched.

"Hope you're hungry. I know a really good seafood place by the marina."

She grinned. "Sure. Count me in."

He laughed, and my nostrils flared.

Then they left.

They fucking left.

I tucked the blunt back into the corner of my mouth, swiveling back to the TV. The whole room fell quiet, and all eyes were directed at me for further instructions, and what the fuck was everybody so upset about?

"Hey, you." I pointed at the girl who Trent had thrown away mid-fuck. She was fixing her hair in front of the mirror next to my gaming rig. I patted my lap twice. "Over here, and bring your friend." I pinned the other one with my eyes. The girl I'd rejected only moments ago. Good thing she'd decided to stick around.

With a giggling girl on each leg, I took a hit of my joint, pulled the first girl's hair so that she was facing me, and pressed my lips to hers. I exhaled, shotgunning the smoke into her mouth. She took it all in with an excited gasp.

"Move it forward." I brushed the bridge of her nose with the tip of mine, my eyes heavy. She smiled with her mouth closed and kissed the other girl on my lap, letting the smoke seep into her mouth.

Trent and Jaime watched me the whole time.

"They're probably just fuck buddies," Trent offered, rubbing his hand over his shaved head. "I didn't hear about this shit until tonight, and Dean can keep a secret like I can keep my pants up at a Playboy-mansion party."

"Yeah," Jaime chipped in. "It's Dean, dude. He's never had a serious girlfriend. He's never had a serious *anything*." Standing up, he shouldered into his navy letter jacket. "Anyway, I gotta head out."

Of course. To pretend to be some loser on a dating site and spend the night sexting Ms. Greene. I swear, if I hadn't seen his dick in the locker room, I'd assume Jaime actually had a pussy.

"But I'm telling you," he added, "don't overanalyze it. There's no way in hell Dean's settling down. He's set on New York for college. You're staying here with her. She didn't get accepted anywhere, right?"

Right.

On top of that, Help hadn't bagged a scholarship so far. I knew that because we shared the same mailbox, and I browsed through her envelopes to see where little Emilia LeBlanc was headed next. So far, it looked like she wasn't going anywhere, much to her dismay.

I was going to a bullshit college in Los Angeles a couple of hours away, and she was staying here. I would come back every other weekend, and she'd still be here. Catering to me.

Serving me.

Envying me.

She was going to stay small and insignificant. Uneducated and opportunity-less. And above all—*mine*.

"I really don't give a fuck." I chuckled, grabbing both the girls' asses, clutching their soft flesh as I moved them toward one another. "Lick each other's tits for me." My tone was flat. They did as they were told. It was so easy to get them to do it, it depressed the hell out of me.

The girls and their tongues were at war. They begged for my

attention like two dogs battling for their lives in an underground fight. They did nothing for me, and naturally, I resented them for that.

"So where were we?" I asked my friends.

"In deep denial, apparently. Jesus." Jaime shook his head, sauntering to the door. He clasped Trent's shoulder on his way out. "Make sure the girls don't do anything too stupid."

"You mean like him?" Trent jerked his thumb toward me.

I squinted at him. But he didn't care. He was a kid from the hood. Nothing scared him, let alone my rich milky ass.

There was rage brimming inside me. Soon, it was going to overflow.

They were so sure they knew me. So sure I wanted Emilia LeBlanc.

"Fuck this shit. I'm going down to the pool." I stood up suddenly, and the girls collapsed, each of them landing on an arm of the chair with a soft thud.

One of them whined in protest, and the other shrieked, "What the hell!"

"Bad high," I offered as a half-assed explanation.

"It happens." The girl who'd fucked Trent a second ago smiled in understanding.

I wanted to beat the shit out of their dads almost as much as I wanted to screw up Daryl. Their availability repulsed me.

"Are you gonna call me?" Alicia-Lucia tugged on my shirt. Hope glittered in her eyes.

I gave her a slow once-over. She looked good but not as good as she thought. Then again, she was eager to please, so probably not the worst lay.

I'd warned her.

She'd refused to listen.

"Leave your number on Trent's phone." I turned on my heel and left.

In the hallway, people made way for me, gluing their backs to the wall, smiling and raising their red Solo cups to me, groveling like I was the fucking pope. And to them—I was. This was my kingdom. People loved my type of evil. That was the thing about California, and that's why I would never leave. I loved everything other people hated about it. The liars, the pretenders, the masks, and the plastic. I loved how people cared about what was in your pocket and not in your fucking chest. I loved that they were impressed by expensive cars and cheap wit. Hell, I even loved the earthquakes and bullshit vegetable shakes.

These people who I hated were my home. This place—my playground.

Murmurs rose from every corner of the hallway. I didn't usually grace these people with my presence, but when I did, they knew why. Shit was going to go down tonight. Excitement filled the air.

"Fell in Love with a Girl" by the White Stripes pounded against the dark walls.

I didn't make eye contact with anyone. Just stared ahead as I sliced through the throng until I reached the storage cellar under the kitchen. I closed the door behind me. It was quiet, dark, like me. I pressed my back against the door, squeezed my eyes shut, and took a deep breath of the damp air.

Damn, that shit Dean brought in *was* strong. I was only half-lying when I said the stuff was bad.

I walked deeper into the room, mentally slamming the door on the rest of the world. On Daryl Ryler. Josephine. And even on people who were only half-villains, like Emilia and my dad. My fingers brushed the weapons on the wall I had collected over the years. I fingered my crowbar, dagger, baseball bat, and leather whip. It occurred to me that one day, hopefully soon, I could give up this collection, which I had never used but owned because it made me feel safer. Mainly, having this shit meant Daryl didn't mess with me anymore.

I was looking for a physical, slow-building fight. I was looking for explosive pain coming out of nowhere. In short, I was looking for trouble.

When I climbed back upstairs to the outdoor pool, empty-handed, I stood over the edge. The moonlight lit my reflection against the clear water. The pool was full of people in swim trunks and designer bikinis. My eyes roamed the place, searching for Dean. He was the guy I wanted to fight. To break his smug boy-next-door face. But I knew he was out with Help, and besides, rules were rules. Even I couldn't bend them. The minute I stepped out there with my sleeves rolled up to my shoulders, I invited whoever wanted to fight me to step forward. But I couldn't ask anyone specifically. They had to volunteer. That was the dangerous game we played at All Saints High to burn time: *Defy*.

Defy was fair.

Defy was brutal.

Most of all, Defy dulled the pain and provided a great explanation for my marred skin.

I wasn't surprised when I heard the thump of Trent's cast behind me. He knew how fucked up I was and wanted to save the night.

"Tell Dean to dump her ass or I will," he said from behind my back.

I shook my head, sneering. "He can do whatever the fuck he wants. If he wants to bang that hillbilly, it's his funeral."

"Vicious," Trent warned.

I turned around and sized him up. His smooth mocha skin shone under the full moon, and I hated him for his ability to enjoy the opposite sex with such carelessness. Fucking random chicks was growing old too fast. And I wasn't even eighteen yet.

"This shit with this chick is gonna drag everyone down a very dark path." He took off his shirt, exposing his huge, ripped torso. He was a bulky bastard.

As always, I kept my shirt on. People eyed us avidly, but I'd never cared about these assholes. They wanted to fill their meaningless existence with something to talk about. I was only too happy to give it to them.

I coiled my fist, cocking my head sideways. "Aw, you care about me. I'm fucking touched, T-Rex." I clutched the left side of my black tee above my heart, mocking him with a fake smile.

Georgia and her airhead crew were watching us intently, waiting for the monster in me to pounce on one of my best friends. I marched past Trent, my shoulder brushing his, trudging toward the tennis court where we fought on most weekends. It was big, secluded, and spacious enough for the crowd to take seats on one side of our makeshift octagon.

"Give me your worst, Rexroth," I growled, trying to calm myself down. Trying to remind myself that Trent and Jaime were right. Dean and Help were just a fling. They'd be broken up by the end of the month. He was going to dump her—hopefully with her virginity still intact—hurt and angry and looking for a rebound. She'd be fragile, insecure, and vindictive.

And that's when I was going to strike.

That's when I was going to show her she was nothing more than my property.

"Come on, T. Move your injured ass to the tennis court. Just try not to bleed all over my fucking grass after we're done."

CHAPTER THREE
EMILIA

THE PRESENT

"Watch where you're going, schmuck!" I shouted as I waited on the corner outside the trendy office building on the Upper East Side.

The muddy stain on my bib-waisted sailor dress, the one with the tiny smiley faces, widened, spreading quickly. I held my cell between my ear and my shoulder, swallowing a frustrated scream. I was puddle-soaked, hungry, tired, and desperate for the walk signal to turn green. On top of everything, I was already late for my shift at McCoy's.

The roar of honking traffic on a Friday night filled my ears. The problem with jaywalking in New York City was that the drivers were New Yorkers too, so they didn't mind running you over if it came to that.

Or soaking your clothes, for that matter.

"What the hell, Millie?" Rosie coughed into my ear on the other end of the line. She sounded like an asthmatic dog. My sister hadn't left her bed all day.

I would've been jealous had I not known why.

"A taxi driver just splashed me on purpose," I explained.

"Calm your tits," she soothed in her own special way, and I heard her shifting in bed, groaning. "Tell me what they said again."

The signal turned green. The animal kingdom that was New York's pedestrians almost ran me over as we all rushed to the other side of the street, ducking our heads under the scaffolding above us. My feet screamed with pain in high heels as I rushed past food vendors and men in pea coats, praying I'd get there before the staff meal in the kitchen was over and I missed my chance to grab something to eat.

"They said that while they were happy that I was taking an interest in the advertising industry, I was paid to make coffee and file stuff, not to make suggestions in creative meetings and share my ideas with the design teams at lunchtime. They said I was overqualified to be a PA but that they didn't have any art-intern positions to fill. They're also trying to 'trim the fat' to stay economically lean. Apparently, I'm just that—*fat*." I couldn't help but let out a bitter laugh, as I'd never been skinnier in my life—and not by choice. "So they fired me."

I blew out air, forming a white cloud. New York winters were so cold, they made you wish you could show up at work wearing the quilt you'd rolled yourself up in the night before. We should've moved back to the South. It still would be far enough from California. Not to mention the rent was way cheaper.

"So you've only got your job at McCoy's left?" It was Rosie's turn to sigh, and her lungs made a funny noise. Worry colored her voice.

I couldn't blame her. I was supporting both of us for now. I didn't make much as a PA, but dang, I'd needed the two jobs. With Rosie's meds, we weren't making ends meet as it was.

"Don't worry," I said as I sprinted down the busy street. "This is New York. There are job opportunities everywhere. You literally don't know where the next job will come from. I can easily find something else." *Like hell I will.* "Listen, I gotta go if I don't want to lose my night job too. I'm already three minutes late. Love you. Bye."

I hung up and stopped at another crosswalk, fidgeting. There was a thick layer of people ahead of me waiting to cross the street.

I couldn't lose my job at McCoy's, the Midtown bar I worked at. *I couldn't*. I glanced sideways, my gaze halting on the long, dark alley sandwiched between two huge buildings. A shortcut. *It's not worth it*, a little voice inside me said.

I was late.

And I just got fired from my day job.

And Rosie was sick again.

And there was rent to pay.

Screw it, I'll be fast.

I ran, my spine vibrating every time my high heels hit the pavement. The cold wind slapped my cheeks, the sting like a whip lash. I ran so fast it took me a few seconds to absorb the fact that someone had yanked me back by the courier bag slung over my shoulder. I fell flat on my ass. The ground was wet and cold, and I'd landed on my tailbone.

I didn't care. I didn't even have time to be shocked or get angry. I clutched my bag close to my chest and looked up at the offender. He was just a kid. A teenager, to be exact, with a face dotted with popped pimples. Tall and lanky and in all probability as hungry as I was. But it was my bag. *My* stuff. New York was a concrete jungle. I knew that sometimes, in order to survive, you had to be mean. Meaner than those who were mean to you.

I shoved my hand into my bag, hunting for the pepper spray. I just planned to threaten him—he had to learn a lesson. The kid yanked my bag again, and again I pulled it closer to my middle. I found the cool can of pepper spray and pulled it out, aiming at his eyes.

"Step back or go blind," I warned in a quivering voice. "I say it's not worth it, but it's up to you."

He flung his arm at me, and that's when I pressed the nozzle. He twisted my wrist violently. The spray missed him by inches. He backhanded my forehead and shoved me away. I felt my head spinning from the blow. Everything turned black as I went under.

A part of me wasn't too eager to come back.

Especially when my vision cleared and I realized my hands were empty. My phone, wallet, driver's license, cash—two hundred bucks I owed my landlord, dang it—were all gone.

I pushed myself to my feet, dirty pavement digging into my palms. One heel of my cheap shoes had snapped when I fell. I grabbed it on my way up. Catching sight of the retreating silhouette of my mugger in the distance, my bag clutched between his fingers, I waved the wooden heel in his direction with my fist and did something that was completely out of character. For the first time in years, I cussed *out loud*.

"Well, you know what? *Fuck* you too!"

My throat was burning from screaming as I limped my way to McCoy's. There was no point crying, though I did feel pretty sorry for myself. Getting robbed and fired on the same day? Yeah, I was definitely going to sneak a few shots when my boss, Greg, wasn't looking.

I made it to McCoy's twenty minutes late. The only sliver of solace was that the grouchy owner wasn't there, which meant that my neck was safe from getting fired for the second time that day.

Rachelle, the manager, was a friend. She knew about my financial struggles. About Rosie. About everything.

The minute I walked in through the back door and met her in the hallway next to the kitchen, she winced and brushed my lavender hair away from my forehead.

"I'm ruling out kinky sex and placing my bet on clumsiness," she said, shooting me a sympathetic frown.

I exhaled, squeezing my eyes shut. I opened them slowly, blinking away the mist of unshed tears. "Got mugged on the way here. He took my bag."

"Oh, sweetie." Rachelle pulled me into a tight hug.

My forehead fell to her shoulder, and I heaved a sigh. I was still upset, but the human touch felt nice. Comforting. I was also relieved that Greg wasn't there. It meant I could lick my wounds quietly without having him shouting at all the waitresses with foam bubbling from his mouth.

"It gets better, Rach. I got fired from R/BS Advertising too," I whispered into her cherry-red hair.

Her body stiffened against mine. When we pulled away, her expression wasn't concerned anymore. She looked downright horrified. "Millie…" She bit her lip. "What are you gonna do?"

That was a *very* good question. "Take more shifts here until I get myself together and find another day job? Get some temp work? Sell a kidney?"

The last one was obviously a joke, but I made a mental note to look into it when I got back to my apartment. Just out of curiosity. *Yeah, right.*

Rachelle rubbed her forehead with her palm, scanning my body. Knowing what I must look like, I hugged my midriff and flashed her a weak smile. I was thin. Thinner than I'd been when I first started working here. And the roots of my lavender hair were starting to show, but they were so light brown, it didn't look too bad. My physical state, especially with the broken heel and stained dress, underlined the mess I was in.

Rachelle's eyes stopped at my fist. She untangled my fingers from the shoe heel I was holding and took a deep breath, closing her eyes. "I'll glue this for you. Take the shoes in my locker and get to work. And smile big. God knows you need the tips."

I nodded, slapping a wet kiss onto her cheek. She was a lifesaver. I didn't even care that she was fun-sized, three inches shorter than me, and that her shoes were two sizes smaller. I bolted for our lockers and slipped into my uniform—a cropped, tight red shirt that showed off my stomach, black mini skirt, and a black-and-red apron with the McCoy's name plastered across it. It was tacky, but the bar was frequented by Wall Street types, and the tips were great.

Pushing the wooden saloon doors open and marching to the

dark, stool-lined counter, I ignored the thirsty—and not for alcohol—looks men sent my way. I was twenty-seven. Seemingly, the perfect age for the meat market New York had to offer. But I was too busy trying to survive to have a boyfriend. My policy was to be friendly with my customers without giving them false encouragement.

"Hey, Millie," Kyle greeted from behind the bar. He had slicked-back blond hair, studied filmmaking at NYU, lived in Williamsburg, and dressed like Woody Allen. Anything to disguise the fact he was actually from South Carolina.

I smiled at him while the regular crowd at the tables, men and women in suits, scrolled through messages on their phones and traded stories about their days at work. "Busy night?"

"Okay so far. Don't freak out," he warned, "but Dee is pissed at you for being late again. You'd better go take care of your tables." He nodded toward the right side of the restaurant.

Dee was one of the other waitresses who worked Fridays with me. I couldn't blame her for being mad. It wasn't her fault I was dealing with personal issues. I nodded and offered him a thumbs-up, but he was already engrossed in the book he was reading under the counter.

It wasn't that bad, working at McCoy's. Our clientele spoke quietly and drank expensively, always tipping 15 percent or more. Swaying my hips to "Baby It's You" by Smith, I ambled to a table in the corner of the room. It was dark and secluded from the rest—my favorite spot because it somehow always lured the best tippers.

I called it my lucky corner.

Two men were sitting there, hunched and engrossed in a hushed conversation. I plucked the menus from under my arm and smiled at their bent heads, trying to grab their attention.

"Hello, gentlemen. I'm Millie, and I'll be your waitress tonight. Can I get you anything while you—"

Him. That's where I stopped. Because the minute the man with the tousled black hair looked up, my heart flipped over, and my mouth froze.

Vicious.

I blinked, trying to decipher the image in front of me. Baron Spencer was here, and to my dismay, he looked a hell of a lot better than I did.

Tall, well above six foot, his long legs stretched to one side, with eyes dark like his soul and unruly raven hair that curled up at the sides, covering his stupidly perfect ears. High cheekbones—always rosy when touched by the sting of the cold—square jaw, and straight nose. Everything about his face was composed and icy.

Only the flush on his porcelain skin reminded me that he was still flesh, blood, and heart and not a machine programmed to ruin my life. The color in his cheeks even gave his dark, brooding features a boyish glint.

I wasn't surprised to see the I-dare-you-to-fuck-with-me expression was still stamped on his face, like an old song I knew by heart. I also wasn't surprised to see that, unlike me, his sense of style had matured with age. Impeccable yet unpretentious. He wore dark-blue jeans, brown Oxfords, a white dress shirt, and a tailored blazer.

Casual. Understated. Expensive.

Nothing fancy, but enough to remind you that he was still richer than 99.9 percent of the population. I always changed the subject whenever my parents tried to fill me in on anyone from Todos Santos, and they never mentioned Vicious. Not in recent years, anyway. For all I knew, he woke up every day to do nothing except dress like a big-shot rich guy.

I couldn't look in his eyes, couldn't even look in his direction. My gaze moved to the man who sat opposite him. He was slightly older—early thirties, maybe?—heavy-set with sandy-blond hair and the sharply tailored suit of a greedy Wall Street broker.

"Anything to drink?" I repeated, my throat closing up. I was no longer smiling. Was I even breathing?

"Black Russian." Sharp Suit dragged his eyes along the curves of my body, stopping at my chest.

"And you?" I chirped to Vicious, pretending to write down the drinks I would've remembered by heart anyway. My shaky hand scribbled blindly, missing my little notepad.

"Bourbon, neat." Vicious's tone was indifferent, his eyes dead when they landed on my pen. Not on me.

Aloof. Cold. Unaffected.

Nothing's changed.

I turned around and wobbled back to the bar in my too-tight shoes, placing the order with Kyle.

Maybe he didn't recognize me. After all, why would he? It had been ten years. And I'd only lived at the Spencer estate during my senior year.

I tapped the edge of the bar with the side of my chewed-up pen. Kyle groaned when he heard Sharp Suit had ordered a Black Russian. He hated making cocktails. I lingered, skulking behind Kyle's shoulder, stealing another glance at the guy who used to make my heart stutter.

He looked good. Lean-muscled and all man. The last ten years were kinder to him than they'd been to me. I wondered if he was just passing through Manhattan on a business trip or if he lived here. Somehow, I thought I'd know if he was living in New York. Then again, Rosie and my parents knew better than to share any information about the HotHoles with me.

No, Vicious was only here on business, I decided.

Good. I hated him so much it hurt to breathe when I looked at him.

"Drinks are ready," Kyle said behind my shoulder.

I spun around. Placing the glasses on a tray, I took a deep breath and started back to his table. My knees shook when I thought about what I looked like in this skimpy little outfit. A cheap-looking cropped top and shoes two sizes too small.

Shame inspired me to straighten my spine and plaster a big smile on my face. Maybe it was a good thing he didn't remember who I was. I didn't need him to know how I ended up being a broke waitress who lived off cereal and mac and cheese.

"Black Russian, bourbon." I placed red napkins on the round black tabletop and set their drinks on top, my eyes darting to Vicious's left hand, searching for a golden wedding band. There wasn't one. "Anything else?" I hugged my tray to my lower stomach, summoning my work smile.

"No, thanks." Sharp Suit sighed, impatient, and Vicious didn't even bother to acknowledge me. Their heads lowered back to the quiet conversation they were having.

I moved on, throwing glances at him over my shoulder and feeling my pulse everywhere, down to my neck and eyelids. Our encounter was anticlimactic, but that was for the best. We weren't old friends or even acquaintances.

In fact, I'd meant so little to him that, at this point, we weren't even enemies.

I focused on the rest of my tables. I laughed at my clients' unfunny jokes, and I drank the two shots Kyle slipped across the bar when my customers weren't looking. My treacherous eyes kept drifting to Vicious's table, though. His jaw was clenched as he spoke to his companion. Vicious wasn't happy.

I leaned my elbows on the bar and watched them closely.

Baron "Vicious" Spencer. Always providing the best show in town.

I watched as he slid a thick stack of papers across the table, pointed at the first page with his index finger, sat back, and stared at the man, his eyes announcing victory. Sharp Suit reddened and slammed his fist against the table, snatching the papers and choking them in his hand as he waved them around, spitting as he spoke. The papers crumpled. Vicious's cool didn't.

No. He remained calm and unruffled as he leaned forward, saying something I couldn't decipher, and the more the blond man got excited and heated, the more Vicious looked uninterested and amused.

At some point, Sharp Suit threw his hands in the air and said something animated, his face as dark as a pickled beet. That's when Vicious's face brightened, and he propped one elbow on the table as he dragged his finger along what must have been a specific spot in the verbiage on the first page of the document. His lips were thin when he said something to the man in front of him, but Sharp Suit looked nearly ready to faint.

My heart pounded too fast, and my mouth dried. Jesus Christ. Vicious was threatening him, and to no surprise to me, he wasn't being shy about it.

"Millie, take five." Dee slapped my ass from behind just then. I jumped, startled. She was back from her cigarette break, and it was my turn.

I didn't smoke, but I usually used the time to talk to Rosie on my cell. I wouldn't be doing that tonight, but I was glad Dee had apparently put my tardiness behind her.

"Thanks," I said, making a beeline to the toilets. I needed to wash my face and remind myself that the day was almost over. I slipped past the sinks and disappeared inside one of the individual stalls where I leaned against the door and took long, steady breaths.

I didn't even know what would make me feel better. Getting my PA job back? No. I'd never liked it much. The accountant I worked for at the advertising agency was a walking, talking sexual-harassment suit just waiting to happen. Having Vicious recognize me? It would only make me more flustered and embarrassed. Having him leave? I was too intrigued by him to want him gone.

I left the bathroom stall and was just about to splash some water on my face at the sink when the door opened and he walked in.

He. Walked. In.

I wasn't scared. Even after everything that'd happened, I knew he wouldn't hurt me. Not physically, anyway. But I was intimidated, and I hated that I looked like a Hooters reject while he… he had an aura about him. When he walked into the room, no matter how dingy and small, you could feel the wealth. The status. The power.

His eyes landed on the cherry blossom mural behind me before they leveled on my face, and my mind raced. His gaze told me he knew exactly who I was and that I was the one who'd painted the mural behind me.

He remembered me.

What he did to me.

He remembered everything.

His eyes met mine, and my stomach knotted. My heart fluttered in my chest, and an urgent need to fill the awkward silence slammed into me.

"Have you come here for forgiveness?" The words left my mouth before I had the chance to swallow them.

Vicious chuckled darkly, like the concept in itself was preposterous. He hadn't made a single move, yet I felt his touch everywhere.

"You're a mess," he said matter-of-factly, eyeing my hair. My lavender locks were all over my face, and a nasty bruise had bloomed on my forehead.

"Nice to see you too." I pressed my back against the wall, my hands against the cold tiles below the mural, seeking relief from the fire he'd lit in me the moment he walked in. "I see you successfully graduated from a bully to a tyrant in the span of a decade."

He laughed, a deep laugh that vibrated against my bones. I closed my eyes and then opened them, drinking him in. A year of him being hateful toward me had trained me well. I stopped caring a long time ago that the joke was on me.

His smile disappeared, replaced with a frown. "What are you doing here, *Help*?"

He took a step forward but stilled when I held my hand up, stopping him. I wasn't sure why I did it. Maybe because it hurt so much that he was seeing me like this. Helpless. Half naked. Poor and lost and small in this big city that chewed you up and spat out the remains once your hopes and dreams died. Filling the small meaningless shoes he'd created for me all those years ago. Becoming *the help*.

"I work here," I said, finally. Wasn't it obvious?

He moved my way again, his posture casual and relaxed. This time I straightened. I tilted my chin up. A waft of his scent—spicy, earthy, clean, and masculine—filled my nose. I inhaled and shivered. He'd always had this impact on me. And I always loathed myself for it.

"Last I heard, you were working on a fine arts degree." He arched a thick, devilish eyebrow, as if to ask *What went wrong?*

Everything, I thought bitterly. *Everything went wrong.*

"Not that it's any of your business, but I did get a degree." I pushed off from the wall and moved past him to wash my hands. He followed me with his eyes. "A thing called life butted into my plans, and I didn't have the luxury of working my way up on an art-intern salary, so I work as a PA. That's what I did until about three hours ago when I was let go. I thought I was having a bad enough day when I walked in here, but"—my eyes swiped his body—"clearly, the universe decided to make it an all-out disaster."

I didn't know why I was telling him all this. I didn't know why I was speaking to him at all. I should've yelled or stormed out of the bathroom after what he'd done to me years ago. Should have called our bouncer and kicked him out of McCoy's. But as much as I didn't like to admit it, I didn't hate him as much as I probably should have. A tiny sad part of me knew he wasn't to blame for my current state. My choices were mine.

I'd made my bed. Now I had to lie in it, even if it was full of fleas.

He tucked one hand in his pocket, using his free one to tousle his unruly hair—even more perfect now that he was all man. I looked away, wondering how he'd spent the last decade. What he did for a living. Whether he had a girlfriend or a wife or maybe even some kids. I'd always made it a point not to ask or listen, but now that he was in front of me, curiosity poked me, begging my mouth to ask these questions.

But I didn't.

"Have a nice life, Vicious." I turned off the faucet, sashaying to the door.

He grabbed my elbow and jerked me in his direction. A jolt of panic and excitement ripped through me. There was no point in shaking him away—he was twice my size.

"Do you need help, *Help*?" he whispered in my face. I hated him for calling me that.

And I hated *me* for responding to his gruff tone the way I did, even after all this time. Goose bumps prickled my skin, and a hot wave crashed inside my chest.

I was breathing heavily, but so was he.

"Whatever it is I need," I said, my voice a hiss, "I don't want it from you."

He pinned me with a wolfish grin. "That's for me to decide," he said, releasing my arm like it was dirty and nudging me to the door. "And I still haven't made up my mind."

I turned around and bolted out of the bathroom, leaving my high school crush turned nemesis alone in the bathroom.

I contemplated asking Dee to serve their table for the remainder of the night—knew she'd have probably said yes, seeing as they reeked of money—but my stupid pride made me want to see this evening through. It somehow felt important to show him, and myself, that I was indifferent to him, even though it was a lie.

Around three rounds of drinks and an hour later, Sharp Suit stood up. He looked frustrated, annoyed, and defeated, feelings I knew all too well from my year in Todos Santos. The man extended his hand across the table, but Vicious didn't shake it or stand up. He just glared at the stack of papers between them, silently urging Sharp Suit to pick them up. The man did and left in a hurry.

I rushed to place their bill on the table and turned around before

Vicious had a chance to talk to me again. He paid with a credit card and vanished from what *used* to be my lucky corner. When I picked up the signed receipt, my hands trembled. I was scared to see how much he'd tipped me. Pathetic, I knew. It shouldn't have mattered. But it did. On one hand, I didn't want to feel like a charity case, and on the other, I wanted…heck, what *did* I want?

Whatever it was, when I picked up the receipt, I knew it wasn't this. My eyes flared when I saw what he'd written at the bottom:

For your tip, go to 125 E 52nd. 23rd floor.

—Black

A crazy laugh fizzed from my throat. I fisted the note into a tiny ball and dunk-slammed it into the trash behind Kyle.

"Lousy tip?" He looked up from his book, confused.

"He didn't leave one." I motioned for him to pour me another shot.

He grabbed the neck of the vodka bottle. "Asshole."

Oh, Kyle, I wanted to say. *You have no idea.*

CHAPTER FOUR
VICIOUS

Plot twists. Guess they kept shit interesting.

I'd be lying if I claimed I'd forgotten about Emilia LeBlanc. But I hadn't expected to see her again. Sure, I knew she was in New York. New fucking York, the home of over eight million people who *weren't* Emilia LeBlanc.

I'd come to the city a week ago with the intention of doing one thing and one thing only—to make the jerk I'd met at McCoy's drop his fucking lawsuit against my company. He had.

Did I enjoy intimidating him? Yes.

Did it make me a bad person? Probably.

Did I care? Not even one bit.

Sergio had caved, but not because I metaphorically squeezed his balls so tightly his future children screamed in agony. He'd done it because I pulled out a detailed draft of a counter-suit, one I'd written myself the night before, on my flight from LA to New York. And I'd aced this motherfucker.

Lawyers had the potential to make the best criminals. That was a fact. The only thing that stopped me from being an outlaw was opportunity. I had plenty of those within the law.

But Help wasn't far off. I was a bad person, a good lawyer, and to some extent, yes, still the same asshole who made her senior year miserable.

Sergio was going to drop the lawsuit, let us keep the client we allegedly "stole" from his firm, and all was going to be well. I was a partner in a company specializing in high-risk investments and mergers. The four of us—Trent, Jaime, Dean, and I—had founded Fiscal Heights Holdings three years ago. They worked the money side while I was the company's lead attorney.

Sure, I liked numbers. They were safe. They didn't fucking speak. What wasn't to like? But I liked arguing and pissing people off even more.

And now I'd found Help.

She wasn't part of the plan, which made the surprise so much sweeter. She was the missing piece. Insurance in case things went south back in Todos Santos. I came here for a merger deal, but I also needed someone to do my dirty work. Originally, I wanted my ex-psychiatrist to help me reach my goal. He knew the whole story and could testify against my stepmother. But fuck, dealing with Help was going to be so much sweeter.

It would probably shatter her innocent little soul. She didn't do revenge. Was never cruel or selfish or any of the things that were the essence of my being. She was kind. Polite and agreeable. She smiled at strangers on the street—I would bet she still did, even in New York—and still had that faint Southern drawl, welcoming and soft, just like her.

I hoped she didn't have a boyfriend. Not for my sake, for his. Whether he existed didn't matter. I'd figuratively shoved him out of the picture the minute I set foot in McCoy's and looked up to find her peacock-blue eyes staring right back at me.

She was perfect.

Perfect for my plans and perfect to pass the time with until they materialized.

A ghost from my past who was going to help me haunt the demons of my present. She had the ability to help, and it was obvious she was in a financial pit. A black hole I could fish her out of, healthy and in one piece, except for her scruples.

I was prepared to throw in a lot of resources to get her to agree to my plan. She was mine again the minute I saw her in her next-to-nothing outfit.

She just didn't know it yet.

EMILIA

My heart was my enemy. I'd known that since I was seventeen. That's why I couldn't stop thinking about him—despite my recent unemployment—when thunder cracked and rumbled above my head.

It had been twenty-four hours since I'd seen him, three hours since I'd fantasized about punching him, and an hour and fifteen minutes since I'd debated, for the hundredth time, whether to tell Rosie about it.

At home, I wormed out of my soaked clothes, changed into dry ones, and ran back down to Duane Reade because I'd forgotten to pick up Rosie's meds. By the time I got back, I was soaked again.

I opened the plastic bag and placed everything on the counter in our tiny studio apartment. Mucus thinners. Vitamins. Antibiotics. I unscrewed all the tops because Rosie was too weak to do it herself.

My sister had cystic fibrosis. Some diseases are silent. But cystic fibrosis? It was also invisible. Little Rose didn't look sick. If anything, she was prettier than I was. We had the same eyes. Blue with turquoise and green dots swirling around the edges. Our lips were soft and plump and our hair the same shade of toffee. But while my face was round and heart-shaped, she had the sculpted cheekbones of a supermodel.

To be a supermodel, though, Rosie would have to stride down the catwalk, and lately, she couldn't even make it from our third-floor apartment down to our street.

She wasn't always sick. Normally, she could function like almost any other person. But when she was sick, she was *really* sick. Fatigued, weak, and fragile. Three weeks ago she'd caught pneumonia.

It was the second time in six months. We were lucky she'd taken the semester off college to try to make some money because otherwise she would've flunked out.

"I bought you clear broth." I took out the carton from the bag when I heard her rustling in our bed. I set the soup next to her medicine and turned on the stovetop. "How are you feeling, you little devil?"

"Like a leech who sucks all your money. I'm so sorry, Millie." Her voice croaked with sleep.

Friends was playing on our ancient television set. The canned laughter bounced between the scant furniture and thin walls, making our Sunnyside apartment a little more bearable. I wondered how many times Rosie could watch without losing her mind. She already knew all the episodes by heart.

She rolled off of the mattress and stood up, moving toward me. "How'd the job hunting go?" She rubbed my back in circles and started massaging my shoulders.

I sighed, dropping my head back and squeezing my eyes shut. *So good*. I couldn't wait to jump into our double futon and watch TV under the blankets with my sister.

"Temp agencies are swamped, and no one is hiring for retail this close to Christmas. Those jobs are already gone. On the bright side, heroin chic is making a comeback, so at least we'll have that going for us." I blew out air. "I guess what I'm trying to say is, money's gonna be extra tight this month."

Everything went quiet, and all I heard were her labored breaths. She slapped a hand over her mouth and winced. "Oh, *fuck*."

Yup. Rosie was no Southern belle.

"Can we survive December? I'm sure I'll get back on my feet soon. By January, we'll both be working."

"By January, we'll most likely be homeless," I muttered, placing a pot on the stovetop and stirring the broth. I wished I had something to add to it. Vegetables, chicken, anything to make her feel better. To make her feel *home*.

"We'll take everything you just bought back and get a refund. I don't need my meds. I feel so much better."

My heart shattered in my chest. Because she did need them. She needed them bad. Her antibiotics prevented lung and sinus infections, and her inhalers opened her airway. Not only did my sister need her medications, she literally couldn't breathe without them.

"I threw away the receipt," I lied. "Besides, I can always get them to raise the limit on my credit card." Another lie. No one in their right mind was going to give me more credit. I was already neck-deep in debt.

"No," she interrupted again, spinning me around to face her. She gripped my hands. Hers were so cold I wanted to cry. I must've flinched because Rosie withdrew them quickly. "It's bad circulation. I'm feeling really well, I swear. Listen to me, Millie. You've done enough for me. Made too many sacrifices along the way. Maybe it's time for me to go live with Mama and Daddy."

Tears welled in her eyes, but she smiled. I shook my head and gathered her hands, rubbing them to warm her up.

"You've only got two years left on your degree here. You'd have to start over in California, even if you could find a program you could afford. Stay. There are zero opportunities for people like us in Todos Santos."

Besides, our parents were still broke. So were we, but I was much better at shouldering the financial burden. I was young and still had fight in me. Our parents were old and worn-out, two sixty-something servants living in California, still in that stupid servants' apartment on the Spencer estate.

It wasn't that bad for us most of the time. Rosie had worked too, until pneumonia knocked her on her butt. The wet, cold fall had made her sicker, and now winter had hit early and we were behind on the heat bill. But spring was going to come. Cherry trees were going to blossom. We were going to get better. I knew we would.

Still, telling her about my encounter with Vicious was out of the question. She didn't need another reason to worry.

"I need a distraction." I rubbed my face, changing the subject.

"You can say that again." She tugged on her lower lip before turning and walking toward my easel in the corner of the small room.

The easel held a half-finished painting I was working on—a sandstorm rising to an inky-black sky. An art collector from Williamsburg named Sarah had ordered the painting. She used to work for Saatchi Art and was still tight with gallery owners all over the city. I wanted to impress her. I wanted to get my foot in the door. I also needed the money.

Rosie knew painting soothed my soul.

She took out the half-squeezed oil tubes, brushes, and wooden palette, mimicking my usual routine when I prepared to paint. Then she swayed her hips to our old stereo, put on "Teardrop" by Massive Attack, and silently made me some coffee.

I loved my baby sister so much in that moment. It reminded me that the sacrifices I made for her were worth it.

I painted as cold December rain furiously knocked on our window. Rosie plopped onto our mattress and talked to me like when we were in high school, exchanging notes about people we went to school with.

"If you could fulfill one dream, what would it be?" she mused, propping her pajama-clad legs against the cold wall.

"Own a gallery of my own," I answered without even thinking, a stupid smile plastered all over my face. "You?"

She picked at the fringe of the pillow she was hugging to her chest. "Get that damn degree and become a nurse," she said. "Wait, scrap that. Jared Leto. My dream is to marry Jared Leto. I'd take a stab at Jared Leto. I'm not even talking about, like, a shallow wound.

I'm talking a full-blown, deep-cut, ER-worthy stab. I mean, we'd be able to afford it. He's doing very well for himself."

I shook my head. She laughed, prompting me to do the same. *Lord, Rosie.*

I knew it was important to box up these kinds of moments, keep them locked away in my heart, and call them up when things got hard. Because moments like these reminded me that my life was hard but not bad. There was a difference between the two.

A hard life equaled a life full of obstacles and challenging moments but also full of people you loved and cared about.

A bad life equaled an empty life. One that wasn't necessarily hard or challenging but was devoid of the people you loved and cared about.

By the time I was done painting, my fingers were numb and my lower back ached from standing in a weird position for hours. We shared mac and cheese and chicken broth and watched "The One with the Lottery" episode of *Friends* for the six-millionth time. Rosie mouthed all the punch lines, her eyes never leaving the TV, and eventually fell asleep in my arms, snoring softly, her lungs wheezing for air.

I was confused. Tired. A little hungry.

But above all, blessed.

Four days passed before I caved and bought a new phone. I didn't want to spend the money, but how else would potential employers contact me? It was nothing fancy. The kind of Nokia from before the smartphone era. But I could text and make calls and even play some old-school games like *Snake*.

I'd been spending the week knocking on recruitment agencies' doors during the day and working shifts at McCoy's at night. Rachelle begged the other waitresses to give me their shifts so I could pay the rent, and even though I was embarrassed, I was mostly just grateful.

Rosie took her medicine, but she was still getting worse, and worry gnawed at my gut.

It was the apartment.

We didn't have adequate heating in our tiny Sunnyside studio, and sometimes it was colder inside than it was out. I often found myself jogging in place, doing jumping jacks to warm up. Little Rose didn't have that option because she was always out of breath.

I didn't know how to get out of the financial hole I'd been digging ever since I'd offered to have her come live with me. She'd wanted to study in New York, so I temporarily gave up on my internship at an art gallery and took the PA job to support us.

That was two years ago.

Stuck in a rut, I needed a miracle to survive until Rosie was back on her feet.

My mind drifted to Vicious and the fact that he hadn't come back to McCoy's. *Well, at least there are small miracles to be thankful for.*

I was mostly happy about it, but an occasional pang of sorrow would pierce my heart at the thought of him. I couldn't believe he hadn't left a tip. He really was a heartless bastard.

It was another cold night, and I was getting back from a double shift at the bar. I held on to the banisters in our building as I fumbled my way up the dark staircase of the Italianate-style brownstone. The hallway upstairs was dark too because the landlord hadn't bothered to replace the dead light bulbs. I couldn't complain since I was late on the rent almost every month.

My arms were stretched out in front of me as I felt my way down the hall. A shriek escaped my lungs when moonlight slanted through the tall window near my apartment door. A large shadow fell across me.

My pepper spray was already out of my new thrift-store courier bag when a light flashed from a smartphone the shadow was holding. Bluish light enveloped the angles of Vicious's face.

He was leaning against my door, wearing a tailored navy sweater rolled to his elbows, black dress pants, and stylish shoes, the leather still wrinkle-free. He looked like a Ralph Lauren ad, and I looked like the girl who cleaned up the set. The visual alone made me scowl at him before he even opened his mouth.

"I'm surprised, Help."

The ever-constant nickname gave me yet another reason to scowl. *Help*.

His eyes dropped to the pepper spray, but he didn't seem fazed by it. "I thought you'd come for your tip."

"You did?" The tension in my body eased as some of the fear rolled off me, but my heart continued pumping furiously for a whole different reason. "Well, here's a tip from me to you—when you single-handedly ruin someone's life, said someone is not too eager to contact you. Especially for money."

Vicious looked indifferent to my bitter tone. He pushed off from my door and strode closer, purposeful and confident, reminding me that he was much more comfortable in his skin than I was in mine. When he stopped, his chest brushed mine, sending shivers to the rest of my body.

I moved aside, crossing my arms over my chest and quirking an eyebrow. "Do I want to know how you found me?"

"Your little friend Rachelle thinks I'm taking you out on a surprise date. Not the sharpest pencil in the box, but then you always had a soft spot for the simpletons of the world."

I looked away from his face, concentrating on the peeling, worn door leading to my shoebox apartment. "What are you here for, Vicious?"

"You said you're a PA," he replied on half a shrug.

"And?"

"And I need one."

I tossed my head back and laughed, not a trace of humor in me. He really had some nerve. My laughter died quickly. "Leave."

I fished my keys out of my purse and stabbed the key toward the lock. He reached for my waist, effortlessly spinning me around to face him. His touch caught me off guard. Suddenly, I felt light-headed. I jolted away from his body and twisted back to the door, hysteria climbing up my throat. I dropped the keys and picked them up. I didn't like the way my body reacted to this man. It always had been—still was—completely out of sync with the way I felt about him.

"Name your price," he growled, way too close to my ear.

"World peace, the cure for lung disease, for the White Stripes to reunite," I shot back.

He didn't even blink. "One hundred K a year." His voice crawled into my ear like sweet poison, and I froze. "I know your sister is sick. Work for me, Help, and you won't have to think about how to pay for Rosie's meds ever again."

How long a conversation did he have with Rach and more importantly—why?

That kind of pay would be amazing, especially for a PA. But my pride—my stupid pride, a monster that demanded to be fed only when Vicious was at the dinner table—snatched the imaginary microphone and did the talking for me.

"No," I gritted out.

"No?" He cocked his head to the side, like he didn't hear me right, and, dang it, he looked good doing it.

"Is this word new to you?" I squared my shoulders. "No amount of money is going to make the fact I hate your guts disappear."

"One hundred fifty K might," he said, unblinking.

Does he need a hearing aid?

His eyes were so dark blue they sparkled like rare sapphires. He thought it was a negotiation. He was wrong.

"It's not about the money, Vicious." I felt my teeth grinding together. "Do you want it in another language? I can write it down for you or even communicate it in the form of a dance."

His mouth twisted into something that resembled a smirk, but it failed to last. "I forgot how fucking fun it is to piss you off. I'm throwing in an apartment within walking distance of the job. Fully furnished and paid for throughout your employment."

I felt the blood rush between my ears. "Vicious!" *Would it be too much to punch him?*

"And a nurse who will be on call for Rosie. Twenty-four fucking hours a day. That's my final offer." His jaw twitched once.

We stood in front of each other like two warriors about to wield our swords, and a sob caught in my throat because, goddammit, I wanted to take the deal. What did that make me? Weak, immoral, or simply insane? More than likely all three.

This man had driven me out of California, out of my *mind*. Now he was hell-bent on hiring me. On elbowing his way back into my life. It didn't make sense. He wasn't a friend. He didn't want to help. His proposition was littered with red flags.

I tried to slam my key into the lock again but couldn't find the keyhole in the dark. Which reminded me I had an electricity bill to pay. Three of them, actually. Fun, fun, fun.

"What's the catch?" I croaked as I turned to face him, rubbing my forehead, frustrated.

He brushed his knuckles over his cheekbone, amusement dancing in his pupils. "Oh, Help, why must there always be a catch?"

"Because it's you." I knew I sounded bitter. I didn't care.

"It may entail some tasks that won't make it into your contract. Nothing too seedy, though."

I cocked an eyebrow. That didn't sound too reassuring.

He quickly caught my drift. "Nothing sexual either. You'll be happy to know, I still see more ass than a proctologist. For free."

For some stupid reason, my heart leapt when I read between the lines. Vicious was single. No girlfriend if he was still enjoying meaningless flings. Vicious was too proud a man to be a cheater. He was an ass, but a loyal one nonetheless.

"And why me?"

"The fuck does it matter?"

"It does to me," I bit out, a last ditch effort to walk away from this deal. "And also because I'm a terrible PA. *Terrible*. I once sent the accountant I worked for to a meeting with another company's file, and I nearly booked his wife a flight to Saint Petersburg, Russia, instead of St. Petersburg, Florida. Thank the Lord for airport codes," I muttered.

"You would have done her a huge favor. Florida is a fucking downer," he quipped, adding, "and your stripper outfit may have made me feel a tad bit guilty."

Liar, I thought bitterly. Yet it was so fitting that he'd found me here. One eviction notice away from rock bottom. Offering me the one thing I couldn't refuse. Dangling the health and security of my family and me in my face once again.

"I don't want to work for you." I sounded like a broken record.

"Lucky for me, you don't have much choice. When reality makes the decision for you, it's easier to accept your fate. Your tip"—he shoved one hand into his slacks pocket and took out a folded slip of paper—"was waiting for you. Next time you're asked to do something, do it in a timely manner. Patience is not one of my virtues."

"What is?" I deadpanned. Still eyeing him suspiciously, I plucked the paper from between his long fingers and took a peek, my pulse drumming wildly.

A check.

$10,000.

Sweet Jesus and His holy crew.

"Consider it a month's signing advance." He looked down at it, his brow furrowing as he examined it along with me. His shoulder brushed mine, and a warm surge lapped across my chest. "Since we agreed on a hundred fifty K, the after-tax will be about right when you start working for me."

"I don't remember agreeing to anything," I argued, but even I didn't believe myself at this point.

I'd taken on so much debt and was living off one meal a day. Not a big one either. I was at war with myself, but deep down, I knew that the money was going to win this time around. It wasn't about greed. It was about survival. I couldn't afford my pride. And my pride, unlike the money, wouldn't be able to feed me, to pay for Rosie's medications, and to make sure our electricity was still on next month.

Vicious reached for my cheek and brushed a lock of hair from my eye, his body so close to mine I could feel his heat. It threw me back to the night we kissed all those years ago. I didn't remember the moment fondly.

"Do you trust me with your life?" His voice was black velvet, caressing me in places he had no business reaching.

"No," I answered truthfully, closing my eyes, wishing it was someone else who was making me feel what I was feeling.

Hot.

Wanting.

Wanted.

Anyone else but him.

"Do you trust me with *mine*?" he asked.

The man was smart. No, smart was putting it mildly. More like a genius. He was cunning and intelligent and always a step ahead of everyone else. He kept his ass covered. I knew that, even though we'd only lived close to each other during my senior year. In those months, I'd seen him walk out of so much trouble. From hacking into teachers' laptops and downloading exams, selling them to desperate students for a ludicrous price, to burning up a restaurant at the Todos Santos marina.

But we weren't kids anymore. We were grown-ups, and the consequences were heavier.

I nodded yes.

"Show up at work tomorrow at eight a.m. sharp, Help. It's the address I gave you at that bar. And don't make me regret my generosity."

I felt a breeze moving across me when he turned the corner and left the hallway, silent as a ghost. I heard the door to my building slamming shut downstairs, and that's when I opened my eyes.

It was a good thing I remembered the address he'd scribbled for my so-called "tip" by heart. I'd somehow inked it into memory, just like everything else about him. My default mechanism with Vicious was to collect everything about him.

And now, apparently, I had a new job working beside him.

I unlocked the door and found Rosie asleep. I was relieved her meds had allowed her to sleep through the commotion we'd caused in the hallway. That was the moment I decided this was the right choice to make.

This was just another stolen-textbook moment.

I had to bow down in submission, take this Big Bad Wolf's heat, and then walk out of the situation with what I needed. But this time, I was going to be the one to leave on my own terms, not his.

That was my promise to myself.

I hoped to God I could keep it.

CHAPTER FIVE
VICIOUS

"I'll fucking ruin her." I rolled a pen between my fingers—Help's pen—the one I'd snagged from her at McCoy's.

She hadn't noticed the pen was missing—she was too flustered to realize what was happening—and that was exactly how I liked her. The pen was chewed on at the top, and it was so fucking typical of Emilia. She used to leave chewed pencils on her desk every single day in calculus class.

I may have picked them up.
I may have saved them.
They may still be in a drawer somewhere in my old room.
Shit happens when you're a horny teenage boy.

I rolled my executive chair back, pushing from my desk and swiveling toward the floor-to-ceiling windows overlooking Manhattan.

People said New York made them feel small.

But I thought New York made me feel pretty fucking big.

From my point of view, I sat on the twenty-third floor of a skyscraper, and I motherfucking owned the whole floor. Thirty-two people worked here, soon to be thirty-three when Miss LeBlanc joined us, and they all answered to me. Depended on me. Smiled at me in the hallway, even though I was an ill-mannered bastard. I mean, how could New York make me feel small when I grabbed it by the balls and made a last-minute reservation at Fourteen Madison Park for tonight?

Some folks were owned by New York, and some folks owned it. I was among the latter. And I didn't even live in the fucking city usually.

"You will not ruin your stepmom," Dean dismissed with a laugh. I was still facing the Manhattan view. He was on speaker. "You've been watching too much *Pinky and the Brain*. Only you don't want to take over the world, you just want to shit on people's lives."

"She texted me last night that she's landing in New York this afternoon and expects me to clear my schedule for her," I fumed. "Who does she think she is?"

"Your stepmother?" Dean's voice was light and amused.

It was four fifteen a.m. on the West Coast, the ass-crack between night and morning. Not that I gave a fuck. He wasn't used to the time difference yet. Lived in New York for the last ten years of his life. And he was chill by nature, the little fuckwit.

"And to be fair, you were supposed to be back in California by now. What's taking you so long?" he asked. "When the fuck are we switching back?"

I heard the woman who was in bed with him—in *my* Los Angeles bed, fucking *gross*—moaning in protest at his loud voice. I licked my lips and twisted Help's pen in my hand. I still needed to tell him that I'd hired her but decided to wait till next week. He had no idea she was living in New York all these years, and I wanted to keep it that way.

One disaster at a time. I had my stepmom to deal with today.

"Not anytime soon. Your staff's been slacking off. I'm picking up the work you've left here."

"Vicious," he grated out through what sounded like clenched teeth.

Our three-year-old enterprise, Fiscal Heights Holdings, was so successful, we had four branches: New York, Los Angeles, Chicago, and London. Normally, Dean was in New York, and I was in Los Angeles. Sergio and his stupid lawsuit had brought me here. I was the one who used my mouth for more than sweet-talking and licking ass. If we needed someone to soften a client, we sent Trent. But if shit got nasty and the situation called for intimidation or legal ruthlessness, I was the one on call.

Meanwhile, Dean was taking the opportunity to check on our Los Angeles branch. We did it from time to time, all four of us. Switched scenery, shook things up. As a token of our friendship, we stayed at each other's places. The four of us co-owned all of our residences. We were a family, and in the upper class, nothing said family like mingled estates and funds.

Normally, I didn't mind, even though I knew Trent and Dean would dip their sausages in every single honeypot within a twenty-mile radius of my condo. Those fuckers had probably bedded half of Los Angeles in my crib, but that's what I had a maid for.

And a PA who made sure the sheets they used were thrown out—or, better yet, burned—before we switched back.

This time, I especially didn't mind Dean staying at my condo. I wasn't prepared to drag my ass out of his apartment either.

Our New York branch was a mess, and I *did* need a personal assistant to sort it out. Sadly for Help, she was going to get dumped right after I was done with her. I couldn't let her work for Dean.

Not that he would even want to see her fucking face ever again.

She was dead to him. From his point of view, deservedly so. Anyway, that was her problem, not mine.

"Wrap it up, Vic." He called me by my nickname. Calling me Vicious in public had become professionally inconvenient in recent years, so now everyone just assumed Vic was short for Victor. "I want my apartment back. I want my office back. I want my fucking life back."

"And I want to live in a place where you don't have to give the taxi driver the exact fucking route like you work for them and not vice versa. Don't worry, I won't outstay my welcome."

"News flash, douchebag." He laughed again. "You already have."

I could hear the woman beside him yawn loudly. "Hey, babe, can we go to sleep?"

"Can you sit on my face while we do?" Dean answered.

I rolled my eyes. "Have a nice day, shit-face."

"Yeah, go eat a rotten ass. But not on my bed," he said, and then the line went dead.

Just in time, as I had a visitor.

"Good morning, Mr. Spencer! I brought you your coffee and breakfast. A three-egg-white omelet and a slice of toast with a side of freshly cut strawberries."

I barely listened to the chirpy voice but turned around in my chair. "And you are?" I checked out the woman in front of me. Her hair was so blond it was almost as white as her big smile. Taller and thinner than the national average. And her suit. St. John, a recent collection.

Maybe I wasn't that far off with the outrageous salary I'd offered Help. Hey, it was New York, after all.

"I'm Sue! Dean's PA." She was still bubbly. "I've been working for you for almost two weeks." Her smile was still creepily intact.

Right. On second glance, she did look familiar.

"Nice to meet you, Sue. You're fucking fired, Sue. Collect your shit and leave, Sue."

Sue suddenly looked crestfallen. I was actually relieved for her. Until now, she'd looked like a bad plastic surgeon had sewn that eerie smile on her face.

Her cheeks paled under her heavy makeup, and her mouth fell open. "Sir, you can't fire me."

"I can't?" I arched an eyebrow, feigning interest.

I woke up my Dell—fuck MacBook and fuck all the hipster posers who preferred Macs, Dean included—and double-clicked on the proposal I was working on. I was staging a hostile takeover, a surprise attack on a company that competed with one of our holdings, and fucking Sue was keeping me from finishing the last tweaks. My breakfast plate was still clutched between her French-manicured fingers, and I was hoping she could leave it on my desk before she left.

I clicked on the side comments I'd made on the Word doc last night, after I left Help's, to make sure my proposal was airtight. My eyes never left the screen. "Give me one reason why not."

"Because I've been working for Dean for two years now. I was employee of the month back in June. And I have a contract. If I've done something wrong, you're supposed to give me a written warning first. This is wrongful termination of my employment."

Her panicky voice grated on my nerves like a bad high on a weekend.

I glanced up at her. If looks could kill, she wouldn't have been a problem anymore. "Show me your contract," I snarled.

She stomped off in a huff out of the glass box I temporarily called my office. It was usually Dean's, and the fucker liked glass and mirrors, probably because he loved himself too much not to check his reflection every two seconds. Sue returned after a few minutes with a copy of her contract. It was still warm, fresh off the printer.

Goddammit, she wasn't lying.

Sue had the right to thirty days' notice and all kinds of fancy shit. This was not a standard FHH contract. I'd drafted the original myself and used every loophole known to man to make sure we had the minimum legal obligations to our employees in case of termination. This PA chick had signed a contract I wasn't familiar with.

Was Dean fucking this girl?

My eyes skimmed over her whip-thin, malnourished body again.
Probably.

"Ever been to LA, Sonia?"

"Sue," she corrected through another unnecessary huff. "And once," she added. "When I was four."

"How would you like to fly there so you can help Dean while he's working in LA?"

Her face turned from annoyed and sad to confused and then elated.

Definitely. Dean was fucking her.

"Really? But doesn't Mr. Cole have your PA to assist him?"

I shook my head slowly, my eyes still on hers. A huge smiled tugged at her lips, and she clapped her hands, barely containing her excitement. Thrilled. Such a simple creature, our little Sue was. Exactly how Dean liked them. He was stupid enough to mistake Help for someone like Sue.

I knew his ex-girlfriend better than he did.

"So I get to keep my job?" Her voice was breathless.

"It's in the contract." I smacked the papers she'd printed, eager to kill the conversation before *she* killed my remaining functioning brain cells. "Now move it. You have a flight to catch."

As soon as she left my office, I picked up my phone and called my PA in Los Angeles. People were disposable. I'd realized it from a very young age. My mother certainly was when my dad replaced her with Josephine. Of course, he'd never acted like a parent, so it was easy to believe that I was disposable too. That's why the idea that no one around me was of much importance was ingrained deep within me.

Not my friends.

Not my colleagues.

Not my PA.

"Tiffany? Yeah, collect your stuff and your last paycheck. You're fired. I'm flying someone else out to replace you tonight."

I wasn't fucking her.

She had a standard contract.

Goodbye.

I saw her on the security monitor near my laptop the minute she walked through the etched-glass doors into the reception area of FHH.

My new PA arrived at eight a.m. sharp, but to say I wasn't impressed was an under-fucking-statement. I'd expected her here at least fifteen minutes earlier. I'd talked to Sue at seven thirty, and I had better shit to do than wait around for Help. But I should've known better. This girl had always been a headache.

I couldn't ignore her when I saw her at that seedy bar, McCoy's. For one thing, she'd been dressed like she was about to climb over my lap and give me a twenty-dollar lap dance. For another, her shoes were too small, and the bra peeking from her uniform was two times bigger than her boobs. Meaning she wore shoes that weren't hers and a bra that used to fit before she'd lost so much weight.

I couldn't help but feel slightly responsible for her situation.

Okay, a lot responsible for her situation.

I'd driven her out of Todos Santos. Then again, no one told her to land her fine little ass in the most expensive city in the whole fucking country. What was she doing living in New York anyway? I had no time to ponder this as I pressed the intercom button.

"Receptionist," I barked—I didn't know her name, and fuck if I cared—"direct Miss LeBlanc to my office and make sure she's got Sylvia's iPad or a notebook."

"I'm sorry, sir, but do you mean Sue?" the old woman asked politely. Through the glass wall, I saw her already standing up to shake Help's hand.

"I meant whoever that chick was who served me breakfast," I growled.

I got back to staring at my screen when Help knocked on my door.

One Mississippi.
Two Mississippi.
Three Mississippi.

After ten seconds, I leaned back in my seat and knotted my fingers together. "Come in."

She did.

She came in wearing a red-and-white ladybug dress—I shit you not—and yellow leggings. I also saw that the heel to one of her shoes was glued on crooked. At least they were the right size this time.

Her hair was still light purple. Good, I liked it that she no longer reminded me of Jo. And her roots weren't showing anymore. Great, that meant she'd made an effort for me since my visit last night. She'd tied her hair into a loose French twist. Emilia stared at me defiantly, not even offering a hello.

"Sit down," I instructed. It was easy to be cold to people. Cold was all I knew.

My last real hug was when I was a kid. My mother. Shortly before the accident that stole her freedom. My stepmother, Jo, pretended to hug me. Once. At a charity event. After my response, she never did it again.

Help sat down, and my eyes glided over her legs briefly. She still had a nice body despite looking like she could use a good meal or three. She had an iPad clasped in her hand. Her eyes were on me. They bled suspicion and disdain.

"Do you know how to use an iPad?" I asked slowly.

"Do you know how to talk to people without inspiring their gag reflex?" she responded, mimicking my tone and cocking her head.

I swallowed down a chuckle. "I see I got someone's panties in a wad. Very well. Start writing. Book me an appointment with Jasper Stephens—you'll find his number in my email, which you should have access to by now. Then a meeting with Irene Clarke. She'll want to meet outside the office. Don't allow for that to happen. I want her here, and I want her to bring the other CEO of her company, Chance Clement. Then send a driver to JFK—my stepmother should land there at half past four, and book me a taxi to Fourteen Madison Park for seven p.m. We're having dinner there."

I continued rattling off orders. "I want you to send fresh flowers to Trent's mom—it's her fifty-eighth birthday—and make sure there's a personalized card with my name on it. Find her address. She still lives outside San Diego, but I have no fucking clue where. Ask the receptionist what I had for breakfast, and make sure it's on my desk every morning from now on at half past eight or earlier. And coffee. Make sure there's coffee as well. Make extra copies of every single document in this file." I tossed a thick yellow file her way.

She caught it midair, still typing on her iPad, without lifting her head.

"Familiarize yourself with what's inside. The players. Their likes and dislikes. Their weaknesses. There's an upcoming merger between American Labs Inc. and Martinez Healthcare. I don't want anything to fuck it up. Including my new PA." I rubbed my chin, my gaze shamelessly gliding over her body. "I think we're done here. Oh, and Emilia?"

Her eyes flicked up, meeting mine from across the desk.

I smirked arrogantly and tilted my head to one side. "Doesn't it feel like we've come full circle? The daughter of the help becomes…" I dragged my tongue across my lower lip. "The *help*?"

I didn't know how she'd react, just knew that I wanted to poke her one more time before she left my office. This woman made me feel uncomfortable, exposed. Fuck, I didn't even know why I'd hired her ass. Well, I did. Still, most of the time she made me feel like I wanted to explode and tear the whole place apart.

Help raised her head proudly and got up from her seat but didn't make a move toward me. She just stared at me like I was a fucking freak. I knew my shirt was stainless and ironed. Black, crisp, and sharp. That I looked presentable. Handsome, even.

Then what the fuck was she staring at?

"You're still here," I said, moving my eyes to my laptop screen, clicking on my mouse a few times without purpose. She needed to leave. I needed her gone.

"I was just thinking..." She hesitated, staring at the reception area through the open blinds of my glass office walls.

My eyes snapped to where her gaze landed—the golden FHH hung inside a bronze circle. There was a hint of a frown on her full pink lips, and despite disliking her, I wouldn't mind having them wrapped around my dick under my desk at some point.

"FHH?" She scrunched her nose in a way that I suspected most men would find adorable.

"Fiscal Heights Holdings," I replied, curt and formal.

"Four Hot Holes," she shot back. "You're the Four HotHoles of Todos Santos. You, Trent, Jaime, and Dean."

"I have no idea what you're talking about."

Just hearing her utter his name aloud made me want to punch the desk. The initials of our enterprise were our little secret, but sometimes, especially when we met once a month for beer and business, we'd talk about how we'd fooled everyone. How people put their hard-earned millions in the hands of a company whose name stood for four football idiots, three of whose rich daddies paved their way to success.

But not Help. She knew. Saw past our bullshit. Guess that was what had always drawn me to her. To the girl who lived off cheap carbs and wore four-year-old shoes but never once fawned over my big mansion and glitzy car.

There were several reasons why I hated her. The first and most obvious one was that I suspected she knew what Daryl and I were talking about in my family's library. That she knew my secret. It made me feel pathetic and weak. The second one was that she looked just like a young Jo. Same eyes. Same lips. Same slightly overlapping front teeth and that Lolita look about her.

Hell, even the same Southern accent, even though I could hear that she'd lost most of it now, after ten years.

Hating her was like atonement to my mother, Marie, for a sin that wasn't even mine.

The third one, though, was part of the reason why I didn't just hate Help, I respected her too. Her indifference to my power somewhat disarmed me.

Most people felt helpless around me. Emilia LeBlanc never had.

I uncuffed the links on my dress shirt and rolled my sleeves up, taking my time and my pleasure in knowing she was watching me. "Now get your ass out of my office, Help. I have work to do."

"Darlin', bless your heart, I swear you look too good!" Jo clutched my cheeks in her cold, leathery hands. Her manicured fingernails dug into my skin a little deeper than they should have, and not by accident.

I flashed her a detached smile and allowed her to lower my head so she could kiss my forehead one last time before everything between us went to shit. This was the most physical contact I'd allowed her over the years, and she knew better than to overstep her boundaries. She smelled of chocolate and expensive perfume. The cloying scent felt rotten in my nostrils, even though I knew other people probably found it sweet.

Finally, she released me from her grip and inspected my face closely. The bluish tinge under her eyes suggested she was recovering from yet another facial surgery. Jo was what happened to the Bond Girl twenty-five years later. Her resemblance to Brigitte Bardot used to be uncanny. Only unlike Bardot, Jo never agreed to this thing called nature. She fought it, and it fought right back, and this was how she'd ended up having more plastic in her face than a Tupperware container.

That was her problem. All the bleached-blond hair, surgeries, makeup, facials, and superficial bullshit in the world—the designer clothes and shoes and Hermès handbags—couldn't cover up the fact that she. Was. Getting. Old.

She was getting old, while my mother remained young. My mother, Marie, only thirty-five at her death. With hair black as night and skin white as a dove. Her beauty was almost as violent as the accident that eventually ended her life.

She looked like Snow White.

Only unlike Snow White, she wasn't rescued by the prince.

The prince was actually the very man who agreed to poison the apple.

The witch in front of me arranged for it to be delivered.

Unfortunately, I didn't realize the truth until it was too late.

"I adore this restaurant!" She fluffed her over-styled hair and followed the maître d' to our table, gushing about expensive shit and mistakenly thinking it passed as small talk.

I tuned her out. She wore the gray "Alexander Wang" dress I'd bought for her birthday—it took me forever to find a cheap knock-off that'd make her rich friends laugh at her behind her back—and a perfectly applied lipstick a shade darker than her favorite red wine, just to make sure she'd look prim and proper, even after her meal.

A part of me was angry at Help for not fucking up any of the tasks I'd given her today. I thought she'd promised to be a shitty PA? If only she'd forgotten to book Jo a driver, I wouldn't be here now.

I trudged through the avant-garde design of the exclusive restaurant, moving past walls made of live plants, French doors, backlit black cabinets, and ornate paneling. For a few seconds, I felt like a kid who was about to endure some punishment he dreaded, and on some level that's exactly who I was.

We sat down.

We drank our water silently from crystal stemware that was as impractical as it was nonsensical.

We flipped through the menu, not looking at each other, murmuring something about the difference between Syrahs and Merlots.

But we didn't talk. Not really. I was waiting to see how she was going to broach the subject. Not that it mattered in any way, of course. Her fate was sealed.

She'd not murmured a word about the reason she'd flown here, not until after the waitress served us our entrees. Then she finally spoke up. "Your father's getting worse. He's going to pass soon, I'm afraid." She stared into her plate, poking at her food, like she had no appetite. "My poor sweet husband."

She pretends to love him.

I stabbed my steak with my fork, cutting into the blood-rare filet, chewing the juicy piece of meat, my face blank.

But my hate for him is genuine and real.

"That's a shame," I said, my voice devoid of emotion.

Her gaze met mine. She shivered inside her fake designer number.

"I'm not sure how much longer he's going to be able to hold on." She rearranged the silverware over the napkin she hadn't placed in her lap, straightening it in a neat line.

"Why don't you just go ahead and spit it out, Jo." I smiled politely, draining my glass of scotch—fuck wine—and sat back, making myself comfortable. This was going to be good.

Squeal, Mother. Squeal.

She took a tissue from her purse, patting the mist of sweat from her waxy Botoxed forehead. It wasn't warm in the restaurant.

She was anxious.

It felt good.

"Baron…" She sighed, and my eyes clenched shut, my nostrils flaring.

I hated that name. It was my father's. I would've legally changed it long ago if it weren't for the fact I didn't want anyone to know I gave a shit.

"You don't need all of his money," Jo said with another sigh. "You've built a multimillion-dollar company on your own. And, of course, I have no expectations about how much I might inherit.

I just need a place to stay. This whole thing has caught me so unprepared…"

I was only ten when Dean's father, Eli Cole, a family law attorney who represented some of the biggest actors in Hollywood, shut Dad's office door for a two-hour consultation on estate planning. Despite being crazy for Jo—or maybe because he was crazy for her and never really trusted himself—Dad insisted on a prenup that protected every penny and gave Jo nothing if she ever filed for divorce.

Death wasn't a divorce, but she was worried about the will.

Neither Jo nor I knew what his will said, but we could guess. My father was a vain old man whose wife was once his mistress, a second violin to his business empire. And me? To my father, I barely existed except as a name that symbolized his legacy, but unlike her, I could help that legacy live on.

In all likelihood, I was going to be in charge of his entire business empire soon. I would hold the purse strings, and Jo was worried that my main vice—vindictiveness—would mean she was going to lose her cushy lifestyle. For once in her miserable life, she was right.

I exhaled, lifting my brows and looking sideways, like she'd caught me off guard. Not uttering a word—it was too much fun to watch her hopeful gaze as it met my armor of indifference—I was about to take another sip of scotch, only to find the glass empty.

"If we find out that he…" She trailed off.

"Left you penniless?" I finished for her.

"Give me the mansion." Her tone was clipped, and surprise, surprise, she was no longer pretending to be warm and motherly. "I won't ask for anything else."

The way she looked at me—like a brat who'd been denied their favorite toy, like she was in a position to negotiate—almost made me laugh.

"Sorry, Jo. I have plans for that mansion."

"Plans?" She seethed, her bleached teeth shining with saliva. "It's my home. You haven't lived in Todos Santos for ten years."

"I don't want to live there," I said simply, tugging at my tie. "I want to burn it to the ground."

Her blue eyes flared, and her mouth collapsed into a frown. "So if it comes to that, you won't give me even one thing, huh? Not even the mansion."

"Not even the fruit bowl on the kitchen counter. Sans fruit," I confirmed, nodding. "We should do this more often, Jo. Spend time together. Dine. Share a nice wine. I had a lot of fun tonight."

The waitress placed the bill on our table, the timing perfect, just like I'd arranged. I smiled, and this time—this one miserable fucking time—my smile actually reached my eyes. I yanked my wallet out of the breast pocket of my blazer and handed over an American Express black card. The waitress took it immediately and vanished behind a black door at the end of the busy room.

"Remember, Baron, we don't know what the will says." Jo shook her head slowly, her eyes hard. "There will be no mercy for those who have not shown mercy to others." She was quoting the Bible now.

Nice touch. I distinctly remembered *Thou shalt not kill* somewhere in there too.

"I smell a challenge. You know I'm always a little silly for a challenge, Jo." I winked and thumbed my collar, widening it. I'd been in this suit for far too long. I wanted to shed it along with this shitty day. My expression remained amused.

"Tell me, Baron, do I need to seek legal representation for this?" She leaned forward, her elbows on the table.

Elbows on the fucking table? Josephine would've smacked me good if it were me with my elbows anywhere near the table when I was a kid. Her brother would've finished the job with his belt in the library too.

I cracked my neck and squeezed my lips together, pretending to think about it. I definitely had legal representation of my own. It was the nastiest motherfucker to ever study law, and it was *me*. I might be cold, heartless, and emotionally handicapped, but Jo knew, beyond a shadow of a doubt, that I was also the best in the business.

I'd spoken to Eli Cole too. He'd agreed to represent me in case my father did leave her something and I needed to scare her off. I wanted her penniless. It wasn't about the money. It was about justice.

The waitress reappeared with my credit card. I tipped her 100 percent and got up, leaving my stepmother alone at the table in front of her half-eaten dish. My plate was clean. My conscience was too.

"By all means, please feel free to lawyer up, *Mother*," I said as I shouldered into my cashmere pea coat. "Frankly, that's the best idea you've had in years."

CHAPTER SIX
EMILIA

TEN YEARS AGO

"Sure you don't want to go back to the party?" I asked Dean between breathless kisses.

He nuzzled his nose into my collarbone, our lips swollen from the last half hour. We'd kissed until we'd run out of saliva and our mouths were numb. I liked his kisses. They were good. Wet. Maybe a little too wet but definitely enjoyable. Besides, we were still figuring out how to enjoy each other. Things were going to get even better with time. I was sure of it.

"Party? There's a party?" Dean rubbed the back of his neck, pinching his eyebrows together. "Cut that shit, Millie. I didn't even notice. Way too busy spending time with a girl who tastes like ice cream and paints like Picasso." His voice was husky and hoarse.

I ignored the Picasso remark because my style was nothing like his, but I appreciated the compliment, I guess. Okay, it annoyed me a little. Because I knew for a fact Dean didn't know even *one* Picasso painting.

God, what was wrong with me?

I liked Dean a lot. He was handsome, with his chestnut man-bun and green eyes. I ran my hand over his bulging triceps, groaning with need when I thought about what they could do to me if and when we decided to take our make-out sessions to the next step.

Soon, Dean was going to ask for sex.

Soon, I was going to agree.

I would be happy to give him my V-card if not for the nagging feeling that this was just another cruel Vicious joke. Surely, Dean wasn't hateful enough to date me just so Vicious could make fun of me later? No, he seemed genuine. The sweet messages. The coffee he brought me every morning when we met at school. The late-night phone calls. The kisses.

When he'd first asked me for a date months ago, I'd politely declined. He'd persisted. For weeks and weeks, he'd waited next to my locker, beside my bike, and outside my family's apartment at the estate. He was relentless and focused yet kind and sweet. Said that he promised not to touch me until I was ready. Said I shouldn't judge him based on his reputation. And claimed to have a ten-inch dick, which meant absolutely nothing to *this* virgin. I might have playfully punched his arm for the latter.

But I was lonely, and he was cute and nice to me. Having someone was better than having no one.

Sometimes, doubt still crept into my mind. I had unresolved feelings toward his good friend. Granted, most of those feelings were negative, but still.

As if sensing my wall of defensiveness going up, Dean leaned into me on my narrow single bed and pressed his lips to my temple. "I really like you, Millie."

"I really like you too." I sighed, rubbing his cheek with my thumb. I'd spoken the truth. The feelings he stirred in me, they were positive. Safe. But they weren't wild. They didn't drive me crazy, and they didn't make me want to act irrationally and unlike myself.

Which was good. I think.

"All your friends are out there. I'm sure you want to hang out with them." I nudged him softly. "You don't have to choose between me and your parties."

But that wasn't the whole truth, and we both knew it.

"I'd rather stay here with you," he said, lacing his fingers through mine.

We both looked at our hands, silently contemplating our next step. The atmosphere shifted into something heavy that pressed on my chest, making it hard to breathe.

"Then I'll come with you." I mustered a smile.

I didn't like Vicious's parties, but for Dean, I was willing to show my face. Even though it was a face no one wanted to see.

People at school still thought of me as an inbred hillbilly. But now, I was no longer bullied. Once it became known that I was hooking up with Dean Cole, no one dared to stuff crap in my locker or mutter hateful words when I walked by. Even though it was difficult to admit, that was a big part of the reason why I liked spending time with my new boyfriend.

He made life easier. Nicer. *Safer*. I wasn't using him by any stretch of the imagination. I cared about him. Helped him with his homework, left "good luck" sketches in his locker last fall before football games, and smiled like a loon every time he walked by me in the hall this winter.

"You'd do that for me, babe?" An easy smile spread across his face. Out of the four of them, Dean was the stoner. He seemed to take everything in stride. Including our relationship. "I knew you were perf." He was already up on his feet, pulling me by the hand. "Now hurry up, babe. I'm dying for a beer, and I've got some killer bud. Trent and Vicious are gonna shit themselves."

I flashed Dean a weak smile through my reflection in my small mirror as I fixed my hair. I liked my hair messy, but no matter what I tried to tell myself, I cared what people thought. I cared, and like everybody else, I wanted to be liked.

I was wearing a creamy oversize sweater, cropped to my midriff and falling off one shoulder, and a pair of cutoff denim shorts. I slipped into my black-and-pink-flowered boots and chuckled when he jerked me to his body and kissed me hard again.

I pulled away after a few seconds, wiping our saliva from my mouth.

"After you," I said.

He stopped, his brow furrowing, a serious expression on his face. "I love that you want to make me happy. Wherever we're going next year, we're going together. Got it?" He was staring at me like I was the sunrise.

It felt nice.

So nice.

I allowed myself to bathe in his warmth, even though it wasn't mine to take.

"Yeah, Mr. Caveman. Got it." I rolled my eyes but smiled.

He kissed me again.

So safe.

He smacked my butt lightly. "Good. Let's move it."

I was ready to be happy with him. I really was.

"Last Nite" by the Strokes was pouring from the speakers as we shouldered our way through the drunken crowd. People were standing, dancing, and making out in Vicious's living room like they owned the place. When my family first started working here, I couldn't understand how his parents allowed him to throw these wild parties every weekend. Turned out they just didn't give a damn. Not about the parties and definitely not about their son.

Baron Senior and his wife, Jo, were never around, especially not on weekends. It was my suspicion that Vicious lived by himself at least 70 percent of the time. I'd been there for over four months, and I could count on one hand the number of times I'd seen him interact with his father.

I didn't even need one finger to count the times he'd interacted with his stepmother.

I thought it was sad.

But that was the exact same thing Vicious thought about *my* life.

Dean and I spent some time in the giant kitchen, with Dean tossing back shots—at least five or six—before he motioned for me to go upstairs with him. I obliged, mainly because I felt weird hanging out in the kitchen where Mama worked, and anyway, I hadn't seen Rosie anywhere on the first floor. I was hoping she was upstairs somewhere. With any luck, without someone's tongue shoved into her mouth in one of the many bedrooms. It wouldn't be a big deal—and definitely not the first time I'd caught her making out with some random guy—but it always made me feel like a protective mama bear.

Upstairs, Dean strode right through the door into the media room, while I hesitated outside, scanning to see if I could maybe spot my baby sister on the landing or in one of the hallways to the right and left.

Truth was, I wasn't only looking for her—I was also looking to avoid the other HotHoles. To say that they didn't like me was like saying the Pacific was slightly damp.

They hated me, and I had no idea why.

"Jaime, my man!" Dean slapped his good friend's back as he entered the inner circle of his friends inside.

They were all standing with beers in their hands, talking animatedly, probably about sports. I stayed in the hallway with the rest of the rejects. I didn't want to go in and give Vicious the opportunity to scowl or say something crude in my direction.

After a few minutes, Dean whipped his head toward the door and noticed I was still outside. I didn't particularly care, if I was being honest. I was talking to a girl named Madison who also rode a bike to school every day. But she did it to get fit and thin, whereas I did it because I was poor and didn't have a car. We were talking bikes when Dean waved me over.

"Babe, what are you doing out there?" he slurred on a hiccup. "Get your fine ass in here before I bite it."

Madison stopped talking and gawked at me like they'd just called me onstage to receive a Nobel Prize. I disliked her at that particular moment.

I shook my head. "Having fun right here, thanks." I smiled into my bottle of water, wishing I could disappear. I didn't want Vicious to notice me.

"Fuck's going on here?" I heard Trent—beautiful, charming Trent Rexroth, who was a nice guy to everyone but me—grumbling from inside the circle. When he raised his eyes and saw me, he looked thunderstruck. "Jesus, Cole. You're such an idiot."

Why was Dean an idiot?

When Jaime noticed I was there, he pinched the bridge of his nose before shooting Dean a dirty look. "You just had to, huh? Douche."

The circle broke, and I caught a glimpse of Vicious, his hip leaning against a desk, a beautiful girl I didn't know by his side. My chest hurt when I noticed how close he was to her. Still, he didn't touch her or even look at her.

What he *was* looking at didn't surprise me. He was staring right at me.

"That's my fucking girlfriend, man," Dean garbled to Trent, ignoring Jaime. "You better shut your pipe if you don't want that pretty face of yours ruined." He turned around, his steps wobbly and uneven, and shot me one of his panty-melting smiles, but his eyes were heavy with drowsiness and alcohol. "Millie, please?" He clasped his hands together, sinking down theatrically and walking the remaining way to the door on his knees. His dimples were on full display, but it did nothing to ease my embarrassment.

I turned a nice shade of tomato red and buried my face in my hands, my fake smile so wide my cheeks hurt. "Dean," I groaned, squeezing my eyelids together. "Please get up."

"That's not what you said just twenty minutes ago, babe. Actually, I think it was 'Dean, does it ever go soft?'" He snorted out a laugh.

I was no longer smiling.

When my hands left my face, it completely wiped the grin off his face. Behind his back, Vicious sent me a death glare, his jaw twitching to the rhythm of my heartbeats.

Tick, tick, tick, tick.

His lips were so thin, they were practically invisible. The first step he took forward made me flinch. He cut through the mass of people in the media room toward the hallway in a few long strides and yanked Dean from the floor by the back of his collar. Dean spun in place, his face colored with surprise, and that's when Vicious slammed Dean's back against the nearest wall, twisting his designer white crew-neck shirt.

"I told you not to bring her here," he whispered darkly, his lips barely moving.

My heart stuttered in my chest.

"What the fuck is wrong with you?" Dean pushed him away, taking a step forward, his every move laced with unrestrained adrenaline.

They stared at each other for a moment too long. It made me think this was going to escalate to a fight, but Jaime and Trent stepped in. Trent pulled Dean toward the door, while Jaime shoved Vicious deeper into the room.

"Enough!" Trent shouted at both of them.

Jaime grabbed Vicious's arms, locking them behind his back. The rage radiating from both of them was thick in the air like suffocating smoke.

"Tennis court." Vicious shook out of Jaime's hands and pointed at Dean, seething. "This time don't cry when I fuck you up, Cole."

I didn't want them to fight. Vicious fought until he passed out. His arms had the scars to prove it.

Trent rotated, marching in my direction and narrowing his gray eyes at me. "Get the hell out of here," he commanded, his big body filling the doorframe, his eyes hooded. He looked royally pissed off.

I couldn't see Dean or Vicious. Whatever was going on, it was a private matter. Dean and I had been together for a couple of months, but I knew the other HotHoles wouldn't help me stop the fight. I'd be wasting my breath.

"When are you guys going to stop acting like I've got leprosy?" I questioned in a low voice, folding my arms across my chest. "Dean is my boyfriend, and y'all have literally never spoken a nice word to me. Why do y'all hate me so much?"

Trent shook his head, a bitter chuckle leaving his lips. "Jesus. You really don't know?"

"I really don't." My face heated again. Was I missing something that was colossally clear?

When he leaned down, his face level with mine, I shivered. "If you think you can rip us apart, you're wrong. Leave Vicious alone."

Leave Vicious alone?

My blood went from zero to boiling in a second, and I was ready to burst. Baron Spencer was everywhere. Where I lived, where I hung out, where I slept, and where I studied. That was fine and not his fault. But he didn't have to look at me the way he did, to talk about me the way he had. He didn't have to bark at me and mock me every chance he could.

Leave *him* alone? No. I'd had enough.

Vicious wasn't only in my life without my permission. He was in my veins. Always close by, like a shadow, haunting me without really touching me every time he was close enough to grab me by the throat.

"Happy to. I don't want anything to do with the guy anyway."

Throwing a look of indifference in Trent's direction, I swiveled and stalked downstairs, through the kitchen and out the servants' entrance. I needed to find Rosie and tell her what had happened. She would make sense of it all.

I was a little mad at Dean for making that crude joke.

I was *a lot* mad at Vicious, Jaime, and Trent for acting like I was a North Korean dictator. They were obviously allergic to me, and though it was never my intention to become the modern-day Yoko Ono, I was starting to believe breaking up with Dean was inevitable.

The HotHoles were such a huge part of his life. If they didn't like Dean's girlfriend—me—that was a serious issue. I was tired of feeling like an STD they were trying not to catch every time I was near them.

I deserved more.

More respect.

More patience.

More acceptance.

Just *more*.

I headed for our apartment and flung the door open. The small living room, like my mood, was dark and cold. Mama and Daddy were already asleep, and when I opened Rosie's door, her room was depressingly empty. She was probably hanging out by the pool with some of her friends. Unlike me, she'd made a few of those at All Saints High. Mostly people from neighboring, less affluent towns.

I entered my room and slammed the door. Pulling my blanket over my head, I closed my eyes, wishing for sleep. I didn't even bother crawling into my pj's, just kicked off my boots. I wanted the night to end and for tomorrow to swallow the memory of it whole.

I tossed and turned, knowing full well I couldn't go to bed with all the music and shouting coming from outside. Lord only knew how my parents slept so peacefully through these parties. I stared at the ceiling, and it stared right back at me. I started thinking about Dean, but my thoughts quickly moved to Vicious.

Vicious. Always ruining everything. Pinning me down, kicking me out, throwing me into an emotional twilight zone. My eyes fluttered in the dark, and I sighed.

The door creaked. My heart stopped. I knew who it was. Rosie would've asked if she could come in. So would Dean. No. The only person who'd never bother knocking, even though he wasn't welcome anywhere near me. He'd walked into my parents' house like he owned it because he did. In his mind—I had no doubt—he owned me too.

"This shit stops now." His voice echoed in my small room, dripping with ire.

Rolling over in bed so my body faced the door, I felt my pulse beat against my throat. I took him in silently, my eyes roaming every part of his body. He leaned against the wall, glaring while I lay in my bed. My heart did something crazy in my chest. Cartwheels or somersaults—I wasn't really sure.

Because he had never been so close.

Never been in my territory.

This was the first time he'd deliberately sought me out, and it didn't feel nice and safe.

It felt divine but dangerous.

Even though I liked the notion of him looking at me while I was in bed, I rubbed my thighs, pushing myself to a sitting position, my back against the headboard. Sonic Youth's version of "Superstar" seeped through my window, and I got drunk on this one perfect moment.

It felt like I'd won something, and I hated that I was flattered. Vicious always seemed so unaffected when it came to the opposite sex. I rarely saw him with the same girl, and he never visited any of his flings at their houses. It was just one of those facts of life every girl at school knew. Girls came to him, and not vice versa.

Yet here he was, in my house, in my room, near *my* bed. Even if he'd come here just to threaten me some more, he'd still made the trip. *I got to him.*

He was in my veins.

But I'd managed to crawl under his skin.

"To what do I owe this pleasure, Vicious?" I mocked. The words felt bitter on my tongue. I wasn't a meanie. Before we moved here, I was friendly. Kind. Now, less so, but still incapable of deliberately hurting someone.

The room was dark, but light poured in from the party outside, invading every inch of space that belonged to me.

Except it actually belonged to him, and Vicious never let me forget that.

He didn't even look at me. Just stared at a mural I'd painted on my wall—his wall—of a cherry blossom tree. His eyes were blank. Turned off. I wanted to grab his shoulders and shake him, turn on the light inside him, make sure someone was home.

Vicious rubbed his jaw, kicking my door shut behind him. "If you wanted my attention, congratulations, you've got it. Now break this Dean bullshit off."

I flung the blanket to the floor and bolted to my feet. My sweater slid down one shoulder, and my plain white bra peeked out. I was too agitated to care. I pushed him with all the strength I could muster, not even a little worried about the consequences. His broad back bumped against the wall, but his expression remained cool.

I took a step back, placing my hands on my hips. "What's your problem with me, huh? What have I ever done to deserve this? I don't go in your house. I don't look you in the eye when I see you at school. I don't talk to you or about you. But it's not enough for you. Look, I don't want to be here either, okay? I never signed up to live in Todos Santos. That's all on my parents. They need the money. We need the money. Rosie has an illness and healthcare's better here, not to mention this place is rent-free. Tell me what you want me to do that doesn't require my family being homeless, and I'll do it, but for Lord's sake, Vicious, leave me alone!"

I wasn't sure exactly when I began to cry, but hot, fat tears ran down my cheeks. I think I must have boiled to the point of overflow. I didn't like that he was seeing me like this, vulnerable and broken, but hoped it would inspire him to be a little less hateful to me.

His eyes dragged slowly from the mural to me, his stare still vacant.

I raked my fingers through my hair, frustrated. "Don't make me be mean," I muttered. "I don't want to hurt you."

"Break up with him," he repeated, curt. "Make it stop."

"Make what stop?" I frowned.

He squeezed his eyes shut. "Emilia," he warned.

About what, I didn't know. But for once, he didn't refer to me as *Help*.

"He makes me happy." I stood my ground because who the hell was Vicious to tell me who to date?

"He's not the only one who can make you happy." He opened his eyes, and pushing off the wall, he took a step in my direction.

My skin was on fire, and I knew what would soothe the burn away, like an aloe balm, but it was wrong. So wrong. So was him ordering me to stop dating Dean.

Then why does a part of me feel pleased?

"Ask me what I want again," he snapped. His voice was like ice rolling on my skin, leaving uncomfortable shivers of pleasure in its wake.

"No." I started walking backward, still facing him. He followed me. A predator stalking his prey, and he had the physical and psychological advantage over me.

I was about to become his next meal, and I had no doubt in my mind—he was going to devour me.

"Ask," he breathed. My back had hit the opposite wall and his arms came up around me, caging me in. I was trapped, and not only physically. I knew there was no way out, even if he'd stepped aside.

"What do you want?" I gulped. I wanted him to make it stop too, and I wasn't even sure what *it* was. But it was there. I felt it too.

"I want to fuck you and watch your face while I do. To see how you drown in me as I hurt you as much as it hurts me to have to see your goddamn face every day."

I sucked in a breath. Not sure how to respond, I raised my hand to slap him across the face. He captured my wrist, stopping me before my palm reached his cheek, and shook his head slowly.

"You need to earn the right to slap me, *Pink*. And you're not there yet."

Pink. My heart stuttered.

I was horrified that he affected me this way. It seemed like no matter what he said to me, he always left a dent. In my brain. In my thoughts. Making me dissect him. But with him here, admitting to wanting to have sex with me…something changed.

We were flush against each other, and I was drunk on his scent and high on his face, and oh my Lord, I knew we hadn't done anything, but it felt so much like cheating. Self-loathing made my stomach churn. I wiggled my wrist free, trying to push past him. But he wouldn't let me go.

"Ask me what I want," he ordered again, his pupils so wide his eyes were almost completely black.

He was following me again, matching me step for step. My wrist was still clasped in his hand, and a part of me wanted to know what it'd feel like to fall into his claws. But this chase was going to end soon.

The back of my knees hit my bed, and the hunt was over.

"What do you want?" I obeyed him, asking the question not because I had to but because I wanted to know what vile thing he'd say next. It was bad. It was immoral. And it was the moment I knew I should break up with Dean. I should've never agreed to date him in the first place.

"I want you to kiss me back," he whispered into my face, his breath tickling my cheek. *So close*.

"But you—"

He shut me up by slamming his lips on mine. They were warm and sweet and *right*. Not too wet and not too dry. His kiss was carnal, deep, desperate, and I felt dizzy—breathless—the weight of his muscular body pinning me to the edge of my bed, seconds from pushing me onto the mattress.

But I wasn't going to cheat on Dean, no matter what I felt. It wasn't who I was. So despite the tingle sizzling down my spine and to my toes, I jerked my head to the side, looking at the floor and pinching my lips together. I covered my mouth with one hand to make sure he didn't try to do it again.

"Get out of my room, Vicious," I said through my shaking fingers. It was my turn to order him.

He stared at me intently for a few heartbeats. I saw him from the corner of my eye, angry, and…defeated? It was the first time I'd hurt him back, and even that was only because I absolutely had to.

I wasn't a cheater.

But not hurting Dean felt like crap because I'd hurt Vicious instead.

It took him a few seconds, perhaps less, to compose himself.

Then he leaned forward. "Ask me again," he said for the third time, a sly smile on his face.

I closed my eyes and shook my head no. I was done playing his twisted game.

"Ask me how she tasted when I kissed her tonight after we threw you out of the media room. Your sister, Rosie." His voice was velvet, but his words were poison, and I crumbled inside.

It hurt me more than I could ever describe because I knew it was true. He sliced through my flesh, leaving pain with every stroke of his imaginary knife.

"Let me give you your answer, Help. She tasted like you…but sweeter."

CHAPTER SEVEN
VICIOUS

THE PRESENT

"It's open."

Help waltzed in, and holy fuck, what the hell was she wearing?

She looked like she'd gotten lost in Keith Richards's closet and barely survived to tell the tale. She wore leopard leggings, ripped at the knees, a black Justice tee (the band, not the philosophical theory), a checked raincoat, and cowboy boots. Her lavender hair was mostly covered by a beanie, and she held two Starbucks coffees, taking a sip from one. She looked like the PA of the CEO of a multimillion-dollar financial company like I looked like a prima ballerina. If this was another way to show me she didn't give a shit, it worked.

"Hey." She slid one of the Starbucks cups across my desk. It bumped into my forearm.

I glanced at it without touching it, returning my eyes to my laptop screen. "What the fuck is this?" I wasn't completely sure if I was referring to her outfit or the Starbucks. Was this Halloween? I checked my calendar just in case. Nope. We were definitely deep into December.

"Your coffee. Your breakfast awaits in the kitchen." She threw her Harley Quinn courier bag across the brown leather sofa in the corner of my office.

It took everything in me not to toss the coffee against the wall and send her on her way back to unemployment. I reminded myself that I hadn't hired Help for her magnificent PA skills or her fashion sense. I needed her. She was a part of a bigger plan, and I was gearing up to execute it. Soon, she was going to be worth the money and the glitzy apartment.

And she is better than my ex-psychiatrist for the testimony, with her big, innocent eyes.

Fuck. *The apartment.* In my quest to convince her to take the job, I threw out a lot of shit I needed to back up now.

I sucked in my cheeks, feeling my jaw locking. "Get me my breakfast," I hissed out.

"No," she replied evenly, clearing her throat and tilting her chin up. "Your highness, I request that you go to the kitchen and have breakfast with your loyal subjects. I believe it's important that you familiarize yourself with your colleagues. Did you know half the floor is sitting there right now? It's French Toast Friday."

She tilted her chin even higher, inspecting me.

Of course I didn't fucking know that. The very notion of getting out of my office and spending time with those people who I didn't know or care about was making my insides bleed.

She stared me down, and I wondered what was going through her little purple head. Actually, I was also interested in the origins of that lavender hair. I didn't hate it. It suited her round face and eccentric style. She knew—Emilia LeBlanc fucking knew—she could bring a man to his knees, so she never bothered with pretty dresses and makeup. She wasn't a tomboy—in fact, today she was even dressed up, in her own weird way. Her hair was always a mess, though, and she looked like one of those urban New York chicks who carried professional cameras around, taking photos of their Pret A Manger breakfasts and pinning them on Pinterest, genuinely believing that they were legit photographers.

And still, I knew Help well enough to recognize that she

wasn't being pretentious. She really was an artist. The best painter I knew.

"Vicious?" she asked.

I slammed down my laptop screen, leveling my eyes at her. "Get me my breakfast. Unless you want to get back to bussing tables in a French maid uniform?" My voice dripped ice. It calmed my nerves a little.

She squinted at me, not budging.

I'd forgotten how hard to tame she was.

And I'd *definitely* forgotten how much it turned me on.

"You won't fire me. You need something from me. Heck if I know what, but if you're so desperate you gave me a job, I have a feeling I can bend you a little too." She waggled her brows and let out a throaty chuckle. "Come on. It'll be fun to meet the people you work with."

I hated that she had leverage over me and that she knew it. Help, of course, was right. We needed each other. She needed my money, and I needed her cooperation. Weighing the situation, I decided to pick my battles.

"Let's make one thing clear so that there won't be any future confusion. I'd hate to kick your ass on your second day, but I also won't hesitate to do so. You're my employee. Hence, I make the rules. The moment you signed that contract, you became mine. You will serve me. You will obey me. You. Will. *Help*. Me. Understood?"

Our gazes locked, and I allowed myself to get sucked into those blue eyes for exactly two seconds. They were Smurf-blue today. Probably not the best analogy, but shit if it wasn't the truth. Help's eye color constantly changed according to her mood.

She arched an eyebrow. "You promise what you want me to do isn't illegal?"

"It's not illegal," I said. *Of course it was illegal.*

"Nothing of a sexual nature?" she proceeded.

I threw her a condescending glance, as if mocking the very idea.

She was going to have sex with me. But of her own free will.

She blinked, clearing her throat. Shaking her head. *So Help needs some help with breaking the spell.*

"Fine. You got yourself a deal. Let's go. But I'm fucking warning you, I hate French toast."

Spending time with my staff reminded me why humans were my least favorite creatures.

We all sat at a round white table, and I glared at my cold toast and egg-white omelet with little appetite. Help laughed a hearty laugh, the type I had never heard before she moved to California, as she showed the geriatric receptionist something on her iPad. They cooed and exchanged grins, and I wanted to know what they were talking about but didn't ask. Then the receptionist said she was retiring at the end of January, and Help jumped at the opportunity to organize her farewell party, as if she was going to be around that long.

Whatever. I wasn't going to burst her bubble just yet.

People made small talk with each other but barely acknowledged me. My employees at this New York branch were timid and wary of me whenever I was here in person, which wasn't very often. They were used to Dean, who might have been a sleazeball but was also a pretty decent boss. I was cold, more detached, and when I got angry, I'd yell at the person who fucked up so loudly the glass walls in the office would rattle.

They treated me like I was a ticking bomb and asked the dumbest, most boring questions.

"So how do you like New York? I bet it's very different from California."

No shit, Sherlock.

"Have you done any of the holiday stuff? Ice-skating in Central Park? Rockefeller at Christmas?"

Fuck yeah. I also took selfies of myself holding the Statue of Liberty in the palm of my hand and hung it over my fridge with an I heart New York magnet.

"How big is the Los Angeles branch?"

Big enough to avoid all the people who work there with me.

I'd always been antisocial. My popularity in high school blossomed through association. I hung out with outgoing people. Trent, Jaime, and Dean lived for the crowd. But me, I still liked the silence. The humming sound of expensive electronics in my Los Feliz penthouse and nothing more. Well, maybe the slurping of a nameless woman beneath me as she sucked on my cock. Specifically, one with a hair color like Help's. That made the fantasy so much more realistic. Anything else was pointless noise I wanted to eliminate from my ears.

"I'm done," I announced to Help after fifteen minutes, getting up from my chair.

She was still engrossed in conversation, this time with the NY branch's chief accountant. He was fairly young for a senior accountant, a preppy New Englander who probably graduated from an Ivy League school. Reeked of privilege. A guy like *me*.

"Emilia…" I snapped my fingers twice, like she was my pet.

Help swiveled her head, giving me her unimpressed look before resuming her conversation with him. At this point, the guy turned mute and kept stealing glances at me like I was the Grim Reaper.

I got him. I did.

I was young. So fucking young to be a CEO. People didn't achieve this level of power at twenty-eight. But the HotHoles and I, we'd had our fair share of shortcuts, what with the ability to invest millions of family dollars in our business from the very first year. Wealth attracted more wealth. And with Jaime, Dean, and me putting ten million dollars in FHH back when we founded the company, we saw a return quicker than the average idiot entrepreneur.

We'd created a monster.

And we were in charge of it.

That made me even more formidable than your usual CEO, and the young accountant knew it.

"If you're not in my office in sixty seconds, I'll just assume you've resigned," I said easily before I turned around and left. On my way back to my office, I kicked the HR manager's door open and proceeded—without even looking at the person who occupied the desk. "The accountant kid—how good is he?"

"Floyd? He's good. Been here for three years now. Mr. Cole never complained." The middle-aged woman behind the desk looked at me like she didn't want me there. That made two of us.

"Send him to my office immediately."

"Is there a problem?"

I closed the door without answering her and then stormed back to my office, where Help already stood. Good. At least she knew that my generosity and willingness to make this work had their limits. She was focused on her iPad and seemed to give zero shits about my semi-tantrum.

"Book a flight to San Diego for this afternoon," I barked. "And arrange for my father's limo to take us to Todos Santos." Without a glance at her, I fell into my executive chair and rolled it toward my laptop, pushing my sleeves up.

"Us? I'll need the other person's name for the ticket." She tapped on her device, the trace of a smile still on her lips.

"The other person is you." My voice was flat.

Her eyes arrowed from the screen to me. "I can't leave my sister."

"I clearly remember you agreeing not to argue with me, Help. Don't start a war with me. I come equipped."

"That was before I realized my sister's health could be compromised—"

I cut her off. "Rosie will have a private nurse attending to her while you're gone. Have my people move her to your new apartment today." I scrawled the address of the building where I was living.

I wasn't stupid enough to tell her I was living in Dean's apartment. The HotHoles had invested in a few smaller units in the building. One was a corporate place we used as backup if we were all in town at once. Also a convenient place to get laid. The apartment was vacant and minimally furnished. That was more than enough for these two.

"And what do you know, this apartment has *heat*," I added, remembering the cold, drafty hallway in her ancient brownstone.

She shoved one of her hands deep into those pink-purple locks and massaged her skull in frustration. Seeing her sweating made my cock twitch. Luckily, I was behind a desk.

She had no way out. This was happening.

"I'll call Rosie and see what I can do," she muttered, her eyes shooting daggers at me. Blue with light purple hair. And that Harley Quinn courier bag.

How could you not want to fuck this chick? Of course I was hard. She looked like a rainbow.

"Here's a friendly reminder. Your sister's not your boss. I am. So you'd better not come back with the wrong answer." I twisted to my laptop when I heard a knock on the door.

"Come in," I called out, and Floyd entered my office, reeking of Brooks Brothers.

"You wanted to see me, Mr. Spencer?" he stuttered, smoothing his starched shirt. He looked like he might've shit his pants.

I was hoping he had because that would absolutely kill any chance of him and Help ever hooking up. I nodded at him while Emilia gave us a hooded glance, wrinkles knitting the corners of her eyes.

"I'll get out of your way, then," she said and turned to leave.

"Stay," I ordered sharply and pushed back, sprawled in my chair. I'd always been comfortable with other people's defenselessness. "Close the door and take a seat, Floyd. You too, Ms. LeBlanc."

They did as they were told, and I took a deep breath. I needed to tread lightly on this one.

But I needed to remind Floyd who was in charge more.

"Who am I?" I asked Floyd before he had a chance even to make himself comfortable in the chair in front of my desk.

He shifted in his seat, rubbing the back of his neck and throwing a glance toward Help before his eyes landed back on me. "The CEO of Fiscal Heights Holdings," he said.

"Try again." I knitted my fingers together, leaning back and tapping my two index fingers on my lips. "Ms. LeBlanc, who am I?"

"A sadistic jerk?" She examined her nails.

And my blood fucking boiled. I felt it bubbling in my veins as I grinned away my anger. Anger that quickly turned into delight. I liked her sass. Floyd, on the other hand, gasped in horror.

"Wrong. Try again." I turned to him. "Your turn."

"Baron Spencer," he said.

"Ms. LeBlanc?" I asked, even though I knew she'd be rude. This wasn't an argument. This was foreplay. She just didn't know it yet.

"The world's worst neighbor? I think I'm beginning to enjoy this game."

"Floyd?" My eyes landed back on him. "One last chance to get it right."

He looked so miserable. Sweaty and helpless and confused. I knew that if this leaked, I was going to get shit from Jaime, Dean, and Trent for the next century. Among us, I was known as the one who always took it a little too far with the staff.

"You're my boss," Floyd stammered, finally—*fucking finally*—getting it right. "You're my boss, Mr. Spencer," he repeated louder when he saw the approval in my expression.

"That I am," I agreed, crashing my palm onto my glass desk. "I'm your boss."

He jumped in surprise. Help didn't flinch.

"And I remind you," I continued, "I've built this company with everything I have in me. I'll be damned if something as foolish and careless as an office fling will stain the reputation of FHH."

Recognition dawned in his expression. Floyd knew where I was going with this. Office romances were something I didn't tolerate. I gave Trent shit about it, and Trent was a childhood friend and the owner of 25 percent of the company. He'd fucked his way into three sexual-harassment lawsuits in three years. I swear, sometimes it felt like 15 percent of our revenue went straight to making sure the employees he fucked and dumped stayed silent.

Sexual harassment, my ass. The women who'd sued had wanted Trent's dick more than I wanted Floyd's stupid-ass, tennis-loving, hipster-glasses-wearing limp body out of my fucking vicinity. There was no way I was letting Justin Timberlake Junior with his secondhand Brooks Brothers suits fuck things up for me with Help.

"Do we understand each other?" I said, glancing between them. "No more flirting."

"Oh, sir!" Floyd looked horrified by the idea. "We were just talking! This is a big misunderstanding. Millie told me she used to work for an accountant. I would never... I've worked so hard to get where I am today. We were mingling, that's all. Actually, I told her about this show I started watching, *Love is Blind*. She said she'd look into it too. Anyway, I have a girlfriend."

Of course he did. And now Help knew that too.

I could see I'd pissed her off. Her lips had thinned into a hard line. Her small hands curled into fists until she had to tuck them between her thighs. She looked like she was on the brink of punching both of us. Her anger turned me on, and I made a mental note to warn her to keep her feelings to herself unless she wanted me to throw her over my shoulder and fuck her against the glass wall of my office.

"As long as you know the drill," I told Floyd, deciding I'd inflicted enough torture on him for one day. I threw my phone on the glass desk, shrugging. "You're excused, Mister...?"

"Hanningham," Floyd said, nodding at me as eagerly as a newly trained dog. "I understand perfectly, sir. It won't happen again." He rushed for the door before I changed my mind and fired him.

After he left, I turned back to my computer and resumed working, ignoring the fact Help was still there, her eyes on me, looking like she was about to stab a stapler into my chest. A grin tickled my mouth, but I didn't let it loose. She was here, she was angry, and she was going to spend the weekend with me in Todos Santos.

Those were the simple facts.

And I was going to fuck her at some point.

This was an assumption, but I was rarely wrong.

"You're pissing me off," she said quietly, her eyes still searching my face.

"And that's turning me on," I retorted, my voice flat. "So you might wanna tone down the hate glares if you don't wanna find yourself being fucked on this desk with the blinds still open."

I was still staring at my screen, working on the merger deal I was eager to get signed before Christmas, but I could see from my peripheral that she had paled. I liked how—once again—I'd gotten under her skin. Quickly.

"You're disgusting," she muttered, still staring at me—but not in a way that suggested she was appalled.

I cracked my neck, opening my browser and checking the stocks on the screen, skimming through the greens and the reds. "That may well be, but I'm balls deep in your fucking head, Help, and there's nothing you can do about it."

Her eyes glittered with rage, and fuck, I was so hard, and fuck, she was so beautiful. This was so on. I was going to fuck Dean's ex-girlfriend, use her for my personal needs, and toss her away when I was done.

And after choosing the wrong guy, there was no doubt in my mind she deserved it too.

"You just gave Floyd a lecture about the interoffice fraternization policy. No mixing business and pleasure." She leaned forward. Her elbow touched my finger accidentally, and she jerked it away.

I met her halfway, erasing the space between us across the desk. "Correction—guys like Floyd won't give you pleasure. Men like me would. Besides, the man likes *Love is Blind*," I drawled, as if this alone was a reason to fire him.

To me, it was.

"You know what your problem is, Vicious? You still haven't decided if you hate me or like me. That's why you act like this every time I'm around other men." There wasn't a trace of embarrassment in her voice. She owned up to this.

What she didn't know was that I knew exactly how I felt about her.

I hated her but was attracted to her. It was really that simple.

"You know what I feel right now, Ms. LeBlanc? I feel like you need to pack a fucking bag and start making the necessary arrangements. You're coming with me to California, whether you like it or not."

CHAPTER EIGHT
EMILIA

"You realize it sounds shady as hell," Rosie said between coughs while I packed all of our worldly possessions and tucked them into plastic trash bags in our studio apartment.

I was going to miss this place. Even though our mattress was located less than a foot from the stove and had a hole in it the size of my head and even though we had to jump to reach the top kitchen cabinets where we stored clothes, it still felt bittersweet to let go.

This was where we'd made memories. Happy, funny, sad, emotional memories. This was where we'd danced to music and cried in front of crap B movies and eaten junk food until our stomachs hurt. Where I'd painted canvases and sold my art for actual money. Where I'd helped Rosie with her nursing degree, staying up nights to quiz her from doorstop-thick books.

Now we were moving to one of the most exclusive luxury buildings in Manhattan, but I was anything but happy about it. I was frightened. I knew Vicious had plans for me, and I was absolutely positive that whatever those plans were, he was going to cash in on my fat salary.

But I didn't want Rosie to worry about it.

"Well, he said it wasn't sexual or illegal, so at least we know he's not going to sell me across the border or make me kill someone." I fake-laughed, balling up another one of my dresses and stuffing it inside a duffel bag.

I was packing up our stuff as fast as I could. I'd changed from work, opting for my black faux-leather tights and pink pom-pom sweater, and I knew I didn't have time to change again before the limo picked me up to head to JFK. But I tried to convince myself that looking plain and messy was the best approach. I didn't want Vicious to get the wrong idea. Even though he was still cold and rude to me, I'd noticed the way he looked at me. It was the same way I'd looked at him when I would sneak into the football field in high school to watch him play all those years ago.

We liked what we saw.

But I reminded myself that this man didn't do relationships. He did destructions. And one of his past projects was my life.

I zipped up the duffel and pulled a few more trash bags from a drawer, throwing canned goods, coffee, sugar, and everything else we had that was nonperishable inside. We were going to take our food with us. Vicious might have advanced me part of my obscenely large salary, but we still needed to be careful with our money. Very much so. Despite the contract he'd made me sign, I didn't know how long I'd last as his employee.

And despite what he thought, I was no fool. I was still going to look for a different job, even if it paid a fraction of the salary. Being at that man's mercy was like getting comfortable inside a golden cage with a hungry tiger.

Rosie followed me with her gaze, still lying on our mattress and coughing into a crumpled piece of toilet paper.

"You're a bold ho, Sis. I can't believe you agreed to work for the Undertaker after what he did to you. It's the second time you've let him buy you." Little Rose was the only one who knew what happened on my eighteenth birthday.

I refused to let her words get to me, though. She was the main reason why I'd taken the job in the first place.

"People do things for lots of reasons. Or do you have another idea of how to pay for our lives in New York?" I muttered.

"I don't care about our money situation. I wouldn't work for Baron Spencer." Rosie jutted out her chin, defiant.

"But you'd certainly kiss him." I turned my back to her, throwing a jar of strawberry jam and a pack of cookies into a bag full of junk food. It was a cheap shot, but I couldn't help myself.

Rosie coughed some more. "That's ancient history. Get over it. I was fifteen, and he was gorgeous."

He still is, I thought bitterly. *And he was mine.*

No. No, he wasn't. Dean was mine. Rosie had kissed Vicious because she didn't know I had feelings for him. And after that night, she'd chased him around like an eager puppy—until Vicious told her he was drunk when he kissed her and that she needed to get over herself.

I remembered that night like it was yesterday. He wasn't drunk. He was stone-cold sober. It was after he saw Dean and me, when he *knew* we were making out. I'd hurt him, so he'd wanted to hurt me back, so he'd kissed my sister.

I turned to face her, and for a moment, I felt a lot less guilty about leaving her with a nurse for the weekend. Then she coughed, and the familiar stab of protectiveness returned.

"Are you sure you'll be okay without me?" I asked.

She gave me a sideways look and rolled her eyes. "Yes, *Mom*."

I knew better than to buy it. She looked pale. Her eyes were red-rimmed, and her nose and upper lip were peeling with dry skin. What was I thinking, leaving her here in New York with a nurse I didn't even know? I realized she was twenty-five and perfectly capable, but she still had a lung infection and a mouth that could start a war, or at the very least get her into a lot of trouble.

"Thanks for doing all the packing for me, dude." She waved her hand toward the mountain of trash bags and boxes that had basically taken over the whole room.

I plopped down on the futon beside her and hugged her tightly. She buried her nose in my shoulder.

"Hey, Millie?"

"Yeah?"

"Don't fall in love with him again. I saw how you reacted after you found out we kissed. What you went through after you left Todos Santos. You can work for him, but you can't let him get to you like that ever again. You're too good for that. For him."

Just as I was about to respond, the buzzer sounded. My heart jumped into my throat, which was ridiculous because I knew it couldn't be *him* at the door downstairs.

"Be right down," I said into the speaker. But when I peered out the window and saw a man wearing a chauffeur's uniform standing next to a big, shiny black car, I froze. It was all happening too fast. I felt like I hadn't had enough time to get myself together. To prepare.

I stared at the driver, a physical reminder of how different I was from my boss. I wasn't used to being served. I'd always been the servant. Me, my parents…

Vicious was right in calling me *Help*. Not that it wasn't rude, but it was the truth nonetheless.

I grabbed the duffel and looked at Rosie. "The movers should be here soon. They'll put the furniture in storage." Another way I planned to hedge my bets. "The nurse will be waiting for you at the new apartment. I arranged for a taxi to pick you up in an hour. Oh, and your medicine is in your backpack." I jerked my chin to the bag I'd packed for her.

Rosie offered another eye roll and threw a pillow in my direction. I dodged it.

"Try not to piss the nurse off," I suggested with a straight face.

"Sorry. I piss everyone off. It's the way I'm wired." She shrugged helplessly.

"Don't forget to take your medicine, and there's a list of restaurants that deliver in your backpack. I put some cash in your wallet too."

"Jesus, dude. Thank God you're not trying to wipe my ass."

Rosie could mock me all she wanted. I didn't care if I annoyed her. But *she* was going to be okay.

And *I* was going to see our parents. It'd been two years. Lord, I'd missed them.

"Please tell Mama I got fat and that I'm dating a forty-year-old biker who goes by the name Rat." Rosie sniffled, patting her nose with the wad of toilet paper.

"Okay. That will soften the blow when I tell her I'm knocked up with twins and have no idea who the father is."

Rosie giggled, coughed, and slapped her hand over her mouth, feigning an *oops*. "I think Mama would like that, actually." She blew a strand of her toffee-colored hair out of her eyes. "Have fun, okay?"

"Hey, it's Vicious. Fun is his middle name."

"No, honey. Asshole is his middle name."

We both laughed.

I grabbed the strap of my duffel and descended the stairs, smiling to myself. I could do this. I could survive a business trip with Vicious without letting him into my pants and, more importantly, my heart. I just had to keep my eyes on the prize.

The money. The means. The key to financial freedom.

How hard could that be?

I met him at the airport.

He wore a long, dark-gray pea coat, charcoal slacks, a cashmere sweater, and his usual scowl. He was standing outside, the freezing New York weather staining his cheekbones a dark shade of pink while he puffed on a blunt.

On the sidewalk of the airport.

I was a little surprised to see he was still smoking weed. He had when we were teenagers, but he was twenty-eight now, a workaholic, and a control freak. Granted, he'd always been a control freak. He just had fewer things to control when we were kids.

I jogged the short distance from the limo to him, rubbing my arms against the cold. I'd thrown an army jacket on over my thin pink sweater, but my thrift-shop jacket didn't stand a chance against December on the East Coast. I stopped a few feet from him and started swaying from side to side to warm up. He noticed but didn't offer his coat.

"You're getting a little old for that," I remarked, slanting my eyes to his blunt.

"I'll remember that next time I give two shits about what you think." He blew a cloud of smoke into the air.

I knew that the HotHoles had always viewed me as the naive Goody Two-shoes girl from the South. They weren't wrong. Even New York couldn't harden me all the way. I'd still never smoked weed or tried any other type of drug. I still didn't use words like "fuck." I still blushed and looked away when people talked about sex in an explicit way.

"You could get into trouble," I continued, nagging. Not that I particularly cared. I just knew it annoyed him, and I liked irritating him. It gave me the false notion that I had some kind of control over him.

"So can you," he replied.

"Get into trouble?" I asked. "For what? Standing next to an ass?"

He stubbed out his blunt against a garbage can, his fingers so white they were almost blue, and flicked the butt to the sidewalk. A luggage cart wheeled by and crushed the remains of the weed into the concrete. Vicious leaned down toward me, and I held my breath, my lungs burning, anything to protect me from his addictive scent.

"If I answer your question," he said, his body close, "you'll get all feisty again. You blush every time you look directly at my face, so I'd advise against asking me about what I have in mind. Don't tempt me, Help. I'd be happy to help you stain your pristine criminal record with a public indecency charge."

Good. Lord.

"For a lawyer, you seem to be begging for a sexual-harassment lawsuit. Why?" I rubbed my hands over my thighs. I started to remember why I'd wanted to slap him half the time when I lived so close to him.

"I'm not sure." His thick, dark eyebrows pulled together. He headed toward the entrance of the terminal. I followed. "Maybe because I know you'll never have the balls to go against me. To *fight* me, Help."

And it was high school all over again.

I should've known.

After security, we turned toward the airline's executive lounge, with me carrying my own duffel and Vicious luggage-less except for a laptop bag. I tried to keep up, but he was taller and faster, and the weight of my bag was slowing me down. He didn't like it.

Vicious glanced at my duffel before groaning and snatching it from my hand.

This wasn't him being a gentleman. He probably couldn't wait to have a stiff drink.

JFK was packed with people. Snow was settling on the runways, and there were flight delays, white letters flashing on the blue electronic screens around us. The crowd was thick, the security people tired and aggravated, but still, Christmas was approaching, and the air was sweet and hopeful.

Seeing my parents this time of the year would be nice, even if we weren't going to spend the holidays together.

I glanced at Vicious. "I feel like we should set some ground rules here. I'm not going to date you, and I expect you to stop threatening men who talk to me. Floyd, for instance."

"First of all, no one wants to date you, Help. I want to fuck you, and by the way you look at me, I know the feeling is mutual. Second, it's my company, so I make it my business to know when my employees are porking each other in the bathroom."

As we breezed into the executive lounge, I blushed so hard I felt as if my cheeks were going to burst into flame. He was being crass again, deliberately so.

"Third, I did you a huge favor. The guy is a piece of crap of the worst variety." He directed us both straight to two plush recliners arranged to face one another.

We both took a seat. There was plenty of food and coffee around, even alcohol—I'd never been in an airport lounge or flown first class, so this was new to me—but neither of us opted for anything. I assumed he was used to this kind of luxury. Me, I was too stunned to make a move. It felt like entering a universe where I didn't speak the language or know the social codes.

"Fourth, you don't want a last name like Hanningham," Vicious finished.

It was so ridiculous I started laughing. Actually, I might've also laughed because I was so nervous to board a flight headed back to Todos Santos. I wanted to see my parents but dreaded seeing anyone else.

A troubling thought stabbed at me. "Will Dean be there? Is he still living in Todos Santos?"

Vicious's jaw twitched the way it did when he was unhappy about something. His grip on the arms of the recliner tightened.

"Dean's in Los Angeles," he answered, glancing at his Rolex.

I was glad I didn't have to see my ex-boyfriend after everything that went down. I eased farther into my comfortable seat, closing my eyes. I wondered if I could catch up on some sleep on the plane. I'd worked a shift at McCoy's last night—I was hedging my bets, not willing to hand in my notice yet.

I felt his eyes on me, but he didn't utter a word.

I liked when he watched me, and that bothered me.

And he was right about sex, and that bothered me even more.

I did want to sleep with him. It was worse than those butterflies that take flight in your chest the first moment your eyes lock on your crush. When I was around Vicious, they flew all the time. But I also knew that I was not a one-night-stand kind of girl. And even though I wasn't morally opposed to casual sex, starting something up with Vicious was an absolute no-no.

We shared a history.

I had feelings for him.

Bad feelings, good feelings…in short, too many feelings.

"Where are the rest of the guys?" I murmured, my eyes still closed.

Yesterday, I'd done my homework. I knew they were all partners in FHH and knew the branches of their company were scattered around the world, but I didn't know who lived where. And Dean living in Los Angeles? That was a surprise. Dean loved New York, talked about living there even when we were teenagers. It was Vicious who always preferred the glitz and plastic, the masks and pretense of Los Angeles. For a cynical person, he really seemed to hate the stark, naked honesty that was a city like Manhattan. In LA, he was another beautiful, empty mask passing for a human being.

"Dean was in New York until about two weeks ago. Then I took over. I'm not sure when we're switching back, but when it happens, I'll go back to LA. Trent is in Chicago, and Jaime is in London."

"You switch branches often?"

He shrugged. "'Bout twice a year."

"Sounds confusing. And pretty dumb," I mumbled.

"Well, I appreciate the insight, especially from someone who's been serving beer for a living."

Silence fell and I looked away, taking in the polished women and suited men around me. As far as I was concerned, the conversation had ended the second he'd decided to act like a jerk again.

"We don't usually switch places for more than a week," Vicious gritted out of nowhere. "Special circumstances kept me in New York."

It was his version of an apology, but I still wasn't satisfied. I only shrugged.

"How long have you been supporting your sister?" His eyes skimmed down my body. Regret swallowed the sarcasm and edge in his voice. He wasn't used to being nice to people. To being civilized, really. Though he seemed to be trying.

I licked my lips, refusing to make eye contact. "Too long," I admitted. "Is Jaime still with…?" I trailed off when I realized it was none of my business.

Vicious's best friend had dated our Lit teacher, Ms. Greene, while we were seniors. Their affair blew up shortly before we graduated, making waves in Todos Santos and a tsunami in our high school. Then he took off with her after the school year ended.

Vicious huffed, and even though my eyes were still averted, I knew he nodded. "They're married. They have a baby girl, Daria. Took after her mom, thank fuck."

That made me smile. "How is he doing?" I asked, knowing it was territory Vicious would feel comfortable with.

"Jaime has assumed the role of the responsible adult out of the four us. When Trent, Dean, and I get out of line, he talks some sense into our asses."

His candor made me turn my head toward him. "You were always good together, the four of you."

A dark smirk found his lips, and he shrugged tiredly. "Until you came along."

It didn't sound like a jab. He said it more matter-of-factly. I wanted to ask him so many questions—*Why me? What was the fixation with me to begin with? Why did you care that I dated Dean?* Vicious was a god among men to the girls of All Saints High. I should never have been on his radar.

I let out a sigh of relief when they announced our flight was boarding. We got on the plane before everyone else. We were scheduled to land in San Diego, a short half-hour drive from Todos

Santos, and would arrive by early evening with the time change. But after explaining everything to Rosie and packing up the apartment, exhaustion found me, lulling me into the kind of sleepiness you can't fight. And anyway, staying awake and dealing with Vicious wasn't an option that I found particularly appealing. The minute I landed in my first-class seat, I nuzzled into the headrest and closed my eyes.

Shortly after we took off, I peeked over at him for a few seconds. His gaze was on his laptop. His eyes remained there, but I knew he sensed me watching him.

"Thank you for giving Rosie a place to stay," I whispered.

His jaw twitched, but he didn't lift his gaze from the legal document he was working on.

"Go to sleep, Help."

And so I did.

CHAPTER NINE
VICIOUS

There were two things I never told anyone about myself.

Number one: I had insomnia. Ever since I was about thirteen.

When I was twenty-two, I saw a shrink to try to fix it. He said past events were responsible for the fact I couldn't sleep to save my fucking life and suggested we meet two times a week. That lasted one month.

Since then, lack of sleep had become a part of my everyday existence. I'd run on zero sleep for a few nights in a row and then pass out for a day or two to make up for it. I'd even learned to control the cycle of frustration. When I left the office late at night, instead of tossing and turning in bed like a junkie craving his fix, I went straight to a twenty-four-hour gym and worked out. Then I'd go back to my empty apartment and read the latest thriller—whatever bestseller crap everyone was talking about—or an autobiography of a public figure I didn't completely hate.

Sometimes I'd invite a woman over. Sometimes we'd fuck. Hell, sometimes we'd even talk. I wasn't against talking to the women I shared a bed with. But I never went out of my way to get them there in the first place.

I had rules, and I didn't break them.

No dinners. No dates. No visiting them at their place. Absolutely no fucking pillow talk.

Things were my way or the highway.

If they wanted me, they knew where to find me. In the morning, I'd get dressed and show up to work, freshly shaved and looking rested. I knew that the pass-out stage would eventually arrive, but I'd become better at sensing when. It didn't make my life easier, but it made the sleepless nights bearable.

Number two: contrary to popular assumptions, I was capable of love.

Sentimental, banal shit? Yeah. But deep down, I knew the truth. I wasn't a monster or a psychopath or a fucked-up sociopath like my stepmother. I loved. I loved all the fucking time. I loved my friends, and I loved the Raiders. I loved practicing law and shaking hands on lucrative deals. I loved traveling and working out and fucking.

Fuck, I loved fucking.

I glanced over at Help. It wasn't easy to ignore her sleeping beside me. So close. Her face stirred the kind of chaos in me I once had tried to tame by doing shit like Defy. Her lips begged me to take them in more ways than one. Her body too. But I couldn't. Not unless it was on my fucking terms.

I tried to work on the pharmaceutical merger deal. I tried to work and saw her shivering in her seat while she slept, goose bumps dotting the delicate flesh of her neck and collarbone.

Tearing my gaze back to the screen, I tried to work again.

But I kept stealing glances.

And I kept trying to cool down the temperature my blood boiled to every time I was near her.

I ended up pulling a blanket over her body. I watched her sleep for forty minutes. Forty fucking minutes. This was bending the rules. What was worse—I wanted to break them all. With her.

I tried reasoning with my cock. There was no guarantee Help would get into bed with me. You could take the girl out of the church in Virginia, but you couldn't take the church out of the girl. Despite her years in New York, I suspected she still wasn't a heavy Tinder user who bed-hopped her way to her next broken heart.

Plus she seemed to hate me just as much as I hated her.

And last but not least—I knew I was about to plunge headfirst into some dirty, nasty shit with my family.

I couldn't afford a distraction. All I wanted was to get the help I needed from her, maybe screw her a few times, and cut her loose.

Make it stop.

We landed at sunset, slicing through sky the color of purple with a gold undertone, just like her hair. The bite of a promising new adventure filled my nostrils when I finally got out of the airport, armed with the girl I'd driven out of this place ten years ago.

Cliff, my family driver, was leaning against the black limo, waiting for us at the curb of San Diego International's baggage claim. He rushed to snatch her duffel—I'd overnighted my luggage straight to Todos Santos—and flung it into the trunk of the limo, firing off pleasantries I didn't bother acknowledging. Emilia followed behind me, her eyes darting everywhere, drinking in the view she hadn't seen in so long.

I knew she'd visited her parents a few years ago when I was already in LA, but that was the extent of it as far as I was aware.

The drive to my father's mansion ticked by silently and gave me time to think and regulate my heartbeats. Cliff kept his mouth shut, probably remembering I was not my chatterbox stepmother. I didn't bother to raise the privacy glass. Help squinted at the side window, pretending I wasn't there next to her.

This weekend was important to me. It was the weekend when I would finally tell my father about my plans.

Help didn't mention the blanket, and I didn't mention how my brain almost fucking detonated when I caught myself doing it. Such a small gesture. Such a huge impact on my mood.

At the eight-car garage behind the house, Cliff pulled her duffel from the trunk.

"I better head to see my parents." She jerked her thumb toward the servants' apartment. "I haven't been here in a while." The accusation in her voice suggested I was to blame for that. "I hope my mother's not in your kitchen. Or am I allowed inside now?"

Another accusation. Hey, I wasn't the one who'd made them live in the servants' apartment. Truthfully, I would have offered them a place inside the house, considering it was empty. It was Josephine who was a fucking haughty snob.

"I'll pick you up at eight."

"Tomorrow morning?"

"Tonight. I have an urgent meeting with my lawyer, and I need you to take notes." She wasn't going there to take notes. Originally, I'd hoped to talk her through my plans for her on the plane, but she'd fallen asleep.

I sometimes forgot that other people slept. An average person would spend twenty-five years of their lifetime asleep. Not me. I was fucking wide awake.

I had been tempted to wake her up on the plane, but she'd looked so out of it, I was sure she wouldn't understand half the crap I had to tell her anyway. And all of it was important.

At any rate, my justification for the trip seemed to pacify Help, and she shot me a polite smile.

She was starting to get comfortable around me. I pitied her.

"I'll have dinner with my folks and see you later then."

She clutched her duffel to her chest and ambled down the pavement leading to her former home beside the garage, while I headed for the iron double doors at the front of the cold mansion where I'd once lived. Before I turned the corner, I twisted my head back toward her.

She was standing outside the door to her parents' quarters. When it opened, she jumped into her mother's open arms, knotting her legs around her thick midsection and letting out a happy squeak.

Her dad clapped and laughed. Soon, the three of them were half crying, half laughing with joy.

When I pushed my front doors open, no one was there. Nobody waited for me. But that was hardly news.

My stepmother was probably already back in Cabo with her friends. Thank fuck. And my father was probably upstairs in his bed, marching his slow way to death after his third heart attack in the last five years.

But this time, his cold, vicious heart was going to lose the battle.

Death. Such a mundane thing. Everybody died. Well, eventually. But almost everyone fought against it. Sadly for my father, he had silent enemies who prowled in the dark.

One of them was his son.

He was so hot on getting rid of my mother—so relieved when she finally died—that he forgot his time would come too. And it did, with a little push from Mother Nature.

Karma was working extra hard with this piece of work. Dad had been in great shape for a sixty-eight-year-old. He ate well, played tennis and golf, and had even cut back on the cigars.

But the work of saints is done through others.

It was time for everyone to get what they deserved for the death of Marie Spencer.

Daryl Ryler was long since dead.

Baron Spencer Senior would soon be dead too.

And Josephine Ryler Spencer would have nothing to live for. *Nothing*.

"Dad?" I called out, rooted to the foyer floor. He didn't answer. I knew he wouldn't. His third heart attack had left him weaker than ever. That was after the stroke he'd had between heart attack two and the most recent one.

Now, he was wheeled by two nurses everywhere and was barely able to communicate anymore. He was lucid, but his speech was gone. His ability to move his limbs had vanished too. My father could barely lift a finger to point at what he wanted or needed.

He once thought of my disabled mother as a burden, a liability that marred his balance sheet… Now he'd become a liability to Josephine.

What goes around comes around.

I dropped my briefcase in the middle of the vast, dark entrance hall—the curtains were always drawn in my house—and climbed up the stairs. "I'm coming for you, Dad."

This was the last time I was going to speak to him.

The last time I would pretend to give a shit.

When I got to his room, he wasn't there. My father hardly ever ventured out of his bedroom when home. His male nurses sometimes took him to the library, and if I didn't find him there, with Josh or Slade, then he was probably at the hospital. Again.

I went down to the library, and sure enough, it was empty. I stood in front of the oak desk and swiped my palm across it. Once upon a time, this had been my mother's favorite room. We used to spend so much time here together. We would sprawl on opposite ends of the sofa, reading silently and occasionally glancing at each other, exchanging grins. I was only six when the tradition began.

Sharing the silence. Our love for everything written.

Even after the car accident, when she became a quadriplegic, we still did this. Only she didn't sit on the sofa anymore. But I'd humor her, reading *Little Women* and *Wuthering Heights* for her aloud. Needless to say, they weren't my style. But that smile… Her smile was definitely worth the hassle.

When she died, Jo and Dad abandoned the room. But then Daryl Ryler, Jo's twin brother, started using it for a whole other reason.

Beating me.

I knew I should hate this room after everything Daryl had put me through in here, but it always drew me back. Because my mother's nurturing smile, a balm to my starving soul, was what I thought about when I entered the library.

Not the way Jo locked me inside while Daryl smacked me with his ringed hand until my chest was cut and bruised. Not how she lied about what happened when he whipped me with his belt until my legs were covered with welts and blood.

Head bowed, I now stared at my hands pressed against the desk. This was a position I knew too well. It's how I'd stood when they punished me.

My palms shook against the wood, and I knew what it meant. I was going to crash soon, the sleep I found so elusive demanding its due. But first, I needed to get Help to assist me with my plans concerning the will, and I also needed to break the news to Dean about her before he found out about it from his dad.

I fished my cell out of my dress pants and dialed his number, tossing the phone on the desk after putting the call on speaker. Dean answered after the third ring.

"You sent me Sue!" he greeted, his voice filled with frustration.

I leaned back. "What's the matter? I got the vibe that you were banging her. Thought you'd be happy."

"As a matter of fact, yeah, I am banging her. Which is why she wasn't thrilled when she walked in on me feasting on someone else's pussy on your office desk."

I scowled. Things like this made me feel less guilty about breaking up him and Help. Did she really need to be with a shitty guy like Dean? Like Trent? Like *me*? We were all cut from the same self-entitled cloth.

I rolled my lip between my fingers, fighting the twitch in my jaw. "You offered her a nonstandard contract without consulting me. What the hell went through your head, you dickbag?"

"Not much, but I can tell you what went on under my belt when I did it."

I actually heard the smirk on his lips.

I sighed, shaking my head. "I'm calling you out on this next time we have our monthly meeting."

"I'm so scared I'm practically pissing my pants here." Dean snorted, still unaffected. "So who's helping you in New York? You fired the mouthy she-devil who worked here. I saw her packing up her stuff yesterday."

Tiffany, my previous PA, was a bitch to work with. Not to me, of course, but everyone else at the office hated her. Almost as much as they detested me. And that said *a lot*.

"I found another PA."

"I bet you did." He laughed. "Let me guess. Old and experienced, gray hair, pictures of her grandchildren everywhere on her desk?"

I heard the echo of a bathroom, a zipper rolling down, and him pissing. *Fucking typical Dean.*

"Actually, my new PA is Emilia LeBlanc," I said, waiting for his reaction.

But there wasn't any.

I didn't want to play his game. I didn't. But after twenty seconds of complete silence, I had to say something, *anything*, so I did.

"Hello?"

The line was dead. He'd hung up on me.

Son of a bitch.

CHAPTER TEN
EMILIA

I changed into something nicer and treated my parents to a restaurant at the marina for dinner. We ordered a bottle of wine, which I could easily afford with my new paycheck, and appetizers as well as entrées. They filled me in on their lives, which, surprisingly, they claimed were a lot quieter and nicer now. Baron Senior was being cared for mainly by his nurses—he was much sicker than I'd realized. And Josephine Spencer was rarely at the mansion and often away traveling.

The restaurant was on a boat called *La Belle* and was a little fancy for my liking. They picked the place. I would have never chosen it. Everyone in town knew Vicious and his friends had set fire to the original *La Belle* during our senior year, but no one knew why.

The food was good, and the tablecloths were the kind of white you see in Tide commercials. I couldn't complain. I had food and wine in my belly and a smile on my face.

Dinner was just a distraction, though. The reason I was here was *him*.

And *he* was dangerous.

"You working with Baron Junior now?" Mama smiled in a meaningful way I didn't like. Her body was fleshy after years of being overworked and filled with home-cooked, fat-laden Southern food she would've never served to her employers, but beneath it all, she was beautiful. "Tell us about it."

"There's really nothing to tell. He needed a PA, and I needed a job. Since we went to high school together, he thought of me," I explained carefully. Calling him an "old friend" would be lying to their faces.

I left out the fact that Vicious had said he needed me to do something shady for him.

That he admitted he had less than respectable plans for me.

That he'd already threatened to fire me twice.

And I definitely left out the part where he told me he'd fuck me against the glass desk of his office for everyone to see.

"He's a fine-looking boy." My mother clucked her tongue in approval, taking another generous gulp from her wine. "Surprised he hasn't settled down with anyone. But I guess that's how it is when you're so young and wealthy. You have the pick of the crop."

I shuddered inwardly. Mama admired the rich. It's something Rosie and I were never on board with. Maybe because we had the misfortunate of attending All Saints High and tasting the disdain and snobbery of wealthy students. The bitterness stayed in our mouths long after we'd left Todos Santos.

"I never liked the boy," Daddy said out of nowhere.

My head snapped to him. My father was the Spencers' jack-of-all trades. He cleaned the pool, handled the landscaping, and was the maintenance guy when something broke down or needed replacing. He worked mostly outside and had gray hair, a sun-wrinkled face, and the stringy, muscled body of a laborer. This was the first time he'd ever spoken about Vicious that way.

"How come?" I probed, pretending to be nonchalant while I poured myself another glass of wine. I was going to be tipsy by the time I got back home, but I didn't care.

"He's bad news. The things he did when he lived here…I'll never forget them." Daddy's lips were pinched in the kind of disapproval that made my heart sink.

I knew my father. He rarely spoke ill of someone. If he didn't like

Vicious, that meant he was rude to him too. I wanted to poke at the subject but knew my chances of getting answers were slim to none. Daddy wasn't a gossip.

I paid the check, even though my parents tried to argue about it, and Daddy drove us back to the house.

My room remained the same as when I'd left it ten years ago. Interpol and *Donnie Darko* posters. The cherry blossom mural, the colors slightly faded—that was what I loved about oil colors, they grew old with you. Some pictures of me with Rosie scattered around. The room reflected my teenage years pretty accurately. Only it didn't have a huge picture of Vicious squeezing my heart until I mentally bled out.

I plopped down on my bed—with its pink floral quilt Grandmama made for me—and drifted into wine-induced drowsiness…

My nap was interrupted by a scowling Vicious standing at my door, dressed in a suit and looking scary as hell. He still hadn't learned the art of knocking.

Which was a perfectly fitting metaphor for our relationship. I was always expected to ask for permission to enter his space, but he was always barging into mine unannounced. Much like how he'd found me at McCoy's.

"It's time," he said, hands in his pockets, giving me his profile. He looked on edge, even more than usual.

I sat upright on my bed before grabbing my handbag from my nightstand, still woozy from sleep. My mouth was dry from drinking too much wine and eating too little food. He didn't budge from the door when I got to it. Just stared at me like a psychopath—the same cold, rich jerk who watched me like I was prey but who still hadn't decided if I was good enough to be his next meal.

And I was still the servants' daughter who wanted him to love her or leave her alone, just as long as he put her out of her misery.

I tilted my head sideways, refusing to pass and risk touching him. "Are you going to let me through?" I huffed.

His eyes, lazy yet brooding, gave me a slow once-over before they landed on mine. He offered a little smile that said *Fight me for it, Help*.

Whatever. I wasn't going to make a move until he got out of my way.

"Remember Eli Cole?" he asked.

Of course I remembered him. He was Dean's dad. A divorce attorney who dealt with high-profile cases and a man who always looked at me with warm eyes when I'd gone out with Dean. He was nice. Sweet. Much like I remembered his son.

I nodded. "Why?"

"Because he's who we're going to see. I need you sharp. Are you drunk?"

It stung, but I only arched an eyebrow and offered him a tight smile. "Vicious, please. We can work this out between us. Think about the kids," I mocked.

Vicious didn't appreciate my joke. He scowled and moved away, allowing me to squeeze past him and walk out the door. I felt his eyes heating my back when he muttered under his breath.

"Fuck the kids. I'll stay for the ass."

In the car, privacy glass isolated us from the driver, blocking every sight and sound in the rear. I stared out the window. Boutiques, art galleries, and day spas, all decorated for Christmas, flashed by in a colorful blur of Main Street holiday lights. This was downtown Todos Santos, where I'd collected empty memories like old receipts. I drew in the condensation on the window, dragging my fingertip along the glass, painting a face of a sad woman. The rain knocking on the window looked like her tears.

The silence was thick in the air, and the traffic and the rain became heavier as we moved through downtown. People were dashing to grab take-out food, shop for gifts, or make it to a Christmas concert.

"Are you getting a divorce?" I finally asked. I twisted my head and glanced at him. He looked every bit the rich finance lawyer that he was. I, meanwhile, wore a retro dress—royal-blue velvet—paired with silver leggings and cowboy boots.

"In a way," he mused, his gaze still hard on the window. Aloofness bled from his eyes. He hated this town. I hated it too. But while I had my reasons—I was bullied, mocked, and ostracized—he was practically a king here. It didn't make any sense.

My heart drummed wilder at his words. He was married?

"Do you want to talk about her?" I asked quietly.

He chuckled, shaking his head, and I closed my eyes, trying not to let his voice stop my heart. It didn't belong there.

"*She's* a dead woman walking. I'm getting divorced from Josephine. My father is going to die any day now. I need to protect my assets and money from his gold-digging wife."

My jaw went slack, and it was at that exact moment when Vicious's head swiveled and our eyes locked.

"Why?" I whispered. I had a bad feeling this was not the whole story. I had an even worse feeling that he was going to involve me in his war somehow. I couldn't afford to take sides. My parents worked for Josephine Spencer.

"His will. He hasn't told either of us what's in it. Jo thinks she can give me trouble and claim some of the Spencer fortune. Whatever the will says means shit. Jo's in for a rude awakening."

"What does she want?" I asked.

He shrugged. "As much as she can get, I assume. The house here. A few more properties in New York and the beach house in Cabo. Some investment accounts my dad played with over the years."

He said it casually, as if it was nothing. For me, it was a lot. More than I'd ever know.

"Don't you have enough money to go around? Does it really matter if you have thirty million or fifty million in your bank account?" It was a genuine question that I didn't know the answer to.

He shot me a condescending look before blinking once, seemingly trying to control his annoyance over my presence. "It's a lot more than fifty million, but even if it were fifty cents, she doesn't deserve a thing. Which brings me to the reason why you're here."

Just as he said it, the limo stopped in front of a house that was all too familiar.

Like most of Todos Santos, Dean's childhood home was more like a mansion, but it was less vast and glitzy than the Spencer palace, and it actually had character—the things that make a house look like a home. Full of color and art and light. Light everywhere. Outside and inside the house. And Christmas decorations. A cone-shaped tree, reindeer, and snowflakes, all LED-lit and mesmerizing in their beauty.

Neither of us spoke nor moved for the first few seconds.

Dean. I rarely thought about him anymore, but when I did, it was fondly. He was a good guy. A goofball, with something more lurking behind that big smile. The jester, the joker, the clown. I never knew whether he was sad or happy. Smart or foolish. Ambitious or a slacker. He kept his cards close to his chest. Even after almost an entire school year together, I hadn't been able to even begin to figure out who he was.

Luckily, Vicious had mentioned that Dean was in LA, so I was in the clear. I wouldn't be running into my old boyfriend tonight.

Still, there was something urgent in Vicious's eyes as he stared at me, and I found myself knotting my legs and clenching my inner thighs, his scrutiny painfully gratifying.

"If it comes to it, I need you to tell Josephine that you're willing to testify in court that I told you about how she polluted my relationship with my father. That she sent me to boarding school in Virginia to get rid of me and paid one of my teachers to report I was violent. Uncontrollable. That she sent her brother, Daryl, by to beat me when I complained. That after I got expelled, her brother moved here and continued those beatings. That Jo claimed I was hurting myself. That it went on for years."

I felt my blood draining from my face and neck, my eyes snapping to him.

"Is all that true?" I gulped.

"I don't see how that's any of your business."

Over the years, I'd thought a lot about the conversation I overheard outside the library. About the man he was with. *Daryl.* I'd replayed the scene over and over in my head a thousand times, but before now, I'd always come to the same conclusion. Vicious sounded like the one in charge. Strong, secure.

It was almost impossible to consider the idea that a guy like him could be the victim of abuse. Had it actually happened? Was any of it true?

"No one would believe you told me anything," I said. "We were never close."

"Pink and Black were." He shot me a hard look. "Principal Followhill holds the records of every fart released in the hallways while she reigned at All Saints High. She has proof to confirm it."

Pink and Black. It was the first time in years he'd acknowledged them, *us*, and bitterness hit the back of my throat. I'd always imagined that if we came clean to each other, it wouldn't be like that. Wouldn't be…so dirty.

"You said this wasn't going to be illegal. Perjury is illegal, Vicious. Very much so."

"What do you know about perjury?"

"Rosie and I are addicted to *Law & Order*. I know enough," I said under my breath.

That made him heave a sigh. "Well, for the money you're being paid, you can take a bullet or two," he muttered.

But for the first time since we'd bumped into each other at McCoy's, I didn't like his eyes on me anymore. Not because he scared me, but because he looked sad. I couldn't bear it. It was physically painful to see those dark-blue marbles shining with something that looked like pain.

"Besides," he continued, "I don't plan to let things ever advance to court. You wouldn't be under oath unless you have to testify. You just need to convince Jo that you're *willing* to testify. She'll never contest the will after you tell her what you know. Trust me."

So this was why he'd hired me as a PA and not anyone else. He needed someone who Josephine would believe had had the opportunity to know him well enough that the story would be convincing.

But I didn't actually know anything. He'd asked me to lie.

I shook my head and grabbed the door handle on my side of the car. "Why do you think that I'd lie for you? That I'd do that even if it were true?"

He blinked once and smiled before opening his side door and stepping out. His eyes weren't sad anymore. Just an empty, pretty shell, like the rest of him.

"Because I said so, Help."

CHAPTER ELEVEN
EMILIA

Dean's house hadn't changed one bit. Still big and warm and welcoming, painting a perfect picture of the privileged guy who had once lived there. After passing by a Christmas tree the size of my New York apartment and a garland in the foyer, we stopped by a large oak door at the end of the hallway. It was the first time I'd been in Eli Cole's office. I didn't know how much he knew about how his son and I broke up, but if he did know the full story, he didn't make it uncomfortable for me. Eli was older, with suspenders and a bow tie, an old-schooler who looked a lot like a professor in a *Harry Potter* movie. He was nice to everyone, always, never rude or patronizing like the rest of this town.

They were qualities that had instantly endeared him to me.

Vicious and I were sitting in plush leather chairs—antique looking and newly padded—in front of his rich, dark wooden desk. Eli didn't have a computer or a laptop on his desktop. Just a stack of papers arranged neatly on one side and a huge library of family law books behind him.

My hands were sweating, and I tangled my fingers together as I mulled over the last words Vicious had said to me before we stepped out of the limo.

Because I said so, Help.

He knew I was weak when it came to him. Knew every time he was around I was in a constant battle with my morals.

Because I'd wanted to kiss him that day despite being Dean's girlfriend.

Because I wanted to lie for him today, just to put a smile on his cruel, beautiful face.

I barely listened as Vicious and Eli discussed prenups and undue influence, wills and precedents for contesting them. Eli retrieved a thick law book from the shelves, and they talked about Jo and Baron Senior, both men hunched over the desk, reading through a decision together. Vicious looked too engrossed in what he was doing to care that I was having a meltdown next to him. So many things swirled in my head, tangling into a headache.

I was torn between Vicious's truths. The one he gave me and the one he gave the rest of the world. And my truth? It was very simple. I didn't know what was right and what was wrong. I just knew the lines between the two blurred when it came to him.

"Millie?" Eli's voice pierced through my thoughts.

I blinked and straightened my spine, smiling politely in his direction. "Yes, Mr. Cole?"

"Do you have any questions about everything we've discussed so far?" Eli knitted his fingers together and offered me an encouraging smile.

I shook my head no. No one had asked me to do anything yet, which was good, because my morals were going to win. Again.

"Everything's clear?"

I licked my lips. "Yeah," I said.

"Good. If not, you're sitting next to one of the finest attorneys I've had the pleasure of meeting. I'm sure he can brief you more about what to expect if this goes to court," Eli said. "Your testimony is Baron's best chance. The statute of limitations for criminal charges has long since expired, but he can still punish that woman. For Josephine, I suspect having no money will seem as bad as jail. It's imperfect justice, but that you can corroborate what he told you is very important. I'm so glad you've offered to testify, Millie."

Offered? Vicious had told him that I was going to help them out without even asking my permission. Oh, heck no.

I tried to soothe my nerves by telling myself that if Eli was so sure and positive about what happened, then maybe lying wasn't so bad. Maybe Jo deserved all of this for abusing her stepson. But then I remembered that before Eli was a nice man, he was a lawyer.

A lawyer who was responsible for a lot of nasty divorce settlements in Hollywood. Cases that were all about money.

He was not to be trusted, just like Vicious.

Eli escorted us back to the front door, and Dean's mom, Helen, kissed his cheek while ignoring me. Maybe she knew more than Eli did about my breakup with her son. Or maybe she simply wasn't as gracious as her husband about forgiving me for what I'd allegedly done.

When we walked to the car, keeping our distance from one another, Vicious said, "And to think that she thought you might someday be her daughter-in-law."

Again, his voice was smooth and casual but his words venomous.

"Aren't you proud of yourself for breaking us up?" I bit out, hoping I sounded just as calm as he was.

He stopped next to the car, ignoring the SoCal drizzle, and opened the door for me. I climbed into the back, scooting to the far corner to put as much space as possible between us. He joined me, but this time scooted closer than he had been earlier. Our thighs were pressed against one another.

I was just getting used to his physical proximity again when he twisted his body toward me and captured my wrist. He guided my hand to his mouth, the hot air of his breath hitting the sensitive flesh of my wrist.

"Dean ever make you feel the way you do right now?"

He stared into my eyes, searching for something. I didn't know what it was, but I wanted him to find it in them. My stare dropped to his lips, and I gulped. I could almost taste them, like that night all those years ago. Soft and warm, against all odds. And right. *So right.*

"Dean ever make you shake the way you are right now, even when he fucked you? Dean ever get you that far out of your comfort zone? Your home? Your precious *morals*?" He smiled at me, his lips a whisper from my wrist, from the heavy pulse throbbing there.

A shiver rolled down my spine, sending electricity to the rest of my body and exploding in my lower stomach.

Suddenly, it felt too hot to breathe in the car.

"Don't lie to me, Help. I can smell your bullshit a mile away. Kind of like your normal scent because you always lie to yourself when it comes to this. To us. I did you a huge fucking favor, breaking you up, and you'll thank me later. Naked. For now…" He pressed the button on the intercom, and his voice turned from a hot whisper to a clipped order, breaking the spell. "Cliff, take us back home."

It was the end of the conversation but by no means the end of the discussion.

CHAPTER TWELVE
VICIOUS

TEN YEARS AGO

Help broke up with Dean, and for the first time in months, I felt like I could breathe again. My reaction to their relationship was irrational, immature, and completely out of line, but still…if I couldn't have her, no one else could. Especially not one of my friends.

Dean seemed a little bummed but not crushed, and every time he glanced her way at school, Trent or Jaime was fast to slap his back and remind him that this was for the best. And it was. If Help were in love with him, she wouldn't have broken up with him. But she wasn't. She said she didn't want to lead him on and that he was a good guy. Said that the situation was too complicated and that the last thing she wanted to do was tear the HotHoles apart.

Too. Fucking. Late. Sweetheart.

For the most part, though, it was a good month. Trent's cast was off, so he was working on rehabbing his leg. A new *Gears of War* game came out. My dad and Jo were abroad—Austria? Australia? I didn't give a shit as long as they were gone. Emilia was lonely and solemn again. And Dean was back to acting like the funny stoner everyone learned to love because they had no fucking choice. I thought it meant that he had gotten over her ass and moved on to someone else.

I was wrong.

I found out just how wrong I was at a football training session at four o'clock on a Tuesday after school. At All Saints, the team trained year-round. We were seniors, graduating in a few months, but somebody had to whip next year's squad into shape. I was doing static stretches on a foam roller with a dozen groaning, bulked-up freshmen as I silently watched him approach.

We'd barely talked to each other since that party. I'd told him I kissed Help. Of course I did. But I left out the fact that she didn't kiss me back because it didn't mean shit.

Yeah, she didn't kiss me back, but she'd wanted to. Still did. The way her thighs clenched, the way her body poured heat into mine, the way she parted her lips and a little moan escaped from between them. The way her soft tits crushed against my hard chest.

She was a terrible liar, and she wanted me.

She was going to have me. Soon.

Dean grabbed a black foam roller and plopped down on the grass beside me, mimicking my stretch, a stupid grin plastered on his face. I ignored him. I didn't like that he'd joined my group. Recently, we'd only felt comfortable in each other's presence if Trent or Jaime was around.

"Hola, Mr. Douchebag. What's shaking?" He beamed like the stupid clown he was. We all smoked, but Dean was the only one who actually looked like a Woody Harrelson–movie dropout, with his chill smile and messy bun.

I answered with a glare and a shrug.

"Think the team'll be any good next year without us?" His elbow poked my ribs harder than it should have.

"Is this fucking small talk? 'Cause I don't do that shit." I squinted at the horizon and plucked a few blades of grass, feeling restless.

Make it stop.

I shifted on the roller, deepening my stretch. It was obvious that he had something to tell me, and it was becoming even more obvious that he was gloating. Whatever it was, he was going to have fun breaking it to me.

"You're right, dude," he said. "We should probably get to the point. So I dropped by your house yesterday. Trent wanted me to give you back your football gear."

I'd lent Trent some gear months ago, before he got injured. I'd forgotten all about it. It wasn't like I'd need it again. I wasn't a football star, off to play in college, and thanks to his fucked-up leg, unless a miracle happened Trent wouldn't be either.

"You weren't home," Dean continued, "so I figured I'd leave the gear by the garage. But then I bumped into Millie. She was trying to fix her bike outside the servants' apartment. She said hi. I said hi back. I may have been a little high. I may have told her she was a bitch for kissing you at that party…"

My jaw clenched, and I felt my teeth grinding against each other. Emilia broke up with him before I'd told him we kissed. He'd never confronted her about it because by the time he knew, she'd already dumped him.

Dean flashed me a victorious smile and patted my shoulder, pretending to clean off some grass. I shook him off.

"Dude, I'm a little embarrassed for you. Millie never kissed you back, did she? She broke up with me to pacify you, you giant, pussy baby—"

That was it.

He didn't get the chance to complete his sentence because I was all over him in a second, throwing fist after fist straight to his face. Fury blinded me, rage consumed me, and my body rippled with fire. I didn't want to hear the rest.

The next thing I felt was Jaime's arms as he yanked me from Dean, but it was too late. Dean already had a split lip and forehead, and his nose looked like it needed to be put back in place. I launched at him again, even with Jaime and the second-string quarterback, Matt, trying to pin me down to the grass. I grabbed Dean by his shirt and pressed my nose to his.

"You back with her?" I demanded, seething.

He smiled through the pain, wiped the blood from his mouth with the back of his hand, and nodded. "Surprisingly, she wasn't happy about you lying to me, telling me *she* kissed *you* back. So here's the deal, Vicious…" He spat blood on the grass and got up but didn't make a move to hit me back. "Millie's my girlfriend. You'd better come to terms with that. You had your chance when she first moved here, and all you did was be a fucking dick to her.

"What the hell did you think was going to happen? She's hot. She's nice. She's fucking kind. Of course guys noticed. I noticed too. I knew you were gonna go batshit crazy on me, and I let you because you're a friend. Hope you got that out of your system." He winked. "Because my nose will be fine tomorrow, but you'll be a fucking mess every time you see us making out in the halls."

I charged at him for the third time on autopilot.

"What the fuck, Dean!" Jaime pried me off him and dragged me toward the blue bleachers overlooking the field.

This time I didn't resist. There was no point. Dean had won, and I'd lost.

"Get the hell out of here before I finish Vicious's job," Jaime roared, and I heard Dean laugh behind us.

That weekend, I had another balls-out party at my house. Dean didn't dare show his face, and I assumed Help was with him. When I showed up at the pool with my sleeves rolled up, a sophomore guy looking to impress one of Georgia's cheerleading crew accepted the challenge and met me on the tennis court.

Defy was fair.

Defy was brutal.

But this time, Defy did nothing to dull the pain.

From then on, everything changed between the four of us. Dean and I weren't on speaking terms. At all.

I toyed with the idea of banning him from my estate altogether—it was completely doable—but decided that I didn't want to look like a total fucktard in Eli Cole's eyes. Besides, if Dean didn't come to Help, Help would go to him, which was just as bad if not worse. The servants' apartment was a lot smaller than Dean's mansion, and Emilia's parents were always around. They had fewer chances to fuck each other if they were here.

But they were steady again, and I saw them every-fucking-where. I saw them at school, at parks, at the mall my dad owned, and sometimes even outside the servants' apartment. To be fair to Help, she never made out with him in public. Not even a kiss. They sometimes held hands, and that alone made me want to go on a killing spree. I didn't understand the burning hatred that flared every time I saw Dean. How it had transferred from her to him all of a sudden.

Trent and Jaime were desperate to keep us all together. I saw where they were coming from, I really did, so we still all hung out together. We sat together in the cafeteria. We nodded hello in the hallway. But we didn't talk to each other much, and the subject of Emilia LeBlanc was tacitly taboo. She was like Voldemort. No one was to mention her name, and Dean pretended like she didn't exist when he was around me. I tried to pretend she didn't exist too, but of course I couldn't.

Because she was fucking everywhere.

I thought about her even when technically I didn't think about her. I thought about her when I worked out and when I hung out with my nonfriends and when I played video games. When I studied and when I fucked girls—Jesus Christ, especially when I fucked girls—until, at some point, I stopped fucking girls altogether because it reminded me that one day, one day soon, Help was going to fuck that douchebag Dean.

I couldn't let that happen. It didn't make sense even to me, but I just couldn't. She was *mine*. It sounded irrational, but that didn't make it any less true. I didn't have to slap my name on her ass when she walked into class that very first day. The way I teased her, taunted her. I was normally too busy with the shit that was going on in my life to bully people. Everybody knew that the new girl belonged to me.

I never in a million years would have dated her or even taken her out. She wasn't worth the trouble. No girl was, and especially not her. Still, she was mine to play with. Case in point, from the very first time her eyes landed on me, she looked at me like she was already mine.

Swallow. Blink. Sigh. Blush. Look away. That was her routine every time I passed by her, even now.

But Dean didn't care.

The fucker just. Didn't. Care.

Maybe that's why I did what I did toward the end of the school year. Help was going to celebrate her eighteenth birthday in a week, and even though Douchebag Dean (the name had a real ring to it) never talked about her in front of me, I knew he was going to take her to a spa weekend somewhere fancy along the coast. It was all so stupid. Help wasn't a spa girl. He should've known that.

If I were her boyfriend, I would have taken her to watch the cherry trees bloom. Or given her new painting supplies because the girl wanted to be a real artist and open a gallery or some shit. Not that I was her stalker or anything, like Jaime was with Ms. Greene before he started banging her. Emilia wore her weird personality like a billboard, proud and loud. From the way she dressed to how she was always covered in paint and doodled cherry blossoms everywhere.

Dean, he just liked the idea of her. Pure and innocent, with her sweet Southern accent, pretty dimples, and boho style.

But I knew her best.

I was in the weight room when Dean and I had our second conversation about her. It had been weeks since I'd planted my fist in his face, but my fingers still itched whenever he was close. This time we were in gym—an advanced weight-training class only open to seniors. We had to bench-press together because we were both late and all the other machines were taken. I was spotting him while he pressed a set at one eighty. He was lifting more than his usual, and I could've sworn he looked a little juiced up.

He grunted like a beast with every push of the weights. My fingers floated below the bar in case his body failed him. I wondered if he knew Help wasn't the type of girl who was into veiny, muscled-bound knuckleheads.

"So you're taking her to a spa," I said. Straight to the point. I didn't have time for fucking chitchat.

He rolled his eyes, his face sweaty and red, and let out a sigh. "It's her birthday. Would you rather I ignored it?"

"I'd rather you break up with her," I answered flatly, my stare blank. There was no point in sugarcoating this shit. He knew I hated their relationship. And despite them being together for months, I knew it wasn't love. I saw the way she looked at him. She liked him, but there was no fire.

Her eyes burned for me. Only for me.

"Be reasonable," Dean muttered. He wasn't so focused on lifting anymore. He still looked red, but his arms shook now, and I felt the strain of the weight and our conversation affecting his body.

I shoved my hands inside the pockets of my light-gray sweatpants. "It's not in my nature to be reasonable. Break this shit off, Dean. You're going to college in New York. She's staying here. Do it now before…" I trailed off.

Before you take her fucking virginity. It had nothing to do with me wanting to mark her first. I mean, I did. Of course I wanted that. But I would've taken Help even if she'd slept with every single guy at All Saints High. It was her I was worried about. I knew she would regret it.

Okay, fine. I wasn't worried about her. I was worried about me.

What the fuck was wrong with me? I was on the fast track to losing my mind. Her pussy seemed to own me, and I hadn't even tasted it yet. All I knew was that I wanted it for myself. Too bad it was attached to that annoying little fool.

"Before what?" he grunted, and his arms shook harder. "Before I sleep with her? How the fuck do you know I already haven't?"

His hands turned white, but his snicker grated on my nerves, sending a rush of annoyance down my spine. He tried to press the bar all the way up and put it back in the handles. Sweat dotted his forehead. He was losing the battle.

That's why we needed people to spot us.

Only I wasn't spotting for him anymore.

Instead, I grabbed the bar and pressed it down toward his throat ever so gently. His eyes widened.

"I wouldn't mess with me, Cole," I warned in a low voice. My gaze was lazy, but my jaw was tense. I couldn't help it. "They call me Vicious for a reason."

"I'm going to school wherever she does, fucktard. I'll stay here with her if I have to. She's mine."

I pressed harder. What the fuck was he talking about, staying here? He couldn't stay here. But then I wasn't in a position to make him leave either, was I?

"Liar," I said, fuming. Goddamn Dean. "Don't fucking lie to me, Cole."

"You watch and see." His neck was purpling, but it did nothing to calm me down.

I pressed harder, and he gagged. People were starting to notice. I didn't care. I glared at him in warning. "Dean…"

Everybody stopped what they were doing to look at us. Everybody. I saw Jaime and Trent from the corner of my eye, pushing their way to us, and knew I was running out of time.

"Vicious…" Dean dared, smiling up at me.

When Jaime finally got to us, I turned around and walked away, leaving Dean lying there with the bar against his throat. Someone else could help him out.

I was so done with this fucker.

So done.

He took her virginity.

He enjoyed it.

I bet she did too.

It was during their spa weekend when she turned eighteen. Leave it to Emilia to lose her virginity less than a day before she legally could. There were candles and chocolate and all kinds of fancy shit that meant nothing to her. I heard all the details because I basically forced Jaime to tell me after it happened. Dean told Trent and Jaime on the fucking phone, like a chick, making them swear not to tell me.

But while Dean was BFFs with Rexroth, Jaime was my closest friend.

When I threatened to tell his mother—Principal Followhill—that he was bumping uglies with our Lit teacher unless he spilled, he'd started singing like a fucking canary.

That's when I made the executive decision that Help could no longer live in Todos Santos. She had to disappear and stay the fuck away from everything and everyone I knew.

I wasn't stupid. I realized that I was preventing her from being around her sister and her parents. Her boyfriend. I was banishing her from everything she knew.

From a comfortable future.

From money and opportunity.

From family Christmases and blue-eyed kids with Dean, who was oh-so-fucking enchanted with her.

From love.

I was ruining her life.

Because. I. Was. Jealous.

Jealousy was a weakness I didn't need and wasn't proud of. But I had to conquer it before it conquered me. That's why, the day they returned from their little spa vacation, I was already waiting for her in her room. I sat on her bed with my elbows on my knees and tried to ignore the fact that everything smelled like her. A weird, heady combination of cinnamon, milky butter, and a singular sweetness that only belonged to her. I wanted it out of my nose, out of my estate, and out of my fucking life.

Yes, she'd driven me mad.

She gasped when she walked into her room and found me there. She didn't know that I knew everything. That she'd fucked one of my best friends. Emilia didn't look any different, but she *felt* different.

She felt out of reach, now more than ever.

"Pink suits you," she remarked in a dry tone, nodding toward the pink flowery linens on her bed. "Who let you in, Vic, and what the hell are you doing in my room?"

No one let me in. Her parents and Rosie had gone to the farmers' market or some shit.

She dropped her backpack by the door and walked over to her dresser, pulling out some fresh clothes. I loved how she was wearing a crop top with the name of a band only she knew and another pair of Daisy Dukes. She looked tan, and a golden necklace was glistening against her soft bronzed skin.

I also liked that she'd called me Vic.

But I didn't like that she didn't even look at me when she said it.

"You need to leave," I said.

"I think that's my line." She sighed. "I need to take a shower and fix myself a sandwich. Whatever you need will have to wait until I'm done. Or maybe until I start taking orders from you."

"I don't mean leave the house. I mean leave this town, this state, this fucking planet."

Maybe not the planet. I didn't want her dead. I just wanted her out of my life.

Help slammed a drawer shut with her hip and squatted down to fish her toothbrush from her backpack. "Let me ask you something. Do you know you're crazy, or do you see yourself as a sane person? I'm genuinely interested in knowing."

She waved the toothbrush handle at me and then dumped clothes from her backpack into the laundry basket in one messy heap.

"I'll give you ten thousand dollars to disappear."

She rolled her eyes. She thought I was joking. "As tempting as the idea of putting a state or two between us is, I have nowhere to go."

"Twenty thousand dollars," I fired back, narrowing my eyes at her. I was going to withdraw the sum from my own account. I doubted my dad would even notice, and if he did, it would still be worth it. I was losing my sanity, fast, because of her.

"No," she chuckled, resolute. "What the hell makes you think I'd do what you're asking?"

I figured she wouldn't just leave because I told her to, so I shrugged and picked up my cell phone, staring at her, blasé.

"I'll fire your parents, and then you'll all have to move back to some shithole in Virginia, and poor Rosie—poor fucking Rosie—won't have access to the nice health-care plan my dad is paying for. That's what makes me think you'll do what I demand." I smirked.

Her eyes turned to slits, and her lips thinned. *She hates me.* I hated myself too. For the both of us. But I couldn't fucking take it anymore. It was too much. *She* was too much.

"You can't do that," she whispered, her hands shaking as she gathered her fresh clothes and toothbrush to her chest. She loved her family so much. Especially Rosie. "They work for your parents, not you. They wouldn't cave to their moody teenage son." Emilia was trying to convince herself more than she was trying to convince me.

"They wouldn't?" My eyebrows jumped as I feigned surprise.

"When's the last time they even bothered being here? Let's test your theory. I'll call my dad right now."

To everyone else, it seemed like I'd always had Baron Senior by the balls. Even though he was too busy doing the New York-Cabo-wherever-the-fuck-Jo-wanted-to-sunbathe route to actually be a parent, he rarely denied me.

I assumed it was because of the guilt that plagued him from what he'd done to my mom.

"Hey, Dad, it's me." I spoke into the phone, swinging my legs up on her bed and crossing my feet at the ankles. I was still wearing my muddy sneakers. My phone was on speaker.

"What do you want, Baron?" There was no mistaking the impatience in his tone.

Help's mouth opened slightly.

I popped my minty gum in boredom, sighing. "Just so we're all on the same page, since you guys are barely at the house anymore, am I correct to assume the staff is under my supervision? Meaning I can hire and fire if someone isn't meeting my needs?"

I heard the splashes of the waves against my father's yacht—*Marie*, after my mom—and ice clink in a glass. Scotch was my guess.

"Yes," he said. "You assume correctly. Why? What's wrong? Somebody giving you trouble?"

I nodded with a triumphant smile even though he couldn't see me. She could, though.

Help's face whitened beneath her golden tan. Upset. Horrified. I was sending her packing at eighteen, with no prospects and no place to go, and I'd threatened to fire her family if she wouldn't leave.

"No, everything's good," I said, still watching her. "Speak soon, Dad." I hung up on the fucker—he and Jo and Daryl were going to pay, but they were a problem for a different day. I snapped my gaze to meet Emilia's.

She tilted her chin up. The contempt she held for me was rolling off her rigid posture in waves.

The silence was suffocating, and so was the idea that I was essentially ruining her life. I was choosing myself over Emilia, my feelings over hers, and it wasn't noble or honorable, but it was who I was.

"Can I finish out the school year at least?" she asked so quietly it took me a few seconds to decipher her request. She was perfectly composed. Proud.

Fuck, she was beautiful when she was strong. I was doing the right thing getting rid of her.

I nodded.

"Leave the week after school ends," I instructed, getting up from her bed. I already missed it. "And it goes without fucking saying that you and Dean are done. This is the second and last time I'm telling—not asking—you to stop this shit. Tell him you're leaving because you've met someone else online. Insist that he never contact you again. One glitch, Emilia, and I promise you, your family won't just lose this job. I'll make sure they don't find another one."

She didn't answer, but I knew she got the message. She wasn't the kind of girl to puss out when it came to her loved ones. Her family was her everything.

When I walked out of the servants' apartment for the very last time, I asked myself if there was a chance Emilia would ever forgive me.

I wondered how much groveling I'd need to do if I ever wanted to get back in her life.

No. The price was too high. We were done.

But so were she and Dean.

CHAPTER THIRTEEN
EMILIA

THE PRESENT

I wasn't gonna do it.

At this point, I didn't even care about the money. I'd never cared too much for it anyway. Sure, I wanted to survive, maybe take a breather from chasing overdrafts, but at what cost?

Nope, I wasn't going to ruin anyone else's life with a lie. Ever. I wasn't Vicious.

I spent my night lying in bed, thinking and analyzing the last few hours. There was a lot to take in. Vicious wanted me to lie and tell Jo straight to her face that if it came down to it, I would testify against her, telling the court he'd told me things he never had.

I was a horrible liar. But a little voice inside me kept asking—*and what if it is the truth?* The answer was always the same—even if it was the truth, it wasn't *my* truth. There were other ways Vicious could get what he wanted without dragging me into his war.

At four in the morning, I finally kicked off my blanket and slipped into my flip-flops. I knew there was no chance I was going to fall asleep after deciding I wouldn't help him, so I might as well just read. I remembered the library I'd always wanted to visit over the years.

This was probably my last chance to see it before Vicious kicked my family and me out. And it's the place I'd been avoiding for ten years straight, always wondering, aching, and peeking through these doors. But no more. I wanted to see what was behind them.

I was done with his blackmail. Done with being bought.

This time, his money would lose.

I entered the mansion through the kitchen, using Mama's security code. It was still the same ten years later.

I tiptoed to the hall, clad in the XL Libertines shirt I called my pajamas, and headed down the ironwood floor, following the same route I had that first time I'd gone to knock on the library door. Vicious would be fast asleep upstairs. I'd read a little, inhale the scent of the old books, calm my nerves, and go back to my parents' place.

I was silent. Which was why my shriek almost rattled the walls when I pushed the door to the library open and found Vicious in one corner, sitting at an ornately carved wooden table with four upholstered wingback chairs. It looked like a study table you'd see in a public library, only much fancier.

He lifted his eyes from the screen of his laptop at my yelp and stared at me long and hard for a few beats until my racing heart calmed a little. Then, wordlessly, he pushed the chair opposite him with his foot in a silent invitation for me to join him. I didn't move.

"What are you doing up so late?" My voice trembled.

"What are you doing trespassing in the middle of the fucking night?" he retorted, his voice calm and tired.

He'd changed into a white designer V-neck and a pair of dark-denim pants or jeans. I didn't need to see them to know they hung low on his body.

"I couldn't sleep, so I thought I'd read a little. Never mind." I spun around, heading back toward the hallway.

He stopped me. "Help." His voice was firm. I halted but didn't turn around. "Grab a book. I promise not to make conversation."

I rubbed my thighs and mentally scoffed at the idea of joining him. Especially after how he'd acted in the car.

"I'm resigning," I said, my back still to him. It was easier that way. I always caved when his eyes held mine. "I can't do what you're asking me to do. Please don't try to threaten me with my parents or Rosie or with starting a third world war. I've made up my mind. I can't lie for you."

I heard the squeak of his chair as he got up, and I closed my eyes. I knew my resolve was going to crack with every step he took in my direction. Because stupidly, I still felt things for Vicious. Things I had no business feeling.

He stopped when he was standing in front of me. I felt his heat rolling toward my body. I felt my body accepting the warmth, drinking it in, enjoying it, despite what he'd done to me.

"Open your eyes," he ordered.

I did. We stared at each other for a few seconds. His eyes were still on mine when he slowly peeled his shirt off his ripped body. I kept my glare on his black pupils, too afraid to drop my gaze. It wouldn't be the first time I'd seen a male torso at such close proximity.

But it definitely would be the first time I'd seen Vicious's.

His white tee landed on the floor with barely a sound. I was hyperaware of the fabric near my bare feet in my flip-flops.

"Look down," he instructed softly.

My eyes drifted south, my gaze slow and wary, taking in the perfect porcelain skin of his neck and shoulders until I landed on his chest. He was hard-muscled and pumped...and covered with scars. Some pink. Some white. All of them old and faded. Long scars. Short scars. Deep scars. Shallow scars. There were many, too many, like a subway window that had been abused over the years. He looked like someone had doodled on his stomach and chest with a Swiss-made knife.

Bile rose up my throat, and I clamped my lips together, feeling my chin quivering.

"Remember when I used to arrange the fights at my tennis court?" he asked, his voice unruffled. "I'm not gonna lie. Part of it was for fun, to unwind. But the other part, Help, was because I didn't want people to ask questions about my scars." He lifted both his arms, showing me the front of his wrists and forearms.

Covered with more scars.

I'd noticed them before, of course, but I'd bought the lie. I'd thought the fights were to blame.

I tried to swallow but couldn't. His scars somehow felt like they were on me. My skin burned for him. "Jo did this to you?"

"No." He ran his tongue over his front teeth. "Her brother, Daryl Ryler, the guy you saw in this library that first day. Jo didn't cut me. After she first married my dad, she just smacked me around. A lot. And then Ryler moved here when I was twelve…" He hesitated, but it didn't look like he was having too much trouble getting the words out. His face was still as emotionless as ever, his speech low and firm. "She'd lock the door from the outside and leave him to 'punish me.'"

I sucked in a ragged breath. I wanted to kill that woman. Even after everything he'd done to me, I wanted his stepmother to die. Then something else occurred to me.

"Did your dad know?"

"I told him, but he was never around much. His business was always his focus. Then, after I got expelled from boarding school and was back here, Jo convinced him I was hurting myself. Cutting. All the rage with 'troubled' kids like me. She even hired a psychiatrist to assess me. One chosen by her, of course. There was talk of sending me off somewhere for treatment. So I learned to keep my mouth shut until eventually I was big and strong enough to fight back. I was sixteen."

My eyes ran over his torso frantically. Shame crawled into me when I realized it wasn't only sorrow I felt. Butterflies flung their tiny wings in my chest, and my nipples puckered. I liked what I was seeing. He was perfectly imperfect. Flawlessly flawed. Most importantly—he was Vicious.

"You never told anyone else? The police? A teacher?"

His dead eyes blinked once. "There wasn't much point by then. Jo and my dad were traveling a lot, and Daryl was barely ever around. Drugs." He shrugged. "He died shortly after you left town. Overdosed and drowned in his own Jacuzzi." He tilted his head sideways. "Shame."

A shiver broke down my spine. I remembered every word of their conversation that first day in the library. *No.* Vicious was incapable of killing someone. But was he really? I didn't want to ask him about it. Both because I wasn't ready for his answer and because it would've caused another moral debate, and my head was aching as it was.

"Vicious…" I was breathless. He moved toward me. Our bodies touched. I wanted to melt into him but knew better than to give in to that temptation. He was so haunted and troubled. And on top of everything else, he was still hateful to me.

For Lord's sake, the man still referred to me as "Help."

Yet when his body pressed against mine, warm and comforting, nothing like the man it belonged to, I couldn't pull away. We were flush against each other, but his arms were at his sides. We were both liars, telling ourselves that as long as we didn't use hands, this didn't count. Only it did. In my heart, it did.

"It's a mess, but it's my mess," he said. "I won't drag you into this shit in court. Jo doesn't deserve a penny, but whatever happens with the will, this stays between her and me." He dropped his eyes to my lips. He was so close, I was almost able to taste the saltiness of his warm, naked skin and the heat of his mouth. "You get out of this unscathed. I know you think I'm a piece of shit, and you have good reason to, but I'm not asking you to perjure yourself. I would never complicate your life like that. Never. I just need you to help me frighten Jo enough to back off if there's a problem with the will."

Torn, I shook my head. "I'm sure your friends can help you just as much if not more."

"They don't know," he said. "I haven't told them. Not about Daryl Ryler, not about Jo. I'm not proud of this, Help. I let them do this to me. For years. You're the only one who knows, other than Eli Cole and a shrink I hired myself a few years ago."

I could have told him a lot of things. That it wasn't his fault. That there was nothing to be ashamed of. That he wasn't alone. But I knew Vicious well enough to know that wasn't what he wanted to hear. He was too proud for a pep talk. What he wanted was cooperation.

"Then ask your psychiatrist," I said.

"That would be very messy, very expensive, and very public. No. This is personal. Private. I want to deal with Jo quietly, and we both know you can keep a secret."

Pink.

Black.

"How do I know you're not lying?" I made my voice stone-cold, ignoring the compliment. But this made sense. I knew what I heard in the library all those years ago. But after Vicious's behavior toward me, I'd chosen to believe it was just an ugly family argument.

"You don't. You'll have to trust me."

"And what on earth have you ever done to make me think you're trustworthy?" I wrinkled my nose, taking a step away. Being so close to him wasn't helping.

The back of his hand brushed my cheek, and my heart leaped. I retreated again.

"I was an asshole, but I never lied to you. Not once. Josephine came after my family's money with her brother, and she did some nasty stuff to get what she wanted. This is payday for her. But not in the way she hopes it will be."

I closed my eyes, shaking my head.

When I didn't answer, he took my hand and pulled me toward a chair. It was five in the morning, and I'd lost my appetite for the written word.

"Stay."

"Why?" I demanded.

"Because I order you to."

"No."

He dipped his head down and shook it, exhaling sharply. "Fuck, then do it because I want you to. It's been a long day. Don't decide right now. Just sit here while I work and get used to seeing my sour-ass face again. I won't try to bribe you again. Instead, I'll ask that you think about what *you*, Emilia, consider as justice. Because I know you're good and I know I'm bad, but at the end of the day, I suspect we have the exact same moral code."

I perched on the chair across from his, but only because I was too shocked to continue standing. Vicious's confession, combined with the fact that I suspected Ryler hadn't really died a natural death, almost paralyzed me completely.

I slowly reached for a leather-bound book on the corner of the table. I raised an eyebrow at him when I spotted the title on the spine. "*Little Women?*"

He only shrugged.

I opened the book but didn't really read anything. Every few seconds, my eyes would drift back to Vicious.

His gaze was still on the screen when he said, "Is there something else on your mind, Help?"

I hated that we were back to what we were before his confession.

"Am I an idiot for sitting here with you?" I asked, honestly interested to know what he made of this whole situation.

A ghost of a smile passed across his face. "You're a lot of things. An idiot has never been never one of them."

"Then what am I?"

"You're..." He looked up, inspecting me. Sometimes people could communicate with a stare alone, and his eyes said *mine*, but his mouth said "Complicated. You're complex. It's not a bad thing."

I wanted to tell him that he didn't deserve my help, that I hated him, but that wasn't the truth. At least not the latter. Even if I was considering lying for him, I didn't want to make a habit out of it, so I just kept my mouth shut.

He tangled his leg with mine purposely under the table, daring me to pull away. I didn't. I liked his warmth. I liked his long, muscular leg laced with mine. I liked how after a few minutes of pressing his leg harder into my calf, he used his knee to nudge my legs apart. I let out a sigh.

But all throughout, he didn't look at me. Not even once. I pretended to keep reading, and he tapped the table with a chewed pen. My hands tightened on the book when I recognized the name printed on the pen's side. I realized that it was *my* pen. The pen I'd used when he came to McCoy's.

Then he lifted his eyes and sent me another relaxed smile. "By the way, I took it upon myself to tell your little friend Rachelle that you won't be returning to the bar for any more shifts. I trust you girls can live off your current salary. You're all mine now, LeBlanc. And you're welcome."

CHAPTER FOURTEEN
VICIOUS

It happened. I fell under.

After staying awake for eighty-four hours straight, my body finally gave in and completely shut down. It happened in my old bedroom, and I barely made it into bed, but I did. I was still shirtless—mainly because I liked how she looked at me when I was working and she was reading. But it was morning, and I knew that I was going to sleep for a long time and that sooner or later, she'd realize that something was wrong. That people don't just disappear for so many hours in the middle of the day.

I woke up thirteen hours later, and it was evening again. There was noise coming from the broad hallway outside my room, and I hoped it was Help, even though I knew it wasn't. I was right, of course. It was my father's nurses, Josh and Slade. They were arguing among themselves about the Raiders and the Patriots, and I was not impressed. The two fuckers had woken me up.

I passed by the beefy men and walked straight into my father's bedroom. He must've been discharged from the hospital and returned while I was asleep. And surprise, surprise, Jo was still nowhere to be found. Guess Cabo was more important than standing by your man in his final weeks. Or days.

The gravity of the situation weighed heavy on my shoulders, but this was what I'd waited for for so long. Ever since I was twelve.

Now, it was time.

Daryl was dead.

Dad was dying.

And soon, Josephine's life would be over too.

I kept the door open. The nurses glanced my way but continued bickering in the hall, flinging their arms around as they talked football.

"Hey, Dad." I smiled, leaning a shoulder against his wall with my hands tucked inside my pockets. I rested my head beside a Charles-Edouard Dubois painting—it was good, but I liked Emilia's shit better—and enjoyed the view.

The man who'd ruined my life looked like a cheap carbon copy of the man he used to be. Completely bald, pallid in color, with a neck like a lizard's, his veins sticking out from his saggy, thin skin. I looked nothing like him and exactly like my mother, which I guessed was part of the reason why Jo hated my guts.

"Don't lie, Son. Jo and Daryl would never do such a thing," he told me when I showed him my scars. My wounds. My pain.

"She locks me in there with him," I argued for the millionth time.

"Jo says you do it to yourself. Is this about attention, Baron? Is that what you want?"

I didn't need attention. I'd needed a different fucking father.

"You hanging in there?" I smirked at Baron Senior now, painfully aware of the men behind me.

He blinked his eyes but said nothing because he couldn't. I, on the other hand, had plenty to say. I knew my words could possibly kill him. I didn't care.

"Sorry I dropped in unannounced. I needed to see Eli Cole about your will."

As far as Dad knew, he and I were on good terms. Last time I'd seen him, I still even feigned interest in his business and his health, but it was showtime. Revenge time. I ambled into his room and took a seat at the edge of his bed. The bastard wasn't going to spill a word about it.

Was I the primary beneficiary?

Was Jo?

There were a lot of fucking millions on the line here. Dad's power was in his money. That's how he'd controlled his wives, and that's how he thought he'd gained my respect. He was wrong. *As usual.*

"You know, it's going to be interesting to see how much you left Jo. You always kept your cards close to your chest. Used your wealth for power. I bet you made her agree to that draconian prenup before you even sucked her tits, huh?" I winked playfully, my lips curving into a slight smirk.

He didn't respond but breathed hard. Yeah, the Spencer men were lawyers by training, and they liked women…but they fucking *loved money.*

"Nah. I bet you did the right thing by her. From your point of view, at least. Not from mine. The fact that you killed Mom kind of changes everything." I jutted my lower lip out, gauging him for a reaction.

Until then, he didn't know I knew. Didn't know that I'd overheard him and Jo talking in the library before it happened.

Dad's eyes grew big and perplexed and then darted to the hallway helplessly, but it was futile. From where the nurses were positioned, the situation looked innocent. A son softly speaking to his ailing father.

"Are you sure your brother will keep his mouth shut? I can't risk anyone knowing. Even a whiff of suspicion could destroy my business dealings."

"Baby, it won't. I promise you."

"I'm not a bad man, Josephine. But I don't want this burden for the rest of my life."

It was a year after my mother got seriously injured in a car accident that left her a quadriplegic. I was nine. Way too young to understand what it meant.

I didn't know what to make of it then, so I'd collected every word said behind the library door where I'd eavesdropped until the puzzle was complete. By the age of ten, I knew that conversation by heart.

By the age of twelve, I also knew exactly what it meant.

"Trust me, Daryl will help you. I'm telling you, darlin', no one will ever know. Anyway, people have no right to judge. You may as well be married to a garden vegetable."

"I don't know, Jo. I don't know."

"Baby," she purred. *"Honey, you can't divorce her at this point. We both know that ship sailed as soon as she had the accident. What's there to think about? You'll be doing her a favor anyway, if you ask me. She can't even scratch her nose anymore."*

"What about Baron Junior? What about my son?"

"What about him?" she snapped. *"Aren't I good enough for him? Trust me, he'll barely remember her when he grows up."*

I stared at what had become of my father since Jo and her brother had entered our lives. I wasn't supposed to be there the day I first saw Daryl Ryler in our house. I came home sick from school, and our housekeeper at the time picked me up from school.

I'd climbed up the stairs and dropped my backpack on the floor in my room, but instead of crawling into bed, I'd wanted to see my mom. The guestroom they'd put her in was across the hall, and it was more like a hospital room than a bedroom. I wanted to read her the poem I'd written in Language Arts and tape it to her wall. She had a whole collection of them.

The stranger didn't see me. The man was leaving her room, and I was about to ask him if he was today's nurse.

"You should be in bed, Baron," the housekeeper had called from the bottom of the stairs. "You have a fever. Make sure not to bother your mother. You don't want to make her sick."

I never got to read her my poem. Twenty minutes later, her nurse—a woman, not the man I'd seen—called an ambulance. Her respirator was clogged.

Coincidence? I didn't think so.

"That's right, Dad. I know about you sending Daryl Ryler to kill her." I grinned and patted my father's stiff shoulder, watching his eyes dancing.

My father looked panicked, but he couldn't move a muscle. Realization washed over his face, and it was my time to strike harder.

"Yeah, about him." I bit back my smile, smoothing the white Egyptian cotton sheets of his bed. "I was thrilled when they found him dead. I figured no one other than your gold-digging wife was going to miss him, and truly, his death was more of a public service when you think about it. How many people has Daryl Ryler wronged? How many felonies has he committed? How many Maries has he killed?"

My dad was still lucid. He must've put two and two together and deduced I'd killed Daryl. As usual, he thought the worst of his son. Oh, fine. Maybe this time I deserved it.

Dad actually managed to move his hand a little, and his whole body shook. His eyes bulged as he gurgled.

"It's too late now. To change the will, switch and give it all to Jo. Not when the doctors are questioning your mental competence. Who knows what's working inside that brain and what's not? No one gives a fuck about what you have to say anymore. I mean, your doctors are pretty amazed you're still alive. Honestly? I'm pretty amazed too. Why did you hold on for so long? You've got nothing but money. Nothing at all. Your work's your life. Got remarried to a woman who hates your guts, and you don't know anything about your son other than the color of his eyes."

The nurses stopped chatting, but when I turned around and flashed them a plastic smile, they resumed their conversation. My head twisted back to my writhing father. He shook so badly, I was pretty sure he was going to die right then and there.

"Doesn't matter who inherits everything. There's no one to protect Jo once you're dead. She'll be alone, defenseless. No brother to help her plot and scheme. Daryl's gone." I chuckled before remembering the expression on Help's face when I told her how Ryler had died. Despite everything, I didn't want her to think of me as a monster. As a killer.

"And you... I will destroy everything you worked for. Your company. Your reputation. Your assets. Your *name*."

His eyes widened to a point they almost rolled out of their sockets. Tubes came out of his nose and wrists. He opened his mouth, but the only thing that came out were incoherent grunts. My father sounded like some kind of primitive animal, a zombie, which wasn't far from the fucking truth. What human being discarded his wife and the mother of his nine-year-old child?

"I came here to say goodbye, Dad," I said, sliding forward on his bed until my body pressed against his. I squeezed his immobile leg.

His gaze screamed horror. There was so much he wanted to say. To shout. To me. To the nurses. But he was trapped inside himself.

"I'm going back to New York. Got more important things to take care of. I want you to know I loved you when I was a kid. It wasn't always like this. But I promise you, now..." I pressed my lips to his ear.

He shuddered, trying to move his arms, but he was paralyzed. From the outside—to Josh and Slade—it probably looked like a sweet moment.

"...I promise to shit over every single thing you've made part of the legacy you worked to create. I'm starting with this cold-ass mansion. I never liked it anyway. Then I'll liquidate the company you built with both hands and invest the money elsewhere. I wish you could watch me burn everything that matters to you, but you won't be able to. So it's probably best that you'll be dead."

With that, I straightened and winked playfully at him. His face was so strained, he was purple. This was how I wanted to remember him. Weak. Defeated. Ruined. I turned around and grinned to the nurses in the hallway.

"Bye, Dad."

Help and I landed back in New York on Monday morning. I told her to go settle in at her new apartment because I knew she was desperate to see her baby sister and, for once, I wanted to stop acting like a douchebag to the woman I actually needed by my side.

Of course, I failed to mention that the apartment I was living in upstairs was actually Dean's because why the fuck did it matter? And because I didn't want to talk to her about Dean. Ever.

I, on the other hand, had a lot of work to do on the merger. FHH was on the verge of merging two of the biggest pharmaceutical corporations in America. Yes, one of them was the one I *did* steal from Sergio and his company, as a matter of fact.

It wasn't fair, but I didn't care about fair. I cared about getting my clients what they needed. And what *we* needed. Besides, it wasn't like Sergio's nonexistent kids and family were going to starve.

Having this massive transaction under our name was going to be life altering, not only financially but also in terms of our reputation. We couldn't let anything screw it up for us.

Even though he'd hung up on me, Dean kept calling me like a desperate ex-girlfriend every day, and I kept on hitting ignore like the bastard who was about to *steal* his ex-girlfriend. Only she was never really his. She was always mine.

Part of the reason for my behavior was to teach him a lesson, and part of it was because I was enjoying the New York office too much to hand it back to him. I would, of course, but not yet. Christmas was approaching, and California Christmas sucked.

Besides, I had nowhere to spend the holiday, and at least in New York I was one of many lonely souls. Dean was going to spend the holidays with his family in Todos Santos, so really, I was doing him a favor.

I arrived at the office in good spirits for a change. I didn't yell at anyone. I didn't break anything. I was nice to the secretaries and receptionists, and I did not lose my temper even once when a guy tried to cut in front of me when I hailed a taxi. I did step on his foot before I climbed into the car, bypassing him nonchalantly. Guess old habits die hard.

When I arrived in front of my apartment building, my phone beeped. I'd received an email with the contract, signed by both of the corporations. Successfully merged. This shit was going to be plastered on every financial website in North America within the hour.

And it was all us. I couldn't contain my triumph.

I didn't even have the chance to stare at the signatures on the screen before Jaime called me. I picked up.

"Fuck. Man, we're rich!" He laughed.

"Richer," I corrected dryly. "And you're welcome."

"Richer," he bellowed in agreement, "and you're a fucking douchebag, bro."

"This isn't news to me," I said, joining his laughter as I heard Mel and his baby, Daria, singing in the background.

"I'm going to celebrate with my family. Speak tomorrow, asshole." Jaime hung up.

Trent called a few seconds later. "Motherfucking God! Is it true?" he shouted and then chuckled.

I rolled with him and snorted out a laugh too. "It would appear that way."

"Listen, I'm at my parents'. We're all gonna head for a pre-Christmas dinner with Dean's folks, but I'll call you tomorrow to kiss your ass about that deal, Vic. Hope you're doing something fun tonight. Bye."

"Bye." I hung up.

But I wasn't.

My friends were going to celebrate with their families, and I was going to sit in an empty apartment that didn't even belong to me and eat takeout or fuck a woman without a last name who I was going to forget a few hours later.

It was depressing.

It was unfair in a whole different way than the unfair way I conducted business.

And it was fucking unacceptable, considering there was something I wanted very much and that was within reach.

Maybe that was how I ended up in front of her door. Logically, I had no business seeking her out. She was my PA and a woman I'd wronged. I should've just left her alone for once.

But I didn't want to. What I wanted was to fuck her and get rid of my weird fixation on her once and for all.

I knocked on her door, hoping to fuck Rosie wouldn't answer.

I pounded my fist on her door again, and this time I heard footsteps. When she opened the door, my first instinct was to jerk her into my body and kiss the shit out of her until her lips bruised. But I couldn't, so I just smiled, tugging on my tie, loosening it. She had paint all over her face, brown and yellow and green. Earth tones. Her temples were misted with sweat, and her crazy lavender hair stuck to them. She wore graphic leggings and a baggy, paint-stained white shirt.

Barefoot.

Natural.

Beautiful.

"Hey," she said. Her earbuds were still hanging from her shoulders by a thin wire. "Sorry, I was listening to some music. I got the email about the merger. Congrats. Do you need me to do anything?"

Yes. Wrap your lips around my dick and suck. Hard.

"Come to dinner with me," I said instead. I was breaking so many rules at once, my head spun like a motherfucker.

(1) No dating.
(2) No dating Help.

(3) No risking getting attached.
(4) No deliberately putting myself in a vulnerable position.

But I wanted to fuck her really bad, just so I could tell myself that I had after all these years, before I went back to LA.

She blinked a couple of times before blurting out, "No." It wasn't cold or cruel. She sounded surprised and a little confused. Still clutching the edges of the fiberglass door, covering it with paint, she elaborated. "It's not a good idea, and you know it."

"The fuck not?"

"Well, I have about five hundred reasons that come to mind, but let's start with the obvious ones—you're my boss and you refer to me as *Help*."

"It's a term of endearment," I fired back. "Which I can drop, if you don't like it. Go on."

She let out a brittle laugh. "When you hired me, you promised you wanted to work together, nothing more."

"Yeah?" I huffed, growing impatient. Did she realize she was turning down what no one else had ever before been offered? "And now I want you to come with me to grab some dinner. I plan to eat a steak, not your pussy."

I may have overdone this one because Help—fuck, *Emilia*—tried to slam the door on me at the exact same moment I slid my foot inside the gap. She smashed the door against my foot, but I didn't care.

"Fine. We'll order in. What's your problem? You need to eat. Besides, Rosie's here too, right? You don't think I'll try to bang you in front of your sister, do you?"

The look on her face told me that yes, in fact, she was quite certain I'd try to bang her in front of her sister.

I might have deserved that.

I lifted three fingers in the air and sloped my chin up. "Scout's honor."

Hesitantly, she cracked the door open, but not all the way. "We can order in, but that's it." She stepped aside, giving me permission to enter her little universe.

I bulldozed into her apartment, into her *life*. The walls and kitchen were minimalist white, the floor a light-colored wood, the design open with very little furniture, white as well. It looked like an insane asylum. There was an easel in the corner of the living room, next to the window overlooking the city, with a big stretched canvas of an in-progress painting. A cherry blossom tree overlooking a lake. It was vivid and sharp, like nature was within reach. Which was a beautiful lie, of course. We were in a concrete kingdom, imprisoned by skyscrapers. Industrial smoke and mirrors.

Interesting. So Help was still an artist. It didn't surprise me. She was actually talented. Her shit wasn't tacky or good in a generic, mainstream kind of way. Her art was thought provoking. But not enough to be borderline crazy. It represented her quite perfectly, actually.

Her back was to me. We both stared at the painting.

"Why cherry blossoms?" I asked, ten years later than I should have. She'd always had a thing for the tree. She painted other shit too; everything she owned had been doodled on: textbooks, backpacks, clothes, arms. But she always came back to the cherry blossoms. Even her hair was the same shade as her favorite tree.

"Because they're beautiful and...I don't know, the blooms are gone so fast." I heard the smile on her lips. "When I was a kid, my grandmama used to take me to DC every spring to the Cherry Blossom Festival. Just me. I used to wait for it all year long. We never had much money, so to spend a day there, to go to a barbecue restaurant afterward... It was a big thing for me. Huge.

"Then she got sick when I was seven. Cancer. It took a while. I didn't really understand the concept of her dying, going away and never coming back, so she told me about the Japanese Sakura. People in Japan travel from all over to see the trees at their prime. Cherry blossom season is short but breathtaking, and after the blossoms fade, the flowers fall to the ground, scattered by the wind and rain. Grandmama said that the cherry blossom was life. Sweet and beautiful but so darn short. Too short not to do what you wanna do. Too short to not spend it with the people…you love." Her eyes closed slowly as she took a deep breath.

She stopped talking, and I stopped fucking breathing. Because I knew what made her stop. Me.

Everything I did.

I prevented her from spending time with some of these people—her parents, her sister—for my own selfish reasons when she was only eighteen.

"Holy cow, I'm a buzzkill." She let out a breathless chuckle. "Sorry."

"Don't be." I swallowed, taking a wide step so we stood flush next to each other, still observing the painting. "Shit happens. My mom died when I was nine."

"I know." Her tone was somber but not anxious. Normally, people didn't like it when you brought up your dead mother. Grief was an uncomfortable emotion to deal with. "That must've been hard."

"Well, you said you were a buzzkill. My competitive side inspired me to bring my A game." I shrugged, my voice even.

"Vicious." She laughed again, this time turning to me, giving me that look teachers give their students when they're disappointed with them.

I grinned. "Dead mother beats dead grandmother every day, and you fucking know it."

She swatted my shoulder but couldn't hide her smile. "You're horrible."

"Horribly sexy. Yes."

We ordered Vietnamese, and I told her how my mom got injured in a car crash and then died when I was nine. The usual details, except for the really sordid stuff about who made it happen. She was covered in paint, so we sat on the drop cloth under the easel. It wasn't my thing, but I didn't mind. The reason I told her about my mom was simple. I didn't want her to bail on my ass if push came to shove. If I was going to corrupt her morally, I needed more ammo.

She cried when I told her about how I found out my mother was dead. My dad was away on an urgent business trip, so our housekeeper told me between my hiccups and sniffs.

There were a lot of reasons why I didn't tell her the whole truth. The one I'd kept to myself all those years. The reasons now weren't that different than what they'd been back then.

I was still ashamed I hadn't realized what Dad and Jo were talking about doing when I was nine. I'd felt guilty all these years, wondering if I could've saved my mom, warned her, told someone.

Which was probably stupid because who would've believed a nine-year-old?

And afterward, if someone did believe me, what then? My mom would still be dead, and it could've been even worse for me. The shame, the pity, the gossip if there was a trial. When your dad sends his mistress's brother to pull the plug on your mother? Yeah, there was no coming back from that sob story. I would've been forever labeled as "that poor kid."

I wasn't anyone's "poor kid." I was a rich man. Powerful in people's eyes, and I intended to keep it that way.

I trusted Emilia. I knew I could confide in her. She'd kept our secret under wraps from everyone in high school. I trusted her to keep the one about my scars too.

The way she looked at me when we sat on her drop cloth—I was pretty fucking sure my nine-hundred-dollar slacks were stained with paint—made me want to tell her the rest. But I didn't want her to think about me what I used to think about myself. That I'd made a mistake in keeping quiet. That none of it would've happened if I'd told someone. That I could've stopped it all before it started. That I was stupid. *Weak*.

"I wish you'd have given me more of a chance to be there for you when I lived there," she murmured, looking down at her thighs and fighting more tears.

I wanted to touch her, but I didn't want a hug. I needed to fuck her until every inch of her flesh was raw.

I smiled politely. "See? We all have our cherry-blossom story." I looked around, suddenly anxious to stop talking. "Where the fuck is Rosie, anyway?"

I was starting to feel the way I did before, when she lived so close I could see into her bedroom window. I couldn't pin that feeling down. Not then and not now. I just knew that it was unacceptable. I had enough fucking fires to put out in my personal life without creating another shitstorm.

She muttered something about calling her sister and checking up on her and got up exactly as the doorbell chimed. She twisted her head to me and quirked an eyebrow, as if to say *what are the odds?* and sashayed to the door to get our food.

The smell of our hot, spicy food carried all the way to where I sat while she made small talk with the guy. Typical Emilia, nice to everyone and their mothers.

Emilia arranged some plates on our makeshift picnic blanket and opened a bottle of wine that she'd probably bought from the Dollar Tree, but dinner was nicer than the nicest ones I'd had in the last couple of years. We ate in silence, and that was okay because Emilia wasn't the type of girl who hurried to fill the air with meaningless chatter. She liked silence.

Like me.

Like my mom.

Then again, it'd been a while since I'd sat down for dinner with someone who wasn't one of the other HotHoles or my stepmother.

"Tell me something bad about you," I said out of nowhere.

"Something bad?" She took a swig straight from the bottle and placed it on the floor next to her thigh, wiggling her pursed lips from side to side. She was thinking.

"Yeah. Something that's less noble than Little Miss Perfect helping her sick sister by working two jobs."

She rolled her eyes at me but smiled, struggling to come up with something. When she did, she seemed half-elated. "I paint with oil paint!"

"Holy fuck, that's badass." I bit my lower lip and shook my head.

She laughed and swatted my shoulder—again—and, *yes*, Emilia LeBlanc wanted to fuck me as much as I wanted to fuck her. It was written all over her body language.

"Let me finish! I'm cautious. I take my time. Oils take a century to dry. You need to open the windows and let them air-dry, but I like how the colors are vibrant and the painting looks so real. Oil paint is actually pretty toxic. It's terrible for Rosie's lungs, but I still use it because I hate acrylic." She sighed, blushing a little.

Hot damn. Help was admitting to doing something selfish. She was definitely cracking.

I placed my hands over my temples and shook my head, feigning shock. "Mind-blowing shit, LeBlanc. Next thing you'll tell me you pay your taxes after April fifteenth."

"I like to live on the edge." She shrugged and sucked a noodle between her lips, using chopsticks.

I almost shoved away the paper take-out containers and pinned her to the drop cloth. *Almost*.

But it was becoming clearer to me that I wouldn't be able to hold myself back for long.

"I'm not all good," she said, slurping more food. I loved how she ate like she didn't give a fuck that I was watching her.

"Nobody's all good, just like nobody's all bad." I licked my lower lip, and she did the same. She dropped her chopsticks and chanced another glance at me. I continued eating, pretending I didn't give a damn.

"Sometimes I think you're all bad," she said, but I knew she didn't really mean it. I knew Emilia LeBlanc well enough to know she saw the goodness in everyone. Even me.

"Care to test that theory?" I slurped a noodle between my lips and winked. "I can make you feel pretty fucking good. Just say the word." She laughed, and it felt good in my chest. Warm, even.

"Is that your official pickup line? If so, I'm half suspecting you're still a virgin." She wrinkled her nose.

Yes, it was on, so fucking on. She was charmed. I recognized it when women were affected. Smelled it from miles away, like a shark out for blood.

I tossed my empty take-out box aside and moved closer to her. She didn't retreat. She wanted it. Wanted my mouth on hers. Wanted my hands buried in her cherry-blossom hair and my body grinding against hers. It was happening. Finally.

I leaned in. She stopped breathing and looked down, waiting... expecting...wanting. It took every ounce of fucking self-control in me to lift my hand and brush her delicate neck instead of pinning her wildly to the floor and ripping her stupid leggings from her thighs.

She released a breath, lolling her head to the side. "I'm going to regret this." Her voice was tiny, like her.

"Probably," I agreed. "But it'll be worth it."

My lips made the journey from her neck to their final destination—to where they fucking belonged from day one. Her warm breath tickled my flesh, and I wanted her to suffocate me with her kiss. I resisted the urge to ball my hands into fists, unexpectedly worried about how this would go down. I was starving for her. My next move wasn't going to be a calculated one, and that was the first time I'd felt that way about anything in a long time.

I was so close that I was able to feel her skin meeting mine, the little lines of her red lips brushing mine, when the door unlocked and fucking Rosie walked in.

Emilia withdrew herself from me immediately before I had a chance to finish the job and started collecting the take-out containers littered around us.

"Rosie!" Her voice was pitched high. "What took you so long? I got you some noodle soup. It will warm you right up."

She quickly disappeared into the kitchen behind a long white wall. I leaned back on my forearms on the drop cloth, staring at grown-up Rosie like she'd pissed in my food. She returned a feisty look in my direction. Oddly, it made me feel like a teenager all over again.

"If you hurt her, I will kill you." She pointed her finger at me for emphasis.

I was perfectly still, giving zero fucks about this five-foot-four gnome firing threats at me like she was Rambo.

"Cockblocking me first *and* threatening me? Should I remind you that the only reason you're not living in a sewer with that rat who trains the Ninja Turtles is because of my generosity?" I slanted my head sideways, flashing her my arrogant smirk. It was the exact one that drove men insane with anger and women mad with lust.

Rosie, of course, was immune to my charm. Using her to get her sister's attention ten years ago had killed every good thought she'd had about me. Not that she'd had many even before we kissed. In fact, I was pretty sure our lips had only locked because she was irritated by my lack of attention. I was the only teenager with a dick at All Saints who hadn't been consumed with impressing her. Of course, I was fully occupied with obsessing over her older sister.

"Generosity, my ass." She walked deeper into the room. Honestly, for a chick who suffered from a congenital lung disease, she looked pretty perky to me. "I don't know what you've got planned for her, but if it's vicious like you, I'm not going to let you get away with it."

I needed to stop this exchange before Emilia came back to the living room and Rosie shit all over my progress with her. Both sisters were feisty, but while Emilia was sassy in a

I'm-a-good-person-but-can-engage-in-fun-banter kind of way, Rosie was more from the I'll-stab-you-in-your-sleep-if-you-piss-me-off school. It was certainly not the only reason why I preferred Emilia to her sister, but it was a part of it. They looked the same, but they didn't *feel* the same. Not by a fucking long shot.

"My intentions are pure," I lied.

"I don't believe you," Rosie snapped.

"Too fucking bad because I'm not going anywhere, so you'd better get used to me." I got up. I was a little woozy from the cheap wine and lack of sleep but high as fuck on everything else that had happened that evening.

My high school obsession strode back into the living room with a bowl of soup and an apologetic smile.

"Vic was just leaving. Our company signed a huge deal today. He needed to brief me about tomorrow morning," she explained.

I hated that she felt like she owed her sister some sort of an explanation.

"I'll see you tomorrow at the office." I smoothed my shirt with my palm.

Emilia nodded but looked a million miles away from where we were just moments ago. That fucking sparkle in her eyes had died. Her sister's face must've reminded her how much of a douchebag I was.

"Again…" Emilia cleared her throat, her tone professional. "Congrats on the merger."

I left with my throbbing dick trying to worm its way out of my pants to the nearest high-class hooker in this zip code. I didn't know New York well enough to have a steady fuck here, but it didn't matter anyway. The storm that brewed in me was going to calm only when my cock was deep inside Emilia LeBlanc and not a moment sooner.

As I punched the elevator button and ran my hand through my hair, something strange dawned on me, and for the first time in years, I had a clear idea of what I wanted from life that had nothing to do with my career, money, or ruining Jo and Dad.

I wanted Emilia.

I wanted to kiss her whenever I felt like it.

I wanted to mark her in a million different ways.

I'd told Rosie the truth. I wasn't going anywhere. I was staying in New York until my dad died, until Josephine became penniless, and until I banged Emilia like I'd wanted to when I was eighteen.

In the elevator up to the penthouse, my phone pinged with a message from Dean.

> Just a friendly reminder—I'll be coming back to New York soon. If I were you, I'd run now before I get to you.

I didn't even grace his bullshit with a reply. Just walked into his apartment, with its tinted floor-to-ceiling windows, and started packing his shit for him, throwing his expensive suits into his designer garment bags.

We weren't switching back anytime soon. Not until I got what I wanted.

He was staying in LA.

Whether he liked it or not.

CHAPTER FIFTEEN
EMILIA

Rosie shook her head, her eyes following my every movement. She didn't need to do anything—I knew what she had to say.

"Shut up about it," I warned, cleaning the area around the easel and giving her my back while she sat at the dining table and watched me in my painting corner.

She kept staring at me, not touching her soup.

I didn't regret almost kissing Vicious. For once in my life, I hadn't played it safe. I wasn't cautious. I didn't paint my life in oil colors. I'd reached for acrylic, quick to dry, and settled on it—whatever *it* was I wanted with him.

"Fine," Rosie bit out. "But for the record, I warned you."

She slid a manila envelope across the white dining table. I opened it and stared at the money, ignoring her while counting it. Instead of feeling happy about selling a painting, I was filled with unease.

Was I about to make a huge mistake by messing around with Vicious? Probably. But I couldn't deny myself what I wanted, and we weren't kids anymore.

This was happening.

He was going to use me, and I was going to use him back.

It was a mistake of epic proportions, I knew that.

And just like any huge mistake, payback was going to be painful.

Sadly, it was a price I was willing to pay.

The next morning, I arrived early at the office. I wasn't sure why, but I wanted everything to be in perfect order.

For the first time, Vicious's coffee and breakfast were waiting for him on his desk.

I closeted myself inside my office—two doors down from his—and booked Rosie a plane ticket to San Diego. I wanted her to spend Christmas with our parents. Truly, there was nothing I wanted more than to tag along with her and make it an epic family week, but one last-minute ticket was expensive enough, and I needed to be financially cautious. In any case, I was certain Vicious wouldn't give me the time off.

Sending Rosie to the other side of the country had nothing to do with her warning last night. *Right*.

After I sent her a text with the surprise ticket, I sorted through Vicious's email. I responded to requests from charity organizers, cleaned up the junk, and flagged messages from investors that he needed to answer himself. His inbox was so career-focused it was almost sad. There was nothing personal except some banter with Jaime and Trent and a clipped question about the merger from Dean. I wasn't snooping. It was part of my job description to keep his inbox in order.

It wasn't a part of my job description to check out his Facebook interactions and read through every single exchange he'd had with a female in the last six months, but I took the liberty of doing that too because…well, because I was just hardworking like that.

I yelped and jumped to my feet when I realized he was standing at my door, staring me down like I was his breakfast.

"Trying to watch porn in the office again?" he said while I blushed. "We have security measures for that. Those websites are blocked."

I let out a nervous laugh and brushed my hair from my forehead. He looked too good to be so evil. Vicious was in another one of his dark suits, but he'd discarded the jacket and rolled up his shirtsleeves, exposing muscular forearms peppered with a smattering of that LA sun and those scars that made my heart beat erratically.

The only thing I could think about was how we'd almost kissed last night and how I'd silently cursed Rosie while I fixed soup for her in the kitchen after I'd had to pull away from him.

I quirked an eyebrow at him and leaned back. "Your IT people are doing a terrible job. I've been watching snuff all morning."

He laughed, and his amusement looked genuine. Rare and brief, like cherry blossoms in the spring. But just like the flowers, it died quickly.

"I didn't peg you for a kink girl, Emilia." He tucked his hands in his pockets. "Whatever floats your boat, I'd be happy to be captain."

"Tacky." I pretended to gag. "And now I'm 99 percent sure you *are* a virgin."

I was teasing him, and I didn't care anymore. Yes, he was a damaged person, but I now knew there might be reasons for that. No, I wouldn't ever forgive him for what he'd done to me. But that didn't mean I couldn't have some fun with him until I dug out of my financial mess. Might as well take him up on every single thing he offered while I could. Because that's essentially what we were doing—using one another.

Vicious's eyes licked my body head to toe, slow and taunting, then landed on my face. "Have your ass in my office in ten minutes. We need to tie up a few loose ends with the merger."

With that, he left, closing the door behind him. I didn't have time to catch my breath before my phone rang. I answered it with a grin.

"Please tell me you're coming with me!" Rosie exclaimed. I was glad she was feeling better and even happier that she was so excited about seeing our parents again.

"Sorry, Little Rose. I have a ton of work, and besides, I've wanted the new apartment to myself ever since I walked in. I'm going to put Panic! At The Disco on full blast, dance naked, eat pizza, and paint while you're gone." Despite a pang of sadness at not being there with my family, this actually sounded like a great idea. It would certainly top our last two Christmases, one of which ended up with me giving Rosie a half-empty bottle of perfume, though she pretended it was brand-new.

"I'm not going anywhere without you, you crazy ho. Not on Christmas."

"Rosie..." I sighed, pushing my office chair back from my desk and standing up.

I spent the next ten minutes in the bathroom, multitasking, trying to convince her and brushing my hair with my fingers, attempting to look good. "You're being ridiculous. I just saw Mama and Daddy. It's been two years since you've seen them. Please."

"Come with me," she insisted again.

"I want to save some money."

"You make a fortune!"

"Now, maybe, but who knows what'll happen in a month or two?"

Silence fell. She knew I was right. I was still looking for another job, knowing this one was only temporary. Vicious said so himself. He didn't even live in New York year-round.

I gave her the final push. "Seriously, do you realize how long it's been since I've had a place all to myself? I'll actually hold it against you forever if you waste the ticket. It's nonrefundable. I don't need to see your sorry face all through Christmas anyway. Go."

"I love you," she said with a sad chuckle.

"Right back at ya, sister." I smiled. "Now go pack. You have a flight to catch in a few hours."

"Okay, but did you tell Mama about Rat? I thought I'd mention I'm adopting a pet snake with him."

"Rat?" I scrunched my nose.

"My biker boyfriend!"

I laughed. "Oh yeah, she knows you're seeing him. Said she'd love to meet him sometime soon and that there's vermin in the Spencers' attic anyway, so the snake will feel right at home."

On my way to Vicious's office, I desperately tried to regulate my heartbeats. What was I doing, wanting to have a fling with the man who'd ruined my life? It was inexcusable. But I wanted him, and I was tired of depriving myself of what I wanted.

I knocked on his door, as was expected of me, and rubbed my hands over my thighs, throwing a glance at the glass reception desk and Patty, who sent me a warm smile. I smiled back.

"Come in," Vicious growled. He was standing behind his own glass desk, his palms flat against it.

"About the merger?" I clutched my iPad to my chest. I felt pretty proud about being able to form coherent sentences, considering my physical reaction to him. "You wanted to go through a few things?"

"Turn around and face the door," he ordered, completely ignoring my question. He was still reading something on his laptop screen.

I frowned. "Excuse me? Why?"

"Because I'm your boss and I tell you what the fuck to do." He lifted his head from the screen, his gaze piercing the thin layer of faux confidence I wore.

His face was expressionless, but his hooded eyes gleamed. The way he looked at me, with his dark-blue irises undressing me item by item, made me want to throw myself at him, like all the other shameless girls from high school. Slowly, I spun and looked at the door, my heart galloping, filling my ears with violent thuds. I was just glad that, unlike the rest of the offices down the hall, his had only a single glass wall. The door in the center was made of solid black wood.

"Is this about last night?" I asked.

"No."

I felt each and every one of his footsteps shaking my core from the inside. My womb clenched, and a hot wave of lust crashed against my pelvis. In seconds, his body was flush against mine from behind, and it was warmer than I remembered. Larger. Even more intoxicating than when he was eighteen. His lips found the sensitive spot on my neck, brushing—not kissing—teasing me with the promise of something more.

"It's about you being a liar when you were seventeen. And it's about you still being a liar when you're twenty-seven. You fucked one of my best friends when really you wanted to fuck me. It's time to make amends, Miss LeBlanc."

He snaked his arm around my shoulder, cupping my cheek and dragging my head back to meet his chest. His lips found my temple, and they smelled of coffee, lust, and him.

"I'm done playing kiddie games with you," he rasped, his voice so low—too low—and I felt his hot mouth moving on my skin. "We're both at the same place now, both single and hot for each other. This is happening. We're fucking. Say yes."

"Vicious…" I started, but then he pulled my hair gently, extending my neck and reaching his free hand to pull my waist, my butt hitting his thick, throbbing erection. My rear was pressed against his groin, and I felt how much he wanted me.

My need for him was just as strong. A warm, heady feeling made my thighs quiver and clench. I wanted to take a bite of the forbidden fruit I'd convinced myself was poisonous. He gave me pain, but ironically, this pain gave me life.

"Say. Yes," he repeated.

I needed to say no but wanted to say yes, so I settled for a little voiceless nod.

"Good girl," he breathed. "I knew you'd come around as long as you didn't have to look me in the eye when you admitted it."

He spun me around, and before I could say something—*anything*—his mouth attacked mine. Every doubt I'd had evaporated.

His tongue parted my lips, this time demanding, not asking, and I remembered how I hadn't allowed that to happen the first time we'd kissed. Now there was no barrier. There was no Dean. No HotHoles and no Todos Santos. Just two hungry, savage adults who wanted to rip each other to shreds.

I wanted to dissolve into smoke, to crawl into him and never leave. It was crazy, but that was how much I craved this man.

His mouth was hot, his kiss ravenous and rough. Like he was trying to erase every trace of every other man who'd ever tasted me—an erratic rhythm that made my heart skip several beats. I was so aroused, I thought I was going to die right there in his arms if he didn't peel my clothes off. But I couldn't ask him for it. For one thing, it was nine in the morning and the floor was packed with colleagues. When he grabbed me by my butt and raised my body so my legs wrapped around his waist, I knew we were seconds from doing something very unprofessional against his office door.

"People might see us," I moaned into his lips.

"And?" His teeth captured my lower lip gently and pulled it into his mouth. He sucked on it hard. His eyes were hooded with something other than boredom.

The fact that it was me who made him this way made my heart flutter.

"And it's grossly unprofessional," I said, voicing my thoughts, but I didn't pull away.

He was right. We'd wanted each other all along in high school. I'd been foolish to try to translate my emotions for him into something with one of his best friends, and he'd been hateful to chase me away instead of claiming me the way he should've.

It was obvious we had no future. Too many terrible things had happened between us. But that didn't mean we couldn't enjoy the present until he was done with his revenge and went back to his life in LA.

"Emilia." His baritone rumbled in my ear. He didn't call me Millie, but at least he'd stopped calling me Help. "I don't give a fuck who sees us, and it's probably better if they know not to fuck around with what belongs to me."

"What about the company rules you warned Floyd about?"

"Fuck the rules. I own the company."

Despite his words and his touch, I managed to place my palms on his chest and push him away. My lips throbbed with our searing kiss, and I felt the thump of my pulse at my temple.

"We can't do this here," I argued, trying to convince both him and myself.

He didn't look too fazed but walked to his desk and grabbed his keys and phone. He pressed his finger to his intercom, his gaze still on me.

"Receptionist," he barked. "Cancel all my shit for today. You've got access to Miss LeBlanc's computer. My schedule's in there."

"Is everything okay?" I heard Patty's soft, feminine voice from the other end of the line.

"I'm taking a sick day, and my PA needs to tend to me."

He hung up and stacked his folders into a neat pile, ignoring me again. I knew exactly what it meant, and my heart raced wildly in my chest.

Tapping my chin, I said, "Sick, huh?"

"Yes." He didn't even look up. "I'm fucking sick of not being inside you, where I should've been a long time ago. Now let's go."

It felt like the walk of shame as we made the long trip from his office to the elevator, with him clasping my elbow possessively, like a guard escorting me from the premises. Everybody was looking at us. And I do mean *everybody*. Eyeing us through the glass walls of their offices, peeking from the kitchen area, and stealing glances from behind the reception space.

I didn't care as much as I probably should have. This wasn't a legitimate job, and Vicious wasn't a legitimate boss. It was an arrangement that was going to be over soon, so I had to grab whatever I could before my time was up.

As we both stepped into the elevator, another suited employee tried to join us.

"Leave," Vicious said simply, and the man walked out of the elevator without even a flinch.

My mouth fell open, and Vicious punched the button that closed the door and slammed my body against the silver wall.

"Now, where were we?"

I was praying no one else would witness the fact that Vicious was a few seconds from screwing the life out of me, but that hope was futile. By the time the elevator pinged open and we stumbled out to the busy lobby of the building, my lip was cut from one of our wild kisses. I was bleeding. To be fair, I'd bitten him first, but I was teasing him. He, on the other hand, was… *Insane* was the accurate word.

Our hurried steps carried us toward the exit, and I knew our apartments were only a short ten-minute walk away, but it felt weird to make this journey on foot while we were so flustered and hot for one another. My panties were so soaked I hoped people weren't able to see it through my Christmas-themed leggings. Luckily, they were made out of a thick fabric.

Vicious continued to guide me by my elbow, which should've felt gallant and flattering, but I had zero illusions about what this was. I knew him well enough, despite all these years, to know romance was simply not on the menu for him. He was as emotionally available as a jackhammer. This was pure lust, exploding after a decade of simmering quietly, brewed by frustration, jealousy, and hate.

Once we walked through the revolving door, rushing down the street through the December chill and the crowds of Christmas shoppers, I started laughing. We were walking so fast that our butts might as well have been on fire.

"Do I wanna know what's funny?" His face looked strained, and I bit down another chuckle.

I shouldn't have laughed. I had blood on my lower lip, and he was sporting a visible erection. But he looked *so* serious. Like he was ushering me to the ER and not to his bed.

"Just the way we're acting, like two high schoolers who just found out one of them has an empty house," I said, fighting another burst of giggles.

He squeezed my elbow, and we cut the corner, almost jogging.

My laughing stopped when we walked through the glass doors to the skyscraper where we lived. Vicious punched the elevator button three times in a row and started pacing, waiting for it to ping open. He ran his hand through his inky-black hair.

"Rosie's home," I said, swallowing hard.

He turned around to look at me, and I swear it looked like his erection was going to break through his zipper or his zipper was going to break his erection. Either way, it was going to hurt.

"We'll go up to the penthouse," he said, shoving a hand deeper into his tousled hair and tugging impatiently.

"She could bump into us in the elevator. Or the hallway. Or…"

Truly, I didn't care about Rosie catching us. I was a grown-up, and besides, we'd both brought men over to our old studio on occasion. When it happened, the other sister would make herself scarce. Nope. I was clearly stalling, and I didn't know why.

"Fine. We'll grab a taxi. The Mandarin isn't that far. It's a long shot this time of the year, but they might have a room or two available. If not, there's always the bathroom at Starbucks." He turned around and started stalking toward the entrance.

I grabbed his hand and stopped him, and our eyes met. "Really, Vicious? After ten years of waiting, that's how you want to do this? In a hotel, in the middle of the morning?"

"Fuck." His jaw clenched and he exhaled, closing his eyes. "What did you think was gonna happen when we ditched work?

That we would catch a Jennifer Lawrence movie under the fucking covers?"

He looked so on edge, I thought he was going to detonate on the marble floor. I flattened my palm against the collar of his dress shirt, and that seemed to soothe him a little.

"I bought Rosie a plane ticket to fly home to see our parents. She's supposed to pick up her meds around six and then go to the airport straight from there. We can still go back to the office and come back here after she's gone."

"Fuck no," he almost spat. "We're spending today alone."

When he didn't move, just stared at me like he was going to take me on the floor, I tangled my fingers together, twisting them. "I could show you New York."

"What?" His brow furrowed.

"Show you New York. Show you where I like to go, where I like to eat. Show you why it's so much better than LA, why Frank Sinatra and Woody Allen and Scorsese rhapsodize about this crazy place with this crazy weather like it's paradise."

"Sweetheart, I don't do monogamy." He tsked like I had asked him if he could part the sea. "And that sounds a lot like a date."

"It's not," I protested, feeling my face heat. "Also, I vividly remember you asking me to go to dinner with you yesterday. What's changed?"

"That wasn't a date. I was just really fucking hungry."

"Well, what makes you think I'd like to date someone as hateful and cold as you anyway?" I tilted my head like a bird, my eyes blazing with heat.

"I don't know. I don't care. *And* I don't do dates," he said again, taking a step back and shaking his head. His cheeks flushed pink, and this time it wasn't only from the cold.

Sweet Jesus and His holy crew.

At this point, I'd had enough of this nonsense, so I decided to kill the conversation. "Really?" I snorted.

"*Really*," he enunciated.

"So if I tell you I want to redo our senior year in one day…to go ice-skating at Rockefeller Center and let you get to second base like two teenagers…" I erased the gap between us, kissing a sliver of his exposed neck, and his breath stilled. "And go eat at P.J. Clarke's and move to third base in the bathroom…" I rasped the words against his hot flesh and dragged my eyes up to meet his stormy ones. "And end the day at a Broadway show where I'd do something very inappropriate under the coat in your seat…" We melted into each other, and sure enough, I felt the swelling in his slacks getting bigger against my stomach. "You'd say…no?"

His face was the funniest thing on earth as it moved from surprised to eager and then finally to turned on.

"Fuck," he muttered, pressing his hard cock against me. From the outside, it must've looked like we were sharing the dirtiest hug ever. "I'm about to go ice-skating for a hand job, and I'm not even sixteen anymore."

"You're totally going on a day date," I joked.

He rolled his eyes but followed me back outside and into the nearest subway station, buttoning his pea coat to cover the massive bulge between his legs. "Lead the way."

Despite my teasing, I didn't really plan to take him ice-skating. But I wasn't going to tell him that just yet. I actually enjoyed watching him sitting opposite me on the subway. Jaw grinding. Brow creased. Eyes locked on mine. We were oblivious to the noise around us—the damp, stinky coats brushing against us, Kindles, paperbacks, and take-out bags that smelled like Asian food and were nudged into our ribs. It was just us.

I couldn't remember the last time I'd spent the day having fun in the city without thinking about picking up more shifts or running errands.

I also couldn't remember the last time I spent the day with a man who made my knees weak, my breath erratic, and my heart feel like it didn't belong to me anymore.

"This means nothing," he said from across my seat, twisting my own words from yesterday when I let him into my apartment.

"I'm asking you to ice-skate with me, not trying to melt the ice around your cold, cold heart," I retorted in the same way he'd responded to me less than twenty-four hours ago.

He cracked a rare smile. "Where are we really going? This isn't the way to Rockefeller Center."

"Always so perceptive, Mr. Spencer." I got up and held on to one of the poles when we reached 77th Street station. He followed me. "We're going to the Met."

At the Met, there was a special exhibition about human anatomy, of all subjects. It was extra realistic and gory too. When we waited in the short line to get the tickets, I told Vicious I'd almost fainted when I saw an Egyptian mummy the first time I'd visited the museum. He laughed and said that he once went to the Mütter Museum in Philadelphia on a school trip and threw up when he saw some of the remains of Einstein's brain.

"Can't blame you. There are some things better left to the imagination…though I can't see myself ever wanting to picture that either." I scrunched my nose as we entered the exhibit.

I choked the little booklet I was holding to release some of the tension from my body. We stopped next to a picture of a real heart, sitting on a white cube. It was bloody and looked fresh, like it was still beating not long ago.

I saw the art in it.

Heck, I wanted to run back home and paint it.

"I was thirteen and all kinds of messed up. The brain just always seemed to me like the most important, intimate part of the human body. Maybe because that's what was left of my mother after her accident. She was paralyzed from the neck down but completely lucid. Still herself."

I didn't utter a word because it felt important to let him speak.

We were both staring at the picture when he added, "I like the way you stare reality in the eye without looking away. You're not a coward, Emilia."

I nodded. "Neither are you. I mean, you're crazy but brave."

We walked a few feet to our right, checking out the next piece. Time moved quickly, too quickly. Four hours into our day at the museum, and I was starving, so I suggested that we go get something to eat. Vicious nodded in agreement. I was surprised we'd gotten this far without him complaining about us being here so long. We walked toward the exit, but then he grabbed me by the collar of my coat and shoved me into a corner behind a wall leading to the bathroom. It was quiet and secluded. Just another dead weekday before Christmas.

His lips found mine quickly as he muttered, "Where's that second base you promised me?"

I linked my fingers around his neck and waited for him to make a move.

I was a good girl.

He was a bad boy.

He knew what to do.

Vicious pressed his lips to mine, kissing me slow and long—teasing this time—before moving away and watching me through narrowed predator eyes.

"Refreshing," he croaked.

I nodded. A good long kiss was better than quick, casual sex. He ducked his head down again for another one, deepening our kiss, and sucked on my tongue *hungrily*, cupping my ass with one hand *firmly*, and brushing my throat with his thumb on his other hand *softly*.

"Did you think about this often? Kissing me like that?" My voice was husky. I felt him nodding even though my eyes were closed. The electricity between us was tantalizing. My body begged for more of him and chased his touch, desperate to be closer.

My obsession. My muse. My enemy.

"All the fucking time, Emilia. I wanted to squeeze this ass…" He clutched my butt, pulling me to grind into his erection, his lips hunting mine with leisurely, playful kisses that both intoxicated and soothed me. "To feel these tits…" His callused thumb dragged from my neck to my collarbone and before I knew it, he kneaded my right breast through my clothes while sucking on my jaw. "To kiss these goddamned fucking lips that smiled for *him*." He kissed me over and over again.

It broke me.

It revived me.

It ruined me.

I didn't even address the subject of Dean because my ex-boyfriend seemed to have moved on just fine. After I bumped into Vicious, I'd peeked at Dean's Facebook, my curiosity and guilt getting the better of me. I saw that he was happy, content, and, unsurprisingly, a whore. It made me feel better somehow. That I no longer occupied his mind.

Unlike Vicious. I was there in his head. I was there, and he hated it. That's why we were kissing right now. Because he kept telling me he hated me, but I—I didn't believe him. Not now anyway.

"Then why were you so hateful?" I wasn't sure if I was mad or smitten with him. My mind zigzagged in confusion every time he was around.

His hard-on was still digging into my "Rudolph the Red-Nosed Reindeer" leggings when he lowered his kisses to my breasts, ignoring me, pushing my sweater down and sucking on my nipples through my bra. I felt him pulsing next to my inner thigh, and I wanted every inch of him to fill me. Craved it. But Vicious's expression grew serious.

"Emilia…" he warned.

"No, tell me. How the heck does it matter anymore? You got what you wanted. I left. So why don't you put me out of my misery?"

He sighed, pulling away and boxing me in with his body, his arms on either side of me trapping me against the wall. His eyes were on the floor. "I was scarred from head to fucking toe. Physically marred. Mentally disfigured. The beatings I took from Daryl Ryler ruined me. I couldn't take my shirt off when everyone went to the beach. I couldn't fuck girls with the lights on. I couldn't breathe without thinking about what a monster I was underneath my clothes, underneath *my flesh*. And then there you were. Pure and scar-free, with your big, kind eyes and honest smile. You were so clean, and I was filthy. I guess I wanted to dirty you up.

"Then there was the Ryler shit. I thought you'd figured out what he'd done to me. I was afraid that you were going to tell people. I couldn't risk that, so I scared you. Then I drove you away. I'm fucked up, Emilia. I know that. I'm not asking you to fix me. It is what it is. We'll fuck. We'll use each other. Until one of us finds someone else they prefer."

He wanted casual. That was fine.

He was light in a dark fog. But I knew better than everyone how bad the gorgeous dancing flames in him could burn. If I treated it as a fling, my heart would be guarded away. His too.

"Have you ever dated anyone seriously?" I practically sighed the question.

We were cooling off. His body became tense and his posture straight. We swiveled toward the exit doors and resumed our journey to the subway. I followed. To say that I was content with his explanation was a lie, but it calmed me down. A little, anyway.

"Never," he said, emotionless. "Have you? Other than—"

"Two serious boyfriends here in New York." I nodded, cutting into his words before he could say his name. Dean hurt him, like Vicious hurt me. I got it now.

"Mmm" was all he said. We slipped into the subway station and were lucky enough to catch a train that had just pulled to a stop. It was packed, but I had a feeling it wasn't the only reason he pinned me to one of the yellow walls with his whole body so that nobody else would touch me.

"Were you in love with either of them?" His lips were dancing against mine.

I shrugged. "How does one really know for sure? They were very nice."

"I see. *Nice*."

That's all his lawyer-self needed to say to rest his case. His cocky smile stayed in place the whole train ride.

Bastard.

We made a stop by Rockefeller Plaza. I told him I wanted to see the tree and watch people ice-skate. Truth was, all I wanted was to push him a little more. Poke at his patience. See how far he was willing to go. Turned out, it was pretty darn far. Further than I've ever known him to go for a girl. That, in itself, stroked my ego in places that made me shiver with pleasure.

Our next stop was Thin Crushed Ice in the East Village. I'd never been to this bar before, but I always passed by it when I went to the paint store for painting supplies and wondered what it was like inside. So, technically, it wasn't a favorite place of mine, but I had a feeling it was going to become one. It looked sexy and dark, with a phone booth for an entrance leading to an open bar with exposed brick walls, taxidermy wearing sunglasses and ties, and wooden ceilings that made it look like we were somewhere far away from New York. The place was full of hipsters despite it only being a little after six p.m. on a weekday.

Vicious slid into one of the black-leather sofas inside a booth, and when I went to sit across from him, he shook his head like I was a rookie and patted the space beside him. I slid next to him, and he hooked his arm over my shoulder. I closed my eyes and allowed myself to smell him—really take him in—enjoying the quiet moment of having him for myself.

When I opened my eyes, he reminded me once again that this wasn't a date.

"Drink." He threw the cocktail menu in my general direction, grabbing his phone and checking his emails. "But not enough so that I won't be able to fuck you on the grounds of you being too shit-faced."

Most girls would have walked away just then. But I knew Vicious had to make up for being vulnerable at the Met, when he admitted to feeling weak. When he admitted defeat.

"With that kind of attitude, sober me wouldn't give you the time of day either." I checked out the food menu and, naturally, craved every single dish. My mouth watered even though I hardly knew what half the items were. They sounded sophisticated. A mix of Asian and Mediterranean. I didn't care what they meant, I just wanted them all in my belly.

When I lifted my head from the menu to ask him what he wanted, I found him looking at me oddly again. He'd been doing that throughout our time at the museum, but I hadn't wanted to ruin our fun day out and ask why then.

"What?" I finally asked.

"Third base is oral, right?"

I rolled my eyes. Just when I was about to answer, the waitress approached our table. She was the mother of all hipsters, with hair like mine and enough facial piercings to pass as a human sieve. She opened her mouth to greet us, but Vicious cut her off.

"Everything." He threw the menus her way, looking back at me but still talking to her. "Just bring everything. Cocktails. Food. Whatever. Everything. Now go."

My instinctive response was to get up and leave before anyone concluded that I was down with this kind of rude behavior. I was wiggling my butt toward the edge of my seat when he jerked me into his body, hard.

"What the heck?" I scowled at him.

"You never answered me." He looked down at me, business-like. "What does third base include? Stretching your pussy with my tongue and getting my dick sucked?"

Good. Lord.

I couldn't believe I used to have a serious crush on this man. And I definitely couldn't believe I'd worried about sleeping with him without having my heart broken. This was going to be easy.

"Vic," I gritted. "Don't pretend like you don't know what third base is."

"I prefer football terminology, seeing as I'm more familiar with the game. Which is why I know I'm definitely going to score tonight."

"Smooth." My face remained unsmiling.

"And thick," he added. "With a slight tilt to the right."

I was about to get up again, but then the waitress approached us with about ten glasses on her tray. Instead of leaving, I tossed down two cocktails like they were shots and swiped my mouth with the back of my hand. I wasn't exactly keeping it classy, but then my boss was probing me about oral sex. Lines were being blurred, and they were becoming blurrier with every ounce of alcohol entering my blood stream.

Vicious took a sip of a beer. Slowly. Completely in control. The hunter was always more calculated and in charge. And then there was me, flailing around like the helpless prey.

"Why have you never pursued a career as a painter?" he asked.

It sounded more like an accusation than a question. Some of the food he ordered had arrived, and I picked at it with my fork, trying a little of everything.

"I have, and I've worked with other artists too. Interned at a gallery here in Manhattan after I graduated. Then Rosie moved in and got sick, so she couldn't hold on to a steady part-time job. Why did you become a lawyer?"

"I like arguing with people."

I laughed at that. I had to agree. "But you chose mergers and acquisitions, hardly a fast-paced, dramatic way to practice that skill," I argued.

He picked up an olive and brought it to my lips. "Open," he said darkly.

I did.

"Now swallow."

I smiled with the olive between my teeth, daring him. He dipped down and kissed me hard, shoving the olive into my mouth with his tongue. It was either choke or swallow. I chose swallow.

He pulled back from me, but his gaze remained on my lips. "Now *that's* good practice. As for law, I have no desire to cover up for other people's fuckups. I'd much rather see how my clients double and triple their investments…and mine. People don't pay me because of my law-school pedigree. I went to a shit college in LA and graduated with people who went to work doing house closings and chasing ambulances. People pay me to make money, and I make a ton of it."

"What's your fascination with money? You have so much."

He leaned forward, picking up a lock of my lavender hair. "Money is like pussy, sweetheart. You can't ever get enough."

"Yeah, and it's made you so happy. You realize you sound like a walking, talking cliché?"

His eyes sparked with something devilish. "I am happy. I've never been happier. It's seven o'clock, so Rosie should be long gone by now. Let's go before I take you up on that offer about third base right here on the table."

"I have one more place I want to stop first," I said.

"Fucking Christ," he gritted. "How about you keep your side of the deal, Miss LeBlanc?"

"I will. Eventually. Patience is a virtue."

"Patience can go fuck itself. Wherever we're stopping, it better be comfortable because I'm tasting you there."

CHAPTER SIXTEEN
VICIOUS

All I could think about was getting into bed with her. I didn't want to talk to her about life. I didn't want to get to know her better. Already I was breaking approximately five thousand different rules by spending the day with her. Every minute spent outside of bed was risky. But it seemed like the more I acted like a blunt, disgusting pig, the more she asked about my profession, my hobbies, my preferences.

People had never given a shit about those things. Ever. Her interest in me didn't make me feel good. It made me feel weird.

We were headed to Broadway next. I prayed she didn't really plan for us to go see a play. I had nothing against Broadway shows, but when one was standing in the way of me and her long-awaited pussy, I was just about willing to burn the whole fucking street down. I'd already started doing the math in my head, calculating the sentence for setting an occupied building on fire. Arson, possibly attempted murder. Those were heavy felonies. What was I looking at here? Hard time. Fifteen years, minimum. Different states varied, but New York was hard on its criminals.

Fifteen years.

Still fucking worth it.

"Vicious!" Emilia snapped me out of my reverie. I walked faster than her even though I had no idea where we were going. I just knew I wanted to get it over with.

"What?" I hissed.

"Did you listen to anything I just said to you?"

Of course not.

"Absolutely."

"Really?" She stopped in her tracks, folding her arms across her chest. "What did I say? Where are we going next?"

It was already past six o'clock, and tomorrow was the last day of work before Christmas. I wasn't in the mood for quizzes.

I looked above her head at the flashing neon sign for a tattoo parlor and blinked once. "You want to get a tattoo," I said flatly.

By the surprised look on her face, I knew I got it right.

"Of what?" she insisted.

"Of…" I gave myself some time to think about it, even though I didn't need any. I knew her. Better than most people, actually. "A cherry blossom tree."

"Screw you."

"That's what I've been trying to do here all day. Where are you getting this tattoo? I don't want it to get in the way of our fuck session."

"Nape of my neck," she replied. "Don't worry, it'll be pretty small."

I nodded, my dick twitching twice. Apparently she got its approval too. "Let's get you inked."

I really was a lucky bastard because the parlor was mostly empty despite it being one of the best places in the city. I didn't know why Emilia chose to take me with her for her first tattoo, but hell if I cared.

She sketched her tattoo on the stencil paper over the counter, the tip of her tongue peeking out of her red mouth as she scrunched her nose and drew. There was a heavily made-up Goth girl leaning against a barstool. She looked at us like most people did. Like Emilia had kidnapped me or like I was her sensible brother. We were so different it was borderline comical. Me with my custom suit, expensive coat, and rich-asshole air about me and her with her burgundy-wine sweater, beanie, Christmas leggings, and army boots.

When Emilia was done and showed her artwork to the girl—it even had coloring and shades—the girl nodded and took the sketch to the back room. Emilia chewed the pencil she'd used, and I took it out of her mouth and shoved it into my pocket.

"Hey, it's not even ours," she protested.

"They don't need this shit with your saliva all over it," I clipped out.

"Oh? And you do?" She grinned.

I didn't reply. She was goddamn ridiculous. A big guy with a black goatee and matching long hair—completely tattooed from head to toe—stepped out of the back room, flipping aside a black-vinyl curtain, and nodded hello to us.

"Name's Shakespeare. 'Sup?"

We all shook hands. Then he proceeded to go over the process with Emilia. Since it was her first time, he explained the full procedure in detail. And when the fuck would this thing be over? It felt like days had passed since we'd agreed on screwing each other.

Shakespeare—whose goatee actually did make him look like an Elizabethan playwright—asked Emilia if she'd like me to tag along and enter the room. She started answering, "Well…"

Which was obviously *not* the right answer, so I answered on her behalf. "I'm coming in."

The tattooist ignored me, moving his eyes between her and me, and tilted his chin down. "He doesn't have to if you don't want."

Fuck him. He made it sound like she was a battered wife.

"Actually, I don't care if he joins us. I know he loves watching me get hurt." She winked at me, but she wasn't smiling, and that thing in my chest sank a little.

Fuck her too.

We walked into the room. The floor was black and white, with red furniture everywhere, and there were framed pictures of Shakespeare's work. He was good. I took a moment to appreciate his ink.

Shakespeare tossed his iPhone across his desk and dropped to his swivel chair in front of the adjustable tattoo table Emilia was already perched on. "What's your poison?" he asked, sending her a wink.

I'm going to cut his fucking goatee off and feed it to him.

Emilia chose "Nightcall" by Kravinsky. He hooked his phone to a USB cable, and the music started blasting from every corner of the room. Shakespeare asked Emilia to take off her sweater and bra and lie on the table on her stomach and to brush all her hair away from her back. She lifted her sweater, exposing her silky olive skin for the first time in front of me. My cock begged for my mind to do something, anything, to lure her to third base like we'd shook hands on.

When she reached for the back of her bra to undo it and turned her back to me, I snapped.

I pulled my wallet out of my pocket. "Here's my credit card." I extended the plastic to Shakespeare, waving it between my fingers like a bribe. "You can use it for whatever you want. Just give us ten minutes alone."

Shakespeare opened his mouth, not touching the credit card, glancing between me and Emilia, who looked just as shocked as he did, if not more. But it was too late to take it back, and I didn't want to anyway.

Come the fuck on, Goatee. Turn around and walk away.

"Anything," I stressed, my face still blank. "Go get yourself a new chair. Or a table. Or ink, whatever the fuck it is you need. My treat. Go order food for the whole building. Buy the stray cat down the road a bed to piss on. I'll give you ten minutes with my credit card if you give me ten minutes in this room with her. Alone."

"Is your boyfriend always so aggressive?" He arched an eyebrow in Emilia's direction, throwing her a questioning look that asked: Do you want me to leave you alone with this asshole, or do you want me to throw him outside and call NYPD?

She laughed her syrupy Southern belle laugh that always seemed to stab straight to the pit of my fucking stomach. "He's not my boyfriend."

Shakespeare's other eyebrow shot up. "You should tell him that. Doesn't seem like he got the memo."

With a huff, I shoved the credit card into his chubby hand and wrapped his sweaty fingers around it. "Hey, Dr. Phil, get the fuck out of here."

Shakespeare did as he was told, the door closed, and it was just Emilia and me. She held her sweater to her braless chest and sat on the table, grinning at me.

"Third base?" She bit her lower lip.

I nodded, approaching her in steps that were restrained and even. I didn't want to pounce on her like a maniac. I mean, I did want to, but I couldn't scare her away. Not after today.

Something had changed, whether I liked it or not. She knew my secrets. Some of them, anyway. I didn't understand why I told her everything I did, but alarmingly, I didn't regret it. Not one bit.

Just when I was inches from her body, watching her bare rib cage rising up and moving down to the rhythm of her heartbeats, I took a sharp right and walked to Shakespeare's phone.

"Where are you going?" Her voice broke midsentence, and I suppressed a chuckle.

"I'm not eating you out to the sound of Kravinsky."

After all, this is Emilia. The most important meal of the day.

And Kravinsky sucked ass, but I wasn't going to argue with her over music. I switched it to "Superstar" by Sonic Youth, the song playing when I'd tried—and failed—to kiss her the first time ten years ago. When I turned around back to her, I saw in her eyes that she remembered it too.

"Apologize," I ordered, striding in her direction once again.

"What for?" Her gaze shifted, and she looked like she was about to throw a punch at me.

"For not kissing me back when you clearly wanted to, you little liar. For fucking one of my best friends. For making that year the worst year of my life since I was nine. Apologize for not being mine when you should've been. Because Emilia, baby…" I tilted my head sideways. "It was always fucking us and you know it."

"I won't apologize unless you do too. For stealing my calc textbook. For treating me like trash…" She sucked in a breath and closed her eyes. "For throwing me out of Todos Santos."

I reached for her, placed myself between her legs, and yanked away the sweater she held to her chest. I stared straight into her eyes. "I apologize for doing all those things to you in high school, but now we're grown-ups, and I think I've met my match. Your turn."

"I apologize for being too fucking irresistible for you to maintain your sanity." She rolled her eyes.

I knew how rare it was for Emilia use the f-word. I loved it on her lips. I stood there staring into her face for a few seconds before I let my eyes drift down. Her breasts were better than I'd expected. Slightly smaller than I'd imagined, but with pinker, smaller nipples. They were truly PPPs.

Perky. Pear-shaped. Perfect.

My pulse quickened, and blood rushed to my swollen cock.

"May I?" I asked. Why the fuck did I ask? When did I start *asking* for stuff, anyway?

"You may."

I lowered my face to her right breast and flicked it with my tongue, tasting her tight nipple, teasing. She sighed and ran her fingers through my hair. My whole back broke into chills. I sucked on her, barely applying real pressure, as I moved my hand to her waistband. I shoved my palm in, moving my finger along her cotton panties.

"Jesus, Vic," she murmured, clutching my head to her chest and loving every moment of it. "Jesus Christ."

I moved to her left tit and sucked harder, and she reacted exactly as I wanted her to, moaning louder this time. That was my cue to nudge her panties to the side. My hand still tucked inside her leggings, I dipped one finger inside her.

So tight.

So warm.

So mine.

"Emilia," I whispered into her mouth before kissing her again. "How many times did you imagine me fingering you when you secretly watched me play football in high school?"

The music was slow and seductive, and we were completely fucking drunk.

Emilia cupped my face and stared at me, her eyes sparkling, like she was awestruck. Alcohol? Hormones? Who cared? She was vulnerable. For me.

"Please, don't." She moaned the words.

"Answer me," I prompted, thrusting another finger into her. She was so soaked. I wanted to tear her stupid leggings to shreds and ride her on the table.

"All the time." Her voice was strangled. "I thought about it all the time and hated myself for it."

The song ended, and I knew we had about five minutes more, if not less. Not nearly enough time for me to do what I wanted to do. So instead of feasting on her pussy, I fingered her faster, plunging deeper into her. She unbuckled me, slipped her hand into my briefs, and squeezed the head of my cock, twirling a drop of precum around it with her thumb. I groaned and devoured her mouth while she jerked me off.

Who would have thought. Emilia LeBlanc from Richmond, Virginia. So sweet. So proper. So fucking out of her mind for me, in this small tattoo shop on Broadway a couple of days before Christmas.

We were rubbing each other and moaning each other's names into our mouths—both of us desperate to make sure it was *real*...

I realized I was about to come all over her Rudolph and his fucking red nose. I stopped her hand on my cock, still homing in on her throbbing clit. What the fuck was I doing? "Don't," I barked. "I'll come."

"And?" She smiled into one of our dirty, hot kisses.

"And I'd prefer not to come in your hand like a twelve-year-old," I said. Barely.

"Ask me nicely, or I'll continue."

Was she fucking threatening me?

"You're going to regret—" I started, but she started pumping faster, and I caved. Like a pussy, I gave her what she wanted. "Fine, fuck. Please."

"Please what?" she teased, and holy hell, she was filthier than I'd imagined. Not at all the innocent little damsel in distress.

"Please..." I cleared my throat. "Don't let me come all over your hand."

That was the moment when Emilia LeBlanc jumped from the table with a naughty grin I'd never seen on her face before and got on her knees for me, her beautiful lavender hair in my fist, pumping my dick as she clasped the head of my cock between her lips.

"Come," she mouthed on my cock.

And I did. Before she even finished the word.

It was stunning, the best thing I'd ever done with a woman in my entire life.

Three hours later, we walked out of the tattoo shop. She had a cherry blossom tree on her skin. It wasn't that small. The nape of her neck was where the brown trunk stood tall, strong, with thick roots adorning her shoulder blades. Pink and purple blossoms caressed her thin, delicate neck.

And I was fucked.

So. Fucking. Fucked.

It was weird to have her in his penthouse.

Over the years, I'd brought girls to Dean's apartment plenty of times. I took them in his kitchen, Jacuzzi, bathtub, the balcony overlooking Manhattan, and even got one flexible Juilliard dancer to do it on his very narrow, very packed wet bar. I didn't think much of it. He did the same in my condo in LA. It was just the way we were. But when we finally got home, at close to midnight, I knew exactly where I had to take Emilia LeBlanc.

On her ex-boyfriend's bed.

It wasn't malicious. Not at all. She was right. This was too important to be done in a hotel or some random Starbucks. This was going to happen in a bed. She wasn't a nameless one-night stand. She was a fantasy, and like all fantasies, she was meant to be savored, cherished, and treated with caution and respect.

Besides, Emilia didn't know it was Dean's bed, and I didn't see how withholding the information from her could hurt her. It made no difference. At least to me.

She looked a little tired in the elevator, so I decided to wake her up by sucking on her neck, mere inches from the bandage covering the pink flowers. I crushed her body to the wall of the elevator and lifted her by the back of her knees, tying her legs around my waist.

"Does it still hurt?" I asked, brushing my fingers lightly over the wrapped-up tattoo. She whimpered into my mouth and dragged her tongue over my lower lip but didn't answer me. I wanted her words. I shouldn't have cared, but I did.

I dry-fucked her, slow and lazy, through our clothes until the doors glided open; then I carried her the rest of the journey to Dean's door while she was still wrapped around me. It was with great sadness that I had to let her go so I could unlock the door, and when I pushed it open, something occurred to me.

I'm a fucking idiot.

"Close your eyes," I ordered. Shit. It sounded like I had a surprise planned for her, but the only thing surprising was that I was a complete and utter amateur. Goddammit.

"Why?" she questioned, sobering up a little from her alcohol-induced exhaustion.

"Because I said so," I snapped.

"Try again. The non-jerk version this time," she said sleepily.

Fuck, it was like behavioral boot camp with this woman. I took a deep breath. "I want it to be perfect," I explained, almost softly.

Her eyes fluttered shut, and I took her hands in mine—I fucking held her hands, another first—and led her to the master bedroom as we passed by pictures of Dean with his extended fucking family, smiling at us from every corner of the room.

Dean had a perfect family life. Amazing parents, two overachieving sisters. The whole deal. But as great as his family was, it wasn't interesting enough for *me* to keep the mementos of them in what was supposed to be *my* apartment. I couldn't explain these pictures to Emilia, and I didn't want to tell her it was Dean's place because I didn't want her to think I was fucking her to avenge what happened when we were teenagers.

Because I wasn't.

I was fucking her because I'd wanted her pussy ever since I first saw her standing outside the library door and knew those peacock eyes were going to haunt me.

I lowered Emilia to the bed and ordered her to keep her eyes closed as I rushed to the living room. I grabbed the framed pictures of Dean and his family and shoved them all into his pantry. There were plenty of them too. All over the living room, hallway, and kitchen area.

Fuck! Why couldn't he have had a shitty family like mine? He could bring a whole FBI unit, fifty CIA agents, and fucking Nancy

Drew to my condo, and none of them would know I lived there. The guy's place was more family-oriented than a Chuck E. Cheese restaurant.

It took me ten minutes to get rid of Dean's crap, and when I walked back to the bedroom, breathless, I saw Emilia lying flat on the mattress, her arms stretched out like a snow angel, snoring softly.

Snoring.

As in not awake.

Snoring.

As in she fell asleep.

Goddammit.

"Thanks a bunch, Cole," I muttered, biting my own fist to suppress a frustrated scream.

This day was for nothing. We weren't going to fuck. Well, not tonight, anyway. It wasn't that today was torture—far from it, I'd mostly had a good time—but the only reason I'd agreed to it was because I knew what was waiting for me in the end.

For a slight second, I contemplated whether I should *accidentally* wake her up by breaking something or turning on the music because I simply *didn't know* she was asleep, but apparently, even my assholeness had its limits.

I covered her with a blanket—again—and strode to the walk-in closet, pulling out my workout clothes. The night was young, and sleep wasn't on the menu for me as usual.

I worked out at the indoor gym Dean's building had to offer and then went back up to the penthouse—she was still asleep—and took a shower. When I was in my jeans and plain black tee, I padded barefoot to the living room and started going over documents for work. There were two agreements I needed to draft before New Year's Eve. Easy peasy. It wasn't like I needed to spend some time with my family.

At four in the morning, I felt her arms wrap around my shoulders from behind as I sat on the sofa, scrolling through one of my clients' files.

"Do you have insomnia?" she asked bluntly into my ear before blowing on it teasingly. "You never sleep. Ever. I'm starting to think you're not human."

"My stepmom seems to share the sentiment." I set my laptop on the coffee table and got up, spinning to face her. She looked how I felt. Pretty goddamn tired.

"Well, do you?" she probed.

"No," I lied. "It's four in the morning. Go back to sleep."

"I'm not tired anymore," she protested. "And my new tattoo burns."

"Pretty sure that's not unusual. And you can go to sleep or let me fuck you, but we're done talking for the day."

"You know what, Vicious? I'm trying. I really am. To take you as you are. But sometimes, even I'm not immune to how horrible you can be." She turned around and walked to the bedroom.

I watched her ass disappear down the hallway before she came back out with her courier bag and threw it across her shoulder. Her shoes were on. Why the fuck were her shoes on?

"Thanks for a mediocre day." She collected her hair into a messy, high bun. "See you tomorrow at the office."

She was leaving?

I felt like a chick. This was the male equivalent of being fucked and dumped. Some men called a taxi to pick up the women they screwed after sex. But she… She just wanted to leave after milking the longest date in the history of dates out of me.

I grabbed her by the ass and pulled her into my body until our noses touched. "Where the fuck do you think you're going?" I breathed hard into her face.

"Home, Vicious. I'm going home."

"You know, Emilia, I feel a little robbed today. Can you see why?"

She blinked at me a couple of times. "You came in my mouth."

"You came on my fingers," I countered. "Yet here I am, still ninety-nine point ninety-nine percent virgin, according to you, waiting for you to pop my cherry."

She threw her head back and laughed, allowing me the opportunity to admire her straight white teeth.

Then she stopped laughing altogether and sighed. "You need help. I'm tired. I'm going to sleep. *In my apartment.* Goodbye."

Without thinking, I pushed my shoulder to her midsection, lifted her up fireman-style, and carried her to the bedroom. This, right here, was what I'd wanted to do to her so many fucking times when I spotted her on the bleachers at one of my football games. I tackled big sweaty guys when really it was a cute fun-sized girl I wanted to take down.

To bring her down with me and drag her to my bed like a caveman.

I sauntered into the bedroom, pinching the sensitive flesh behind her knees and breathing her in. A throaty giggle escaped her.

I knew she had a great view of my ass. I also knew she was not going anywhere. Not this time. It was happening.

"Let me go, Vic," she ground out. Lying. Again. She didn't want to leave, and we both knew it. I didn't answer. "I'm not going to sleep in your bedroom."

Dean's bedroom, but again, there was no reason for her to know that at this point.

I threw her on the bed and then bit my lip as I watched her sprawled on it, staring at me wide-eyed. Her purple hair was everywhere, and it was about to be tangled in my fist.

"That really hurt my tattoo." Her hands moved to the back of her neck instinctively before she remembered she shouldn't touch it. She rubbed her thighs instead.

"Strip for me," I croaked. It sounded almost desperate to my ears. "Now."

"I'll take the non-jerk version, please." She started with this again.

"Fine. Please take off your clothes." I pressed my palms together. I'd have gone down on my knees if I needed to. I didn't want to do it myself. I wanted her to come to me willingly. To ask for it. For what she clearly wanted all those years ago.

To stop lying.

For the first time, I wanted her to invite me in, not to be the one to burst through her door.

"No," she said, smashing my fantasy to pieces.

"No?" I lifted one eyebrow. "Then I guess I'll have to chew them off you."

"Be careful" was all she said, nodding.

Stupid tattoo.

I lowered myself to the bed, grabbing the hem of her red sweater and slowly peeling it off of her, inch by inch. Every sliver of skin was important. Like a blunt at the end of a stressful week, like a meal after days of starvation.

I. Was. Going. To. Savor. This. Woman.

She moaned when her sweater fell to the floor, and I licked an arrow straight to her belly button. I used my teeth to get rid of her stupid leggings and cotton panties while she watched me in awe. Then I unsnapped her bra between groveling kisses.

She was naked.

She was mine.

This was happening.

I got up, standing on my knees on the bed, and simply stared at her for a few seconds, taking it all in. I was going to fuck this girl until there was nothing left for the next guy who came after me.

Hell, just thinking about it made me want to kill him.

I crawled onto the bed between her thighs and placed my groin over hers. Grinding slowly, building pressure, I kissed her mouth deeply and licked her neck, her shoulders, the hollow at her throat. She sighed and grabbed my ass through my jeans, kneading, before unbuttoning the denim and pushing my jeans down along with my boxers. My flesh met her hot skin, and she was smooth, smoother than I'd imagined all these years. When she grabbed my shirt, I clasped her little hand in mine and bit her wrist softly.

"I don't do shirtless," I whispered. It was the truth. No shirtless. No dates. No relationships. Those were the rules.

She shook her head no. There was something almost violent about that movement.

"You're not going to have me unless the shirt comes off."

I didn't budge. I didn't want to tell her to fuck off. For once in a very long time, I didn't want to deal with the consequences of being an asshole. But I didn't want to take off my shirt either.

"I don't care about your scars, Vicious," she stressed, searching my eyes. "They make you *you*."

A moment ticked by. I took a deep breath. I'd never fucked a woman with the lights on. Ever. By the time I started having sex, my skin was already so stained with Daryl's abuse, I couldn't bear it. The shame. The weakness it conveyed. Letting her fingers run freely against the bumpy scars was like giving up something that was completely mine.

"No," I said.

"Yes," she insisted, cupping my cheeks and pressing our lips together. I frowned, breathing her in, my eyes squeezing shut, but Emilia continued.

"We've waited a long time for this. I want the real thing. Not the watered-down version. And the real thing is not only beautiful. It is also ugly. I want your truth."

The head of my cock was already poking at her entrance, so I tried to convince myself I didn't have any other choice.

Yes, I hated my scars. They were pink against my white skin, impossible to miss, and loud, so fucking loud. But my need to be inside her was louder, to the point I was going to go deaf. I groaned and pulled the shirt over my head in one fast movement. Like removing a Band-Aid. I was about to push into her when she stopped me again.

"Condom," she warned.

Right. *Right*.

I reached for the nightstand and patted inside the first drawer, knowing Dean kept them there. It was the first time I'd forgotten about wearing a condom since I started doing it, and I didn't like it at all. My mind was not in the game when Emilia's pussy was involved.

After tearing the wrapper and sheathing my cock properly, I closed my eyes, finally sinking into Emilia LeBlanc. Her nails clawed into my back softly. I tensed when I felt the scrape on my old wounds, but I let her. I was sinking into *her* while she was sinking into *me*.

"Breathe," she whispered into my ear.

I thrust once, surprised at how surreal it felt. I never gave two shits about what women thought of me in bed. But with her, it somehow mattered.

She moaned, encouraging me to go on, stroking my marred flesh. Yet she didn't make me feel like a freak. Not Emilia. She never made me feel that way.

I thrust again, picking up the pace.

She writhed under me, arching her back, asking for more. We were compatible. I knew we would be. Her skin warm and soft. My hard body enveloping hers perfectly. She was sweet and wet for me, and tiny, but not so tiny for it to be painful for her.

I thrust again.

"Vicious," she cried out, digging her fingers deep into my skin. Creating new, temporary marks that I loved. That I wanted to exhibit proudly. To wear like fucking trophies. "Oh my God."

I thrust again.

It felt like stepping into heaven and closing the gates behind me. This was it. I didn't want to leave. Not this bed, not this city, and, worryingly, not even this girl. I felt her quivering beneath me, and my arms flexed as I pushed into her.

Again.

And again.

And again.

I closed my eyes, sighing, feeling her. Not just her body. *Her*. The girl from the servants' house with the gabby mouth and the hearty laugh who ate like boys weren't looking and always carried the faint, pleasant smell of sweet butter.

Then I felt my balls tighten and the familiar welling pressure through my shaft.

No.

I froze. This was not happening. Not with her, and not at all.

After a few seconds of me failing to move, Emilia nudged me, still trapped between my arms. "Vic? Are you okay?"

My jaw flexed. I was the opposite of okay, and fuck, *that* was a first too. She wasn't kidding when she joked about taking my virginity. I'd pretty much experienced everything I had avoided during my youth all in one day and in one night—at twenty-eight years old. And I hated it.

"If I move, I'll come," I said, and *flex* went my jaw again.

She laughed with her whole body shaking, a happy laugh that wasn't mean or judgmental.

"Then do. We've got all night. I'm not going anywhere."

For the first time since I was fifteen and *did* lose my virginity, I came in less than ten minutes. Usually, I was famous for my stamina.

But usually, I didn't go to bed with the woman I was obsessed with.

We did it three more times before the sun came up, and those times I redeemed myself, my reputation, and my cock's dignity.

Still, it dawned on me that Emilia now had an even worse secret on me than knowing about Daryl Ryler.

I'd come after five seconds.

Like an amateur.

But hell, it was worth it.

It was a good morning.

Christmas lights decorated every building and tree in Manhattan, and the streets smelled like vanilla Starbucks coffee. I picked myself up a cup of the good stuff on my way to the office—sans the vanilla because, surprisingly, I still had my balls—while Emilia went downstairs to shower and dress for work. The idea of buying her a cup crossed my mind for exactly two seconds before I crushed and burned it. She was not my girlfriend. She was not my friend. She was not even my fuck buddy. She was just a woman I'd screwed until I took what I wanted from her.

And she'd done the same to me.

Even so, the morning was cold but crisp, and the office was nearly empty. Most people already had taken off outside the city to visit their families. I enjoyed working in silence but knew that unfortunately my deadline was approaching. Dean was sure to return to New York sometime after Christmas, reclaiming the office I'd stolen from him, and that meant I needed to get my ass out of this place and take the LeBlanc sisters with me.

Emilia couldn't stay here. She had to serve me. After all, I needed her cooperation with Jo.

When I saw her in the security screen, I found myself taking one last sip of my coffee and throwing it in the trash, smoothing my shirt with my palm.

She passed reception and paused in the hall, looked toward my office. Our eyes locked through the glass wall, but neither of us smiled. She offered me a little wave and disappeared behind her own door. Thank God she didn't think she could barge into my office and act like my girlfriend all of a sudden.

I was swamped with work for four hours before I saw her name on the screen and answered my cell phone.

"Yes?" I asked.

"I'm hungry. Are you hungry?"

"Only for your pussy," I deadpanned.

Silence.

"On a scale of one to ten, what are the chances of me convincing you to go to McDonald's with me for lunch?"

"Zero," I fired back without thought.

"Come on," she said. "You tore me away from my parents."

"Are you going to guilt me into doing shit for you all the time? Because by now, you should know I don't have a conscience."

But that wasn't necessarily true, and even I was beginning to admit it. The more time I spent with her—especially after the Met, where I admitted why I hated her so much—the more I realized I'd made a mistake forcing her to leave Todos Santos. A mistake I wouldn't repeat if I could turn back time.

"I'd go there alone, but the lines are always so long, and I won't be able to do that and pick up your lunch in time."

I had the same sandwich every afternoon. She already knew my routine.

"Too bad" was my response.

"Or…" Her voice was hesitant. She was nibbling on her lips, I knew, and my cock swelled. "You could give me a two-hour break today. You know, because it's practically Christmas Eve and all."

"No," I said, and then realized I had the opportunity to kill two birds with one stone. It was negotiation time. And I was really good at negotiations.

"Get in my office, Miss LeBlanc. Now." I hung up.

When Emilia walked into my office, I stopped her before she reached my desk.

"Stay by the door."

I wasn't particularly against people seeing us fuck. I didn't mind the crowd, but the lawyer in me knew it could result in a lot of paperwork. She stood by the door and watched me, a playful smile grazing her lips.

"You needed to see me?"

"No. I needed to taste you," I corrected, closing the merger folder on my computer and getting up.

She stood still, pressing her back to the door, her face tight and wary. She hugged her arms to her chest and watched me. My predatory steps made her eyes narrow, and I loved how impatient she was, her foot tapping against the wood of my floor. When I reached her, her hand moved to my slacks and she cupped my balls.

I stopped her with a *tsk-tsk* and a shake of my head. "Fucking wet and ready for me, even from across the hallway." I smirked. "Don't you need a little foreplay?"

"I'll have the non-smug, non-jerk version please. And objection." She blushed. "Lack of foundation. You have no way of knowing that."

She was lying. Again. My pretty little liar. I shoved my hand under her dress and nudged her boyfriend shorts, which I knew she wore because she gave zero fucks about whether I might favor lace to them—Emilia was a sensible 100 percent cotton girl—and thrust two fingers into her at once.

Soaked.

Dragging my fingers deliberately slowly from her tight sex, my eyes holding hers, I brought them to my mouth and sucked them clean, my lips quirking into a smile. "Fine, I'll rephrase. Is it true that you're always wet for me, Miss LeBlanc?"

She rolled her eyes. "We've been sleeping together for less than twenty-four hours. So at this point, yes, I guess I am."

"And is it also true that because of that, you'll do non-work-related tasks for me, even if you don't want to?"

She halted. "That depends on what the tasks are and whether you'll go to McDonald's with me."

I licked her neck and collarbone before dropping to my knees. Thank fuck she'd worn a dress today. Thank fuck it was long enough so that she didn't wear leggings underneath. And thank fuck she was wet enough not to resist my request.

I peeled her panties from her body, pressed my thumbs to the lips of her sex, and opened it wide, kissing it gently while still holding her heated gaze. "I will go to McDonald's with you if you do as I ask," I promised.

"What do you need me to do?" She toyed with my hair, sighing in pleasure.

I peppered kisses all over her sex before sliding my tongue into it, flicking her clit with my thumb. She groaned, tugging on my hair harder and melting into the door. I pressed her flat against the wood. Then I grabbed her thigh and draped it over my shoulder for better access and plunged my tongue deeper into her, thrusting so fucking hard I felt her thighs quivering. Her pussy tightened against my mouth, and she moaned so loud I knew people were bound to hear.

And I wanted them to. Because there'd be less paperwork if they did. Consent wasn't an absolute defense against sexual harassment, but it never hurt.

"Scream my name," I ordered.

She arched her back and pressed herself into my face, and hell, I loved how her pussy smelled and tasted on my tongue.

"Vicious!" she moaned, crying out again and again. "Oh my Lord, yes. Please. More."

She gasped when her orgasm slammed through her tight little body, and she clenched so hard around my tongue, I thought I'd never be able to pull it out. But I did. I stood quickly, unbuttoning my slacks and ripping a condom open with my teeth at the same time.

"You were going to ask me something?" she murmured, still coming down from her high.

I didn't answer. Instead, I thrust into her and pounded her against the door, her back colliding with the wood again and again, the noise leaving no room for any doubt about what was going on. I wanted everyone on the fucking floor to know.

"Come back to LA with me," I said, gripping her ass tightly and going at her more furiously than ever before.

"What?" It sounded like she was yelling at me, but if she was that pissed off, she wouldn't be bucking her hips forward every time I drove into her.

"This city has nothing to offer you. Come to LA when I switch back. Work for me. You'll get to see your parents all the fucking time. I'll get to bang you until you're all stretched out. It's a no-brainer for both of us, Emilia."

"No," she chanted. "No. No. Rosie's school's here."

"She can transfer," I groaned, and shit, no woman had ever felt so good.

"I love New York," Emilia panted.

"You haven't even been to LA. You'll like it more."

"I'm not leaving," she said, to which I replied, "Fuck, Emilia, fuck!" slamming my palm above her head but continuing to slide into her at the same time.

The thought of parting ways with her in three or four days was a reality I knew I had to face. I needed to go back to LA, and she wanted to stay here. I didn't need her for my plans until my dad dropped dead. Then I'd drag her ass back to California to scare Jo off before my dear stepmother got any ideas about claiming my dad's money.

But I couldn't…

I wouldn't…

Fuck.

I thrust harder into her and felt her clenching around me. I was close. So was she. She loved torturing me. I couldn't believe we'd once mistaken her for an innocent little Southern girl. She was wicked mean deep inside.

"You think you can do without this?" I ground into her body until every inch of her flesh burned. I knew she was probably still hurting from the tattoo, so I grabbed her head and pushed it to my chest, swirling my tongue around the shell of her ear, as I made sure her throbbing inked skin was nowhere near the hard wood. The door, not my cock.

And since when do I care?

She moaned again, her hips rolling to meet more of me, demanding I bury myself deeper inside her, and I did. The hallway outside the glass walls on either side of the doors was quiet, and I knew why.

Let them know. I didn't give a damn.

"I was just fine before you came here." She grazed my chin with her teeth and sank her claws into my back, her nails scraping through my dress shirt. "And I'll be all right when you're gone. You drove me away, Vicious. You don't get to order me back just because you've had a change of heart."

We both came at the same time and grabbed on to each other like we were about to collapse on the floor. It took us at least a full minute to recover from our orgasms, gasping while holding each other tight. She didn't giggle or smile like she had last night when we'd gone round after round after round. I didn't see the charm in our situation either.

Things were starting to change already, and I didn't know what to make of it.

"So…" She was the first to speak, clearing her throat. "McDonald's?"

"Deal's off. You said no." I got rid of the condom, tossing it in the nearby trash can, tucked my shirt back into my slacks, and straightened my tie. I turned around and walked back to my desk. "Go get my turkey and cranberry sandwich, Miss LeBlanc. And be quick. There's a lot of work to be done before Christmas, and I expect you back here within thirty minutes or less."

My eyes dropped back to my computer and the merger file I was reading through when I heard the door to my office slam shut.

I was pretty sure I also heard her mutter "Jerk."

CHAPTER SEVENTEEN
EMILIA

I had it coming.

Literally and figuratively, I'd created this mess.

Honestly, I was beginning to suspect I simply had a thing for jerks. Or at least this particular one. Case in point: Dean had been charming, nice, and polite to me, and I'd dumped him not once but twice. Vicious was hot and cold, brutal and rude, yet I'd jumped into bed with him. Four times in six hours. And some of those times weren't even in a bed, which was a definite first for me.

What was wrong with me, allowing him to nail me against his office door?

I saw the way everyone looked at me when I left his office to get his lunch. Patty followed me with her gaze and cocked one eyebrow as I made my way to the elevator, rearranging my dress with one hand and flattening my messy hair with the other.

Then I grabbed Vicious his stupid sandwich.

If I was honest with myself, though, I had to confess I did almost come when he invited me to relocate to Los Angeles. Not because I would entertain the idea of ever moving there—this was a matter of principle; he'd kicked me out and had no right to order me back—but because he'd wanted me around.

I swirled the coffee in my Styrofoam cup with my chewed-on pen and watched him through the glass wall from across the vast reception desk where I hung out with Patty. The place was dead, but he still insisted that we work the full day.

Vicious was pacing in his office, talking on the phone, which was on speaker, always on speaker, though we couldn't hear a word from outside.

Patty asked if I could go into his office really quickly and see if she could leave early because she needed to start preparing food for Christmas Eve tomorrow.

"Come on, doll," she prompted. "My grandchildren need their nana's shortbread. They don't like the stuff you buy at the grocery store. We all know it's crap."

"Why don't you go ask him yourself?" I frowned. The answer was obvious, but I knew she mistakenly assumed he'd be nicer to me.

"Please?" She was sitting in her chair, clasping her hands together, her eyes begging me from behind her thick reading glasses. "I just want to see the smiles on their faces when I surprise them. Their mother is going through a nasty divorce right now. They're really looking forward to this dinner with me."

I remembered long ago Christmases when I'd baked with my own grandmother.

"Fine. I will when he finishes his call."

Patty turned her computer screen around for me to see. It was already three o'clock. "I'm not going to beat rush hour as it is. The subway will be packed. Please," she said again.

I heaved a sigh and approached Vicious's office on heavy feet, like I was on death row. I knocked on the door, and he turned to scowl at me, which I figured was his version of an invitation to come in. Despite the fact we had just had sex against the very door that now divided us, I didn't feel comfortable walking into his domain. He was still talking on the phone, his hands on his waist, oozing power and manhood.

I reluctantly walked in.

"Well, did she steal your dick while you were asleep?" Vicious spat into the phone, motioning for me to take a seat in front of him with his finger.

I obliged, throwing a look behind my shoulder and seeing Patty toss her hands in the air, exasperated.

"No," I heard a male voice grumbling from the intercom.

"Did she rape you?" he continued, his face twisting impatiently.

"Well…no." The guy he was talking to sighed.

"Did she milk your cock with a juicer, slip your balls into her purse, steal your semen, and run away?"

"No, no, no!" the guy shouted, annoyed.

"Then I'm sorry, Trent, but she didn't trick you into shit. You willingly fucked her without a condom, and now she's fucking you legally. I know it's not what you wanna hear, bro, but if the baby is yours, you're done."

My heart pumped hard in my chest. Trent had gotten someone pregnant, and apparently he wasn't too happy about it. Vicious glanced at me before punching a remote. The blinds in his office automatically closed, and the room darkened.

Crap. Patty probably wanted to kill both of us.

I opened my mouth to tell him why I came in, but he waved me off.

"She wants five hundred thousand dollars to get an abortion," Trent grumbled.

My mouth almost fell to the floor, and Vicious walked around his desk, tilting my chin up and pressing my lips together with a wink. He didn't seem too worried about his friend.

"Well," Vicious said, "I'm not the guy for moral advice, but everything about this offer screams *fuck no* to me."

"I can afford it," Trent said, but he groaned.

"I know." Vicious placed one of his knees between my thighs and spread them apart, bending down to where I sat, fingering the hem of my dress, which rode up just enough for him to inspect my panties intently, like he'd never seen them before. "Question is—do you want to?"

"What, you think I should let her have the baby? Should I remind you that she's a stripper with a weakness for coke?" Trent sounded like he was seething.

Vicious flipped my dress up completely, and lowered himself so his face was pressed against my sex. My hands squeezed the armrests of the chair as he inhaled deeply with a wolfish grin and kissed my underwear.

"Sounds like a catch." He bit my clit gently through my boyfriend shorts and slowly dragged his teeth across me, his hooded eyes on me the whole time, watching me squirm in pleasure. "So what did you call me for exactly?"

He was losing his interest in Trent's problems, his attention shifting to the spot between my legs.

"Legal advice."

"I'm not a family law attorney, but my best advice to you as a friend is to use a condom next time and try fucking chicks who are more or less in your tax bracket. Best way to avoid getting dragged into baby-mama drama. Now, excuse me, but my snack for the afternoon has just arrived. Merry Christmas, *bro*." With this, he snaked his hand behind him to his desk, lifted the receiver of his office phone, and slammed it, his head moving back between my legs.

"I'm not in your tax bracket." My brows raised and curved.

He flashed me a devilish grin. "You hate me too much to ever want to have my baby. There's no better contraception than a woman who wants nothing to do with your sperm."

I rolled my eyes and smoothed his dress shirt. "Listen, Patty wants to leave early to get a head start on the Christmas Eve meal she has to prepare."

"Okay. Who the fuck is Patty?" he asked, in all seriousness.

My nostrils flared. "Your receptionist."

"No one leaves early," he snapped, resolute. He lowered himself back to my groin.

"Vic…" I dragged him by his tie to me and pressed my lips

against his. He immediately reciprocated, sucking on my lip and licking every corner of my mouth. Our lips broke apart in a wet pop.

"Mmm?"

"Please. A little Christmas spirit wouldn't kill you."

"But going soft on my employees just might kill my company."

"It's not even your branch," I argued. "She's Dean's employee, and not for long. She's retiring next month."

He pulled away and looked at me. That seemed to pacify him.

"Why are you so good?" His thumb rubbed my clit through my panties absentmindedly.

"Why are you so bad?" I retorted, teeth chattering with pleasure.

"Because it's fun."

"You should try being nice. It's even more fun."

"Doubt it."

He was still rubbing me. I hoped he was going to let me come or stop talking because I couldn't have this conversation while he played with my body like it was his favorite toy.

"So can I let Patty know she can go?"

"Only if you let me fuck you in my Jacuzzi tonight."

"That sounds like blackmail." I bit my lower lip to suppress a moan.

"No. It sounds like fun."

It was futile to try to sway him against the idea. I wanted it just as bad as he did, if not more. I had nothing to do when I got back home. It was the night before Christmas Eve, and it wouldn't be difficult to abandon my original plans for the evening, which consisted of making myself ramen noodles and painting until I passed out.

"I'll tell Patty you wish her a merry Christmas." I got up while he did the same with a groan.

He leaned against his desk, his hard-as-granite cock pointing at me through his dress pants.

I swiveled my head one last time, my hand on the doorknob, and grinned. "You do realize everybody is going to look at me funny because you closed the blinds on us?"

"You realize I've never given two shits about what people think and I'm not about to start now just because Patty and Floyd need something to talk about besides stuffing recipes." He waved me off impatiently, going back behind his desk and plopping down in his chair. "Oh and, Emilia?"

"Yeah?"

"Make me another fucking cup of coffee."

We broke his bed.

I don't know how it happened, but we did. It was after we ordered a pizza and polished off two bottles of wine. I was tipsy, happy, and giggly when I climbed on top of him. I thought his bed could take it. It was solid oak, after all. The bed cracked, and the mattress sank to one side. We followed. He caught me by the waist and jerked me to his chest so I wouldn't roll to the floor, but it still made my heart beat ten times faster.

"Even your bed wants us to stop." I laughed, pushing myself off him by flattening my palms against his scarred bare chest. This time he didn't even twitch when I ran my fingertips over the long pink ridges.

I got up and strode to his bathroom. The door to the master bathroom was open, and the mirror in front of us revealed that he was propped on one hand, his eyes on my naked rear as I made my way to the shower.

"I told you we should've done it in the Jacuzzi."

"And I told you two times was enough. I was getting prune skin. Hey, Vic?"

"What?"

I turned around and met his eyes. He smiled a real smile, and my heart fluttered because from him, these kinds of smiles had to be earned.

I basked in it for a few seconds and then took a risk. "Would you like to…come down for dinner tomorrow evening? It's not a date," I hurried to stress, my cheeks flushing. "I just figured we'll both be alone here in New York, and I didn't want… I mean, I thought maybe—"

"Sure," he cut me off. "Seven sound good?"

"Sounds great." I licked my lips, feeling oddly happy.

He turned away, grabbing his phone from his nightstand, probably checking his emails. His eyes were on the screen when he said, "I don't eat mushrooms or any type of fish."

"Duly noted." I started running the water in the shower, waiting for it to get warm, and padded back to get a fresh towel from the linen closet by the door.

"It can be a date," he muttered from the bedroom, and my head swung toward him.

"What did you say?" I hated that it made my body feel like I'd just gotten off a roller coaster.

"I said it can be a date if you want it to be." He still stared at his phone hard.

I shook my head, smiling, and closed the door behind me. After I finished my shower, he wasn't there. I padded my way to the kitchen, still wrapped in nothing but a towel, but he wasn't there either. The apartment was big, too big for one person. I started peeking into rooms, looking for him. He couldn't have gone out. I'd only spent ten minutes in the bathroom, and he looked tired and very much naked when I left him in bed.

Feeling wary, I got dressed before I started calling out his nickname around the house and dialing his number on my cell. Every call ended with his voicemail. What the hell was going on?

Finally, when I was about to give up and head back to my apartment, I spotted him behind the couch. On a plush silver rug, lying on the floor, fast asleep.

He was wearing his black briefs and nothing else, his thick

lashes fanning his cheeks. He looked like a kid. A beautiful, lost, exhausted boy.

Oh, Vicious.

I wanted to help him into his bed. But I had a feeling he hadn't told me the truth about his insomnia, and if I woke him up, he wouldn't fall asleep again. I gathered blankets and pillows and covered him from head to toe. After I tucked him in, I hesitated, but the last thing I needed was for him to wake up and find me staring at him like a groupie while he slept.

Not that I didn't want to. And that was an even bigger problem.

By the time I walked into my living room downstairs, it was three o'clock in the morning. The easel stared at me from across the room, a half-finished painting of a laughing woman with flowers in her hair, demanding my attention. Instead, I walked to my bedroom, pulled out an empty frame and a staple gun, and stretched a canvas before positioning it on the easel. I changed into my painting tee, tied my hair in an elastic, and stared at the white fabric.

And stared.

And stared.

And stared.

By the time I finally started working on it, it was morning. I didn't stop painting until the early afternoon. I didn't sleep. I didn't eat. I barely breathed. And with every tick of the clock that passed without him around, I started thinking more and more about what we were. Who we were. He'd treated me horribly in the past, but right now…he brought color into my life.

Acrylic? Oil? It didn't even matter. He always thought of himself as blackness, but the truth was he injected so many different pigments into my existence.

To have dinner with him on Christmas Eve, it felt important somehow. Not so casual like the rest of the things we did.

Vicious was right. I was a liar.

Because I told myself I could do casual.

When there was nothing casual about what I felt for him. Not even one bit.

It was a hassle to go shopping on Christmas Eve, but I wanted to get him something. Anything, really.

Vicious was big on music, I remembered that from when we were teenagers. In fact, the only thing we'd seemed to have in common was our mutual love for punk rock and grunge. Maybe that's why I smiled like a fool as I strutted my way from the record shop with a Sex Pistols album tucked under my forearm. I knew he was going to get the joke. *Sid Vicious*.

They actually had a few things in common. Their white skin against their black hair, their flippant attitude, and their zero-fucks-given approach. I just hoped Vic being Vicious didn't make me his Nancy.

As I prepared the essential DVDs to watch after dinner (it wasn't Christmas without *It's a Wonderful Life* playing in the background as you struggled your way through a food coma), I thought about Vicious as a child. What Christmases must've been like for him. I didn't have his money or his power, but I did have a family who loved me. Who catered to my every emotional need when I was a kid.

I only celebrated one Christmas in Todos Santos, but I remembered that his dad and Jo had spent it on a Caribbean vacation. He went to Trent's on Christmas Eve, but I think he'd spent Christmas Day at home. Alone.

Even then, Vicious was too proud to be a charity case. But he wasn't too proud to know what pain felt like, and it couldn't have been easy for him to see us from across the property. Our laughter carried all the way to his house, surely. Mama and Daddy were loud on the rare occasions they had a few drinks, and Christmas was when Rosie and I always had our Christmas carol contest. Our house was full, while his was empty. Same with our hearts.

Mine overflowed.

His echoed.

Oh, Vicious.

It took me an hour and a half to muster up the courage to go upstairs to the penthouse and knock on his door. Before that, I just sat in front of a table full of the yummy dishes I'd spent what was left of the afternoon preparing. I'd made mac and cheese, Cornish hens, a green bean casserole, and my mama's cornbread dressing recipe. I'd even bought an eggnog cake. Nothing with mushrooms. Nothing with fish.

But he hadn't arrived.

I sat in front of the table and waited like an idiot because I was too anxious to watch TV but also too proud to go check on him. Then I remembered that the last time I saw him, he was completely out of it, sleeping on the floor, and guilt washed through me. I should've stayed with him. I should've made sure he was all right.

On my way to his penthouse, in the elevator, I cleared my throat several times because I didn't want my voice to break when I spoke to him. Somehow, I still didn't want him to see how affected I was by him. I knocked on his door three times and rang the doorbell twice, but nothing happened. I turned around, about to walk away, when one of the building's receptionists walked out of the elevator with a wrapped gift and flowers. She headed straight to his apartment door. A set of keys jingled between her fingers.

She greeted me with a polite smile. "Happy holidays."

"Thank the Lord you're here." I almost threw myself at her. "I think something's wrong with him. Can you open the door? We need to see if he's okay."

"Who, Mr. Cole?" Her brow furrowed.

What?

"No." My voice chilled significantly. "Vic…Mr. Spencer."

"Oh. Him." Her lips pinched as she pushed the key into the hole. "I saw Mr. Spencer leave very early this morning with a suitcase. He's probably flying back to LA. He's already stayed in Dean's apartment for much longer than usual."

"Dean?"

She blushed. "I mean Mr. Cole. I deliver his packages for him when he's not around. He gave me a key."

My mouth dried, and I blinked. "This is Dean Cole's apartment?" I confirmed, feeling dumb. Not only about the question. About everything.

The girl nodded, her smile still wide. "Sure is." She sauntered past me and just before the door closed in my face, she said, "Again, happy holidays, Miss LeBlanc. Hope you have a good one."

But it was too late. It was already a horrible Christmas. The worst I'd ever had.

I was about to take the stairs back down to the apartment. There was no way I was waiting around for the elevator, and I didn't want to get in with the receptionist because I feared I'd cry in front of her. I felt pathetic enough without adding the cry-in-front-of-a-stranger humiliation into this mess.

My steps toward the door leading to the stairway stopped when I heard my phone singing in my back pocket. I fished it out, my heart slamming against my chest, wanting out, out, *out*.

I begged for it to be him. Begged for him to have an explanation. Begged for all of this to be a mistake. He couldn't have been so *vicious*. There was no way.

Staring at the screen for a second, disappointment gripped every ounce of me when I saw Rosie's name, before the feeling was replaced with shame.

Vicious was no one. Rosie was my family.

"Merry Christmas!" Rosie, Mama, and Daddy greeted in unison when I pressed the phone to my ear. I smiled despite the pressure in my nose. I was crying, but I didn't want them to hear.

"Hey, y'all! I miss you so much! Merry Christmas!"

"Millie!" Mama shouted in the background. "Please tell me your sister is not dating a biker named Rat!"

I did my best to sound like I was laughing, even though the emptiness spreading in my gut was numbing every emotion in me, even the pain.

"Rosie," I scolded. "Stop messing with Mama's feelings."

We talked for about ten minutes, me still standing on the edge of the stairway, before Rosie took the phone to her room and dropped her voice to a whisper.

"Millie," she said, "I thought you should know something about Vicious."

It seemed like my heart stopped beating when she said his name. Hope and dread filled me in equal measure.

"Yeah?"

"Baron Senior died."

I dropped my phone to the floor, my mouth falling open.

Jo.

The will.

His father.

Everything clicked like a gun hammer, and the invisible weapon was pointed at my temple. It was showtime for Vicious.

But was I about to become his prop?

CHAPTER EIGHTEEN
VICIOUS

"Fucking finally," I said, flinging the door to Trent's red Range Rover open before climbing in. It was a nice rental, considering he was only here for the holidays from Chicago. I tossed my Ray-Ban Wayfarers aside and shot him a look.

"Fucking finally? I got here twenty minutes before you landed." Trent threw his vehicle into drive.

He looked like crap. Well, by Trent standards anyway. The fucker was easy on the eyes. With mocha skin, a rugby-player build, and other shitty qualities that made women cream their panties, he was probably the best-looking guy among the four partners of FHH. Only now he had red-rimmed eyes and a three-day stubble, and he needed a haircut. Yesterday.

"I was actually referring to my father dropping dead," I said, twisting to the back seat and retrieving my black-leather Armani messenger bag.

I was also referring to the fact that I'd gone through travel hell. Everything went to shit the minute I got the phone call about my dad's death. I was in such a hurry to catch a flight, I forgot my charger. My phone died, and there were no available flights to San Diego or LA for hours upon hours. Finally, after I landed, I'd been able to buy another charger and called Trent to pick me up.

I pulled my phone out and checked for calls and messages from

Eli Cole. There weren't any. Just two missed calls from Emilia. She could wait. First, I needed to know when we were going to read the will. No point in contacting her until I knew how soon she needed to fly her ass to Todos Santos. It was crucial she be here on standby, ready to spring my trap on Jo. The raging erection I had every time I thought about Emilia had nothing to do with it.

"Can you focus for one fucking minute on anything other than your goddamn inheritance?" Trent said.

He was still pissy about knocking up that stripper chick. I rolled my eyes. "Right. How is Valenciana?" Valenciana was the stripper. And, sadly, that wasn't her stage name.

"She's okay, we've decided to... That's not what I meant! What I meant is you should be sad about your dad passing away."

We were heading into a traffic jam out of San Diego and toward Todos Santos. I wondered if Jo was going to be home and, if so, if it was too early to kick her out.

"Trust me when I say he earned my hatred fair and square."

"This seems a little out of nowhere. You never spoke one bad word about him before."

I fought another eye roll. "What am I, a fucking fifteen-year-old girl? Which reminds me, where is that fucker, Dean?"

"At his parents', of course. It's Christmas Eve, and if I were you, I wouldn't be surprised if he dropped by to say hello. And fuck you very much for hiring his ex-girlfriend. Now what the hell is that all about, Vic?"

"I needed a PA," I gritted out. It had been ten years. They were together for a semester and a half. It drove me crazy that Dean made it out to be what it clearly wasn't.

"She was his first and last serious girlfriend," Trent accused.

"And she was mine," I said flatly, shoving a blunt I fished from his glove compartment between my lips and lighting it in his car.

The windows were rolled up—it was winter, after all—and zero fucks were given on my part. It was Trent's fault for butting into my business.

Trent tapped the steering wheel. "Goddamn you. Give me a hit." I passed him the blunt.

He inhaled before returning it to me. "You keep saying she was yours"—smoke poured from his mouth—"but did you ever tell her that? All you did was talk shit about the girl and bully her every time she came near you."

"Excuse me, but have you grown a vagina since you found out about becoming a father? What is this crazy talk about feelings?" I exhaled smoke from my nostrils. "When's Jaime landing?"

My best friend was flying in from London for my father's funeral.

"Christmas Day. He'll leave Mel and Daria at home."

I nodded. I knew he would.

"Think you can shut up about my PA and focus on trying not to fuck your way into another mess till then?" I scowled at him.

Trent shook his head and hit the accelerator, swerving onto the shoulder of the road. He breezed up the side of the congested highway, his jaw tight. "Fuck you, Vicious."

"Honey, I'm home!" I announced when I walked into my father's cold mansion. Soon to be mine. Soon to be no one's after I burned it down.

Okay, fine. Technically, I was probably going to use a wrecking ball. After that, I planned to use the land to build a nice library named after my mom, Marie Collins. Not Spencer. His last name was unworthy of her.

No one answered my greeting, so I climbed upstairs to my old room and pulled out my drawers, packing up before I said goodbye to this goddamn place. Most of the shit in my old room was football related.

I wasn't a very sentimental person. I found letters I'd received from dewy-eyed teenage fangirls, an eight-year-old blunt I'd forgotten to smoke, and Emilia's chewed pencils. They were at the bottom of my bottom drawer. I was about to throw them into the trash can beside my old bed when I decided, why waste them?

They were fucking pencils, I reasoned with myself. They didn't have an expiration date.

As I packed, I got a phone call from my father's attorney. I'd been chasing his ass along with trying to reach Eli since I'd gotten the call about Dad dying. Goddamn holidays and people who had real families. Dad took his last breath alone. Only Slade was there to tend to him. The other nurse was celebrating Christmas Eve with his family. Jo was spending the holiday with a so-called friend in Hawaii.

She wasn't there for him, like he wasn't there for my mom.

I wondered if Jo had ever loved him. Really loved him. I knew nothing about relationships, but something told me the answer was no. Something told me that my mother was murdered not because of a great love but because of pure greed.

"Hello?" I pressed my phone to my ear.

Mr. Viteri, my dad's attorney, was a man of few words. "The day after the funeral," he said.

It didn't seem too long a wait.

"Who else are you sending a copy to?" I asked. Not that it mattered. Wills were public records.

"You, Josephine, and your dad's brother, Alistair."

Alistair was irrelevant. He was sixty and lived an ordinary life on a ranch in a small town in Texas. If anything, I was planning to split the funds with him, though I knew he didn't care about money. Lucky bastard. But now I knew for certain Jo was in the will.

"Can you send my copy to Eli Cole? His house, not his office?" I asked.

I heard his Sharpie as he scribbled down the address. "I'm sorry for your loss, Baron," he finally said because that was what he was expected to say.

"Thank you, that means a lot," I said, for the exact same reason.

I finished packing, took my stuff and my sorry ass to the Vineyard, the nearest five-star hotel, ordered room service, and got drunk on whatever was in the mini bar.

I was eager to see Jo's face when I confronted her about knowing everything she and Daryl did. When I forced her to give up every single penny my father left her.

I was eager to have Emilia by my side again. Catering to me. Assisting me. Fucking with me.

Rubbing my hands together at the very idea of what was to come, it dawned on me that the idea of flying my PA to Todos Santos was just a little more exciting than seeing Jo's face crumpling with agony as I laid the new laws of life in her fucking face and stripped her of the money she wrongfully claimed to be hers.

I picked up the phone and called my PA.

To say I got no response would be an understatement.

She didn't take my calls and didn't answer my text messages either. Not on Christmas Eve or Christmas Day or the day after. I dialed, I hit send, and each time my phone sat there silent, I wanted to smash something. Although, to be completely fair, my messages were less than welcoming.

What the fuck happened to your phone? Answer me.

He dropped dead. I need you to come here. Call me back.

I wonder how blasé you'll be when I bend you over and fuck the rudeness out of you for not answering your boss for three days in a row.

It felt ridiculous. The sitting. The waiting. The craving.
That needed to change. I needed a distraction from this woman.
And I knew just how to change it.

"Just leave it outside," I yelled to room service from inside my suite.

It couldn't be anyone else because the only person I'd invited to my hotel—Georgia, my high school casual fuck—was already inside the room. She was also pissing me the fuck off with her annoying, whiny voice. The years hadn't been good to her. Sure, she worked out and was always wrapped in the latest designer number, but everything about her was self-involved, plastic, and overdone.

I needed to throw her out before she made a move on me. Ridiculous, considering I'd asked her here so I could fuck her and the aching memory of Emilia from my system.

So I'd called one of my old flings to distract myself until I had the will in my hands. So what?

Georgia was sitting on the sofa across from my chair, still babbling about something that happened at Todos Santos's country club five years ago. I wasn't listening—I lit up a blunt.

"...and I was shocked, Vic, so shocked. I mean, it was one thing that she didn't want to donate to my charity, but to shamelessly accuse me of founding a whole organization just so Dad would look better during his senate campaign—"

"Why did you break into Emilia LeBlanc's locker that day?" I cut her off suddenly, smoke fanning out of my flared nostrils.

I was physically unable to hear any more of the boring shit she was feeding me. Downstairs, in the hotel bar, where we'd had a drink, I'd convinced myself that I didn't mind her annoying voice and annoying facial expressions and annoying *self*. Alas, I was wrong. I minded all of those things. A lot.

"Emilia LeBlanc?" Georgia twirled a strand of her hair with her finger, blinking at me. Her mascara was too thick and obvious. It didn't really help my disinterested cock.

"Yeah. Don't pretend like you don't remember her." I blew smoke to the ceiling and twisted my wrist to check my Rolex.

"I do remember her. I'm just surprised you do." She arched an eyebrow.

I stared at her, expressionless, rubbing my thumb on my temple with the same hand that held the blunt. "She found her calculus book in my bag, remember?"

Georgia huffed. "Because you took it from me and threatened you'd ruin my life if I ever did it again!"

"You had it coming, sweetheart. You acted like a little brat," I countered without even blinking.

There was another knock at the door. Who the fuck hired this kind of idiot? Why couldn't they just leave the food outside?

"Get the fuck out of here and take my dinner with you!" I shouted. I wasn't hungry anymore. And I definitely didn't want her to stay to dine with me. But what I really didn't want was to touch her. It wasn't unusual for me to throw out a perfectly good one-night stand if I wasn't in the mood. But it was definitely the first time I got annoyed to the point that I wanted the woman out of my life for good.

"Vic, what is this?" Georgia smiled uneasily, shooting up from the sofa and striding over to me.

I took another hit from my blunt and watched her. She placed her ass in my lap, and I shook my head slowly, my eyes dead. "Move your ass, pronto, Georgia. Off."

Another knock on the door, and this time it was a brutal blow to the wood. I got up to answer, and she scrambled to her feet just in time. I didn't care if she landed on the floor.

She grabbed my free hand and squeezed it. "I was a little wild. So what? We all were. That was adolescence. We grew out of that phase."

"I don't want to see you again," I told her, setting the joint in the soap dish I'd appropriated from the bathroom. "You were a nasty bitch to her, and I suspect you're still a nasty bitch to whoever was unlucky enough to stay in this goddamn town. This was a mistake. I want you to leave."

I marched to the door with balled fists at my sides. If this was another hotel staff member whining in my ear that this was a no-smoking room, I was going to make them bleed. I swung the door open, ready to bark at the person in front of me. Then I froze.

"Welcome to California, motherfucker." Dean pushed me back into the room and walked in like he owned the place.

Dean was slightly taller, slightly bigger, and slightly handsomer than me. His light-brown hair was cut short and preppy these days, and his style was a little more elegant than mine. He loved full suits in eccentric colors, just like the Joker. He also loved pissing me off, just like everyone else in my life.

"Hey, Georgie. What's up?" He winked at her.

"I was just leaving." Georgia collected her purse from the round table where I'd sat just moments ago and shouldered past us, making a beeline for the door.

I watched her bony, annoying ass disappear into the hallway and closed the door behind her.

Dean was inside, making himself comfortable, pouring himself a glass of something alcoholic from the minibar and whistling with a smile on his face. "I'd ask you if you want something, but I'm afraid you'll think I care."

I pressed my shoulder to the wall and watched him, my hands tucked in my pockets, waiting for him to get to the point. "That's it? Not even 'Sorry that your dad passed away'?" I mocked.

Dean turned to face me, tossed back a full glass of whiskey, and then pointed it at me. "You're forgetting you had endless meetings with *my* dad at his office. You think I didn't do the math? I know the drill, Vic. You hate your father. You hate Josephine. You hate the whole world. Came here for the money and the estate, didn't you?"

Wrong, asshole. I came here for revenge.

Dean refilled his empty glass. "Where's our little friend, Millie LeBlanc?"

"Where she belongs. In New York at the penthouse. In my bed,"

I lied. "Well, technically your bed." I tucked the half-smoked blunt between my lips and lit it casually. "Don't worry, though. I'll reimburse you for the mattress and frame, which we broke, by the way."

He didn't look surprised. Why would he be? He knew I wanted her. Wanted her body. Wanted her virginity. Wanted it all. He took it from me, and it was a dick move. That was common knowledge. Trent and Jaime still gave him shit about it when we got drunk. And let's not forget that if Dean and Emilia were truly meant to be together, Emilia wouldn't have been so fast to pull the breakup trigger every time I blinked her way.

Truth was she didn't want him. She wanted *me*.

"She was mine," Dean said gruffly, downing his second glass of whiskey.

Jesus. I threw my head back and laughed. There was no way he actually believed that, right? "Come on. Don't lie to yourself."

Dean slid his eyes over my face, contemplating his next move. He wanted to get to me. To hurt me without punching my face and making a mess. I didn't say a word. Didn't move. On some level, I did deserve to be punched in the face for this. Just like he deserved it when we were in high school. It was my time to take a hit for my betrayal.

Finally, he opened his mouth, a sly smile playing on his face. "Does she know you're a heartless bastard?"

I shrugged. "She went to school with me for a year."

He downed a third glass, and I hoped he wasn't going to pass the fuck out on the carpet. I actually wanted to keep my relationship with his father intact.

"Did she ask about me?"

"No. Why would she? Did you ever try to find her?"

"She told me not to." Dean's eyebrows collapsed into a frown.

"Yeah, well, thanks for keeping her entertained until I came along," I said, waving him off.

I just wanted the conversation to be over with. He was going to beat me up, obviously. And I was going to take it because I deserved it. We were just wasting time. But Dean didn't make a move toward me. Not yet. Just when I thought he was going to pass out on the bed, he turned around again and chuckled.

"Wait, do I not get a 'thank you' for breaking her in for you?"

Fuck it. He was asking for it.

I was the first to swing a fist at him. I slammed my knuckles into his nose, and this time I hoped his doctor wouldn't be able to fix his pretty face. He grabbed me by my shirt and flung me across the room. I flew backward, crashing into the TV mounted on the wall. Dean tackled me, planting his shoulder in my stomach, pressing against me until I heard the screen crack behind us. I groaned and threw a jab to his jaw but held myself back from doing more.

I fucking deserved it.

And I knew it was going to hurt.

He poured punches to my face, and I took them all. Then he hurled me on the floor and hammered my ribs with his pointy shoe. Again, he was no Daryl. He was a friend, and I'd fucked up. I'd certainly given him a piece of my mind and my fist when he was the one chasing Emilia.

Writhing on the carpeted floor with him, I bit my lip to stop a moan of pain. Everything throbbed. But hey, I had this shit coming.

"You really fucked my ex-girlfriend?" he roared from on top of me, his voice laced with fury and disbelief.

It was easier to forgive an enemy than to forgive a friend. I knew that all too well.

He was hurt. So was I when I'd found out they'd started dating.

Truth was he was a dick for going out with her then, and I was a dick for doing her now. But she wasn't his obsession. His vice. His fucking Achilles' heel.

"I did. If I were you, I'd squeeze in a few more punches before you go because I'm not going to stop fucking her. I'm going to *own* her."

He kicked me again, and I managed not to curl into myself. I knew it was the last time because he was bleeding from his nose and needed to stop the stream and reposition it before it got swollen. Scarlet blood dotted the beige carpet, and I knew I was going to have to pay for this crap.

"Get up," he ordered.

I braced myself on the edge of the bed, scrambling to my feet.

Dean smiled, smoothing his bloodied shirt. "You look good," he remarked.

I knew I probably had two black eyes and a cracked rib. I nodded. "So do you. Fucking terrific. Anything else?"

"Yeah, actually." He leaned against the desk where my laptop sat and gave me the same victorious expression I'd mastered over the years. "I'm interested to know: How the hell do you think this is going to play out? Your next stop is Los Angeles, and I'm moving back to New York. But hey, man, don't worry. I'll take care of her in my office." He thumped his chest and winked.

My body shook with rage, but I reminded myself that he was just taunting me for being an asshole to him. Still, this had to stop. "Just get the fuck out before I do something that will cost us millions and years of meetings in stuffy courtrooms. Go."

He didn't budge. He didn't look amused anymore either. I sucked in a breath.

"Fire her, Vicious. I don't want her in my branch, and I don't want her in yours either. This girl fucked off with another guy when we were kids and didn't even bother to return my calls."

No, she didn't. She left because I made her leave.

"Not happening," I said, even though I had no idea what to do. She wasn't coming to Los Angeles, that much was clear, and Dean would never let her continue working at the office in New York. I didn't know how I was going to keep her. I just knew I fucking had to.

"Yes, it is," Dean responded calmly, his nose still bleeding all over the carpet. *Goddammit.* "The girl screwed me over."

"She didn't," I finally roared. I threw my arms in the air, using what little control I still had in me not to go at him again. I spotted my lit blunt burning a hole in the bloody carpet behind Dean. He noticed where my eyes landed and crushed it with his designer monk straps.

"She didn't screw your life over. I did," I repeated less heatedly. "I sent her off with twenty thousand dollars. In exchange, she promised she'd tell you she ran away with someone else, specifically stressing that she didn't want to hear from you ever again."

"Why would she listen to you?" He crossed his arms over his chest, skeptical, his brows arched.

"Because I threatened her. I told her I'd fire her parents. Her sister, Rosie, is constantly on meds. They needed the money."

Silence fell between us, heavy and loud.

"You're such a sick psycho," he mumbled.

I said nothing because it was an observation, not a question.

"It doesn't change shit, though, Vicious." Dean finally moved to the door, and when we stood side by side, me squeezing the handle and him on the threshold, our eyes met. "You're saying goodbye to Millie and firing her, or I'll make sure you're kicked off the board. Good night."

CHAPTER NINETEEN
EMILIA

Rosie got back from Todos Santos on Monday morning, all smiles and stories about Mama's new sewing machine and Daddy's weird fascination with *Stranger Things*. I had to admit, Little Rose had never looked better.

I smiled through my heartache and tried to look like someone who was not losing her mind over a man who'd specifically and repeatedly told her that he was only looking for casual sex.

We talked. For long minutes, maybe even an hour, but I didn't listen. Not really. The room spun around me, like a ballerina on her toes, round and round, and in the blur, there was only him. His dark eyes. His scowl. His air.

He was taunting me, even when he wasn't there.

"Did you see Vicious?" I finally asked, my words hurried. I hated that my voice was hopeful, and I hated that every single thing I learned about him made me crave him even more. It was all so stupid, and I was an idiot who needed to face the truth—I had feelings toward the man who was notorious for lacking them.

Rosie shrugged. "He dropped by and packed up some of his stuff from his old room on Christmas Eve after we called you. I offered my condolences, and he, in return, offered me his middle finger. He looked pissed off. I mean, he always looks pissed off, but this time he also looked like he wanted to maybe go on a shooting spree and spare no one, kittens and puppies included. You know what I mean?"

"Of course. It's his usual office look," I said dryly.

"Speaking of which, why aren't you at work? Oh yeah, the funeral's today. Did you get an extra day off? Or better yet, did you quit?"

I stared at the floor, my teeth grinding together. "Still deciding."

Truth was my mind was already made up. It was easier to accept Vicious's job offer when we were only two consenting adults with a shared past that was less than pristine. Ever since I'd found out what he really wanted from me—to break the law, to lie for him to Jo—paired with how he'd now sent those typical demanding texts, I finally felt as disposable as he always wanted me to feel when we lived next to each other.

But what really hurt the most was that he took me in my ex's bed. That was the most humiliating part. The part I was desperate to forget but never could.

She chuckled, but it didn't bloom into a laugh. "Please tell me you didn't sleep with him while I was gone."

My face reddened, my cheeks answering the question for me.

My baby sister knew everything about me.

Every little secret and dirty thought that passed through my head.

I would have eventually told her, but it was obvious that she didn't need a verbal confession in order to put two and two together.

"Millie, hon." She rubbed her forehead in frustration. "I told you not to fall in love with him again. He is majorly screwed up. Not fun screwed up, either. Not like Justin Bieber. More like…Mel Gibson. He didn't even look sad about his dad dying. Just like he couldn't wait to get the hell out of there."

I swallowed. "People deal with grief in different ways." I knew why he hadn't looked sad—because he wasn't. But I couldn't tell Rosie that Baron Senior had let his son be abused. That was Vicious's secret. *Our* secret. And as sad as it was, sharing a secret with him was holding on to some intimacy between us I wasn't sure even existed anymore.

"Why are you defending him?" Rosie shook her head in disbelief. "Listen to yourself. He's wronged you so many times. Made you break up with your high school sweetheart—twice. Kicked you out of Todos Santos. Hired you to do something shady for him. What more do you need?"

I nodded faintly, sucking in air and falling into a hug that was waiting for me from my baby sister. I told her about Dean's apartment and Christmas Eve and our day date, all the secrets that were mine to tell.

"Asswipe," she said as she stroked my hair while I bawled into her shoulder, feeling my bones and muscles turning into jelly.

But I didn't tell her about Daryl or Jo or even the will.

I couldn't stop lying when it came to Vicious.

Lying to the world, and especially lying to myself.

The day of the funeral passed slowly, with me perched on the couch eating Fruit Roll-Ups and watching a Gene Kelly movie marathon. I wanted a good, likeable male character to drown in since I was trying to forget a particularly vicious and broody one.

Yes, I was hurt, though not vindictive about what Vicious had done.

I was tempted to answer his calls. His dad had just died, and no matter the circumstances, no matter what he'd felt about him, Baron Senior was still his last living family member.

But every time I made a move to my phone, Little Rose snatched it from me and shook her head.

"No." She stood up in the living room and growled—actually growled—at me.

"He is going through so much," I mumbled, but it was weak and bitter. Two things I prided myself in not being. Well, usually.

"He doesn't give a damn, and you know it."

"Give me the phone." I was getting tired of saying this. "This is ridiculous. Just because my precious ego has been wounded doesn't mean he deserves this treatment."

But this time, Rosie's face brimmed with anger. "You should tell him that. He was at the hotel bar at the Vineyard last night, the night before the funeral I might add, with Georgia, sipping drinks. My friend Yasmine works there. She served them herself. They took the elevator up to his room."

My expression must've given away my disgust because Rosie handed me back my phone.

I had no one to blame but myself. No one.

I felt my chin quivering. This was what he did to me, Vicious. He broke me. Again and again and again. I tried to stay away, but every time he came for me, I caved.

But not anymore.

Rosie was right.

He was toxic, poison, and he was going to kill everything beautiful in my life if I let him. He was the storm to my cherry blossoms.

This only strengthened my resolve to cut him out of my life once and for all. I flipped the finger to the flashing screen every time Vicious called me and refused to show him any type of mercy.

CHAPTER TWENTY
VICIOUS

The funeral was exactly the shit show I expected.

Josephine attended her husband's burial decked out in a Cabo tan, a black Versace dress, and fake tears. Dean showed up and stood by his father's side, paying his respects but not looking at me. And Trent and Jaime spent the ceremony trying to console me while stealing glances from me to him.

The condition of Dean's nose and my black eyes were a dead giveaway. They knew exactly what had happened. I felt like they held me responsible for everything but didn't want to bring it up, seeing as I was mourning.

Sort of.

I felt nothing actually. My dad's existence only burdened my conscience. Every day he was alive had reminded me that my mother wasn't.

A lot of things were buried when my father's coffin was lowered into the hole. One of them was my frustration with him. But not the hatred. The hatred stayed and, with it, my turmoil. An unrest no one was supposed to know about.

It was a tragedy, but it was my tragedy. I didn't want anyone else to know.

When I got back to the hotel, I sent Emilia another text telling her to call me. *Now.*

I'd have the will in my hands tomorrow. It was time for her to pack a bag and get her sweet ass on a plane. I was also planning on telling her she'd need to stay in California for at least a couple of weeks and help me in LA. I was even willing to throw in an extra few hundred thousand to sweeten the deal. Hell, at this point I was going to give her whatever the fuck she wanted.

But Emilia still didn't answer.

Did she cower, deciding she wouldn't lie for me? It felt like a betrayal. Bitter and heavy on my chest, on my tongue, everywhere we'd touched.

I threw my phone against the wall. It smashed, webbing the screen with countless cracks. The logical thing to do was to ask my PA to replace it with another one, only I didn't have a fucking PA at that moment. I needed her, and she wasn't there. I needed her, but I knew I'd die before admitting that simple fact aloud.

I walked the green mile from my rental car to the Coles' mansion. Time moved sluggishly in those moments. Or maybe too fast, I couldn't decide. This, right here, is what I'd lived for, for years. This, right here, was the end and the beginning of something.

The will.

The verdict.

The grand fucking finale.

Before I knew it, I was in Eli Cole's home office, and even before the envelope containing the will arrived, a bad feeling gripped me. The stale room, stuffed with law books and old leather *and* an old man, felt like the wrong place to be.

Eli wasn't overtly nice to me anymore. Not impatient either, but instead highly professional. When he ushered me over to a chair, he didn't refer to me as "son" as he often did, and he didn't insist on serving me coffee or tea when I told him no the first time. Instead, he looked at me like he knew I'd fucked up his son's face, and that made me restless.

After the messenger delivered the will, he rubbed his nose with the back of his hand, slid his reading glasses on, and cut the envelope with a letter opener, utterly silent. My posture on my seat in front of his desk was guarded and tense. I followed his pupils as he skimmed through the verbiage. He was quiet, too quiet, for the longest time, and I felt hot blood whooshing between my ears.

Jo had looked so fucking smug at the funeral. She hadn't exchanged one word with me. Didn't try to beg…

But then I was so careful…

So cunning…

So agreeable to my dad all those years, up until our last encounter before he died, when I told him…

"Baron…" Eli kept pulling at an imaginary goatee, like he was trying to rub the concern off his face. His tone told me what I didn't want to hear.

I shook my head. This was not happening. I didn't need the fucking money. I made millions myself. Not a fraction of what my dad had, but still.

It was about Jo not getting away with fucking murder.

It was about not walking around the world feeling hollow and cheated.

It was about *justice*.

"Give that to me." I reached for the file and snatched the will from his hand. I flicked through the document as fast as I could, my pulse hammering so furiously I thought my heart was going to explode. Hell, half the shit I was reading didn't even register. But there were two things that stood out to me immediately.

First, the will was handwritten. It would be almost laughable if it weren't for the fact it was, indeed, my dad's handwriting and dated well before he got sick. I flipped to the final page to the signatures of the two witnesses. I didn't recognize either name, but that wasn't unusual. Lawyers often called in their employees to act as witnesses.

Second, there was a disinheritance clause.

"He put in a fucking disinheritance clause!" I punched Eli's desk on a dry scream.

The more I read, the more my blood boiled. He'd appointed Josephine to be the executor. But that didn't bother me as much as the main deal: Josephine Rebecca Spencer (née Ryler) was to inherit his entire estate. I was getting a measly ten million dollars.

The disinheritance provision meant that if I were to challenge the will in any way, I'd get nothing. Just an extra *fuck you* to his beloved only son.

Jo had just become filthy rich in her own right.

And I had just been reduced from an almost-billionaire to a man who was still rolling in it but wasn't going to make any *Forbes* lists anytime soon. Not that I cared. The money didn't mean shit. Revenge did.

I said nothing while Eli watched me, his face wrinkled and wary. I'd been blindsided.

My father knew all along that I hated him. Hell, maybe he'd even suspected my plans. I didn't know how or why, just that Josephine was a step ahead of me all this time. I gulped down a sour ball of anger.

Eli came around to my side of his desk and sat beside me in a second chair. Plastering the will back onto the desk, we both read through it with hunched backs. The will was dated in June, ten years ago. My mind whirled with so many different emotions.

A bad year. A bad month.

"Anything weird happen around that time?" Eli echoed my thoughts. "Anything that could make your father change his mind about the provisions he set up in the prenup?"

My father had been open about the terms of the prenup. She got nothing if she ever filed for divorce. He used his money to keep her married to him, controlling her with the threat of being penniless.

So she'd stuck around. I wasn't surprised he'd left her something after all these years. But everything? It looked like Jo was the one controlling him all along. That shouldn't have been a surprise to me either. Fucking Jo. She'd been whispering in his ear again.

The will was dated shortly after I finished high school. After I threw Emilia out of California for good and everything went to shit. After I went off the rails completely…

Ten years ago was when Daryl died.

"Yeah." I crushed the will between my fingers. "Jo was going through a difficult time. Her brother died. She may have strummed my dad's emotions. I just…" I took a deep breath. "I guess I've always hated him, but it still hurts to know he hated me too."

"I don't understand why he's always favored Josephine over you, but it's time to move on with your life, son." Eli knew what my friends didn't.

When I was twenty-two, the HotHoles all came back to Todos Santos for Thanksgiving. We all stayed at Dean's house and got plastered. I'd just gotten accepted to law school, so I thought it was a good idea to wander into Eli's study in the middle of the night and look through his shit. He was there, and I was so drunk, so lost, so sad, that somehow I'd ended up confiding in him about the abuse.

I'd kept my mouth shut about my mother's murder, though, just like I had with Emilia.

I chose to handle justice myself, and I did. Until today.

Everything was collapsing. I was a walking, talking ghost. A no one. A man without a cause.

"Don't let what they did to you define you. Find something else that makes you tick." Eli's voice shook with emotion. He didn't care anymore that I'd fucked up his son's face. Because my life was so much more fucked up than Dean's ever would be. "Live, Baron. Live well. Don't look back. And don't ever visit that place again."

He was talking about the mansion I'd planned to burn to the ground. The place where I was going to build a library to honor my mom.

When I walked out of Eli's office, I collapsed on the steps leading to his patio and lit a joint. I fished out my cracked phone and called Emilia. She didn't answer.

I called her again.

And again.

And again.

Then I started leaving voicemails. Voicemails that didn't make any sense and that I knew for a fact I was going to regret. Her message greeting was her singing in her sweet voice, followed by a breathless, girly giggle when she got to her punch line:

"Hey, this is Millie! Wanna hear a joke? Knock, knock! Who's there? Not me, so leave a message and I'll get back to you as soon as I can!"

I don't know what your fucking problem is, Help, but you need to get back to me because…because I'm your boss. I pay you good money. I'm waiting for your call.

"Hey, this is Millie! Wanna hear a joke? Knock, knock! Who's there? Not me, so leave a message and I'll get back to you as soon as I can!"

Are you mad at me? Is that it? Is this because I didn't pick up the phone when you called? Should I remind you I had important shit to deal with because my dad had just died? Besides, I was up-front with you the whole time. This is not a relationship. It's two people fucking the obsession out of each other. Get back to me. Now.

"Hey, this is Millie! Wanna hear a joke? Knock, knock! Who's there? Not me, so leave a message and I'll get back to you as soon as I can!"

Emilia! What the fuck!

Then, out of the blue, my phone vibrated in my hand. I let out a sigh and felt a little warmth finally seep into my chest. I swiped the damaged screen quickly.

"When you get here, I'm going to deny you every fucking orgasm you almost reach for a whole week," I growled.

A throat cleared on the other end of the line. "I'm afraid that won't be necessary, Baron." It was Jo, and her voice sounded amused. "Remember when you said we needed to do the dinner and wine thing more often? Well, I'd just love to see you tonight for a meal. Do you prefer red wine or white?"

My jaw clenched, and I would have hurled the phone across the patio if not for my need to hear from Emilia. I hung up and screamed until Keeley, one of Dean's sisters, came out and dragged me into the house to calm me down.

For the next twenty-four hours, I was coddled and fussed over by the Cole women like a pussy, while Dean came in and out of the house and shot me dirty looks.

"Fire her," I heard him singing from his kitchen at one point while his mother sat next to me in the living room with a cup of tea and recounted every single family catastrophe she could recall and how things had somehow miraculously gotten better.

"Fire the girl, fire her now," he continued, undeterred.

She was driving a new wedge between Dean and me, and she wasn't even taking my calls. Hell, who knew if she was even down with helping me take Jo down? I seriously doubted it. No, I was on my own.

I thought I was going to use Emilia LeBlanc, but I was no longer able to control my plans for her or for me. She was the only person I wanted to speak to when my world collapsed. No matter the outcome of the will, I couldn't see letting her walk out of my life. Not again.

I sat in her ex-boyfriend's living room, my face squeezed into his mother's chest like a child, and realized that it was too late to back out.

I no longer *wanted it to stop*.

I was going after her.

And fuck the consequences.

CHAPTER TWENTY-ONE
VICIOUS

Two days after I read the will, I heard Jaime let himself into my wrecked hotel suite with the key card I'd given him so he could come and go as he pleased.

"Jesus. How long has it been since you let housekeeping in?"

Dean's blood was still on the carpet.

I lay on the unmade bed, smoking and staring at the ceiling. Jaime threw a paper bag on the nightstand beside me before taking out bottled water, wrapped sandwiches, Tylenol, and other crap he thought I needed. I'd gotten wasted with him and Trent after I left Dean's because who the fuck wouldn't after they'd just been disinherited.

I puffed a cloud of smoke, and he grabbed the joint from between my fingers, put it out, and yanked me by the collar of my stinky white shirt.

His nose crushed mine. "You're still a millionaire. You're still young, rich, and healthy. And all you can think about is your stepmom getting your dad's dough? Big fucking deal."

He had no idea of the truth, and I didn't want to let him in on the reason why I'd collapsed like a fucking pussy at Dean's house. I just narrowed my eyes at him. "No one asked you to save me, Prince Dickbag."

"So what are you gonna do, man?"

I sat up straight on the edge of the mattress and tugged at my hair. "New York," I said, wishing the joint were still lit. "I'm gonna go back to New York."

"I suspected you'd say that." Jaime took a seat next to me. He smelled good. Of soap and life.

I used to smell like that too before life fucked me over.

"You can't go back to New York, Vic. It's Dean's branch. He's already pissed off with you for the Emilia shit you pulled. You can't work there with him right now, and anyway, who the hell is going to run the office here?"

"I don't give a fuck. I'm going to New York to claim it as mine."

"You mean to claim Millie as yours."

"No," I lied. "I mean I want to work in New York. I'm sick and tired of LA." I jutted out my chin, daring him to argue. I was a stubborn bastard, and he knew it.

Jaime threw his head back and laughed, and I felt anger bubbling inside me. What was so funny about this situation? His laughter died down, but only after a full minute.

"Listen to yourself, Vicious. You're obsessed with this girl. You're *in love* with this girl, always have been, ever since you realized she's not afraid of or impressed by your bullshit. You bump into her in New York and the first thing you do is hire her. You're in deep denial. You want *her*, fucking everything about her. You don't need to steal Dean's office. Just tell her."

I shook my head again. It didn't make sense. Or at least, I didn't want it to.

"I'm going to New York."

"Dean's gonna be pissed," Jaime said for the millionth time.

"Too bad. Plane reservation's already made." That was as far as I had gotten.

I needed a plan. I needed it fast.

I started with a call to HR in New York to tell them that Emilia LeBlanc was on paid leave. She wasn't going to show up at work without some in-person persuasion—I gathered as much from her not taking any of my calls, texts, or emails. In the meantime, I asked the HR manager to inform me if Dean tried anything fishy with her job, and I made sure I had access to all of Emilia's employee records, just in case.

Which also gave me access to her company email. It was just like high school—me thumbing through her mail to see what plans she had next.

I saw she'd already contacted a recruitment agency to have another PA on standby in case Dean or I needed someone next week. Honestly, even that annoyed me. She was clearly pissed at me, and she couldn't even do that all the way without making sure everyone around her was nice and comfortable. Me included.

I wasn't too worried. It wasn't like she could go far. I knew where she lived, and she had no job prospects except wriggling into that slutty waitress outfit again. Otherwise, she wouldn't have taken a job with me in the first place.

On New Year's Day, I boarded a plane back to New York. I didn't know what I was doing or where I was staying. Dean was back at his apartment, and it was clear Emilia didn't want to see my face.

Too bad for her.

In Manhattan, I checked into another hotel and didn't even bother unpacking this time. All the utilitarian rooms blurred into one another. Hotels poisoned the soul. Lucky for me, mine was already tarnished.

After a quick shower and a shave, I decided it was past time Emilia explained herself. I went to Dean's building and waltzed in using his electronic key. I knocked on her door three times and paced the hallway outside her apartment, raking my fingers through my hair.

Nothing.

I knocked again, this time banging my fist against her door. "For fuck's sake! The least you can do is face me in person. I'm still your boss!"

Just as I finished the sentence, the door flung open, and Rosie stood on the other side.

"Where's your sister?" I felt my jaw twitching.

She hugged the door, her chin stuck out. "Actually, I didn't open the door to answer your stupid questions. I opened the door to tell you that you're not, in fact, my sister's boss anymore. She found a new job. We're moving out on Sunday. Thanks for nothing, douche." She smiled sweetly and tried to slam the door in my face.

I had to shove my foot between the door and the frame, just like I'd done the first time I came to see Emilia. The LeBlanc sisters definitely didn't like my presence.

"Where is she?" I repeated. I didn't believe Rosie about the new job. This wasn't happening. She wouldn't have given up her high-paying job at FHH…would she?

Fuck. Of course she would. This was Emilia.

"No," Rosie said. "She doesn't want to see you anymore. First, you make her break up with her boyfriend and force her to leave California…" She trailed off, awarding me with one of her infamous go-fuck-yourself stares. Her voice dropped an octave. "Then ten years later, you sleep with her in his bed. Whatever revenge tour you're on, she doesn't want any part of it."

Shit. She knew about Dean.

But I knew Rosie wasn't talking about the real revenge I was after, with Jo. That was a good sign. Emilia had kept my secrets.

I shouldered my way into their apartment, scanning it for her. She wasn't in the living room, but endless cardboard boxes were, and they were already sealed and ready to be moved elsewhere.

Rosie wasn't lying.

Not about moving away and probably not about Emilia finding another job.

"I need to talk to her," I said.

Rosie shook her head. "Vicious, please. She'll never admit it, but I can tell she cares about you. Too much. And if there's even the smallest slice of goodness in you, you'll leave her alone. You guys are toxic together, and you know it."

"That's bullshit," I fumed. "We're not toxic together."

Though I knew she was right. I was missing a few pieces. A few chips I needed in order to be able to love like a normal person does. That's why I liked breaking things and why I especially enjoyed breaking Emilia. She was the purest thing I'd ever met.

"Where is she?" I asked again, not making a move. I wasn't going to leave until she told me, and I think she knew it too. "Where's your sister? I need to speak to her. We can do this shit for hours, and I still won't stop asking until you give me an answer."

Rosie looked down. "She's gone to an open gallery night by the Hudson. The Height of Fire exhibition. She starts work at a gallery there on Monday. A woman she sold a painting to who used to work at Saatchi really loves her work and…"

I didn't give a fuck about the rest. I just turned around and stalked for the door, but Rosie jumped on me like a little ninja, clasping her hands around my midsection. I spun around, staring at her coldly. She winced, as almost everyone did when I used that look on them.

Everyone but Emilia.

"Please don't, Vicious. She's the strongest link in our family. She takes care of me. She is the reason my parents go to sleep at night trusting that we're okay in New York. You can't weaken her. She is our wall."

I shook my head and left.

Like the fucking wrecking ball I was.

CHAPTER TWENTY-TWO
EMILIA

The night was rainy and cold, almost cold enough for snow but not quite. I was glad for the coat I'd invested in with Vicious's money. I didn't even feel guilty.

My new boss, Brent, a man in his late thirties, lived near the apartment we were about to vacate, so we'd shared a cab and then had a quick drink while he filled me in on what to expect at the exhibit.

My new job at the gallery was just an internship, and the pay was awful, but when Rosie saw the look on my face, she'd basically forced me to say yes. My baby sister was feeling much better and was picking up her old job as a barista once we moved. A job where the tips were great and the owner was flexible with the hours she could work.

I tried not to give myself too much crap for agreeing to work for Vicious in the first place. My situation was dire, with Rosie's health and everything, but never again. I was glad it would be over this weekend after we moved into our new place. I was eager to release myself from Vicious's painful claws.

It was the new year, and he was my resolution. I was done with him.

Brent and I hurried the short distance to the gallery through the horrible weather, and I heard a familiar voice that made my heart stop.

"Emilia!"

My first instinct was to not turn around, to keep on moving, especially since my new boss was there. But I wasn't capable of ignoring anyone. Not even him. I spun slowly on my heel, the sleet lashing both our faces as I drank Vicious in. He ran across the street to get to me, his whole body tensing when he noticed Brent next to me.

"Who the fuck is this tool?" He scowled.

Oh, God.

I blushed furiously, turning to Brent with a crimson face. The last thing I wanted was for my new job to start off this way. I inwardly cursed Rosie for telling Vicious where I was because I knew he had no other way of finding out I would be here. Then I proceeded to also inwardly curse Vicious for failing to notice Brent's boyfriend was standing right behind us.

"I'm so sorry, Brent. Please don't mind him." I kept moving, my eye on the entrance door ahead.

Brent quirked an eyebrow but thankfully didn't say whatever was on his mind at that moment.

Vicious chased us, his long strides catching up with our hurried steps with ease. "I don't care who this fucker is. We need to talk."

"Please turn around and walk away before this evening ends with a restraining order. I'd hate for it to ruin your glowing finance career." My face was dead serious and my voice so cold, I wasn't even sure it belonged to me.

We were power-walking on the sidewalk as he jogged beside us on the street, his hands tucked into his wet coat. I refused to glance at him because I knew I'd surely cave if I did.

"It's important," he said, ignoring my threat.

"Not as important as my career."

"I'm not leaving this spot until you talk to me."

Brent was looking all kinds of uncomfortable beside me, his expression begging for cues about how to respond: Did I need help? Did I want some time alone with this guy?

Sleet slashed down angrily and blew icy needles in my face, each like a sharp slap.

I narrowed my eyes at Vicious. "Stand here if you like. Turn into an icicle. I'm going inside to work."

I let the doors swallow Brent and me and even managed not to look back once as I tramped into the gallery. Over the next two hours, I downed three glasses of champagne and discussed art with avid collectors. But not even my new job and Brent's animated nods at everything I said made me feel better. My mind kept drifting back to Vicious and the fact that he had returned to New York.

The evening dragged. I was so angry—furious, to be exact—that he'd managed to ruin this for me too that I spent the majority of my time plotting how to strangle him in my head as I patiently mingled with strangers and chatted about the merits of the paintings up for sale.

When it was time to leave, I ordered an Uber to pick up Brent and me. Twenty minutes later, the driver texted to inform us he was waiting outside. We waltzed through the doors—I was able to see the yellow car from across the street—when a big shadow appeared in my peripheral vision.

Vicious.

He was soaked, wet to the bone, standing in the blowing sleet, glaring at the entrance door to the gallery, rubbing his palm over his ice-covered hair.

I sucked in a breath and wheezed. Had he been standing there the whole time? His clothes were heavy with water and his cheeks no longer tinged pink from the cold. He looked blue. Shivering. Freezing.

"Go." I nodded to Brent, pointing at the cab. "I'll catch another one. I have to deal with this."

"You sure?" Brent pulled up his coat hood to shield his head from the sleet. He didn't appear too eager to discuss my love life with me in this weather. Rightly so.

I used my hand as a visor to shade the sleet from my eyes and nodded. "Absolutely. He's just a high school...friend." The lie felt sour in my mouth. "I'll see you tomorrow."

Brent gave Vicious another curious look. He must've looked like a complete loon to him. After a brief beat, Brent disappeared inside the taxi and it drove away, red lights dancing as they chased the night traffic of New York.

The sleet was stabbing at our faces as we stood in front of each other, but I didn't say a word. He looked at me helplessly, a lost puppy, and I wondered how I hadn't seen it earlier. The complete and utter nakedness of his feelings. The pain. The ache. All the things that made Vicious vicious.

"You waited here the whole time?" I swallowed a sob. Because it really was sad, underneath all the anger I had for him.

He shrugged but didn't answer. He still looked a little perplexed. Like he himself couldn't believe he'd done what he just did. Waiting for me in a winter storm.

"I don't want to help you with Jo," I said. I didn't, but I still wanted him to get justice. I tried to convince myself that Vicious had other options to explore. His ex-psychiatrist...Eli Cole...

"Not what I'm here for. She's inherited every single penny my dad had." His voice was as detached as always. I barely had time to process this new information before he dropped another bomb. "Don't quit."

"I already have. Sent my resignation letter in the mail. Thought it'd be better this way, seeing as Dean is back and everything." I watched as he squeezed his eyes shut, like this was another blow he wasn't expecting.

I knew Dean was back in town because he'd left me a Post-it Note on my door informing me that my "steady dick" was out of town but that I could still go up to the penthouse and ride in another rodeo if I was feeling lonely.

Disgusting prick.

"Why?" Vicious asked.

"Why?" I almost laughed. The real question was why I'd agreed to work for him in the first place. "Because you have issues, Vicious. You treat everyone around you like crap. You had sex with me in my ex-boyfriend's bed and then you took Georgia up to your hotel room the night before your father's funeral."

You know, in a nutshell.

"I don't give a shit about my father. You know what he let Jo do to me."

"So you rushed home for the money? You disappeared without a word to me. I thought you were hurt or sick when you didn't show up on Christmas Eve for dinner and didn't answer my calls."

"I was out of it when I got the call about my dad," he seethed, barely moving his mouth as he took a step closer. Our chests brushed, shivering against one another. "You were right, okay? I do have insomnia, and I sometimes lose a grip on things. Then my phone was dead, and I forgot my charger. Happens to people all the time. And Dean's place? Yeah, it was a shitty thing to do, but was it really the end of the world? Did you fucking die?" He crooked one eyebrow.

I almost laughed. He looked so dead serious. Like *I* was the one making a big deal out of nothing.

"And about Georgia..." he continued. "You and I aren't exclusive. We established that long before I touched you."

My heart sank. Pain filled the space between us like a black hole we were both scared to fall into. "You did. And now I'm telling you that I don't do nonexclusive relationships. I'm asking you to accept that, respect that, and leave me alone. You made it perfectly clear that I'm not your girlfriend. And that's fine. But I don't think we should keep in touch. We're bad for each other. Always have been."

I took a deep breath, thinking about my eighteen-year-old self. Alone and scared, staring at the world through wide eyes and erratic heartbeats, with no one to look after me but myself. The bus rides from city to city. The "I'm okay" letters to my family. The hurt, the shame, the pain. All Vicious's fault.

"You know…" I smiled sadly, ignoring the sleet that threatened to freeze us to the sidewalk. "I used to think of you as a villain, but you're not my villain. You're your own villain. To me, you were a lesson. An important, brutal lesson, nothing more and nothing less."

I lied because I wanted him gone. Because I wasn't a good person at that particular moment. Visions of him clawing Georgia's dress, the same one she wore ten years ago, assaulted my imagination. After he touched me. After he *marked* me.

"I've already secured myself a job at the gallery. This time, you don't get to make the rules. This time, Vicious, you lose."

That night, I did something I hadn't done since the day I moved out of my parents' house. I pulled out The Shoebox. Everyone had *that* shoebox with their little sentimental secrets. Mine was different because it wasn't full of things I wanted to remember. It was full of things I wanted to forget. Still, I'd carried it everywhere with me. Even to New York. I tried to convince myself that I'd taken it with me because I didn't want anyone to find out about it, but the truth was it was hard to let go of what we were.

Of what we could have been.

In a small and tattered Chucks shoebox lay the reason why I fell in love with Baron "Vicious" Spencer in high school.

It was a tradition at All Saints High to have an anonymous pen pal from the same school and same grade for the whole year. Participation was mandatory, and the rules were simple:

No foul language.

No dropping hints about who you were.

And absolutely no switching pen pals.

Principal Followhill, Jaime's mother, thought it would inspire students to be nicer to one another because you could never be sure that you weren't actually talking to the pen pal you'd established a written friendship with. It was surprising how such an old-school, dated game stuck. People didn't actually mind writing to their pen pals, it appeared. I saw the looks on people's faces when the designated teacher for that day slid envelopes into their lockers, wishing they could pounce on said teacher and ask them who the heck their pen pal was. It was useless, though.

Principal Followhill was the only one who knew who was writing to whom.

But the students never did. The letters were always printed, not handwritten, and we were supposed to sign with fake names to keep our identities hidden.

All the same, I grew attached to my pen pal from the very first letter I received during the first week at my new school. Maybe it was because no one gave me the time of day at All Saints High. Black had decided to start our conversation like this:

Is morality relative?

Black

It was a philosophical question an eighteen-year-old wouldn't normally ask. We weren't supposed to share our letters with other students, but I knew for a fact most pen pals talked about school, homework, the mall, parties, music, and just regular stuff, not this. But it was the beginning of the year, and I was feeling hopeful and pretty damn good about myself, so I answered:

It depends on who's asking.

Pink

We were only required to exchange one letter a week, so I was excited to get a letter back in my locker only two days later.

Well played, Pink. (Technically, you're breaking the rules since I can tell by your name that you're a girl.) Another question coming your way, and this time, try not to get around it like a pussy. When is it okay, if ever, to disobey the law?

Black

I actually giggled for the first time since I'd gotten to Todos Santos. I licked my lips and thought about the question all afternoon before I wrote back a response.

Well, Black (and I fail to see how Pink is any different from Black. Clearly, you're breaking the rules too because I can tell by your name that you're a guy), I'll give you a straight, surprising answer: I think it's okay to disobey the law at times. When it's a necessity or an emergency or when common sense overrules the law.

Like civil disobedience. When Gandhi went down to the sea for salt or when Rosa Parks took a seat on that bus. I don't think we're above the law. But I don't think we're below it either. I think we need to be level with it and think before we do things.

P.S. Calling me a "pussy" is breaking the no-foul-language rule, so technically, you're practically an anarchist in the realm of this pen-pal world.

Pink

The answer came the same day, and it was an all-time record. Nobody was overeager to write more often than they had to, but I liked Black. I also liked the anonymity of the project because I was starting to believe that Black, like everyone else, was treating me like crap daily just because I was the daughter of servants. I could use a friend.

I'm semi-impressed. Maybe we should break more rules by you coming to my house tonight. My mouth is not only good for talking philosophy.

Black

I flushed red and crumpled his letter, throwing it into the trash can next to my bed in my room at home. Here I thought I was talking to someone who was actually funny and smart, and all he wanted was to get into my pants. I didn't answer Black, and when I absolutely had to send my weekly letter, I responded with:

No.

Pink

Black, too, waited until the very last day before he answered me next time.

Your loss.

Black

The next week, I decided to stop playing games and write something lengthy. It was a bad week. The week when my calculus-book incident happened. Vicious took over my thoughts, so I tried to quiet him down by thinking of other things.

Do you think we'll ever crack the riddle of aging? Have you ever wondered if maybe we were born too soon? Maybe one hundred, two hundred years from now they're going to find a cure for death. Then everyone who lives will look back at us and think, "Well, they were screwed. We're going to live forever!" Mwahahaha.

I think I might be a pessimist.

Pink

He answered the next morning.

I think it's more likely that those people will have to deal with the wrecked, polluted world we left them because we did fuck-all and partied hard when they weren't even a sperm and an egg yet. But to your question, no, I wouldn't want to live forever. What would be the point in that? Aren't you hungry for something? Don't you have dreams? What weight and significance do your dreams have if they don't have a deadline? If you don't have to chase them today because you can do it tomorrow, in a week, a year, or in a hundred years' time?

I think you're just realistic and possibly weird as shit.

Black

I didn't write him the next day because I was getting ready for another important exam, though I was planning to write him that evening. But it was too late. Black wrote another letter.

I didn't mean it in a bad way. Your weirdness isn't a turn-off.

Black.

I bet that's just a pickup line to try to ask me to come to your place again.

Pink

I sighed, hoping this wouldn't mean another dry spell from letters. But Black wrote me after two days.

You only get one chance, sweetheart. I'm not going to ask again. You missed the train. Besides, I have a nagging feeling that I know who you are, and if that's the case, I don't want you anywhere near my bed or inside my house.

Can wars ever be just?

Black

My heart pounded fiercely in my chest for the whole day. I looked around in the hallways, trying to catch someone who might've looked at me funny, but no one did. Everybody acted the same way. Meaning they either ignored me or sneered at me. Other than Dean. Dean was hitting on me constantly. I wanted so badly to tell him no, wanted to explain that it was a bad idea, that I had feelings for his friend, but even I knew how pathetic that sounded. Falling in lust with your bully. Craving someone who found you disgusting.

Either way, I didn't answer Black. I'd decided I'd give him a curt answer when I absolutely had to and steer the conversation elsewhere like last time. But I couldn't. Because another letter came the following day.

I asked you a question, Emilia. Do you think wars can be just?

Black

Now I *definitely* knew who he was, and every time I sat next to him in Lit class or saw him down the hallway, I looked the other way, somehow feeling angry with myself for talking to Black so freely. It was like Vicious had an intimate piece of me, now that he had access to my unabashed truths. Which was, of course, stupid. And as if there was any doubt left, my next letter from Black came to me two days after, but it wasn't waiting in my locker. It was sitting on my desk, in my room, at the servants' apartment.

Why do you never fight back? I stole your book. I bully you. I hate you. Fight me, Help. Show me what you're made of.

Black

We exchanged blank pages for the remainder of the month. My letters to him were devoid of words, though I sometimes doodled something offensive when I was particularly bored. His letters to me contained nothing at all. I sometimes smelled the pieces of paper he sent me. I sometimes rolled them between my fingers, knowing he'd touched them too.

And then I started dating Dean.

I felt bad about it the whole time, but I did it anyway. I wasn't using him because I did like him. I didn't love him, but love wasn't something I necessarily thought I should feel at such a young age. It might've been easier to think that Dean didn't love me either. Besides, we were good together. We had fun. But we both wanted to go to out-of-state schools, and it made things lighter and less serious between us. At least I thought so.

Shortly after I started dating Dean, Black began writing again.

Can you tell the difference between love and lust?

Black

I humored him, not because I wanted to but because I relished every chance I had to talk to him.

Lust is when you want the person to make you feel good. Love is when you want to make the other person feel good.

Pink

The next time I got a letter from him, my hands shook. And they would continue to shake for the next few months as Black crawled into my soul and took a seat in the pit of my heart, making himself comfortable.

And if I want to hurt the person, is that hate?

Black

I answered:

No, it's pain. You want to inflict pain on the person who caused you to hurt. I think if you hate someone, you just want them gone. Do you really hate me, Black?

Pink

It was the bravest question I'd ever asked him. He took the whole week to get back to me with that one.

No.

Black

Do you want to talk about it face-to-face?

Pink

Another week passed before he answered.

No.

Black

We ping-ponged for the remainder of the year, talking about philosophy and art. I was dating Dean, and Vicious was sleeping with everyone else. We never mentioned our real identities again. We never admitted to one another, not in person and not in the letters, that we were who we were. But it was becoming clearer that we were compatible.

And every time I saw him walking down the hallway with his lazy smirk and a harem of cheerleaders or his football crew trailing behind him, I smiled a private smile. A smile that said that I knew him more than they did. That they might hang out with him every day and attend his stupid parties, but I was the one who really knew the important things about him.

Even when he tried to kiss me that night, we didn't discuss Black and Pink. If anything, the next week, he wrote to me as if nothing had happened. As if Vicious and Black were completely different people.

The one and only time he'd admitted to being Black was on the day I left Todos Santos for good. Our pen-pal project had ended weeks before, but I still found an envelope on top of my suitcase. The handwriting was unfamiliar, but I still knew who it was from. The outside said:

Open when you feel like you might forgive me.

I still hadn't opened it.

Not even after we had sex because I knew that wasn't about forgiveness. That was about satisfying my need for him. And now? Now I still couldn't forgive him, but finally my curiosity had won out over my self-control.

I pulled the last letter out of my shoebox, the paper yellow and brittle, and read it.

You were always mine.

Black

CHAPTER TWENTY-THREE
VICIOUS

I waltzed through the double glass doors of FHH, ignoring the stunned faces of the New York employees who'd thought they didn't have to deal with my sour ass anymore. My face was relaxed, my posture poised. I was the same old Vicious, regardless of what I was dealing with in my personal life. The office was buzzing with post-holiday phone calls, overlapping chatter, the noise of working printers and people slurping their lukewarm coffees from their stupid "Best Dad/Mom/Grandmother" mugs.

I strode with purpose to Dean's office. I couldn't work inside there right now for the obvious reason—it was occupied by Dean—but I didn't plan to leave NY because there was nowhere else I would rather be.

After I saw her at the exhibit, as I sat in the lukewarm bathtub and tried to get the feeling back in my numb, icy feet, I'd made up my mind. I wasn't leaving until Emilia LeBlanc came with me. Even if that meant she was a package deal with her big-mouthed little sister, Rosie.

Emilia, my makeup is revenge.
Yours is forgiveness.
You're better than me.
I don't deserve you.
But I'm going to take you anyway.

But Jaime was right. I was acting like a fucking tool when it came to her, so the least I owed myself was not to let her slip through my fingers because of that this time.

Opening the door to Dean's office without knocking, I breezed straight in and planted my ass on the chair directly in front of his desk.

He sat there, talking on his phone and deliberately not paying any attention to me. He scribbled something on an FHH notepad as he spoke. "Of course. I'll let Sue know, and we'll send someone over as soon as possible. It shouldn't take long to draft something like this."

Sliding the notepad across his glass desk, he pointed his finger at what he wrote, offering me a smirk.

You look like shit

I snatched the pen from his hand, grabbed the notepad, and scribbled something, lifting it for him to see, right next to my dead expression.

Sue looks like a bad fuck

He chuckled, still engrossed in his phone conversation. "Well, actually, I do have a contact person in Los Angeles. He's one of FHH's CEOs. His name is Baron Spencer. Sue will leave his contact details along with our proposition. Sound good?"

I gave him the notepad and pen, and he scribbled, tearing the paper from the pad and slapping it against my chest. I plucked it from my suit and read.

Your stepmom is a bad fuck. We're not switching branches

It was my turn to write.

Fine. I'll join you here. Mind if I sit on your lap?

He looked up at me, and I winked.

We were back to being rowdy teenagers. Before Emilia came to town and shit all over our relationship.

"Excuse me, Stephen? Sorry to cut you off. I have an important call on the other line, something personal. Can I get back to you in ten minutes? Thank you. Okay. Thanks. You too. Take care."

He slammed his phone down on the desk. I noticed there were a few people peeking curiously from the reception area in the direction of his office and itched to close the automatic blinds but knew better than to step deeper into his territory. He would've pissed right there in the middle of his office if it were appropriate.

"Emilia resigned," he hissed out, opening a drawer and throwing her letter of resignation my way.

I didn't make a move to pick it up.

"I know," I said with a shrug. "She can do whatever the fuck she wants. I'm not going anywhere without her, and I need more time here."

"Tell me…" Dean leaned in, lacing his fingers together. "How would you have reacted if I did the same to you? Told you I drove your high school sweetheart from our town just because I couldn't see her with you and then went ten years later and fucked her in your office, your bed, your fucking everything? Right in your face. How would you feel about that, Vicious? Because I'm starting to believe that you're a sociopath for not understanding the depth of the betrayal. True, the two of us were never as tight as you are with Jaime and I am with Trent, but we were still, in the grand scheme of things, brothers."

It was my turn to lean forward. "I'm a bastard, Dean, but you knew. That night, at my party, before she came looking for you so you could go on your first date? You knew how I felt about it. But you went and did it anyway. I was angry with you for years, but I get it now. She was worth it. Emilia is a compulsion. You just want her, consequences be damned.

"Although when you dig deep and think about it, you have to admit I was there first. Her heart beat for me, and you saw it. You saw it in class. You saw it in the hallways. The way she looked at me in the cafeteria. You saw it in the way she came to our football games, but only when I played, even though you played every single week while I sat on the bench most of the season. She never showed her face on those blue bleachers until after I made first string. We all knew. Jaime knew. Trent knew. You and I knew. I think the only person who didn't realize it was Emilia herself. You've moved on. You would never settle for her today, and you know it. You like the variety too much."

He considered my words, tilting his chin down in acceptance. "We can't both be at the same branch. The LA office is too important to be neglected, and having the two of us in the hallways here is going to result in a power struggle we don't want. But, Vic, I'm so fucking mad at you, I can't even look at you right now. Not only for what you did when we were eighteen but also for what you did in my bed. In my house. With *her*."

My jaw clenched, but I didn't dare look away. I stared at him so hard I thought we were both going to pounce on each other again. My left eye was still purple and his nose was still bruised from our hotel incident.

Dean was the first to open his mouth. "Make it worth my while to sit around in Los Angeles while you chase Millie's ass and beg her to forgive the assholeness that is you."

"Name your price." I knew there were sacrifices to be made, and I was willing to make them. It was justifiable. I got it. I'd fucked up, and I needed to atone for my sins.

"Sell me ten percent of your shares." Dean shrugged. "And I'll pack a bag and wait it out in LA for six months."

"That's seven million dollars' worth," I ground out.

Each of us held 25 percent of the shares. We had equal power. Buying out my shares was buying me out of my power, my influence, my everything. I wanted to laugh in his face, but he looked too serious to fuck with. By the way his hand clenched his phone as he tapped it against his lips, I knew he meant business.

"Fuck that shit. I mean, really, Dean?" I huffed. "It's not like I fucked your sister."

"I actually suspect you did fuck Keeley at some point, but I'm not going to ask you about it for your sake. You asked me to name a price, Vicious, and I did. Take it or leave it."

"Five percent," I shot back. I was so used to negotiating that I thought maybe I could sell him something I could buy back for double or triple the price.

"Ten percent for six months, and if you try to negotiate one more time, I'm taking this offer off the table, and we both know what's gonna happen."

Yes. Trent and Jaime would fly out to New York to babysit us again. Then Jaime was going to drag my ass back to Los Angeles like I was a kicking and screaming toddler and I'd lose her. Forever.

She was mine. I didn't come this far just to turn around and walk out of this again.

"Fine," I said, finally. "Ten percent. I'll draft the contract tomorrow."

"No need. I'll ask my lawyer to do it," Dean said. "I don't trust your ass with anything anymore. Oh, I want you to keep Sue. You're right. She is a mediocre fuck, and she wants me to meet her parents, even though I told her I never want to date. Ever. In. My. Life."

"Fine." My nostrils flared, and I closed my eyes. This was a fucking nightmare.

But Dean continued, undeterred. "I also don't want you in my apartment. You won't be fucking my ex-girlfriend in my bed anymore. You can take the apartment you gave Millie. It's vacant now anyway."

I didn't say a word, processing it all. My expression must've been crestfallen because Dean's smile only grew wider by the second.

"Shit, man, you're going to do this, huh? For real." He threw a foam ball at me.

I didn't blink or reply. Goddammit, I was making a deal with this joker.

Dean got up from his chair and leaned into my face. "How far are you willing to go for this girl, Vic?"

I ran a hand through my hair, tugging hard at the roots. "Well, I think I'm about to find the fuck out."

The next couple of days were busy. I signed the contract Dean's lawyer had drafted (not his dad—a sorry bastard fresh out of law school who drafted a contract littered with enough loopholes and ways out for me to play with when the time came), and I moved my shit into Emilia's apartment downstairs. Dean was scheduled to head to Los Angeles at the end of the week. We told his staff that I was staying in order to recruit two more lawyers to our New York branch and that I needed to train them. It was only a half lie. This had been in the works for months now, but I was never set to train them in New York.

People bought it. Though I didn't know why we needed to explain anything. They fucking worked for us.

Jaime lost his shit when he heard I only had 15 percent left in the company.

And Trent laughed and said he didn't feel sorry for me after treating him like an asshole when he confided in me about knocking up that stripper.

I gave Emilia two days. Two fucking days before I came for her. Finding out where she lived was no issue. Fiscal Heights Holdings still had to send her a paycheck for her last week of work, and our personnel head had her new address.

I decided to personally deliver the check because I was nice like that.

Truthfully, I had no fucking clue what I was doing. I knew I was pursuing her, that I'd given up a lot to stay in New York for her, postponing my revenge on Jo and putting my personal goals on the back burner, but I didn't understand any other part about this. I tried not to label what I felt for her. I tried not to read too much into it. As I said, Emilia was an impulse. Currently, all I knew was that I was acting on it. On my instinct. On my need. On something feral and basic.

She'd moved to a run-down neighborhood in the Bronx.

Her apartment was just above a Chinese joint that smelled of grease and sweat and had bathroom tiles on the walls. All around on her block, I saw old cars with busted windows and windshields. Gray, wet trash lined the gutters, and string-thin, wide-eyed women carried groceries in a hurry to escape whatever danger was waiting for them around the corner. It was one thing to live in a zip code that wasn't exactly desirable because you had cash flow issues but a completely other thing to live in a neighborhood that looked like it had one of the highest crime rates in the city.

What the hell was she thinking? She and Rosie screamed prey. They were small, beautiful, innocent, and alone.

I waited outside the door that led upstairs for two hours before she came back home. It was boring as fuck, so I spent my time reading emails and making phone calls. I stood out in this neighborhood like a sore thumb. But I didn't give a shit.

Emilia approached the building, and when she realized that I was there at her front door, she rolled her eyes and sighed. "Go away, Vicious. You're like a puppy begging for me to adopt you and take you home. Only significantly less cute." She scrunched her nose.

I didn't grace that shit with an answer, just pulled out her check from my breast pocket and handed it to her. She plucked it from between my fingers, her eyes skimming over it. There was a brief moment where I thought she was going to throw it back in my face, but then she must have remembered how poor she was.

"Thanks," she murmured, slipping the check into her messenger bag.

"I don't like you living in this neighborhood." I took a step closer.

She crossed her arms as she took me in. "Then it's a good thing it's none of your business."

"Since when are you so cold?"

"Since you barged into my life again and I was stupid enough to let you in—*again*—and I promised myself there won't be a third time. What do you want, Vicious?"

That was a good question. I bit my lower lip and took in her little body in her yellow-and-red-checked coat.

"I want to fuck you again," I admitted with a groan.

"Fuck me or use me so you can take revenge on your stepmom?"

"It's not about that. Fuck the money. Fuck my stepmom," I said, realizing it was the truth. I didn't care about all those things. Not when I was about to lose Emilia.

If I hadn't already.

"I don't believe you."

"I'll never ask you to do anything about it ever again. All I ask is for your time so I can explain."

"Thanks, but no thanks." She inserted her key into the lock and was on the stairs inside with the door shut before I had the chance to do my usual move of shoving my foot into the gap.

I banged my fist on the painted metal. At least the door looked sturdy. "Now that I know when you get back from work every day, I'm going to wait for you outside the subway and see you home safely."

She laughed from the other side, a cold laugh that she'd learned and mastered because of me. Because of everything I'd done to her.

"If you want to waste your time, be my guest. I'm not going to forgive you. And even if I did, I wouldn't want to be with you."

"We'll see about that." I waited for another response, but this time there was only silence. I grinned quietly to myself. The push and pull were back. She could push all she wanted, but she was going to be pulled back to where she belonged. My arms.

I was still eyeing the door when a skinny white guy who was a veteran junkie, judging by his rotten teeth and lost eyes, shuffled for the door, holding a plastic bag. "You live here?" I growled.

He nodded, confused.

"Third floor. 'Sup, man. You lookin' to score?"

"No, douchebag, I'm your motherfucking nightmare. Stay away from the girls on the second floor. Tell your junkie friends and anyone you know in this goddamn shithole the same thing." I shoved five hundred-dollar bills into his hand. And fuck, why was it muddy? I didn't even want to know. "For every day they're safe and left alone here, you'll get another hundred. Deal?"

His eyes widened in disbelief, his jaw falling. I don't think he'd heard a coherent sentence in a while. "Sure, man. Sure."

I turned around and walked away, hoping it was worth it.

It had to be.

I had a feeling it would be.

CHAPTER TWENTY-FOUR
EMILIA

True to his word, Vicious waited for me at the subway every day at eight p.m. sharp. That's when I'd appear from the freezing station and join him on my street. We would walk in silence.

At first, he tried talking to me about my day, my new job, my new boss, trying to milk info out of me about my life. I was having none of it. Finally, we settled into a routine where we didn't say a word until I got to my door. Then he'd watch as I fished out my key and opened it. Every day, exactly a second before I closed it behind me, he'd asked the same thing.

"Hear me out? Ten minutes, that's all I'm asking."

I'd say no.

And that would be the end of it.

After the first couple of weeks, he changed his script from "ten minutes" to "five minutes." I still said no. I probably should've been more insistent about telling him to get lost and stop following me, but the truth was it really was a bad neighborhood, and I was grateful for him seeing me to my door every night.

They surprised me, his determination and dedication to the cause, whatever that cause might be. We'd only spent a couple of days of bliss in bed together, so the fuel to his lust was bound to run out any day now, right?

A part of me still suspected it was just another one of his games.

Vicious was a terrible loser. He'd proven this over and over again. When he wanted something, he took it, leaving bridges burned and scorched-earth battlefields behind him. I could only imagine what he had planned for Josephine now that he'd read the will.

I wasn't sure what he wanted from me. Even more, I didn't trust myself not to give it to him again. But it soothed my sore pride that he was there every day. Especially after Georgia. Still, not enough to hear him out.

A month after we moved out, Dean came by our new apartment. He looked good, if you liked the hot-shot, all-American Bradley Cooper look. Which I thought I did, but apparently, I was more of a brooding, all-consuming-jerk Colin Farrell type of girl. It was a Saturday, and I was just getting ready to go to the corner grocery. I swung my door open, and he stood there, with his huge smile and wavy Hollywood hair.

"Sweet Jesus! Dean," I said, clutching the door tighter, remembering the Post-it Note he'd left me. "If you're here to taunt me, don't worry, Vicious beat you to it, and he is pretty persistent."

"Millie," he said in a tsking tone, pushing my door open and walking in like he owned the place.

He was wearing a white turtleneck, dark denim, a gray tweed overcoat, and that I'm-better-than-you smirk the HotHoles were probably born with. Dean stopped when he spotted Rosie sitting on the couch, reading something on the old iPad her school had provided her. His eyes narrowed at her and mine narrowed at him.

Oh, no way.

"Well, hello, Rosie. You grew up to be eye candy." He winked at her. I gagged.

"Well, hello, Dean. You grew up to be an arrogant bastard." She winked back at him, wiggled her shoulders in a sassy way, and added, "No, wait, you were always an arrogant bastard. My bad."

"Why are you here?" I demanded, swiveling Dean's shoulders so he faced me. I didn't like it. The electricity in the air when Dean looked at Rosie. It was the same thing I felt when I was standing next to Vicious.

I thought a lot about how I'd feel if Dean walked into my life again, especially since I'd started sleeping with Vicious. I thought I'd feel shame, hurt, and regret, maybe even sadness. But with him standing in my living room, all I felt was anger and a little annoyance. He looked at me like we were strangers, not exes.

To some extent, we were both.

Dean trained his gaze back at me reluctantly, like Rosie was the reason why he'd come here in the first place. "Right. I just wanted to let you know that for what it's worth, I fully support your relationship with Vic, and I'm not saying that because he kicked me out of New York to stay here and chase you like a puppy and begged me to talk to you."

It sounded more rehearsed than a Broadway show.

I cocked an eyebrow at him and folded my arms over my chest. "You don't care?"

He shook his head. There was something light about him. Not just his body language but his expression too. I believed him.

"We were kids. He was jealous, and you were…" He licked his lips, considering his next word.

He was still my first. My first lover. My first boyfriend. My first sexual partner.

Dean's eyes dropped down as he finished softly, "And you were with the wrong guy. I never should have stepped between the two of you, but I did, and I don't regret it for a second. We were a good couple, Millie, but Vicious and you…"

Another pause. Rosie listened closely behind us. Her face told me she was pretty sold too. Dean just had it in him—the ability to sound genuine and believable, no matter what he said.

"You were obviously meant to be together. Even if I didn't completely believe that before, I do now because of the sacrifices he made for you. That's a first. And a last. Give him a chance, Millie. He deserves at least that."

I loved the silence that followed Dean's speech. We all processed it. Everything that had been said. Without being dramatic, Dean told me that he was okay with what Vicious and I did. With what we were and weren't. With what we could have been or could be, if I still wanted to.

"You should probably stay for coffee," Rosie said then, still reading on her iPad.

"Nah." He shrugged, jerking me by my shirt into a big suffocating hug.

It felt nice.

It felt safe.

But mostly, it felt platonic.

"If I stay, I'll hit on your sister, and that'd be really messed up, now wouldn't it, Millie?" he whispered into my ear.

And just like that, the touching moment was gone.

I had a blast at my new job. Brent was talented and worldly and knew everything about everything. We talked art every day and got ready to throw another event, an exhibition in which we planned to show twenty contemporary paintings about nature and love.

One of those paintings was going to be mine.

And it was going to be quite interesting too. It wasn't a cherry blossom tree, like I'd thought I'd paint.

But it was definitely a true definition of the word *love*.

Rosie had started working as a barista again. She was feeling well. We ate pasta a lot but sometimes bought ground beef and made meatballs. She understood how much the exhibition meant to me, so she let me paint into the late hours of the night while locking herself in our bedroom. (We only had one, and we happily shared it.) I opened all the windows, even though it was still cold, and hoped for the best.

There were so many questions I wanted to ask Vicious. How come he was still in New York? What happened with his father? Was he poor now? Well, not poor, obviously. More like unfilthy-rich. And what were his plans for Jo?

But I bit my tongue and said nothing every time I poured myself out of the station and saw his tall, broad frame, wrapped in a delicious suit and overcoat. He'd nod curtly and join me as I walked.

Two and a half months after he started escorting me home, it happened. The inevitable moment I'd expected but dreaded.

He wasn't there to see me home.

My face fell and my muscles slacked when I realized he wasn't waiting for me. It wasn't so bitterly cold anymore—though nowhere near warm—so I shook myself out of my coat and walked a little too fast out to the street to inspect it. Maybe I'd missed him. Maybe he'd gone around the corner to the Turkish grocery store to get himself a cup of coffee. He liked their bitter, muddy coffee. Every time he came early enough, he treated himself to a cup and drank it while he was waiting for me.

He also read the *Wall Street Journal* and checked the Asian stock exchanges on his phone. It was almost like he made this arrangement about his downtime with himself.

I looked around, my eyes gliding over the brick buildings, the throng of people hurrying everywhere, the old brewery staring back at me, and the industrial buildings rising from the dirty, crumbling concrete.

He wasn't there.

My heart sank. I should've known his little mission had an expiration date. There was only so much a man could take, and especially a man like Vicious, who'd never had to beg for a date before. I'd refused to give him ten minutes of my time to listen. Not even five. He had every reason to stop coming.

I knew all that, but it didn't make me feel any better.

I plugged my earbuds back into my ears, shoved my hands into my pockets, and made my way to the apartment, passing by all the junkies sitting on the sidewalk against walls and holding cardboard telling their sob stories. I always fumbled in my pocket and gave them some change. And I always tended to give the change to the people with the dogs.

I crossed the street and jaywalked back to my apartment, almost reaching the entrance of my building, when I saw him. He jogged from the direction of the subway, looking a little flushed. *Vicious*. I bit down my smile and tugged the earbuds out of my ears. When he was about a foot from me, he stopped, straightening his tie with his hand.

"Hey," he said. His hair was a disheveled mess, and I liked it. I liked it a lot.

I remembered how it felt in my hands when he went down on me in Dean's office. I cleared my throat and nodded. "Are you okay?" I asked.

"Yeah, yeah. I just wanted to let you know that next week, on Thursday, I won't be able to make it. Something came up. I'll call a taxi and make sure it picks you up from work."

"No need," I said. "You owe me nothing. And besides, I have an exhibition at work that night. I'll probably stay until late anyway."

He shot me a weird look, tearing his eyes from my face and focusing on the building behind me, like he was trying to remember something. "Give me five minutes of your time?" he asked, as he did every single day, five days a week, excluding weekends.

"Nope. Bye, Vicious." I turned around and slammed the door in his face. Admittedly, it didn't feel good. It felt really bad the first time I did it, and as time passed, it had become worse and worse. I now absolutely hated myself for doing this to him.

But still, I did it.

Because protecting my heart over his had become my priority.

The problem was I had been right all along. Loving someone was essentially wanting to make them feel good, not the other way around.

No matter what Vicious felt for me, I knew exactly how I felt about him.

And I didn't hate him. Not by a long shot.

It was almost a week later when I received the call. Afterward, I took an early lunch break, jumped into the subway, and bolted straight into Vicious's office building. The receptionist in the lobby knew me from my brief time as Vic's PA and let me in. When I walked into the reception area of FHH, however, I was met with a new face of a young receptionist who'd replaced Patty.

I knew Patty had already retired because I kept in touch with her, mainly by email, so this wasn't news, but I didn't have time for pleasantries.

"I need to see Mr. Spencer." I knocked on the reception's counter with my knuckles, not offering any further explanation. Every hair on my body stood on end, and hot shivers ran down the length of my spine. I was that angry.

The receptionist, pretty and bored and disinterested, batted her eyelashes a few times at me. "I'm sorry, ma'am, do you have an appointment?"

"I don't need an appointment," I breathed out, flinging my arms in the air. "I'm his...his..." What was I to Vicious, exactly? Friend? *No.* Lover? *Ha!* Ex-neighbor? But I was more than that. I shook my head, not really feeling like dwelling on the subject right now. "He'll want to speak to me. Please, just tell him Emilia is here."

"I can't do that, I'm afraid." Her tone was not in sync with my mental and physical state. She looked so jaded and sleepy, and I felt like a kernel of popcorn about to pop at any moment. "He doesn't want any interruptions when he's working."

"Look..." I leaned over the counter, seriously tempted to grab her by the collar of her white shirt. "I know he's a jerk and you're afraid that he'll be even more of a jerk to you if you disobey his rules. But I'm telling you. If he finds out I was here and you didn't let me in, he'll fire you. Just like that." I snapped my fingers. "So please, just tell him I'm here, waiting for him."

She stared at me with a peculiar expression before punching in his extension and bringing the phone to her ear.

"Sir? I have a woman named Emilia here for you. She says it's important." She waited a few seconds, muttering a "mmm-hmm" punctuated with a nod, before her head snapped up, her gaze meeting mine.

"He said he doesn't know any Emilia, but he does know a girl named Help."

Darn you, Vicious. I rolled my eyes and leaned my elbows against the counter. "Tell him it's important and that he's a bastard."

Her mouth hung open and her light-brown eyes stared at me like I'd just tried to recruit her to the SS.

I repeated myself calmly. "Tell him that."

She did.

And it almost made me forget how angry I was for one second. A faint smile tickled my lips.

A minute later, Vicious pushed his door open and appeared in the hallway in front of his glass wall. It took me less than a second to realize his new receptionist had a serious crush on him. She swallowed hard when her eyes swiped over his body, and then she shot me a hate glare when she saw the look on his face when we locked eyes.

"Missed me?" He offered one of his cocky smirks as I strode toward him.

"Not quite." I gave him a shove back into his office.

He didn't put up a fight. If anything, he grinned like an idiot and winked at the receptionist meaningfully while my back was to her as he walked backward. I slammed the door in her face and then pushed him to sit on his office couch and crouched down so that we looked at each other. He was still grinning like I came there for another make-out session.

"Your stepmom fired my parents because I worked for you," I said evenly.

A frown replaced his smile. "What a bitch."

I nodded, feeling hot tears welling in my eyes.

"How did she even know?" he asked.

That one was easy. I'd thought about it on the train on my way here.

"My mom mentioned it to her. Look, Vicious, they have nowhere to go. Your stepmom's their only reference. They've lived and worked on your estate for ten years. What do I do? I'd fly to them, but the exhibition… I mean, I could. I *would*. It's just…" I shook my head.

Vicious considered my words for a few seconds, looking down at his hands, before shooting me a resolute glare. "I'll take the next flight to San Diego and sort it out."

My eyes widened. "Didn't you say you have something on Thursday?" It was already Tuesday afternoon, and no matter what his plans were, it was a long shot to make it in time for whatever it was he'd wanted to do by then.

He shrugged. "I'll postpone my plans."

"What were they?"

"Does it matter?"

I considered his question for a second. Did I have any right to ask him what he was doing? No, seeing as I kept pushing him away, not even giving him the chance to explain himself to me for five minutes.

I shook my head. "Thank you. Can you keep me posted?"

He arched an eyebrow, which I imagined meant "What the fuck do you think?" and strode to his glass desk.

Being back in his office reminded me that not long ago, we were different. For a fraction of a second, we were together, and it had felt divine. Not nice. Not safe. Not taken for granted. It was short and beautiful and painfully memorable. Like the tree I was obsessed with.

"Anything else?" He fell into his executive chair and didn't try begging for more of my time. He pressed a finger to his intercom. "Sue, book me the earliest flight to San Diego and get me my turkey and cranberry sandwich. Also, for fuck's sake, tell the girl at the reception to stop sending me 'Have a good day' cards. We all know my days are shitty because this city is a motherfucking downer."

He hung up the phone and tilted his head back to me. "You're still here. Do you want your PA job back?"

I shook my head quickly. "I'm just not sure how you can be both nice and compassionate and a terrible asshole all at the same time," I muttered.

He smiled. "It's a hard job, but someone's gotta do it."

CHAPTER TWENTY-FIVE
VICIOUS

It was time I came face-to-face with Jo.

I needed to. Not because of closure or to talk about it or some psychological bullshit, but because I needed to deal with what she'd done. She'd tricked my father. She'd sent her brother to kill my mother. And now she'd revealed her true shitty personality again by firing Emilia's folks.

This had to stop.

It had to stop a long time ago, but now I didn't have time to stew in my anger for her anymore. I had to act.

My plan wasn't sophisticated. It wasn't brilliant. It was actually borderline stupid. But it was the only one I had at this point.

A part of me hoped Jo wasn't there when I got to town because it would've made things a lot easier, but I knew that more than likely, she was there and waiting for me.

The flight to San Diego passed quickly. I had so much shit to catch up on, seeing as I'd slept through the majority of the day two days ago—hence my lateness to Emilia's commute home. At least I saw the complete and utter relief on her face when I finally made it, albeit ten minutes late, when she was already at the door.

Our private driver, Cliff, was no longer at my disposal, seeing as my father no longer owned the car, so I took a cab to Todos Santos and called Dean on my way there. We were still cold to each other, but being the new majority shareholder of FHH—something neither Jaime nor Trent liked one bit—had made Dean fucking agreeable for a change. He was no longer falsely heartbroken over his ex-girlfriend, and if I didn't know better, I'd think he actually loved the LA life.

"Where's a good Mexican place to eat in this city?" he muttered when he picked up the phone and then yawned. It was seven in the morning. Jesus fuck.

"Pink Taco. Listen, I need a favor."

"Another one?" Dean groaned.

I could practically hear him rolling his eyes on the other end of the line, and it grated on my nerves. I could also practically hear a woman in my bed moaning for him to lower his voice.

And then another one.

Two. *Goddammit, Dean.*

"Spit it out." He sighed.

"I'll be at your place tonight, ten or later. We'll party all night. You're throwing a big-ass party at my condo, and you must invite a ton of people. I'm talking at least fifty."

"And why the fuck?"

"Dean," I warned. I hated it when he asked questions. He never asked the right ones. "Just do it."

"Fine, asswipe."

I hung up the phone just as I entered the estate. The codes were the same. Jo hadn't bothered changing them for some reason. Maybe she, too, thought it was time we took the gloves off and addressed each other. She didn't know I was privy to what they did to my mom. I think she just assumed I hated her because she was competition. Unfortunately for her, it wasn't the truth.

My first stop was to see Emilia's parents at the servants' apartment. I knocked on their door and walked right in. They were packing. Her mom, Charlene, shoved their tacky tablecloths and family pictures into a box while her dad swept the floor. Like fucking Jo deserved them cleaning their house before they left.

"You need to come with me," I told them. I didn't ask them how they were doing because the answer was fucking obvious, and I didn't offer my apology because it wasn't my fault Josephine was a nasty piece of work. Instead, I offered solutions. Fast ones. "I booked you a room at a hotel and rented a space for your stuff in a self-storage warehouse outside town. Come on, the taxi's waiting."

Emilia's mom was the first to react to me. She stopped what she was doing, walked silently to where I stood, and slapped me across the face. Hard. I guess she did what both her daughters tried to at some point, so I had this coming.

I cocked my head to the side and watched her. Tears streamed down her face freely. Such a change from Emilia, who always held back. Even though Emilia looked like a young Jo, she looked nothing like either of her parents.

Charlene looked tired and worn-out.

"What have you done to my daughter?" Her voice shook.

I looked her in the eye. "I did to her exactly what she did to me, but I promise you, I will take care of her from now on. That is, if she'll let me."

It was Emilia's father's turn to join the conversation, and my heart stopped when I watched him walking over to me. I'd never cared what any girl's parents thought about me. Ever. But there was something about this guy that made me want to beg him to give me a second chance.

His brows were knitted, and his eyes twitched. "I never liked you," he said simply.

I nodded. "Can't blame you."

"I don't want you near my daughter, Baron. You're not good for her."

"See, this is where I beg to differ." I strode deeper into their living room and picked up two of the big suitcases. Moving back to the door, I motioned with my head for them to follow me. "I'm going to sort out the Jo situation and secure you two another job, but in the meantime, you'll have to respect her wishes and vacate the premises."

It was an order they didn't have much choice except to obey. They followed me across the pebbled walkway in the front garden to the taxi waiting outside the gate. I tipped the driver two hundred bucks to check them in because the LeBlanc couple had never checked into a hotel before, which was again a painful reminder of how humble Emilia's upbringing was and how she still didn't give a fuck about my wealth.

After I made sure the LeBlancs were on their way to the Vineyard, Todos Santos's best five-star hotel, I strolled into the mansion that used to be mine like I still owned the place. The house was open, meaning Josephine was there. I went straight to the kitchen, and when I didn't find her there, I checked the pool.

She was tanning, lying on a sunbed, wearing a huge pair of designer shades and a skimpy bikini that screamed *I'm still young*. And lied.

I paced quietly in her direction and took a seat next to her. I was still wearing my suit. It was early morning, and the sun was not even fully out, not to mention that it was mid-March, but I remembered Jo talking with her society friends about how a natural tan always beats the machines and tanning creams. She'd freeze her ass outside for a glimpse of a sunray.

"You think this is going to defrost your cold heart?" I asked evenly.

I guess her eyes were closed because the minute I started speaking, she jumped and almost hit the sunshade behind us. She scooted to a sitting position, yanking the shades from her face and scowling at me. "What are you doing here? I'm calling the police!"

She could call the police, but really? On her stepson? It wasn't breaking and entering. And I wasn't aggressive in any way.

Yet.

I leaned back on my sunbed and crossed my legs, staring at the kidney-shaped pool. Jo loved swimming in it. I wondered if she would still be keen on using it if she knew how many teenagers fucked in it during my badass high school parties for four years in a row.

"I thought you said you wanted to do dinners and wine more often," I said, my tone still calm.

Water mattresses floated on the surface of the massive pool like weightless ballerinas, different colors, shapes, and sizes, and it all reminded me of a Bret Easton Ellis book. The rich assholes. The bitchy stepmom. It was all so fucked up to the core. Not that I was making excuses, but I really had had a miniscule chance at turning out differently than I did.

"You didn't come here to spend time with me, and no matter what you have to ask, the answer is no. I don't want them on my property anymore. They're too old for the job anyway." Josephine lifted a glass of ice water and brought the straw to her lips, her movements ladylike and gentle.

It was funny hearing this from her. Emilia's parents were the exact same age as Jo. The only difference was the LeBlancs actually worked for a living. They weren't the useless ones. She was.

"That's fine. Charlene is going to cook for me in LA, and Paul needed to retire two years ago." I still needed to find a place for them to live, but otherwise, I doubted Dean would have a problem. "I actually came here to let you in on a secret." I offered her a smile.

She stopped sucking on her straw and arched an eyebrow. "Oh?"

"I know what you and Daryl did. I know what my dad agreed to do. Know how my mother died. I. Know. Everything."

It was beautiful to see her face whitening and her teeth chattering when the weather and my cold words finally caught up with her body. The glass shattered on the tiles, tiny ice cubes flying everywhere. She opened her mouth, no doubt about to deny the accusation.

"Please, Josephine. No more bullshit. The only reason I spared you from justice all this time was because I didn't deserve to get dragged through all this shit along with you." Besides, the plan was always to make sure Josephine would be left with nothing to live for too.

And it almost happened.

No husband.

No brother.

No family.

No nothing.

Except money.

"I was weighing my options in New York, trying to figure out what I want to do about the whole situation. Well, I think I finally made up my mind." My voice was so light, but her expression darkened.

Everything was strained and wrinkled. She stared at me in complete horror and shock, clutching the tough canvas of the sunbed. "Baron..." Her Botoxed lips quivered. "I don't know what makes you think I had anything to do with your mother's death—"

"Don't lie to me." I blinked once, watching her intently, then shook my head. "I heard your conversation with my dad. Heard the little heart-to-heart you had with him. You're pretty convincing, aren't you? Well, you've never fooled me. It was a matter of when to strike, not if."

"You misunderstood. I promise you I will rehire the LeBlancs, and you and I should talk about the will. It wasn't fair that you father left everything to me. We can reach a financial settlement. I can..."

I tuned her out. She thought it was about the money. How sad was her life? I leaned forward, taking her face in my hands. Gentle. Her breath hitched. Her eyes widened. I was close to her. Leaning into her. Our knees brushing together. Bile bubbled up my throat when I smiled at her serenely. Sickly. Acting like the psychopath she always thought I was.

And maybe I was a psychopath. Maybe she was the person who made me one.

"Jo?" I asked, my voice soft. "Do yourself a favor. Leave this house tonight. I would also advise against sharing this conversation with anyone. You were brave, Jo. So brave to tell my father that Marie was better off dead than alive in her condition. I'd like to see how brave you are if I go to the police. It's true you might even still get away with having her murdered. But are you willing to take that chance?

"Now, get back to your precious tan." I patted her cheek, getting up from my seat. "Who knows? It just might be your last."

Ever since I was a kid, I'd had dreams, vivid dreams, about burning down my father's mansion. I just knew it had to be done. I knew it would soothe the pain, make it go away. Not all of it, but enough for me to live. After I grew up, I even believed that it was the root of my sleeping problems. I just wanted the place to cease to exist, along with my memories of Daryl hitting me, Jo and Dad's conversation, and everything else.

But the Spencer mansion sprawled over twelve thousand square feet. It was huge and made of bricks, not exactly the easiest thing to set on fire.

Still—you never know until you try, right?

The servants' apartment was only about a hundred feet from the main house, not too far away, and while Jo came in and out of the main kitchen several times a day, she'd never even knocked on the LeBlancs' door once. So, after I said goodbye to a shocked Jo, I went back there.

I walked into Emilia's room, nonchalant as ever. I hummed Kravinsky's "Nightcall" because it finally dawned on me, albeit out of nowhere, that Emilia liked the song because it was about *me*. I collected everything I thought she'd miss. Framed pictures. Mementos from high school. Her favorite boots. Tucking everything that wasn't already packed by her parents into a box.

I spent the next three hours carrying all of the LeBlancs boxes to an SUV in the garage and making three trips to the storage warehouse outside town.

Emilia's box, though, I kept for myself.

All that time, I saw Jo through the vast French doors of the mansion's kitchen. Pacing, tossing back glass after glass of wine, and losing her shit. Then, when I was finally done, I turned on the gas burners of the stove in the pool house—all four of them—and left.

I wouldn't do the burning down myself. I needed an alibi. But it was going to happen. Finally.

If Jo decided to stay in the house and burn down with it, that was her problem, not mine.

I'd warned her.

Now I had one more mission before I went back to New York—win the LeBlanc couple over.

CHAPTER TWENTY-SIX
EMILIA

"Have you seen the news?" Rosie flopped on our small sofa beside me. The couch came with the place. It was small, but it was fun to sit on an actual seat when watching TV. Rosie clicked on buttons until she reached a news channel. A mansion we knew all too well was on fire, the roof collapsing into the dancing flames. I stared at it for a long time, knowing exactly what it meant.

Vicious.

When we were seniors, he'd set fire to *La Belle*, the yacht that was also a restaurant that belonged to another football player who'd become an enemy of the four HotHoles. Vicious liked fire. Maybe because he was so cold, he liked the warmth twirling in his palm. It had his signature all over it.

I grabbed my phone from the coffee table and jumped to my feet, dialing his number. I wanted to make sure my parents were okay. That *he* was okay. He answered on the fourth ring.

I stopped whatever it was I was going to say because I heard he was somewhere noisy. A party? A restaurant? I heard women giggling and men shouting. My heart sank to my stomach.

"Hey," I croaked. "Is everyone all right? I saw there was a huge fire in your old neighborhood." I kept it vague because I knew there was no way he was going to tell me the whole story over the phone. Or maybe even ever. Tucking a lock of my lavender hair behind my ear, I clasped one hand behind my neck and paced the apartment.

"Your parents are at the Vineyard." He was curt, as always, even when he was chasing me every day. I made a memo to thank him for the taxi that had waited for me today, when he wasn't able to walk me home. "I'm taking them to LA tomorrow. I need someone to be in charge of the catering at the Los Angeles branch, and your mom's perfect for the job."

I closed my eyes, breathing hard. The last thing I wanted was his charity, but my parents weren't proud people. They just wanted to work and earn their way. I pinched my nose with my fingers, hating that I needed his help and was going to accept it, even after everything we'd been through.

"Thanks," I said. "Well, I'll let you go back to your party."

"Bye," he said, as if nothing had happened. As if he didn't save my butt...*again*.

"Wait," I hurried to get out before he hung up. The line was still there, but he didn't say anything. I rubbed a hand against my thigh. "When will you be back in New York?"

"Can you just admit you miss me? It's not that fucking hard." I heard the smile in his voice.

I cringed. I did. I missed him. I hated that he wasn't here today.

"I'm willing to give you your five minutes." I dodged his accusation.

"Ten," he argued. Even after all this time.

"Eight," I retorted. It was all a game. I'd have given him as many hours as he needed to explain everything to me.

"Terrible negotiator," he said in a tsking tone. "I would've taken five in a heartbeat. Good night, Em."

Em. A tentative smile curved my lips. I knew it would stay there for long hours afterward.

He called me Em.

On Thursday, I wore a white-and-gold floor-length dress to the exhibition, letting my thick, wavy hair fall against my bare back. Brent rented me this dress—*rented!*—knowing how important the exhibition was for me. I couldn't sleep all night thinking about it. I tried to convince myself that it wouldn't be a big deal if no one bought my painting. It was going to be the first time a painting of mine would be on display and for sale in a gallery—a prestigious one too—and I was with some of the best artists in New York. I should've just been happy with the fact that my painting was there.

On the pristine white wall.

Looking at me. Smiling at me. Demanding my attention.

I couldn't focus on anything but that painting.

That afternoon, I'd spoken to my parents on the phone. They were already in Los Angeles and were living in an apartment in the same building as Vicious's penthouse in Los Feliz. I didn't want to know how many apartments the HotHoles had purchased over the years.

Mama was still upset about what happened at the Spencer mansion. "The worst part"—her voice shook again—"was that they think what caused the fire was our stove. I never leave my stove on. You know that. I check it three times before I go to bed every night. I'm telling you, Millie, it wasn't us."

"I know," I said, brushing my hair in front of the mirror, minutes before Brent picked me up. "It wasn't you. I know that. But who knows? Maybe Josephine came in? Maybe one of the other people who worked for her?"

I left Vicious's name out for obvious reasons.

Mama sighed. "What if they think we left it on on purpose because she fired us?"

"Well, does anyone actually know that she fired you?"

"No."

"Let's try to keep it that way," I said.

"Your boyfriend said the same thing."

"He's not my boyfriend." I was getting a little tired of repeating this to everybody, mainly because I wanted the opposite to be true.

"Well, I have to go, Millie. Dean is taking us to buy some things for our apartment. It's really nice. Big. But all the neighbors are so young. It's really weird to live here."

Dean was helping them out? I bit my inner cheek but didn't say a word. That was the main thing about the HotHoles. They were such assholes, but deep down, they had great hearts.

"Enjoy, Mama."

And now, here I was, living my dream, or what was supposed to be my dream. I stared at my painting again, clutching a tall glass of champagne and taking a deep breath. Rosie should've been here, but she'd taken a double shift at the café. She didn't want to do it, but she was covering for a sick coworker, and Rosie knew how it felt to get screwed over by illness. She didn't want the girl, Elle, to get in trouble.

It was fine. I didn't need anyone to celebrate with me. Besides, I had Brent.

A tall, beautiful woman in her early fifties approached me, wearing a black cocktail dress, a pearl necklace, and red lipstick. She smiled as she studied my painting on the wall.

"Nature or love?" she mused. She just wanted to start a conversation and had no idea I was the *ELB* who'd signed the bottom of the painting. Emilia LeBlanc.

"Definitely love. I mean, isn't it obvious?" I quirked an eyebrow.

She laughed breathlessly, like what I'd said was utterly funny, and took a sip of her wine. "To you, maybe. Why do you think it's love?"

"Because the person who painted it is obviously in love with the subject."

"Why not the other way around?" She turned to me with a cunning smile. "See his face." She trailed her manicured finger close to the canvas. "He looks happy. Content. Maybe he is the one who's in love with the person who painted him. Or maybe they're in love with each other."

I blushed. "Perhaps."

"I'm Sandy Richards." She extended her hand to me, and I shook it.

Sandy looked like a rich woman and not necessarily because of her outfit. There was an air about her. In that sense, she reminded me of the man in my painting.

"Emilia LeBlanc."

"I knew it." Then she pointed at the initials at the bottom of the painting.

There was no point denying it. Besides, I was proud of this painting. It was the canvas I painted on Christmas Eve. I'd thought about keeping it and making something else for the exhibition, but the truth was I didn't want Vicious's face staring back at me every day. Every time I closed my eyes, he was there. I didn't need another reminder of my obsession with him.

"Are you sure you want to sell it?" Sandy pressed the cold glass against her cheek, her eyes moving to the painting again.

I nodded. "Never been so sure of anything in my entire life."

"He's beautiful."

"All beautiful things pass on," I said. *My own personal cherry blossom.*

"I'll buy it then," she said, hitching one shoulder up.

My mouth dried, and I blinked away my shock. "You will?"

"Sure. There's something about him. Not in a model type of way. Just…interesting looking. But what I really like about this is that you captured the storm in his eyes. He's smiling happily, but his eyes…they look tortured. So troubled. I love this. I bet this guy has a good story."

"Nah, he's an asshole."

I heard the voice behind me and twisted immediately. Vicious was standing there, in one of his navy-blue suits that made my heart thump and sparked a nagging ache between my thighs.

Disbelief washed through me. He'd made it to my exhibition. And...what on earth was he holding in his hand? It looked like some sort of a ticket.

I didn't know how to react. I wanted to jump on him, to kiss him hard, to thank him for being there, but that's not who we were. Not at this point and maybe not ever. I reminded myself that last time I'd asked him what he wanted from me, his answer was to fuck me. I needed to be cautious with my heart this time.

Vicious walked over to us, ignoring Sandy, pushing his hand into my styled lavender hair, his lips ridiculously close to mine. The chatter around us stopped. I felt Brent's eyes on us. Sandy's eyes on us. Everyone's eyes on us.

So this is what he had planned for Thursday. He knew. He wanted to be here all along.

"Ask me what I want," Vicious murmured into my face.

The public display of affection from him—not sexual, not bullying, but pure, naked affection—filled my chest with warmth, but I tried to swallow down my hope.

"What do you want?" I turned my gaze to meet his, and suddenly, we weren't in New York, in a gallery full of people. We were in my old room. Ignoring the party and the world around us, a world that we constantly disregarded when we were together.

"I want you," he said simply. "Just you. Nothing else. Only ever you," he breathed out in pain, closing his eyes. "Fuck, Emilia. You."

I wanted to kiss him hard like in the movies, but this was reality, and I was an employee and an artist who still had to carry herself in a certain way. But I hugged him close to me and inhaled his unique scent, allowing myself to get drunk on it. I held back all the emotions that flooded me. The relief. The happiness. Wariness and love. So much love.

When we finally pulled away, I looked down to his clutched hand. "What's that in your hand, Vic?"

"This? I saw something I liked, so I bought it when I got here." He opened his fist and showed it to me.

It was a receipt for my painting. My heart stuttered.

He squeezed my hand in his and smiled. "It's gonna look so fucking epic in my bedroom, don't you think? I could fuck you and stare at myself as I do it. That's some Napoleon shit right there."

It was the best night of my life.

Because Vicious not only stayed the whole night but also allowed me to soak in the recognition I had received. He stood beside me most of the time, cradling his tumbler of whiskey, surfed on his phone, and occasionally took a picture of me when I was smiling or laughing with someone. He acted like a boyfriend. But not just any boyfriend. The boyfriend Vicious was supposed to be and never was.

And when the night ended and I turned around, about to tell him that I wanted to take it slowly, that I couldn't give him only my body anymore because it came as a single package with my heart and soul, he beat me to it.

Vicious ushered me to a taxi, planted a soft kiss on my forehead, and slammed the cab's door shut, motioning for me to roll down the window. I did.

"I thought you'd try to take me home." I arched a playful eyebrow.

"You thought wrong. Your pussy doesn't interest me right now. Your heart does."

Always so crude, even when he's sweet.

He tapped the vehicle's roof. "Try to sleep despite the adrenaline. You rocked this shit, Emilia. I'm proud of you. I'll pick you up for lunch tomorrow at twelve. Good night."

CHAPTER TWENTY-SEVEN
VICIOUS

The universe was rooting for me that week.

Dean had stopped being a pussy-ass motherfucker and decided to help me out. He not only threw a party complete with dozens of people who spotted me, in the unlikely event that Jo was going to explore prosecuting me for what happened to the mansion, but he actually took the LeBlancs to get furniture and go grocery shopping. It was with mixed feelings that I'd watched his interaction with Charlene because the fucker was charming and she actually liked him. I could see in the way she looked at him that she wished her daughter had stayed with him. She was going to have to get used to me.

Josephine was not on the premises when her house burst into flames. I'd asked a guy I knew to drive by on his Harley, wearing a ski mask, and throw a firebomb near the garage. He did.

Two hundred thousand dollars, it cost me.

But the Spencer mansion was gone. Wiped from the face of the earth. The scars on the blackened, muddy ground were the only proof that it had ever truly existed.

The next morning, my stepmother sent me a formal text informing me that she was moving to Maui. I texted back that she should leave her inheritance where I could fucking see it because she wasn't going anywhere, hell included, with my money.

She didn't reply, but the message was clear. I'd won. She'd lost. At life. At death. At everything that'd mattered.

It wasn't easy to get back to New York in time for the gallery showing. I had to bribe someone who flew coach to sell me his ticket. I paid double the price, but I made it to the exhibition. And when I got to the gallery, unsure of what I was going to say to her, she did all the work for me.

She'd painted me.

Not only did she paint me (and arguably gave me a better nose than the one I was born with), but it was also what I was doing in the painting that made me smile like a sleazeball. I was holding a joint and laughing into a nonexistent camera—though my eyes were still mine, kind of sad and dark and fucking scary—and I wore a simple black T-shirt that said "Black" in white. The background was stark, stupid pink.

I was her black.

And she was my pink.

I decided to buy the painting in a heartbeat, dragging her boss aside. *Gay, thank fuck.* He was there with his boyfriend, Roi. By that time, I noticed Emilia was standing next to my image, talking about it with a woman, and I hoped I wasn't too late to buy it myself.

I wasn't.

Emilia didn't know it yet, but she was going to paint another painting, of herself wearing a pink shirt against a black background, and I was going to hang it next to mine.

The next day, I arrived at the gallery promptly at noon. She was standing in the doorway in a blue-and-white sailor dress and orange pumps, waiting for me with a smile. It looked so simple. Her, on this spring day, giving me what I wanted so easily. It didn't look so easy while we were in high school. But I could see now that Trent had been right the night I'd found out she was dating Dean. I dragged everyone into a lot of dark shit because I couldn't admit to myself this one simple fact.

All I wanted was for her to be mine, but I kept thinking—believing—that I wasn't enough. That something so broken couldn't possibly deserve someone so whole.

I maintained my pace from the coffee shop where I'd been waiting, taking my time to appreciate the fact that she was waiting for me at the other end of the block. She lost her patience and sauntered in my direction, barely containing the grin on her face. When we were inches from each other, we both stopped. I wanted to kiss her, but it wasn't time yet. So I tucked a lock of hair behind her ear and swallowed.

"Let's go."

We took a taxi. It was spring. It was gorgeous. The only good thing about New York City, other than the fact that Emilia LeBlanc lived here, was what I was about to show her.

"Where are we going?" She munched on her bottom lip.

"Ice-skating," I deadpanned. "Then I want to get a giant tattoo of an asshole on my forehead because it symbolizes me."

She laughed that throaty laugh that made my cock twitch. "I can draw something out for you," she said with a wink.

"I'd like that."

The cab stopped on the edge of Central Park West, and we hopped out. I didn't bring anything with me but my story. Nothing for a picnic. Not even a fucking blanket to sit on. I hoped it was enough. Emilia flashed me a Mona Lisa smile that widened into a full beam when I grabbed her hand and led her to the blossoming cherry tree near the little bridge. The tree was in full bloom. It was especially beautiful, just like her, and she stood and gazed at it in silence.

I'd rehearsed this moment yesterday just before I got to the gallery. Tracked my steps to make sure I knew exactly where the tree was located and made sure it was actually blooming. Central Park was huge, and I didn't want to mess it up. No more messing up with this woman.

She turned to face me. "Cherry blossoms?"

I shrugged. "I guess I can see what the fuss is all about."

We sat under the tree.

The notion of telling someone everything, even her, was crippling. The lawyer in me wanted to drag me by the collar away from this. But the lawyer in me was dead near Emilia LeBlanc. Fucking her against my office door had pretty much proven so.

She looked at me expectantly before blurting out, "Listen, you don't need to explain yourself to me. You are who you are. I knew who Vicious Spencer was before I decided to work for you. Knew you'd pursue me. Knew you would ask me for things I might have a problem doing. And you were right, we weren't exclusive. As much as it hurt, you had every right to sleep with Georgia—"

"You think I slept with Georgia?" I cut her off incredulously, frowning. "I didn't touch her. I tried. Trust me, I did. But she wasn't you. And I know you don't expect me to give you answers, but I'm going to do it anyway because there's a small part of me that thinks that maybe, just maybe, you'll give me a chance afterward."

But there was a bigger part that suspected she was going to call the police and hand me over. Still, I had to do this.

Silence fell between us. My eyes landed on the grass as I spoke. It was easier that way.

"After my mom got injured in that car accident when I was a kid, everything changed. My parents' marriage was never the greatest from what I can remember, but it was after Mom became disabled when we stopped being a family. No more dinners together. No more vacations. He barely even spent time with us anymore. Drowned himself in work. When I was nine, my dad finally decided to leave my mother for Josephine. They were having an affair, but he couldn't divorce the poor crippled wife, right? So Jo convinced him to send a man to make her go away. The man was Jo's brother, Daryl Ryler."

Emilia gasped, and she took my hand in hers.

I continued. "I overheard my dad's conversation with Jo—back then she was his secretary, and because I was nine, I wasn't sure what it meant. I let it slide. Then a few weeks later, I came home from school in the middle of the day because I was sick. Saw Daryl leaving my mom's bedroom in a hurry. She died that day, and Josephine and my dad got married a year later." The words tasted bitter in my mouth. I still hadn't gotten over the fact he hated me so fucking much that he'd left me with practically nothing.

"After what happened to Mom, it felt almost evil to be happy. And Daryl…he eventually became a fixture in our home. Like an old, tattered, ugly-as-hell piece of furniture you wanted to get rid of. He was a drunk and sometimes a junkie—cocaine was his weakness—and he was sadistic as fuck. I was young and broken, and it was easy to drag me to the library and beat the shit out of me and cut me. I had no one to complain to. They'd murdered the only person who loved me."

"Jesus," I heard Emilia mutter as she sniffed loudly and clutched my hand in a death grip. Her eyes were already welling up. "This is horrible, Vic."

So am I, I thought.

"I thought about turning to the police and telling them about the whole thing, but by that point, I knew it was me against the world. Besides, it became personal. I knew what I was going to do. I had a plan. But as I moved toward it, I guess I became hardened. Too hard to notice everything that was beautiful and soft around me."

Enter Emilia LeBlanc. I knew what was going to leave my mouth next, and I tried to convince myself that it wasn't a terrible mistake. Emilia wasn't my girlfriend. She wasn't even technically my friend. And I was going to admit something to her, knowing I was putting my balls in her hands, hoping she wouldn't squeeze them to death.

"There was a game to be played, and I played it well. When you and I saw each other for the first time, Daryl had already stopped showing up at my house. He was coked-up again, and my dad had told Jo to take his keys away. Anyway, he hadn't abused me in a few years. I was big by then. Maybe six two, six three, and a baller. He was just a frail junkie who was losing his hair, but he thought he could still intimidate me. When I found you outside the library, I thought you'd heard too much, and the worst part was, when I looked at you, all I saw was Jo. You had her lips and her hair, her eyes and her posture. It made me want to hate you."

Emilia wiped her silent tears with the back of her hand and nestled her head in the crook of my shoulder. I let her. I took a deep breath of the fresh air, closing my eyes. I was going to do it.

"After you left Todos Santos, everything got worse. We were no longer in high school, and I was no longer a king. No one to play Defy with anymore, which made my frustration with the world simmer. Especially toward my stepmom and her brother. I wanted to kill Ryler. To fucking end him. I showed up at his house. I didn't even have to kick the door in. He was in the backyard in his hot tub, relaxing, his eyes shut."

I told her how I killed him. How I strode nonchalantly toward him, sat on the edge of his hot tub, and dropped his phone, which was on the wooden deck, into the water.

The autopsy said Daryl drowned to death in a drug-induced stupor. It was an airtight story. It was also the right one. He had drowned…but I gave him the drugs to put him out.

After I was done, I stilled, not even daring to inhale my next dose of oxygen.

She didn't stand up and walk away.

She didn't scream at me.

She didn't make a sound.

She just tensed next to my body and brushed her hand along my arm, prompting me to continue. I released the breath I was holding in my lungs and did just that.

"Then it was time to deal with Josephine and Dad. The gold digger deserved to lose what she'd schemed so hard to have. The fact that my dad got sick took care of most of it. My plan was simple. My dad worked himself to death to create a business legacy. All I wanted was to confront him before he died. Let him know I knew all along about my mom and that I was going to get rid of what he'd built, starting with the mansion I hated."

"You burned down the house," she finished gently.

I nodded, my chin digging into her temple. I felt lighter somehow. I hoped it wasn't going to bite me in the ass the next time Emilia and I went against each other, which was bound to happen because that was the way we operated. She jerked her head from my chest and stared at me. And I let her. Because I had nothing to hide anymore.

"You did so many horrible things to avenge your mama," she whispered. A tear escaped her right eye.

I nodded. I'd have said I was sorry, but that would've been a lie she didn't deserve hearing.

"And you're telling me this because...?"

"Because I trust you. Because I want to know if there's still a chance you can know who I am, who I really am, and still..." *Don't say love me, don't say love me, don't say love me.* "Be with me."

"I want to be with you," she confirmed without hesitation, and fuck, it just got a whole lot warmer. "I know that they damaged you, and I still want you. I don't even want to fix you. I just want you as you are. Broken. Misunderstood. Jerk. I want the real version, the dark version, the one who made me the saddest I've ever been in my life but also the happiest."

Now is the time.

I pressed my lips against hers, and they were warm, and they were right, and they were *mine*. We kissed under the cherry blossom tree until I felt our lips were seconds from cracking before she pulled away, blinking at me. I got up and offered her my hand.

She took it.

She fucking took it.

Knowing what I'd done, she was still there. What's more, she was still strong. That was the true beauty about this girl. She never cowered. She always stood tall and thought for herself, knowing what was right and what was wrong in *her* universe. Always.

That's what Pink said all those years ago. That we weren't above the law, but not beneath it either.

There were people around us. Cycling and setting up picnics, taking pictures, and walking their dogs. The place was buzzing with life, but I had just finished talking to her about the death I'd caused. I knew she still had a question in mind, so I waited, allowing her to voice it.

"What are you going to do about Josephine?" Her eyes jerked to me, and I smiled.

"I'm going to punish her where it hurts. I'm going to take her money."

It was pretty amazing how fast six months could pass. I was in no position to talk shit about Dean because he stayed true to his word, sticking to LA and even helping Emilia's parents settle in while I was courting their daughter.

Yes, that's right, courting.

I had no idea how we went from fucking in my office in every position known to man to me holding her bag while I escorted her from the subway to her shitty apartment every night, but it happened. I asked her if she wanted to move in with me, along with Rosie, back to their old apartment in Manhattan, the one I occupied now. I had more than enough space for the three of us, but after she said no, I never brought the subject up again.

We were going to do things her way. I got it. Her way sucked, but I needed to start learning how to play other people's games if I ever wanted something meaningful.

We didn't explicitly say out loud that we were dating, but we certainly weren't fucking, and still we saw each other every day. It went without saying that our weekends were booked, and we spent them together. Rosie tagged along more often than I would have liked, but I bit the bullet. We went to museums and to the movies. We took walks and even went to Coney Island once. Rosie brought a date along when that happened—a greasy guy named Hal—so I had a few hours to smuggle Emilia behind a building and make out with her until she had concrete burns all over her back from me grinding against her.

Rosie kept teasing me about the Hamptons, asking what kind of rich person I was if I didn't have a house there, until finally I caved and rented a place for the weekend, but not before I ran the idea past Emilia's baby sister and told her that if she was not bringing Hal along, I'd be dumping her sorry ass on the road on the way to the beach house I'd leased.

The week before the beach trip, we visited the cherry blossom tree again. The flowers had long died by then, which was kind of depressing to think about, I guess. Worse, spring was almost over, and I knew I was running out of time.

That night we finally got into bed again, and it was nothing like our first times.

Rosie needed the apartment in the Bronx because her boyfriend was sleeping over at theirs. A perfect opportunity for me. I asked Emilia if she wanted to sleep at my place, and she said yes. I didn't arrange a fancy candlelit dinner or get her flowers because that would've been lying, and I promised myself I wasn't gonna lie to her. But I did order us some Vietnamese from that place she liked and bought some booze. She came over after work and kicked off her high heels—lemon yellow with green dots—muttering something about how she was five seconds from caving and pairing sneakers with dresses like the rest of the female lawyers and accountants of NYC.

I grinned and poured her a glass of wine. I was already in my jeans and T-shirt. "Mmm, women in suits and sneakers. The antidote to an erection."

She laughed and threw one of the heels at me playfully, purposely missing me by a few feet. I cocked an eyebrow, striding over to her and handing her one of the full glasses of wine.

"You're aggressive lately. Must be all that sexual tension." Without giving her the option for a comeback, I turned around and started opening take-out boxes, fixing our plates.

She took a sip of the wine, and I felt her eyes on my body. "How are you sleeping these days, Vic?" Her tone was sweet and seductive.

"Like a fucking baby. Thanks for asking."

I'd somehow managed to snag some more planned sleep recently, mainly because I no longer had to worry about everything. Jo was my only loose end, and I was going to deal with her soon enough. Everything else was running smoothly. I slept every other night, which was huge progress. I don't know how it'd happened. Maybe it was the fact that I had someone by my side now.

She tilted her head slightly and stared at me almost dreamily, and I loved her for it.

Shit. I did.

She untangled my fingers from my glass of wine and placed it on the kitchen island as she linked her arms around my neck, and that's when I realized that all this time, all this fucking time I was chasing her, I was actually loving her.

I loved her when I hated her.

And I loved her when I didn't want anything to do with her.

I was so crazy about her, the lines had blurred together. Feelings were mixed, emotions twisted together.

I was stealing her pens and pencils when actually I was desperate for her words.

All of them. Every letter and syllable. Every silly doodle.

It was clear to me then, in a generic white kitchen I didn't particularly like, in a city I hated, in an apartment I was supposed to vacate in three weeks' time, that I was in love.

A love that was worn and old but still burning.

"Ask me what I want again," I said softly, and she grinned, pressing her lips to my chest through my tee.

"What do you want?" she murmured. Her hair smelled fantastic. Like flowers and how my fucking pillow was going to smell tonight.

"Nothing. I'm done wanting things. I have everything I need now. Ask me how I feel."

"How do you feel?"

"In love." I breathed hard, burying my face in her hair. "I feel in love, and it's you who I love. So fucking much."

We didn't eat our dinner. Instead, I carried her to my new bed, one that Dean had never slept in, and placed her on the mattress, on her stomach, watching her heart-shaped naked ass and all that purple hair fanning her back and my pillows. I leaned forward, kissing her tattoo and dipping my hand between her legs, running a finger over her slit. She shivered in pleasure but waited, motionless.

I purposely waited this time. Waited for it to feel right. To show her this wasn't a fling.

I licked my way slowly from her neck to her tailbone, where I stopped and propped her ass up by raising her knees. She was on all fours now, twisting her head behind her shoulder to see what I was doing. I stole a desperate kiss and guided her face so she was facing the headboard again.

"Don't you trust me?"

"I'm just starting to." She laughed breathlessly, and I sank my fingers into her again, feeling her grow wetter.

I borrowed some of that heat and swirled it around her nub, my finger pads stroking smoothly, and felt her pussy rubbing into my hand desperately. I placed one hand on the small of her back, nailing her down.

"Don't move."

"You're always so bossy," she moaned but complied. This time I didn't forget to put on a condom. Hell, this time I didn't forget anything. Slowly, I sank into her from behind while still working her clit. It felt good to be inside her again, but it felt even better to know that this time, it meant something.

At first, I went in slowly. Desperately slowly. Teasing her. Frustrating her purposely.

"Vicious," she begged, her head falling to the pillow as she let out a sigh. "Please."

"Please what?"

"Please don't torture me."

I picked up speed inside her, still not giving it to her the way she wanted it. Emilia liked to be pounded. She liked it rough and angry. Which was why we were so compatible in the first place.

"I think you like to be tortured." I leaned forward, whispering into her ear. "I think you always liked it. Very much."

The first wave of pleasure slammed into her, and her knees and elbows gave in. She collapsed, lying on the bed now, but I still pumped into her hard, my fingers still working her clit. I was relentless. And after depriving myself of her for so long, I had good reason to be.

"Up," I instructed. My voice held its usual cold tone.

"I don't think I can." She sounded just about ready to pass out.

I tugged her up so her back met my torso, cupping one of her bouncy breasts as I fucked her from behind, brushing her nipple with my thumb over and over, rubbing it in circles while sucking on her tattoo.

"Do you know how you feel?" I growled into her neck. I was going to come any second now, I knew it, and some orgasms, you knew it was same old, same old. But this one? It felt like a first. A once-in-a-few-years epic peak.

"Good?" she asked.

"That too." I smirked into her hot, sweaty flesh, licking it to taste her again. I was riding her so hard I knew she burned everywhere, but it was for me, so I didn't care.

I used one of my hands to support her while playing with her tits and the other to grab her knee and spread her leg to the side for better access, and then pounded harder. She yelled louder. Everything between us throbbed.

"You feel like redemption. And do you know what that's like?"

I flipped her over, but I was still at it, and she was shaking with what might've been her third orgasm.

"No. Tell me."

I came inside her hard, feeling my release inside her warm, tight pussy.

"It's perfection, like you."

I fucked Emilia so hard, my back looked like I'd fought a fucking grizzly bear by the time we were done. The woman sure knew how to use her claws.

When we collapsed back on the bed, she rolled over on top of me and whimpered, "I love you."

"I know," I said. Because I did. Because who else would ever put up with my bullshit if they didn't love me?

"It scares me," she added.

"Don't let it. I promise I'll protect you from anything. Even from myself."

An hour later, I was already dragging her out to the balcony—hey, it was a hot day outside, almost summer—sitting her naked ass on the dining set and pushing her legs wide with my shoulders. I ran my tongue along her slit teasingly, hardening in my briefs again. I slid my hand between her legs and pinched her clit. It was good to feel her flesh against mine again. And at least now I knew that the vacation I had booked in the Hamptons would be a fuck-fest.

"People can see us," she told me, and not for the first time. She was right, of course. We were on the twentieth floor, but so was pretty much the rest of Manhattan.

"Fuck 'em," I said, eating her out, filling her with my tongue and fingers at the same time.

She cried my name, and I loved it on her lips so much, I nearly burst. Her mouth hung open for the rest of the time as I plunged into her with my tongue. After she came once more, I stood up and lowered her body so she was flat against the table and fucked her raw, the dining set dancing under her ass, until we both found our releases.

When we ate our cold dinner at the dining table inside, I decided I was going to use my new trait of being honest and just give it to her straight.

"I sold ten percent of my shares in Fiscal Heights Holdings to Dean in exchange for six months in New York."

Silverware clattered on the table, and silence filled the air.

I continued, "That was back in January. I have three more weeks before I need to pack a bag and move back to Los Angeles. I'm not going to ask you for shit because I know you have your life here and that you love your job, but…I'm just letting you know."

Her eyes shot up, and she choked on her dim sum. They glittered with different emotions, which I was still too much of a dick to recognize. But I was fairly sure she wasn't pissed off at me this time.

"Three weeks?" she repeated.

I nodded, solemn. "I can try to sell ten percent more of my shares, but there's no way Trent and Jaime will let that happen. It'll put their asses at risk too."

She drank more wine, probably to buy herself some time. After polishing off the whole glass, she winced. "Thanks for telling me."

I didn't know what I was expecting. Actually, I did. I expected her to say that her job could go fuck itself, she was moving with me.

But then why would she give up on her career just so I could chase mine?

"Sure. Are you gonna eat that last dim sum?" I pointed my chopsticks to her plate. She shook her head, suddenly looking sad. I picked it up and stuck it in my mouth, chewing so I wouldn't have to talk anymore. "Good stuff."

CHAPTER TWENTY-EIGHT
EMILIA

"And again, I'm so sorry," I parroted my own words for the twelve hundredth time, twisting my fingers together as I stood like a punished kid in Brent's office. It was all white, other than the paintings hung on each wall of the room. They were beautiful.

One of a strawberry field.

One of naked men wearing fancy dress shoes.

One of a gun crying.

And one of a cherry blossom tree.

He stared at my painting and sighed, pushing his reading glasses up his nose.

"I'm not sure what to tell you, Millie, other than the obvious. You're making a huge mistake."

I would have argued, but there was no point. He was probably right. How many girls would have left everything they knew and loved—their city, their dream job, *their sister*, for a guy who kicked them out when they were eighteen? Not many. Yet I was that girl.

I was everything illogical and reckless, everything stupid and irrational…because I was his.

So I continued standing there, tapping my foot nervously. Brent got up from his seat, pushing from his white desk, and strode over to me. It was different than standing in front of Vicious when he was my boss.

Because now I wasn't scared, just sad. Sacrifices were like vices. You made them, gave up something good, in order to get something better.

"What will Rosie do?" he asked. He didn't know my sister all that well, but he'd met her a couple of times and knew our story. I shrugged. That was the most painful part. The part that made me feel like a traitor.

"She met a guy. Hal. She's staying here in New York. Wants to enroll back in nursing school, anyway."

Brent gave me a look—that look that said *See? You should stay here too*—but I dismissed it by fixing my eyes on the naked-men painting.

"I'm so sorry I disappointed you," I said. Which was true.

"You didn't." Brent leaned into my face, sighing. "I'm just hoping you're not going to disappoint *you*."

I made my way to Vic's office right after I handed in my resignation. On the subway, I thought about the fact that I'd never resigned from so many good jobs in such a short amount of time. Ever. But I knew what I wanted, and what I wanted was to move to Los Angeles. I'd never been there, but it didn't matter. He was going there. My parents were there.

LA was my home, and I hadn't even been there yet.

I sauntered into Vicious's office, and as usual, his receptionist gave me the stink eye, though at this point she knew better than to try to stop me from getting inside. Over the past few weeks, I'd walked in that door countless times and, embarrassingly, produced noises she could hear perfectly while I was there. Noises that clearly gave away the idea that I was engaged in some grueling cardio activity. Vicious didn't have a treadmill in his office, so she knew exactly what we were doing.

"Hi." I nodded to the receptionist.

"Mmm," she answered back, flipping through a glossy magazine with a picture of heavily photoshopped Selena Gomez on the cover.

I missed Patty. I'd only worked there one week, but it didn't stop me from getting attached. She was fun, even when she'd twisted my arm so I'd ask Vicious to do things for her.

It took the young receptionist exactly three seconds to realize where I was heading, and when she finally snapped from her gossip-induced haze, she jumped from her seat and waved her arms at me.

"You don't want to go in there!"

I'd stopped knocking on Vic's door long ago. Since he took me to see the cherry blossom tree, to be exact. It was as if after that, there were no secrets between us.

I arched an eyebrow and stared at her questioningly. "Why?"

She shook her head, looking exasperated and stressed all at the same time. "He's...he's with this woman. It's been loud the last half hour."

She was kidding me.

"What?" I felt my face whitening. The receptionist pushed her hair back. She was sweating. She looked like she wasn't sure what she should do. This was serious.

"I don't know, I hope he's okay. I..."

Before she could finish her sentence, I twisted the door handle and breezed into his office.

It *was* loud in there, but he wasn't the one doing the screaming.

And he *was* with someone.

The last woman I expected to see.

Jo.

Josephine was standing over his desk, her manicured fingernails clawing at the glass, yelling loudly, while Vicious sat perfectly still in his executive chair. His eyes tore from her to me, and he gave me a private smirk peppered with a wink. It said "nice to see you" and "don't get too attached to those panties because I'm going to chew them off you in a second" all at the same time.

His chin rested in his hand, and he went back to staring at Josephine, who turned around and scowled at me.

"Can't you see we're in the middle of a conversation?" She jerked her head to me and seethed.

I walked over to her silently and slapped her. Hard.

Violence is never the answer. But it felt good when directed at the woman who'd orphaned the man I love.

Shocked silence filled the air after the *thwack* of my palm before Jo brought her hand up and rubbed the pink flesh of her cheek.

"I hate you," I said, staring at her through a curtain of unshed tears. "And I will protect him from you. Any way I can."

She made no move, too astonished to react.

"It's fine." Vic waved her off dismissively, rising from his chair and striding in my direction.

I still eyed her like she was trash I forgot to take out, and he placed a kiss on my cheek and collected my wild hair into a ponytail, releasing it over one of my shoulders.

"Emilia knows everything, and I mean every fucking single thing, so you can talk freely in front of her."

I still couldn't seem to unglue my eyes from Jo. We did look alike. Sort of. And it made me sick to my stomach. Oh, how Vicious must have felt when he saw me day in and day out and all he could think about was the woman who was responsible for his mother's death.

I hugged him and then slowly moved to her.

"Why are you here, Josephine? Are you begging to get thrown into jail?" I asked.

She blinked at me once, like she was sure I was incapable of actually talking just because I wasn't the proud owner of a thousand overpriced designer dresses.

"I came here for negotiation, not to get ripped off." She pointed at Vicious animatedly. "I'm not giving you everything."

"You are, unless you want to get charged with murder." He loosened his tie.

I stayed rooted to the floor, too stunned to do anything. He was so calm all the time that I'd mistaken his indifference for a lack of feeling. But I was wrong. Vicious was full of feelings. He was a walking, talking ball of feelings. Just because he didn't wear his heart on his sleeve didn't mean his heart wasn't bleeding.

"Baron, if you think I'm stupid, you're dead wrong. I know exactly what you did. I always thought the timing of my brother's death was odd." She wheezed, blinking. "I always maintained there was something off about you. Told your dad you were a psycho."

Vicious shrugged. "This is fucking adorable. You do understand that your opinion has zero weight in court, right, Miss Delusional? What you need is a little thing called hard evidence. Got some of that?"

"Well, n...no—" She started, and he cut her off.

"I heard you plotting the death of my mother with my father, and my body is covered in scars. Now take a moment to let that sink in." He paused dramatically. He was mocking her, knotting his hands behind his back and taking a deep breath. He then proceeded. "You had a motive. And Daryl was no angel. Then there's the weird will my father left behind. For no reason whatsoever and without informing his lawyer or me, he disinherits his only son. Viteri told me the new will was mysteriously found in his safe deposit box after he died, and both witnesses who signed it are dead."

"That has nothing to do with me. A coincidence. As for these other wild accusations, you never said a word to anyone until now. A jury will know you're lying." She got in his face, her skin pale, her brow shiny with a thin layer of cold sweat. "*You* have no evidence against me."

But he did.

He had me.

I waved my hand in the air with a smile. "Actually, during our senior year, Vicious and I were pen pals. School obligation. He told me everything about you and Daryl's abuse in those letters. School records show that it's true, and I even kept the letters in a shoebox. Still got 'em," I said with a shrug. "My parents knew what was happening too."

Vicious turned around and stared at me, a little stunned. He wasn't expecting that. That made both of us.

I'd lied for him.

He fisted his hand and chuckled. "Holy evidence, Batman. Jo, that's a lot of evidence against you. I'm going to have a field day burying you alive. In fact, just watch as I dedicate my next couple of years to sitting in court watching you sweat. And I won't stop with the will. I'll have my mom's body exhumed. It's amazing what they can test for even years after the fact. I personally know of a pharmaceutical giant that has amazing capabilities. You don't even have to be convicted of my mom's murder. I'll sue you for wrongful death."

The only audible sound was the humming of the AC and me swallowing hard. Jo, crestfallen, shaking and unbalanced, clutched her waxy cheek. Hard.

"You can't leave me with nothing. Give me two million."

"Not even a penny," Vicious countered. "And I know about every single bank account and vintage vehicle my father had. You're walking away with about two grand and the few clothes that didn't burn up, so you'd better make immediate plans to go to the unemployment office in Hawaii because you'll be strapped for cash soon. Oh yeah, that's right, you've never had a job since you weaseled your way into my family's life. Guess it's time to start looking for one."

Josephine looked white, so white I thought she was going to faint. She let out a scream, a frustrated cry that echoed and bounced against the walls, running toward him and pounding her fists against his chest.

He let her.

Then he held her when her knees buckled, and she collapsed

into something that resembled a hug. It was all so surreal. I didn't know what to make of it. I was guessing none of his employees knew how to handle it either because I saw the curious stares through the glass wall.

"I can't," she mumbled into his chest, clutching on to his clothes, letting her makeup stain his pristine baby-blue dress shirt. "I can't go back to being poor. Baron, please. Baron, I will die."

"*Shh…*" He patted her head in a way that was almost fatherly. "It's over, Jo. You had a nice ride, but you hijacked the fucking vehicle. Did you really think you would get away with it? What am I saying? Of course you did, you stupid little thing. But it's done. The war is over, and the good guys won."

"You're not a good person," she sniffed.

He grinned.

"My mom was."

I ended up sleeping at his place that day. I still didn't talk to him about my resignation. It seemed inappropriate to talk about anything other than what happened with Jo, and besides, he had a lot of phone calls to make to Eli Cole, Mr. Viteri, and other people who were going to handle the mountains of paperwork involved with Jo relinquishing her claim to Baron Spencer Senior's estate.

Vicious even made sure his stepmother was going to give back the jewelry and designer dresses she'd retrieved before the house burned down. Every single one of them. I was actually surprised he didn't alert every pawnshop on the East Coast not to deal with his stepmother. He was busy avenging. Busy being bad. And I let him.

That night, we had sex like we used to before he flew to Todos Santos. Brutal. Hungry. He was detached, but I didn't care. I knew he'd come back to me eventually. And he did.

The next morning, I woke up to find a breakfast of Greek yogurt and fruit waiting for me. Vicious always ate like a rich person. Which meant he wasn't big on carbs and he liked his protein lean and his vegetables organic.

"Where are my eggs and bacon?" I pouted at the table like the food personally offended me, but internally I was smiling. He'd arranged a table full of coffee, orange juice, and carefully cut fruit while I was busy snoring.

Vicious threw a cool glance over his shoulder from the kitchen and raised one eyebrow. "Holy shit. You stayed the night. Didn't I call you a taxi?"

I grinned and held my stomach as I pretended to laugh and then sat down and dug into the yogurt. My mouth was full when I spoke. "So I need to tell you something."

"Okay, but I need to tell you something first." He turned around and walked to the table, holding his coffee cup. His jaw twitched once, and he swallowed. "I want to strike another deal with Dean. I was thinking of maybe extending my stay for another six months, but I wouldn't be able to give him another ten percent. I would if I could, and fuck the company and my shares in it. It's not the money. But Jaime and Trent would never sign on for this shit. Maybe I can convince Dean to sell some of his shares to them—"

I stopped him right there because he was talking nonsense, and even though I appreciated the gesture, I didn't want to watch him flushing his career down the toilet just so I could explore mine.

"I resigned," I said serenely.

He raised his eyes to meet mine. There were hope and confusion in them. "What?"

"I resigned. I'm coming with you. Rosie is staying here with Hal. I asked her to join me, but she wants to give their relationship a try, and besides, she would never live anywhere other than New York. I told her she didn't even give LA a chance—"

He cut me off. "Emilia, no disrespect, but who gives a flying fuck about your sister? Rewind. You're moving with me to Los Angeles?"

I got up from my chair on wobbly legs and smiled sheepishly. "Surprise…?"

He grabbed me and flung me in the air like I was a little kid, spinning me in place, his face happier than I'd ever seen it. I took a breath between kisses, knowing it was going to develop into something more, something a lot more, to tell him what my condition was. Because there was a condition. And it had to be fulfilled.

"One thing," I said.

"Anything," he promised.

"I want you to let Rosie rent back this apartment. I don't like her living in a bad neighborhood. I think she and Hal are going to move in together anyway, so they can probably afford the rent."

"They won't have to afford the rent. Maybe a few hundred dollars for legal purposes, but not the whole thing. I promise you. And she can stay here, yes. I'll make sure of it."

I nodded. "So I'm going to be an LA girl." There was a beat of silence. We both smiled.

"I love you." He grinned like the boy I was once so desperate to impress.

"I loved you first," I teased like the girl who knew deep down he always liked her too.

"Not possible." He kissed me hard, his tongue sliding into my mouth. Then he leaned back. "I loved you since you told me your friends called you Millie. Even then, when I caught you eavesdropping, I knew I wasn't gonna call you that because you weren't going to be my fucking friend. You were destined to be my wife."

EPILOGUE
VICIOUS

TWO MONTHS LATER

"This is stupid," I said, hands in my pockets, still leaning against the wall outside the birthing room. I hated Chicago. I also hated New York. Come to think of it, I pretty much hated everywhere that wasn't Los Angeles or my fiancée's pussy. Lucky for me, I lived in both places.

"It can take up to two days." Jaime blew out a breath and rubbed his eyes, pacing back and forth. "Melody was in labor for eighteen hours before she had Daria."

"Dang." Emilia snapped her head from the sketchpad on her knees and swiped her eyes along Melody's tiny body.

My former Lit teacher, now my best friend's wife, was sitting next to us, reading on her Kindle. Her eyes shot up from the screen. A smirk formed on her lips. "Oh, yeah. And I was induced. Fun times."

"I'm never having kids." Emilia shook her head, her mouth falling open in shock. She wore baby-blue jeans and a green tank top, and her pink hair had flowers in it.

I lifted an eyebrow and jutted out my lower lip. "Thanks for the news. Next time, break it on national television."

I didn't care, though. The last thing I wanted was to share my soon-to-be wife with someone else. And kids could be demanding. We had ten years of acting like two idiots to catch up on. Maybe in three, four, six years. In the immediate future, though? No fucking chance.

She sent me a sly smile. "We've discussed it. You hate kids."

"Hate is a strong word. I don't care for them." I shrugged. "And fuck, I can't believe Trent is going to be a dad."

Just as I said it, a doctor in green scrubs—or were they blue?—passed us by in the hallway and shot me a dirty look. Guess I should be more careful about dropping the f-bomb every two seconds in this place.

"It's ridiculous," Jaime agreed.

We heard footfalls, and Dean appeared down the hallway, running in our direction, clutching the hand of a young woman I didn't know. I couldn't decide who was a bigger whore, him or Trent. Although now that Trent was going to be a dad, I guessed a lot of things were going to change for him.

"What did I miss?" Dean breathed out.

"Nothing, other than basic social skills." Jaime shot him a dirty look and then glared hard at the chick he'd brought along with him. "No offense to the lady, but is this really an appropriate place to bring your date?"

"Cut him some slack." Emilia yawned from her chair against the wall, continuing to doodle. Cherry blossoms. Her favorite. Mine too. "Nobody cares other than you."

My phone rang in my hand, and I groaned. "I have to take this."

Emilia smiled warmly and introduced herself to the girl Dean had brought along. She was always nice to the chicks Dean and Trent dragged to whatever social events we all attended, even though she knew she'd never have to see them again. That was Emilia. The sweetest. The nicest. And…mine.

I stuck one finger in my ear to block the noise from the commotion in the hallway and leaned against a wall. "Hello?"

"Yeah," I heard Mr. Viteri say—he still wasn't a man of many words. "I spoke to your financial adviser. So you're putting aside six million dollars for that gallery on Venice Beach?"

"I want to make the offer tonight," I confirmed. "Buying the whole complex."

"Under your name?" Viteri's tone was cautious, borderline helpful.

I shook my head, even though he couldn't see it. "Emilia LeBlanc. My fiancée."

"I remember," Viteri gritted out, annoyed. "The same fiancée you'd like to marry without a prenup. Do I need to voice my opinion about this matter again, Mr. Spencer?"

"No."

I loved her. I loved her so fucking much there was only going to be one way out of this marriage other than death, and that was if Emilia woke up one day and decided to fuck every single guy on my phone's contact list. Even then, I might forgive her.

I used to think people who didn't sign prenups—rich people who didn't plan ahead—were too stupid to have so much money in the first place. The natural selection of the upper classes. That's what I'd called it. But now I understood. I understood why they did it.

They didn't want to think about the what-if.

They didn't want to consider failure.

Because to them, it simply wasn't an option.

All I knew when I got down on one knee under a cherry blossom tree on our trip to Japan was that this time, Emilia wasn't going anywhere. Ever. Unless it was with me.

Accepting the fact that you loved someone was much harder than falling for that person. It took time. And courage. But when I finally took that time, found that courage, when I finally let my guard down, I'd discovered something spectacular.

I wanted to create a world and fill it with her throaty voice and her smiles. With her laughter and peacock eyes and crazy wardrobe.

She was a happiness capsule I took every day to ensure I was able to sleep, eat, and live well.

And I did all those things. Thanks to her.

I got off the phone and strode back to where all my friends were gathered. Dean's date sat next to Emilia and gushed about her drawing. I puffed my chest out in pride.

Dean elbowed me and tilted his chin to Emilia. "You guys next? Kids?"

"Fuck you," I said, like he'd suggested death and not the creation of new life.

"By the way, I thought about it, and I'm willing to sell you your shares back. Figured you did enough groveling to everyone you owed an apology to."

"How much?" I asked, turning to the wall, shielding my hands as I rolled myself a blunt. This whole thing was too much. Trent becoming a father was too fucking much. I made a mental note to make sure child services was going to visit that baby on a monthly basis with these two as her parents. I placed the tobacco and weed inside the rolling paper, spreading it evenly with the pads of my fingers.

"Seven point five million, plus an apology." Dean hitched one shoulder.

"Eight without an apology," I said.

"Eight with an apology, just because you're an asshole who can't be bothered to do the right thing."

I laughed. "Seven point five with an apology," I repeated. "Do you want me on my knees?"

"Only if you suck a dick as good as your girlfriend." He waggled his brows, and I punched him on the arm. Hard.

"The fuck!" He winced.

"I heard that," Emilia said from the chairs beside us, reassuring me in her sweet voice. "He's lying. And FYI, fiancée now." She wiggled the fingers of her left hand.

Huge, fucking huge diamond. Pink for my Pink, of course.

"I know he's lying, baby. Come with me to the roof?" I asked.

She nodded and got up, leaving her sketchpad behind. When the doors to the elevator closed behind us, I placed the blunt in my pocket and slammed her against one of the walls, kissing her hard. She moaned into my mouth, and soon her hands were in my hair, my hands were on her waist, and we were two bodies becoming one despite our clothes.

"What do you want?" she asked me.

I needed to think of something fast. Over the last couple of months, we'd turned the question into our little joke. *Ask me...what do I want?*

I thought about it quickly before saying, "I want it to be black."

"You want what to be black?" She was panting.

I shoved my hand into her jeans and rubbed her clit through her panties. We were so fucked if the elevator had cameras.

"Your gallery on Venice Beach," I said.

She stopped kissing me. Stopped clawing at my hair. She jerked her eyes up and inspected me, suspicious. "No," she said.

"Yup," I responded. "I never understood why galleries are always so fucking white, you know?"

"Vic." Her lips trembled, and her eyes glistened with tears. Happy tears. Because now I made her happy. All the fucking time. "I love you so much, sometimes I feel like it's not even real anymore," she admitted.

I knew exactly how she felt. "It's real, and it's ours."

I smoked weed while she danced on the roof and threw me smiles every now and again. I watched her with a smile. Life was good. It was about to get even better soon, when this woman became completely mine.

And it was *right* because Dad was dead, Daryl was dead, and Jo was living in a studio apartment on the outskirts of San Diego, working as a waitress, doing double shifts. She never made it back to Hawaii. Sometimes she tried to message me, begging for a loan. I never answered.

We spent no more than ten minutes up on the roof before going back down to the maternity floor, where we were all waiting for Trent's stripper to give birth, but no one was in the hallway. No one.

"You sure we got the right floor?" Emilia looked around us, confused. It looked like the right place. Then again, the problem with hospitals was that everything looked fucking identical.

We spotted her sketchpad on the chair down the hall just as a plump nurse breezed out of a room, squinting at the clipboard in her hand. "Friends of Vasquez and Rexroth?"

We both nodded.

"Congratulations, a healthy baby girl. Let me show you to the room."

We practically jogged after her. The nurse knocked on a door and waited, and then Trent said, "Yeah?" and she let us inside.

Emilia went in first, but I held her hand, right behind her. Trent looked good. Happy. Fucking glowing, even. He held a tiny little thing in his hands, wrapped in a white blanket, with a light-pink-and-baby-blue wool hat on her head. She looked so peaceful and sweet. Valenciana was lying in her bed, speaking in Portuguese with her mother, who sat beside her.

"Brazilian, African American, and German," Trent said, introducing his baby to us, and Emilia squeezed my hand.

"That's a pretty long name. How about we use the initials and call her Bag for short?" I quirked a brow, and Trent laughed.

It was hard to tell, but I thought his daughter might be as good-looking as both of her parents, which was terrible news for the rest of the male population. Her skin tone was a light brown, and her eyes were grayish. Like Trent's.

"That's her heritage, dickwad."

"Trent!" everybody in the room shouted in unison, and I grinned like the asshole that I was.

"Tsk, tsk," I said, shaking my head. "So what are you going to call her?"

He handed Emilia the baby without asking her if she wanted to hold her, but by the smile that almost split her face in two, I knew she was game. She clutched the baby tightly to her chest and cooed.

Then Trent looked at Valenciana, and she looked at him. Something passed between them. I knew they weren't together. Even more than that, I knew this baby probably wasn't an accident. Trent was one of the richest people in his Chicago zip code, hot as fuck, and was bound to become even richer as we expanded. But none of it mattered right now because it was clear that despite everything, they were both committed to this baby and loved her a whole fucking lot more than some married parents loved their kids.

"Luna," they both said.

Emilia was close to fainting from happiness. She smiled and cooed some more and held Luna closer, mumbling about how it was a perfect name for a perfect girl.

Finally, it was Melody's turn to hold the baby, and she took her from my fiancée before the latter managed to run away with her. The room was buzzing with excitement and laughter, and I kicked back, sat next to Emilia, and smiled.

This was my family.

My fiancée.

The HotHoles.

And even the nameless chicks they brought with them.

"I changed my mind about babies," Emilia said through the chatter, leaning into me. "Maybe not right now or in a few years, but down the road, I want it. I think I really want it. What do you say?"

I smirked. Emilia LeBlanc of Richmond, Virginia, was asking me to put a baby in her.

Then I shrugged and leaned back into her. "Don't worry. I won't stop trying to impregnate you, even after you get pregnant."

She laughed.

"Deal?" I asked.

"Deal."

BONUS SCENE
VICIOUS

THE FIRST TIME VICIOUS AND EMILIA MEET AT HIS LIBRARY

Who the fuck is she?

Standing at my library's doorstep was a girl I'd never seen before, yet was around my age. She looked frightened. Big, cerulean eyes peering back at me in horror, like she was the one who had just taken a beating from her abusive so-called "uncle." My back was still hot from Daryl's belt, the welts searing my skin like rings of fire. I needed a cold shower, a cigarette, and a stiff drink. And no fucking company, thank you very much.

Which brought me to my original question—who was this chick?

"What the fuck?" I tapered my eyes at her, baring my teeth predatorily. Rather than answer the question, she turned a nice shade of tomato-red, her eyes flaring into saucer-like plates. She ducked her head, staring down at her dilapidated sneakers, pink cherry blossoms doodled on them by hand. I catalogued her outfit in my head. *Poor.* Not from Todos Santos.

Her face said it all. She'd heard everything that had gone down inside.

Fun-freaking-tastic.

"Have you been listening?" I demanded, straightening my spine to reach my full height and fill the doorframe. I was six-two and beginning to flesh out with muscle mass. I didn't want her to see Daryl. Didn't want her to get the wrong impression. Even if the wrong impression was the correct one.

"I didn't hear anything, I—I swear." Stuttering, she shook her head desperately. Those two blue pools of fear clung to my face like plastic wrap. "My mama works here. I was looking for her," she hurried to explain.

The penny dropped, right along with my amused expression.

Emilia LeBlanc.

She was going to start the new year at my school next week.

The help's daughter.

And my new fucking enemy, starting right now.

I examined her again, now that I had a name to attach to her face. I'd overheard my stepmother, Jo, moaning to her friends over margaritas that the LeBlanc daughters were, "pretty, but basic. Kind of like a French bulldog in a Birkin bag. Mother looks like a hag, as expected."

Emilia didn't just look like a good girl; she looked holier than Jesus Christ on a damn cross. With her modest, church-girl clothes and strawberry red lips pressed together tightly, which I bet she hadn't let anyone kiss. *Yet.* Maybe I was going to change that. After all, she now knew my darkest secret. It was only fair I'd saddle her with a dark, clandestine one of her own. Something she wouldn't want out in the open. And I could think of nothing more horrible than shacking it up with the most ruthless guy in All Saints High. My reputation preceded me, and it said one thing—*Vicious*.

"What's your name?" I stepped forward, erasing the little space between us. Her scent trickled into my nostrils. Of cherry blossom, summer sun, and baked goods. Of wholesomeness I normally found repulsive. I knew her name, but I didn't want her to know I'd done my due diligence before she'd moved in. She needed to know her place. That place, in case there was any confusion, was nowhere fucking near me.

"Emilia." The little shit actually extended her arm for a handshake, like we were in our thirties or whatever. She swallowed hard, mustering a smile. "My friends call me Millie. Y'all can, too."

Y'all.

I stared at her hand like she'd just offered me a flaming bag of crap, and she withdrew it with a wince. She was rocking on her toes now, bottom lip trapped under her white teeth awkwardly, and if I were capable of feeling, I'd probably feel bad for her. She was too easy a target. Even so, I was going to exploit her until there was nothing left to use. Because she deserved it.

And because she looked like a nice, solid distraction.

Emilia LeBlanc was simple, but so was the desire running through my veins when my eyes landed on hers. The warmth she stirred in my chest, spreading down into my stomach, left no room for doubt—I wanted my dick inside this girl.

"You're fucking done, *Emilia*," I growled, imitating her Southern accent. "Wrong fucking place and wrong fucking time. Next time I find you anywhere inside my house, bring a body bag, because you won't be leaving alive."

With that, I thundered past her, brushing my shoulder against hers to just check if it really was craving I was feeling toward the little, helpless creature. Desire zinged up my spine like a lightning bolt. This was new. And not unwelcome. Other than Daryl's beatings, I rarely felt much of anything these days. But now I felt something urgent and carnal—the need to jerk off from the mere sight of the new girl who was my family's help.

I left her behind me, mouth agape, figure frozen, and strode upstairs, knowing her eyes were trained on my back the entire time. That my black shirt was sticking to my muscles, glued together from the blood of Daryl's merciless welts.

I knew where to find her. Right under my nose. And I had big plans for her.

I was going to detect her weaknesses, her likes and dislikes, the things that made her tick.

Then I was going to use them against her.

Empathy for the enemy was a deadly vice. She needed to be terrorized thoroughly and cruelly to ensure she would take my secret to her grave.

And if it meant killing the little vixen's soul in the process—well, so be it.

My plans for Emilia were perfect. Bulletproof. Until the asshole whose face I wanted to shoot opened his damn mouth and ruined everything.

"That's one piece of fine ass right there." Dean smirked behind his Aviator shades, lazily sailing on a pink flamingo floatie in my kidney-shaped pool. The water twinkled under the sun like thousands of pale sapphires. "So hot she contributes to global warming," he hissed out, sucking in a breath. Dean was lathered in enough tanning oil to lube an elephant into a keyhole, sporting a deep tan and Baroque Versace swim trunks. The only reason I was friends with the vain fucker was because Jaime and Trent seemed to like him, and because he tolerated my brand of asshole when most people didn't.

I daggered my gaze behind my Wayfarer sunglasses in the direction he was staring at. Emilia and her sister, Rosie, were making their way from their beat-up car to the servants' house. Emilia was clutching a stack of thick books to her chest, while Rosie was twirling around as she blabbered animatedly. The two sisters were like oil and water. Black and white. Russell Wilson and an actual footballer. Though I found neither particularly palatable, at least Emilia didn't make so much noise all the time. She was easy on the eyes and difficult on the soul. Whenever she was around, I felt...*restless*.

While the annoying horniness she stirred in me would not seem to go away, neither would her aversion to my existence. She seemed to be hating me just as much as I hated her.

"Which one?" Jaime, who was playing a game on Switch next to me on a lounger, didn't bother ungluing his eyes from the device.

"Both." Dean let loose a gravelly laugh, plucking a beer bottle from its holder on the flamingo and taking a sip. "You know in the Bible, when Jacob lifts up the veil and realizes it's Leah he is marrying, not Rachel, and gets all bummed?" His voice scraped my nerves like a nail over a blackboard, making my fists ball at my sides. "Let's just say I'd be good with either one of them warming my bed." He traced the tip of his tongue over his lips. "Or, you know, squirting in it."

I felt my nostrils flaring as I took a deep breath. What a piece of shit.

Since when do you care about lewd comments? a voice inside me chuckled.

Great. Even the voices in my head couldn't fucking stand me. *Shut up, voice.*

"Millie looks like a garden gnome." Trent's eyebrows slammed together as he took a sip of his beer, laying on the lounger next to me. "Small and fragile, always wearing something bright." Even hearing him using her nickname made me want to break something. Preferably his spine. I didn't like it when people found her attractive. I didn't like it when people found her *un*attractive, either. Couldn't they just pretend she didn't exist like I did? Was it too much to ask?

"Oh, come on." Jaime elbowed Trent, laughing. "You so would, bro."

Trent hitched one shoulder up. "If she asked really nicely, and I were in a charitable mood."

"When are you *ever* in a charitable mood?" Dean snorted.

"Never."

They both laughed. I imagined their heads speared on Jo's William Sonoma steel skewers. My jaw ticked, but I kept my mouth shut.

"Rosie looks like a supermodel." Dean finished off his beer, stuck it in the drink holder, and rolled into the pool for a dip. His sunglasses floated over the surface as he swam underwater for a few seconds, then reemerged next to us, bracing his elbows over the edge of the pool. He spat water over his shoulder and back into the pool. "I would let her piss into my eyes and say thank you."

Trent shook his head. "Rosie's a smoke show, but I would be too afraid to touch her, with her illness and everything." Rosie had cystic fibrosis. I didn't fully understand the level of sick she was. I just knew her older sister coddled her to death.

"More Rosie for me." Dean shrugged off Trent's comment, his stare scurrying to the sisters again. They were loitering outside their door, seemingly looking for something they'd dropped on the pavement or under the bushes. The key, maybe. Or Rosie's fucking filters. Who knew.

"Heard Millie got asked to prom by Miles Westaire," Dean said.

"Get the fuck out." Jaime let out a disbelieving chuckle. "With Vicious as her knuckle-popping warden? Even Westaire is not that dumb."

"Source: trust me, bro." Trent chuckled into his beer bottle, shaking his head. Like Trent would ever consider taking *anyone* to prom. He was too laser-focused on his football and studies for a steady girlfriend. Plus, pussy was plentiful. Why would any of us want to settle down?

My mouth twitched into a snarl. "She doesn't seem like his type," I drawled out. But the truth was, Emilia was everyone's type. She had that aura about her, like rays of sunshine ran in her veins instead of blood. She was cheerful and happy and a team player. And she had an ass worthy of every love poem ever written.

"Actually, that makes sense now that I think about it." Jaime finally lifted his head up from the Switch screen, snapping his fingers. "He's been salivating over her ass for weeks now. I always make sure I keep an eye on him when they're in the same radius to ensure he doesn't hump her leg or some shit."

Agitation jam-packed my gut, my eyes ping-ponging between the three of them. Dean dipped his head in the water, resurfacing with a yawn. "Wouldn't be the first leg he humps. Westaire puts the perv in pervert."

"Wouldn't trust him with a cotton ball, let alone a chick during prom." Jaime shook his head.

"Yeah." Dean stroked his chin. "Hope Millie's friends warned her off."

Wouldn't count on it. Most of Millie's friends envied her for her looks, her grades, and how she didn't give two shits about being popular.

"Bro, cut this shit out." Trent put a hand on my knee, and that was when I realized I was bouncing my leg furiously, eager to...what? Rearrange Miles's facial organs? Threaten him? Keep every single person with a dick Emilia didn't refer to as "Dad" out of her way?

But why not? It had seemed to work the past three weeks or so. Westaire just needed a friendly reminder. No other guy was dumb enough to ask her out. They all knew I would destroy their lives if they as much as breathed in her direction.

I got up, grabbed the keys to my Maybach, and left without a word to the sound of Dean, Jaime, and Trent cackling behind my back. "Aw. Sir Cunt-a-Lot is here to save the day!" Dean called out.

"Millie's knight in black tee armor," Trent cooed.

"Leave him alone, guys," Jaime mocked. "He's in his Deep Denial Over Millie era."

Assholes. I unlocked the car, throwing the door open and firing up the engine. Miles lived just down the road. *And not for long, if he's going to make a move on Emilia.*

The engine roared to life. The Bluetooth connected to my phone, the sound of "Scars" by Boy Epic blasting through the air-conditioned space. My foot hit the accelerator, blood pumping in my veins when a small figure in a white-and-pink-checked mini dress ran in front of the car and crashed against the hood, a thumping sound filling my ears. I pumped the brake so hard the back of my head slammed into the headrest and almost punctured my skull. *Emilia*.

The *fuck* was she doing?

I was out the door and rounding the car so fast it didn't even take me two seconds. On the ground lay Emilia LeBlanc, knees dusted with gravel, shielding her face with her arms. My eyes ran over her exposed flesh, looking for blood or any visible injuries. I found nothing but a few scratches. And yet. *And yet*. My heart had pumped more in one minute than it had the entire goddamn year, wrestling its way up to my throat.

No. Nothing had happened to her. She looked fine. Then why the fuck didn't my pulse get the memo?

"Are you seriously injured?" Squatting down, I gathered her by the backs of her knees and her waist, picking her up carefully. "Because we have fucking insurance for that, so don't try any funny business."

I was about to walk her back to her cabin when she decided she didn't want a truce. She sent her small fist straight to my jaw. I managed to dodge her, putting her down on her feet. "You swine!" She panted hard, throwing another swing my way, nearly catching my cheekbone, but not quite. She was a lover, not a fighter, no matter how feisty she was. "You could've killed me."

"Trust me, if I could have, I would have." I scowled, my jaw ticking in annoyance. "Besides, you jumped into the street."

"You thrust into my *life*!" She threw her hands up in the air, exasperated.

Scowling at her, I pointed out, "You were the one who moved

into my fucking property, Emilia. Don't come at me with emotions, I only deal with facts."

Her nostrils flared, and she looked genuinely angry. "I came here to stop you."

"Stop me from what, driving my 500k car?" I arched a skeptic eyebrow. "I'm half-tempted to finish the job, Help. No creature this dumb deserves to live. Survival of the fittest and all."

"You're not going to warn Miles off of me, Vicious." She swung her index finger in my face, wagging it. "I'm done letting you mess around with my love life."

Her *love life*? We were barely seventeen. We didn't have any love life. What we had was awkward make-out sessions with people we didn't even like to try to figure out the mechanics of sex.

More accurately, it was what *I* had been doing. Emilia was a goodie two-shoes. A goodie two-shoes I made sure was radioactive at school to anyone with working eyes and a penis.

"How do you know I was going to go to Miles?" I stuffed my hands into my front pockets, my frown deepening. There was no point in denying I was going to warn him off. In fact, he'd be lucky to get away with it without a missing tooth or a broken nose.

"Dean told me." She parked her hands on her waist.

Motherfucker.

"I'm going to say yes," she said, resolute.

I ran my fingers over my hair and counted to ten, then to twenty, and finally, to a million. Nope. Didn't work. I was still pissed off to the max. "You cannot go to prom with Miles."

"Why?" She knotted her arms over her chest, jutting one hip out.

Yeah, fucker, why?

I had always been good at arguing, though, so pulling a reason out of my ass wasn't hard. "He once got Savannah drunk and took her V-card. He is not a nice guy."

That wasn't even a lie. Miles was a grade-A douche.

Her face softened at my words. "What?"

"Ask Sav. Or anyone else in our grade, for that matter. It's a well-known fact. There were police involved. Hush money from his parents. He took pictures and sent them via Telegram to the hockey team. You name it—he did it. He was lucky not to be expelled from school." The fact that Miles' grandfather was a former senator had not hurt.

Emilia's pretty mouth hung open. "That's why my friends told me he was a bad idea."

She believed me. I was an asshole, not a liar. I nodded. "He is not a nice guy."

"You're not a nice guy, either," she pointed out.

"No," I agreed. "But I'm a fair one." My heart was still beating a thousand times a minute. What the shit? She was *fine*. Whole. In one piece. Right in front of me. Sassing back like the pain in the ass she was.

"And yet, you wouldn't want to see me go to prom with anyone else." She curved a delicate eyebrow, studying my face intently. "Not just Miles."

Uh-uh. She didn't actually think she stood a chance, did she?

I leaned forward, getting into her face, catching a waft of the scent that always reminded me of Japanese gardens and fresh cinnamon rolls. Our noses nearly touched. Her eyes were wild. Dark-rimmed irises the palest shade of blue. "Emilia, sweetheart. I couldn't care less if you went to prom with Michael Myers, just as long as you'd stay the hell away from me."

"Is that why you're going to give Miles a warning?" Her stare didn't waver, and her voice didn't shake. Over the weeks that had followed our first encounter, Emilia had surprised me. She wasn't the scaredy cat I'd thought her to be. She'd showed resilience and spine, the kind of character that could be forged through suffering and endurance. That little girl from Virginia who couldn't afford holeless shoes? She wasn't going to break, no matter how hard I bent and arched her. And that made her even more fascinating to me. I'd never met anyone who could stand up to me like she did.

"I'm going after Miles because I do not like my property

damaged." I flicked her chin, smirking ever-so-slightly. "And you are mine, Help. No damaging my goods. But don't mistake my possessiveness for affection. I wouldn't piss on you if you were on fire."

"You just said you wouldn't mind me going to prom with Michael Myers. Make up your mind."

"Why should I? I don't owe you jack shit, much less an explanation. Now, don't you have a bathroom to scrub or something?" I looked around with boredom, signaling the conversation was over.

Her eyes flared, and the anger igniting behind her pupils made a pleasant shiver run down my entire body. If I couldn't have her interest, I'd settle for her wrath. The warmth felt all the same, and attention was attention. Fuck the semantics.

"You are disgusting, Baron 'Vicious' Spencer."

"That may very well be, but you are mine, and you know it. There is no escaping me, Emilia. You can run as far as you want, try as hard as you can, and I'll still be there, waiting in the wings, watching over you, controlling your life."

She looked stunned at my crass words as I slipped back into my car and threw it into drive again. I rolled down the window, flinging a casual elbow as I stared her down.

"This is not over," she warned me.

"Agreed. It'll be over when I tire of you. In the meantime, try not to get run over while I'm gone. Oh, by the way." I stuck my hand into the front pocket of my pants, rummaging through it and producing the keys to her house. I tossed them, and she caught them in the air. "This what you and Rosie were looking for?"

"You bastard," she whispered.

The car bolted down the curved pavement of my mansion, out of the cul-de-sac and toward Miles Westaire's house.

Because even though I knew Emilia wouldn't go with Miles to prom, that still didn't mean he deserved to keep his nose intact.

Nobody messed with Emilia LeBlanc.

No one but me.

SINNERS OF SAINT CHARACTER INSPIRATION

Baron "Vicious" Spencer—Sean O'Pry
Emilia "Millie" LeBlanc—Emilia Clarke (with pink hair)
Jaime Followhill—Austin Butler
Melody Greene—Juliet Doherty
Trent Rexroth—Jesse Williams
Edie Van Der Zee—Dove Cameron
Rosie LeBlanc—Alexandra Daddario
Dean Cole—Chris Pine
Roman "Bane" Protsenko—Brock O'Hurn
Jesse Carter—Shailene Woodley

DEFY

A SINNERS OF
SAINT PREQUEL

To Jaime Steinman-Jones and Kerissa Blake

PLAYLIST

"Secretly"—Skunk Anansie
"R U Mine?"—Arctic Monkeys
"Under Your Spell"—Desire
"Colors"—Halsey
"Crazy In Love"—Nightcore
"Whistle for the Choir"—The Fratellis
"Halo"—Texas
"Atomic"—Blondie

NOTE

Originally, the anchor symbol was not used by those on the water but by people on land. During the early years of Christianity, Christians were under heavy persecution by the Romans. To show their religion to other practicing Christians under the watchful eye of the ruling people, they would wear anchor jewelry or even tattoo anchors on themselves. The anchor was seen as a symbol of strength as anchors hold down ships even in the stormiest of weather. It was also a popular symbol because of its close resemblance to the cross. Anchors were also used to mark safe houses for those seeking refuge from persecution.

CHAPTER ONE

I snailed my way out of the principal's office toward the SoCal midwinter clouds. Anger, humiliation, and self-loathing coated every inch of my soul, creating a film of desperation I was desperate to scratch away.

Rock. Meet. Bottom.

I'd just found out All Saints High was not going to renew my contract as a teacher next year unless I pulled my shit together and performed some magic that'd transform my students into attentive human beings. Principal Followhill said that I showed zero authority and that the literature classes I was teaching were falling behind. To add fuel to the fire, last week I'd received notice that I was getting kicked out of my apartment at the end of next month. The owner had decided to remodel and move back in.

Also, the sexting partner I'd bagged through a questionable dating site had just fired me a message saying he wouldn't be able to make it to our first in-person date because his mom wouldn't give him her car tonight.

He was twenty-six.

So was I.

Being picky was a luxury a woman who hadn't seen a real-life cock in four years really didn't have.

And as a matter of fact, other than a few short flings, I'd never had a relationship. At all. With anyone. Ballet had always come first. Before men and before *me*. For a while, I'd actually thought it was enough. Until it wasn't.

When did it all go wrong?

I could tell you when—right after I started college. Eight years ago, I got accepted to Juilliard and was about to fulfill my dream to become a professional ballerina. This was what I'd worked for my whole life. My parents had taken out loans to pay my way through dancing competitions. Boyfriends were deemed an unwelcome distraction, and my only focus was joining a prestigious New York or European ballet company and becoming a prima ballerina.

Dancing was my oxygen.

When I said my goodbyes to my family and waved at them from the security point at the airport, they told me to break a leg. Three weeks into my first semester at Juilliard, I literally did. Broke it in a freakish escalator accident on my way down to the subway.

It not only killed my career dreams and lifelong plan but also sent me packing and back to SoCal. After a year of sulking, feeling sorry for myself, and developing a steady relationship with my first (and last) boyfriend—a dude named Jack Daniels—my parents convinced me to pursue a career in teaching. My mom was a teacher. My dad was a teacher. My older brother was a teacher. They loved teaching.

I *hated* teaching.

This was my third year of teaching and my first—and, judging by my performance, only—year at All Saints High in Todos Santos, California. Principal Followhill was one of the most influential women in town. Her polished bitchery was formidable. And she absolutely despised me from the get-go. My days under her reign were numbered.

As I approached my twelve-year-old Ford Focus parked across the aisle from her Lexus and her son's monstrous Range Rover (yeah, she'd bought her son, a senior, a fucking luxury SUV. Why would an eighteen-year-old need a car so big? Maybe so it could accommodate his giant-ass ego?), I decided my situation couldn't possibly get any worse.

But I was wrong.

I slid into my car and started backing up into the almost-empty parking lot, slipping back toward the two pricey symbols of a small dick. At the exact same moment, Mr. Living with His Mom texted me again. The green bubble flashed with GOT THE CAR. R8DY TO SEX IT UP? accompanied with approximately three thousand question marks.

I got distracted.

I got annoyed.

I bumped straight into Principal Followhill's son's SUV.

Choking the steering wheel and gasping in horror, I slapped my hand over my heart to make sure it didn't shoot out of my rib cage. Shit. Shit. *Shit!* The thud that filled my ears and shook my car didn't leave any room for doubt.

I'd done to his SUV what Keanu Reeves did to the movie *Dracula*. I'd fucking ruined it.

My fight-or-flight adrenaline kicked in, and I briefly contemplated whether I should hit the gas, assume an alias, and flee the country to hide in a cave somewhere in the Afghan mountains.

How was I going to pay for the damage? I had a big deductible, and there was that notice at home about my last insurance premium being late. Was I even covered? Principal Followhill was going to kill me.

Mustering my courage, I peeled my sorry ass off my seat. Technically speaking, Jaime's precious black SUV wasn't supposed to be parked in the teachers' lot. Then again, Jaime Followhill got away with a lot of shit he wasn't supposed to, thanks to his looks, social status, and powerful parents.

I circled around to find my cheap car's ass that was kissing his Range Rover's back quarter panel, leaving a dent the size of Africa.

Suffice it to say, *now* things couldn't get any worse.

But I was wrong. Again.

Bending down, I squinted at the destruction, not giving a damn about the fact that my brown knee-length dress danced in the air, exposing my new lace panties. There wasn't anyone else in the parking lot to see them, and it wasn't as if I was going to be flaunting them in front of Mr. Living with His Mom tonight.

"Oh no, no, no..." I chanted breathlessly.

I heard a guttural growl. "Next time you bend over like this, Ms. G, make sure I'm not behind you, or it'll end up on *National Geographic: When Predators Strike.*"

I slowly straightened, pushing my glasses up the bridge of my nose and scowling at Jaime Followhill as I took him in.

Jaime looked like the love child of Ryan Gosling and Channing Tatum, and I was not making this shit up. (Side note: This would be a great idea for an MM romance novel. I'd totally read it, anyway.) Sandy-blond hair tied into a low, messy bun, indigo eyes, and the body of a male stripper. Seriously, the kid was so ripped, his guns were the size of fucking bowling balls. He was a walking, talking cliché of the prom king in a nineties movie. A baller who had every girl's attention at All Saints High...

And his eyes were now on *me* as he strode closer to his very smashed ride.

He wore a tight gray Henley shirt that made his biceps and pecs stand out, slim dark denim, and high-top shoes that looked so expensive and tasteless you just knew Diddy had to be behind that design. He had a few bruises on his arms and a fading black eye. I knew where he'd gotten them. Rumor was he and his stupid friends beat the shit out of each other on the weekends in a fight-club game they called Defy.

Guess Pretty Boy wasn't too rich to be pushed around. I wondered if his mother knew about Defy.

"Well, fuck me to the moon and back." He stopped a few inches from our cars, releasing a wicked grin. It looked like the two cars had melded together. Like his SUV was giving birth to my ugly car through its rear end, and now the SUV's significant other (Principal Followhill's Lexus) was demanding a paternity test.

I taught Jaime, and he was one of the few kids who I could count on not to yell/scream/throw crap at people in English Lit. He wasn't a good student by any stretch of the imagination, but he was too busy with his cell phone to make trouble in my class.

"Sorry." I released a pained breath, my shoulders sagging in defeat.

He lifted the hem of his shirt and rubbed his perfect six-pack, stretching lazily and yawning at the same time. "Seems to me like I fucked your car up, Ms. Greene."

Wait…what?

"You…" I cleared my throat, looking around to make sure it wasn't a prank. "You fuck—I mean, you damaged my car?"

"Yeah. Bumped right into your ass. Pun intended, obvs." He kneeled down, frowning at the spot where our two vehicles met. He brushed his tan palm over the shiny paint of his SUV.

Jaime made it sound like he was the one who'd crashed his car into mine. I had no idea why. He wasn't even in his car. He'd just walked up. Maybe he wanted to blackmail me?

I considered myself a respectable teacher with a moral compass. But I also considered myself someone who would prefer not to bathe in the ocean and sleep in her car. That was exactly what I would need to do to survive the financial blow if I admitted to being at blame for hitting his expensive car.

"James…" I sighed, clutching on to the gold anchor necklace hanging around my neck.

He shook his head and raised his hand in the air. "So I screwed up your ride. Shit happens. Let me make it up to you."

What. The. Heck?

I didn't know what game he was playing. I just knew that he

was probably better at it than I was. So, in true Melody Greene fashion, I turned around and walked straight back to my car, essentially running away from the situation like the little pussy that I was.

"Whoa, not so fast." He chuckled as he grabbed me by the elbow and spun me around.

My eyes darted to his palm on my flesh. He lowered his hand, but it was too late. Butterflies somersaulted in my stomach, and my skin prickled with need. I was hot and bothered by one of my pupils.

Only Jaime Followhill wasn't just any pupil. He was also a sex god.

There was gossip in the hallways of All Saints High to prove it, enough stories to compete with the length of the fucking *Complete Works of Shakespeare*. And those weren't the only things that were long and impressive about the guy if the rumors were true.

Followhill made me almost as uncomfortable as his mother did. Only difference was his mom inspired fear in me, while he poked at my most sensitive spot. He made me feel embarrassed.

That could be because my eyes always drifted his way while I taught his Lit class. Like a moth to a flame, I always noticed him, even when I didn't want to. I was worried he knew that too. That I was looking at him in a way I shouldn't be when he was dicking around, messing with his phone.

Not like a teacher.

But like a woman.

"I said I dented your car." His blue eyes shimmered with intensity.

Why was he doing this? And why the fuck did I care? This kid received more pocket money than I had in all my savings combined. If he wanted to shoulder this, I should just accept.

Was it a better grade he was after? Doubted it. Jaime was a senior on his way out the door. I'd heard his rich ass had landed a spot at an excellent Texas university (see: Mommy Dearest), where he'd play football and probably fuck his way into some kind of a whore Guinness World Record.

"You did," I said, swallowing. "And right now, I'm running late. Please step out of my way."

We mentally shook hands on that lie, our eyes hard on one another. I had a feeling I was digging a hole. A hole in which I was about to dump a ton of dark shit that'd land me in hot trouble. I was striking a deal with the devil's spawn. Even though I had a good eight years on him, I knew who he was.

One of the Four HotHoles.

A self-centered, privileged princeling who ruled this town.

Jaime took another step my way, his body flush with mine. His breath skated over my face. Mint gum, aftershave, and musky male sweat that made me oddly heady. I was so unprepared for this that my face twitched.

I took a step back.

He took a step forward.

Bending his head down, he moved his lips close to mine. To my horror, my knees buckled, and I knew exactly why.

"I owe you," he murmured darkly. "And I'll make sure you get to cash in on that debt. Soon. Very soon."

"I don't need your money," I sputtered, my womb tingling with fuzzy warmth.

His mesmerizing eyes widened, and he flashed me a dimpled smirk. "It's not money I'm going to give you."

How could someone so young be so arrogant and self-assured? I felt his thumb stroking my stomach, barely touching, teasing, making me quiver through the thin fabric of my dress. It was like he'd shoved his whole fist into me and attacked my mouth with his.

I licked my lips and blinked, astonished.

Holy shit.

Holy. Fucking. Shit.

Jaime Followhill was hitting on me. Blatantly. In the parking lot. In plain sight.

I wasn't a troll. I still had a dancer's body after all, green eyes, a nice California tan, and soft chestnut curls. But I didn't exactly give the cheerleading crowd a run for their money.

Tripping backward, I swallowed a groan, feeling my pulse everywhere, eyelids included. "That's enough, James. Drive safely, and please be sure to do your homework for tomorrow," I had the audacity to say.

I tucked myself back into my Ford and then accidentally bumped my car into the Range Rover one more time before I fled the scene, smearing the ugly dent into a long, wide scratch. From the rearview mirror, I watched as he cocked his eyebrows at me in a challenge.

I drove so fast I swore my curls transformed into a dramatic blowout by the time I parked under my building.

At home, I slouched on my couch in front of my phone and waited for Principal Followhill to call to tell me she was firing my ass and suing me for every single penny I had. Or, in my case, *didn't* have.

Long hours passed, but the call never came. I crawled into bed and closed my eyes at ten p.m. but couldn't sleep to save my life. All I thought about was that gorgeous asshole, Jaime Followhill.

How he smelled like the hottest guy I'd ever been near.

How he looked like the most delicious thing in the world when he rubbed his tan six-pack.

How he helped me out of a shitty situation without flinching, knowing that his mother would probably crush me for this, and now...*he wanted something back.*

On paper, he was still a kid, but every other part of him felt like a man this afternoon.

It so defied logic, it was unnerving, almost infuriating when I thought about it.

This morning, I'd woken up with the impression that I hated the Followhills.

But after this afternoon, there was no denying it—there was at least one Followhill I wanted to get *very* friendly with.

CHAPTER TWO

Here was all you needed to know about Todos Santos: it was the richest town in California and, as a direct result, home to the most entitled teenagers in the world. My students knew I couldn't fail them. Their parents had enough power to strip me of my citizenship and banish me to an oxygen-deprived planet. These kids did whatever they wanted during class, much to no one's surprise.

The day after the car incident was different.

I taught six classes. The first five had gone better than expected, meaning I didn't have to slap anyone with a detention slip or call an ambulance/911/a SWAT team for assistance. But it was the sixth and last class that changed my life forever.

I sashayed into Jaime's class—following another barking session from his bitchy mom—into an echoing silence I wasn't used to. Everyone was seated, nobody threw anything, and Vicious, Jaime's BFF, hadn't cut anyone's face and adorned their forehead with a satanic symbol just to burn time.

Normally, this was the part where I had to contain the wrath and deplorable behavior of the Four HotHoles. (Hot Assholes, as they were dubbed by everyone in Todos Santos.) It was three months before graduation, and they were all seniors, a possible excuse for their behavior. Except they'd been this way since the first day.

There was Jaime, who spent my class texting the whole world

and drawing the attention of every girl who wasn't tongue-deep into Trent Rexroth, the underprivileged mocha-skinned football star, who made out with random chicks in the back. He once had a girl sucking his cock under his table in calculus. I kid you not. There was Dean Cole, the airheaded stoner who enjoyed pranks and annoying me in equal measure, and, finally, Baron "Vicious" Spencer, the World's Biggest Jerk.

Vicious was by far the worst. He made good on his name. So goddamned cold and sullen all the time that people nicknamed him after Sid Vicious of the Sex Pistols. He had coal-black hair, expressionless eyes, fair skin, and the kind of rebellious anger that could electrify you to the point of the chills. The permanent twitch of his clenched square jaw made girls wet their panties from fear *and* lust. He was a jock, like all the HotHoles, but he was leaner than the rest, not as muscular. But scarier. Definitely fucking scarier.

That day, Millie LeBlanc, a sweet girl who was the most frequent target of Vicious's wrath, arrived three minutes late. I tilted my head, signaling for her to take a seat. I felt bad for her. Her parents had dragged her all the way from Virginia her senior year to take jobs as live-in servants at one of the town's many mansions—Vicious Spencer's house, to be exact.

As always, she strode right in the psycho's direction and took the empty seat beside him as if she didn't know or care who Vicious was. My soul shouted an extended "*Noooooooo!*" when I saw how he was watching her. *He will grind you up and feed you to his pet snake,* I wanted to warn.

But Emilia just lifted her head, offered a polite smile, and drawled a Southern "hey, y'all" in the direction of him and the other HotHoles. Vicious blinked slowly, intrigued by the idea that she dared to speak to him without permission, and his expression clouded into a taut frown.

"Motherfucker, did you just 'hey, y'all' me?" He let out a feral growl. "Please tell me it's a fucking safe word you're using now because some new boyfriend shoved the Confederate flag up your ass, pole included. Otherwise, don't ever fucking 'hey y'all' me again."

Wow. That was more words than he'd spoken all year.

Millie sighed and said, "I'm only trying to be polite. You should try it sometime."

"I don't do polite," he retorted, a rare smile tugging on his lips. Usually, he seemed to despise her, but he was studying her so intently, it looked as if he was the one who'd like to shove numerous things up her perky little butt.

"Leave him alone, baby doll." Trent, the guy next to her (who took a breather from letting the chick next to him suck his thumb), glanced from Dean to Vicious. "Vicious, stop being a—"

"A raging fucking asshole," Jaime finished from behind them, scraping his chair back and towering over their heads, his sculpted muscles flexed to the max.

Goddammit. It was the first time my workday had ever been blissfully uneventful. The HotHoles just had to ruin it.

Before I could warn everyone off with an impotent threat I'd never follow through with, Jaime galloped toward Vicious and pinned him to the nearest wall, his fingers laced firmly around Vic's neck in a death squeeze.

"Where's your loyalty, man? Leave it be, okay?" Jaime tightened his hold on Vicious's neck.

"James!" I raised my voice, flying up from my chair and banging my palm over the desk. "Back to your seat, now!"

Vicious looked thoroughly amused, rolling his head on the wall and laughing like a maniac. Jaime and Vicious were best friends, but they were also two alphas with a shitload of testosterone and hormones coursing through their veins.

They were also the inventors of Defy. The teachers and high school staff didn't know too much about Defy because it went on at Vicious's house parties over the weekends, but we got the general idea. The game was simple: Our students challenged each other to bloody fights and beat the shit out of each other. For fun.

Defy was supposedly voluntary, but I didn't doubt people were afraid enough of Vicious to indulge his whims, however ridiculous or dangerous.

"Make me," Jaime challenged me on a whisper, his eyes narrowing into slits and zeroing in on my face, his fingers still digging into the neck of an amused, bluish Vic.

Jesus Christ. I never touched Followhill when it came to detentions and tardy slips. His mom was the fucking principal, and she already hated my guts. But he'd cornered me. I had to react.

I clutched my necklace.

Why was he doing this? Yesterday, he eye-fucked me to unconsciousness and back. And now…he…he…

Oh, shit. Now he's cashing in on the debt.

He didn't want me to back down. He wanted me to accept his dare. Was I going to take the bait? It wasn't like I had much choice. I owed him big-time for the Range Rover. Whatever it was he wanted from me, it was already his.

"You've just landed yourself in detention for the next week, starting this afternoon." I pulled open the drawer of my wooden desk and started filling out the detention form.

Everyone fell silent. I'd never done this before. Not to a senior and definitely not to James Charles Followhill III.

From the corner of my eye, I watched as Jaime finally let go of Vicious's neck. Vicious made a sucking sound and grabbed his junk, motioning to Jaime, laughing as he strode back to his seat. Other students slapped his back and looked between them, slipping notes. Probably bets on an impending Defy fight that was about to go down this weekend.

I smacked the detention slip on Jaime's desk, and he jerked his eyes up, beaming a smile at me so sinister my panties melted into gooey, sweet liquid. We both knew what I was doing.

Awarding him with one-on-one time with me, exactly what he wanted.

Accepting an arrangement that'd put me in a fragile, potentially disastrous spot.

I was saying thank you to him for threatening my class, telling them to behave, so that he'd be the only person in detention for the next week.

And at this point, there was no denying it—I was allowing myself to free-fall headfirst into the end of my career, doing somersaults on my way down.

Jaime Followhill had celebrated his eighteenth birthday three days before the parking lot incident, which made the chain of recent events even more suspicious. Had he waited to hit on me? Why? He could have any girl in school. (After Trent Rexroth had a taste, of course.)

I'd already spent my lunch break roaming his Instagram page like there was no tomorrow. His timeline was a pointed reminder that he was eight years my junior. He had pictures from summer camp, for fuck's sake. He was always sporting a dimply smile, tan muscular forearms, a stunning pair of bright blues, and a ton of friends.

Jaime had everything, and I had nothing. He had a coddled past, a cushy present, and a dazzling future. I, on the other hand, was already tainted with career failure and headed toward a life of scrambling to stay employed and out of debt. We didn't make sense. Even for a fling.

But I was too selfish and vulnerable to say no. Besides, having him would be like sticking it to his mom without really letting her know about it.

Win-win, right?

That afternoon, I slipped into the classroom where detention took place, noting that the wooden door to the room had a window.

I wasn't surprised to see the blond HotHole was already there, sitting in the front row, jingling his car keys—and our secret—between his strong fingers with a smirk, haunting me with his teal eyes. Gulping, I sat down at the teacher's table and took out my laptop and some exams I needed to grade.

"Put your phone in your backpack, Jaime." I wet my lips, my eyes focused on my paperwork.

He did as he was told, but I felt his lingering gaze licking me everywhere. My self-consciousness levels were so high I was on the verge of throwing up. I acted like I was about to commit a crime. In a way, I was.

After a few minutes of me pretending to type absolutely nothing on my laptop and him staring at me with a cocky smile, like he was about to devour me at any second, I grunted, "Why don't you do your homework? I'm sure you can do something constructive with your time while you're here." He had two hours to burn, and my face couldn't be *that* fascinating.

But I swore I heard him mumble, "Sizing up my prey is constructive."

My head bolted up from my screen, and I shot him a dirty look. "Excuse me?"

He tilted his chin up, flashing a row of pearly whites of the Hollywood variety. "Ms. Greene, this is going to happen."

I knew what he meant.

"I have no idea what you mean," I snipped. *Pshh.* Playing games with an eighteen-year-old. I promised myself that after today, I was going to take a long, hard look at my life. Preferably while enjoying a generous glass of wine. Well, not a glass, maybe more like a bowl.

Jaime leaned forward on his elbows, his huge arms spanning his whole desk. The devious twinkle in his eyes assured me, once again, that his age was merely a number. Hell, he'd probably slept with more people than I'd *kissed* in my entire life.

"Yes, you do. You know," he said with a smile that was arrogant yet forgiving. Who was the grown-up here? Who was corrupting whom? I swallowed.

My eyes dropped to my keyboard, and I struggled for a steady breath. I was shit-scared and turned on. Apparently, this was the perfect combination to make me produce small moans resembling a cat in heat.

"Why me?" I asked.

Jaime remained motionless, but his stare nipped at the sensitive flesh of my neck, tickling my lower abdomen. "Because," he said slowly, his soft lips parting as he drank me in, "I want to fuck a teacher before I go off to college."

And just like that, ladies and gentlemen, my quivering thighs and glassy eyes suffered a bad case of ice-cold bucket of rage.

Standing up and folding my arms, I pinched my lips together to make sure a curse didn't escape them. "I'm sorry, James. I don't seem to register half of the things you've said today because it sounds like you're begging to fail my class and get kicked out of school."

Now it was his turn to stand, and I shrank back toward the whiteboard when I remembered he had a good nine inches on me (also in his pants, if that prevailing rumor was right.)

"Sweetheart," he said, following that with a *tsk-tsk* of his tongue, his confidence unnerving. "Give me your worst. Fail me. Throw me in detention for the rest of the year. We both know it won't affect my graduation or my future. You'd only be shooting yourself in that lovely, sexy-as-fuck foot of yours."

His eyes moved to my legs, and he took a step forward. My throat constricted with an unfamiliar need to bite something. Preferably this HotHole's butt.

"The damage to the Range Rover is around eighty-five hundred dollars, thanks for asking," he continued, straight-faced.

Another step. *Thump, thump, thump* went my heart. I was a flower and he was a rare sunray, and we were drawn to each other, reluctantly, unwittingly, disastrously. Every cell in my body sizzled, begging for his touch.

Jaime wanted to fuck a teacher, so what? I wanted to fuck a baller.

We were two sensible grown-ups making a conscious decision… only he wasn't really a grown-up, was he? And I was anything but sensible to get into this mess.

But he had leverage on me.

And those piercing blue eyes.

Besides…I wanted him. He was the first thing that had made me feel giddy in a while. Since Juilliard, to be exact.

How sad was that?

"Jaime," I croaked. "I'm sure there are other teachers you could… work your charm on. How about Ms. Perklin?"

She was about three centuries old and smelled like used dental floss, but I wanted to gauge his reaction, postponing what was beginning to feel inevitable. Jaime stopped when our toes touched, his dimpled smile broadening, the black eye barely visible. I might have an easier time rejecting him if he weren't a female lubricant, I thought while admiring his masculine jaw and high forehead.

"Correction…" His lips brushed mine as he leaned down, and I shivered and stepped back, aware people might see us through the door's glass window. "I don't only want to fuck a teacher. I want to fuck my Lit teacher. She's got sass, great ass, long legs, and even though she thinks I haven't figured her out, I know that behind the prissy disguise is a woman who curses like a sailor and can outdrink anyone on my football team."

Damn right I could. They were only teenagers. I had impressive binge-drinking mileage. Eras of destructiveness caused by dark times of depression. *But I digress.*

"Do you want us both to get kicked out of All Saints?" I inhaled, patting my sweaty palms on my navy polka-dot dress. Someone had to talk sense into this boy. Too bad it was *me* we depended on. My willpower was nonexistent in those days. I had very little to lose at that point, if at all.

He grabbed me by the waist and spun us around so his back

shielded my whole body from the windowed door. He pulled me into him, and my body melted against his like hot butter.

"I won't tell," he whispered into my neck, making me shiver with pleasure. "Neither will you. A nice short fling, Ms. G. I'll move to Texas to play college football. You'll move on to an ugly-ass accountant with a good heart or some shit. Someone to make babies with. That's all. Now what do you say, Melody?"

I was about to say *dream on* but didn't have the chance.

Jaime dove down, his sultry lips breathing into mine. "On second thought, don't say a word. I'll see for myself."

Jaime Followhill kissed me, the most intoxicating kiss I'd ever had. The minute his mouth slammed over mine, my toes curled inside my sensible pumps. It wasn't just the urgency of his hot mouth or the sweet taste of his gum but also his drugging male scent. He invaded every inch of my pores, kissing me like he had something to prove, a point to make. I grabbed his smooth-cheeked face with abandon and inhaled, while he opened my mouth with his tongue and devoured me like I was his fucking last meal.

His tongue attacked mine, owning my mouth, licking every part and swallowing my needy moans. I wasn't surprised when his hand dug into my ass and he yanked me into his erection. He rubbed himself against me, shamelessly jerking off on me, grabbing one of my hands and placing it against his impressive cock.

It was wrong.

It was wrong, and I'd be lying if I said I didn't like how wrong it felt.

Whether I was corrupting or being corrupted...I loved how it made me feel.

My heart drummed with excitement and fear. I knew part of the thrill was the possibility we'd get caught. It felt like swallowing an eight ball of speed and washing it down with a dozen shots of vodka.

Hot fucking damn. Jaime Followhill had some moves.

"Anyone can see us," I muttered into another dirty-hot kiss. The space between us was already charged with sex, reeking of juices we barely kept hidden behind thin clothing. I was soaked and ready, and he'd released those male hormones that make teenage guys' rooms smell like jizz and sweat. Only on him, the smell was pretty magical.

"You're covered by me," he murmured into my neck, nipping my skin with his teeth and moving south. His tongue sliced through the valley of my swollen breasts like an arrow.

"Not true." My face was now on display for anyone to see.

"Meet you at your place in an hour."

"You don't know where I live." I hungrily skimmed my hands over his iron chest.

Jaime pulled away and gave me one of his mischievous grins.

Jesus. He was a stalker too? I had to admit, I found it hot as hell. One of the sexiest guys at school…stalked me. Why did I have to be a teacher? Shit like that never happened when I was a student.

"No." My voice was resolute. With every second his lips weren't on mine, the fog of a building orgasm faded, making way for logic.

Hello, logic. You killjoy, you.

"Ms. Greene…" His forehead and nose were crushed against mine. We both panted, eye to eye, chest to chest. "You're about eight minutes too late to walk out of this arrangement. This…" His hand ducked under my dress hem and up between my thighs, and a finger traveled along my wet slit through my plain cotton underwear (no lace today), stroking, not pushing, in a torturous tease. "Is mine until school ends. I will eat it, fuck it, play with it, and sleep in it if I want to. And I want to. I wanna do all those things to you."

What horrified me the most about Jaime's statement was that I knew he was going to get his way. I had agreed to it before I'd even walked into detention today. He had too much power over me, and not only because of his social status. I'd always been aware of his beauty and powerful presence, but up until now, I had used them to resent him. Now that they were offered to me, all bets were off.

"We're going to be exclusive. If I catch you spreading those toned legs for anyone else, he's gonna regret he was born with a dick."

Oh yeah? Was he going to resist all the temptation that was swarming around him like bad BO at Coachella?

As if reading my mind, he added, "My cock will only have two homes. Your mouth and your pussy. Ass, too, if you're feeling adventurous."

Mother of God.

"Detention's over. Take your stuff and leave," I gritted, taking one step back and then another.

He followed me and dipped his head, biting my neck before straightening and snapping his fingers. "Get in your car and drive home. I'll join you soon." He smacked my ass, turned around, and left, leaving a whiff of his singularly masculine scent.

I stood there, mouth agape, his taste still on my lips, the tingling of his touch still between my thighs as I rolled one thought around in my head: *Oh, Melody, you are so fucked.*

Luckily for me, I was about to get fucked even harder.

CHAPTER THREE

I didn't go home.

Going home would be admitting defeat. I might technically have let Jaime take the blame for the car, but I hadn't initiated anything sexual with him. That was all on him.

What made my decision even easier was bumping into his mother on my way out.

I was headed to the parking lot when I spotted Principal Followhill watching me through her office window. I stabbed the entry remote, hysteria controlling my movements as I considered making a dash for my car when her icy voice seeped from the open window.

"Ms. Greene. A word?"

There was a soundless moment when I saw my life flash in front of me, and sadly, it was a short, shitty movie consisting of me sprawled out on my old couch watching *American Ninja Warrior*, showing up to family events dateless, and attending a weekly support group for former athletes (most of us were in various stages of drunkenness).

Fun times.

If Principal Followhill knew what had happened in detention, she was going to remove every internal organ in my body, restuff it with dynamite, and blow up the whole school. That's how much she hated me.

"Sure." I smiled big, throwing my arms in a *why not* gesture and walking back toward All Saints.

Why not? Because she wants to kill you and because you just made out with her teenage son.

The minute I entered her office, I knew she was onto something. Her usually smooth, Botoxed forehead looked like it had collapsed into a heap of extra skin.

"Sit."

I did.

"Ms. Greene, do you know why you're here?"

I was so nervous, I couldn't breathe but somehow managed to shake my head no. Her office alone scared the shit out of me. It was so big yet suffocating, with its heavy furniture of cherry-stained wood and burgundy leather and its oxblood walls, everything a deep red, like Carrie had paid a visit there on prom night and lost.

Principal Followhill stood near a painting that probably cost more than my rent, her arms behind her back, and closed her eyes, exhaling. "The incident with my son, James."

Oh no. Please, no. I wasn't ready to die. I had so many things to see and experience. Most of them between the sheets with her barely legal son, but still.

Jokes aside—I was pretty sure I peed myself a little. I was terrified. Not of getting fired, but of the consequences of pissing off someone with Principal Followhill's clout. My parents taught in the school district adjacent to Todos Santos. This was their home, and they were a vital part of this small, judgmental community.

I was about to screw my family because of a brief kiss.

"Principal Followhill, I can explain," I rushed to say, jumping up from my seat.

She launched in my direction and shoved me back into the chair. If I wasn't so consumed with guilt, I would've been floored that she touched me.

She held up her hand, her face pale. "No, you listen to me. James is a brat. Don't you think I know that? What he did to your car... He should have left a note after he hit you, not driven away. It looks bad, but he simply panicked. He explained it all to me. No need to file a police report. I assure you he's very, very sorry, and he's going back to the student-parking lot from now on. I'll write you a check for your repairs, and I'll of course compensate you for the inconvenience as well. I'll be damned if I'll allow one reckless decision to tarnish my son's reputation." She reached for her Hermès bag and plucked out a checkbook.

My eyes followed her movements like she was performing some trick of dark magic. Of course, I was a problem. She wanted it fixed, so she threw money at it. *At me.*

She didn't know about the kiss. All she knew was that Jaime came back home yesterday with a banged-up Range Rover and his own version of what happened in the parking lot. He'd kept his side of our deal.

"This little car mishap is not to leave these walls. Do you understand, Ms. Greene?" Principal Followhill bent down and scribbled on the check, her mouth twitching in annoyance. "You have a mouth, in case you didn't notice. You could use it and say something."

Why do you hate me? I wanted to scream. *What have I done to you?* Though I already knew the answer. She hated me because I wasn't royalty. I wasn't someone who was born and bred in Todos Santos. I was an outsider, contaminated and mortal, with middle-class parents. On top of that, I was a weak link who—because of my above-mentioned disadvantages—couldn't control my classes.

"Understood," I sniffed.

She fingered the check she'd written for me. Despite my best intentions, I plucked it from between her French-manicured nails and peeked. Ten K. Way, way more than necessary. *Bribe.*

We were all corrupted now. It made me a little less remorseful about making out with her son.

Jaime was blackmailing me.

And I was blackmailing his mother.

My parents always said money made people twisted and immoral. I used to think they were exaggerating. I was starting to believe that they weren't.

I stood up, smoothing my dress and jutting out my chin. Principal Followhill held my gaze but tugged at her ear. *Nervous. Desperate. Clueless.*

"All is forgotten?" Her lips barely moved.

"All is forgotten." I nodded, walking out of her office $10,000 richer.

I drove straight to a local bar.

After all, I had some money to burn. *And dirty little secrets to forget.*

CHAPTER FOUR

I wobbled back to my apartment building at midnight, my breath stinking of Bud Light and stale peanuts. Trying to fish for my keys, I halted in front of my door in the darkened hallway, rummaging through my loaded handbag. When I finally felt the sharp edge of the key, I jerked out my pointe shoe keychain, and it clunked to the floor. Blowing a lock of my hair from my face in frustration, I sighed. It was going to be a bitch to retrieve. I was getting too old to get tanked.

But I didn't even have to bend down.

Because someone else picked my keys up for me. From behind.

My heart throbbed faster, yet I stilled, feeling the warmth of another body pressing against mine. The air pulsated with the vitality of an impending fantasy that was about to be fulfilled.

Fear and lust filled my veins with adrenaline and dopamine. The overlapping feelings made me heady, excited, and aroused.

Crap. I couldn't resist him in my current state. His erection dug into my ass, and I swallowed.

I watched his hand unlocking my door from where he stood behind me. His warm lips whispered into my ear, "Get in and get naked." It was an order.

The door flung open with a little push from his hand. I wanted to cry in excitement. Correction: I did actually cry in excitement. There were tears of joy in my eyes. What can I say? Booze and eighteen-year-old jocks who are hung like a horse made this girl hella happy.

I practically skipped into my living room/kitchen, which was decorated with brown boxes and my old couch. I had to move to hell-knows-where next month and was already starting to pack. Seeing my life crumbling, stuffed into half-filled cardboard containers, only made my decision to have sex with my student easier. It wasn't like I was ruining anything substantial I'd built. I was a loser, practically homeless and soon-to-be unemployed. An outcast. Jaime took the edge off the reality of my future.

I felt his huge form pacing behind me, ready to pounce at any moment.

I pulled off my polka-dot dress and threw it on the floor. Turning around, I looked at him for the first time, smiling under my lashes. Jaime did not return the playful smile. In fact, his brows were knit tightly together and his jaw so clenched, it looked like it was about to snap. He had a cut lip and dried blood coating his nostrils.

He fought. Again. Probably with Vicious, judging from the nasty welts and purple bruises.

"What happened to you?" I swallowed.

He ignored my question. "This is how you repay me for fixing up your shit, Ms. Greene?" His voice was dark and serious. Not at all like an eighteen-year-old student's.

"Jaime." My tone danced unevenly. Jaime…what? I stood him up. Even though I never did agree to meet him at my place. How long had he been waiting anyway?

I was standing in my bra and underwear in my living room, dealing with a cranky teenager, and was pretty fucking sauced. Another low I didn't think I was going to stoop to. I hugged my own waist, covering some of my skin.

"I like your bra," he said hoarsely, but it did not sound like a compliment. *It sounded like a threat.*

I looked down to examine the pink lace.

"It's my favorite. Victoria's Secret." I licked my lips, sounding dumber than an Adam Sandler character. I was so out of my element. Jesus. What the fuck was wrong with me?

"Come here," he demanded, pointing at the floor.

I paced in his direction, my eyes bugging out at the thrill. He was wearing dark Diesel jeans and a black muscle shirt with his gym's name on it. And flip-flops. I loved men who could pull off flip-flops. His bun was spectacularly messy too.

When I got to him, I looked down. No toe hair. A keeper.

"Down on your knees, Greene." His voice still had a menacing edge to it.

Where did that come from? He was usually a pretty playful guy. In an I'll-fuck-you-over kind of way. I did as I was told because… well, because at this point, I was pretty much the Followhills' bitch. *Sit, bend, cash checks, forget secrets, kneel down*. I was lucky they hadn't asked me to scoop dog poop from their front lawn.

"I have a blow job with your name on it for making me wait here like a soft dick." He brushed a brown curl from my face.

"I don't do blow jobs. I have a really bad gag reflex," I answered truthfully. Seriously, I'd found out about it the hard way during high school. Never had a corn dog or a banana since.

Calm and collected, he unzipped and lowered his jeans, releasing his hard, swollen cock out of his Calvin Klein black briefs.

Holy shit, it was beautiful. Not nine inches like the cheerleaders were whispering about in class (they sucked at geometry, that should've been my first clue) but almost—it was just picture-perfect. Postcards-and-stamps worthy. He had the sleekest, smoothest shaft, a prominent head, and a thick velvety vein. And a tilt. To the right.

Perfect, perfect, perfect.

And he fucking knew it, the bastard. That was why he displayed his dick to me like it was the *Mona Lisa*.

I took a brief moment to process the fact that I had my student's one-eyed snake staring right back at me in the middle of my tiny empty apartment. Worst part? *Still giddy and excited.*

My throat bobbed.

"Maybe I can make an exception, since you took a bullet for me and all." I rolled my eyes, feigning amusement. But there was nothing amusing about that cock. It was serious. Things were about to go down, literally and figuratively.

The only problem was…I didn't know how to give head. I think Jaime figured it out himself because he tugged my hair toward his groin.

"Start licking," he instructed.

I did. His flesh was hot and silky under my keen tongue. I circled his cock's head hungrily with my eyes closed, feeling it jumping in delight to the movements of my mouth. After a minute, Jaime picked up my hand and curled my fingers around the base of his shaft. Would you look at that? My Lit student was giving me a sex-ed lesson.

"Pump," he groaned.

I did. I wondered how many of my female students had sucked him off. Probably a lot. I wished I could say I didn't care, but that would be a lie, so I tried to convince myself I cared because it made me feel inexperienced.

"Now suck, in and out," he whispered, grabbing the back of my head and moving it back and forth.

Every time I went in, his cock hit the back of my throat, and I struggled for air…but I loved it. My underwear was once again damp with want. Logically, I knew this wasn't okay. But if it was so wrong…why did it feel so right?

Jaime kicked one of his flip-flops off and dug his toe into the fabric of my underwear. It was humiliating…and so fucking hot. He used his toe to lower the waistband of my undies with a loud growl. Once my sex was exposed, his toe homed in on my clit.

"Shit, fuck, Jaime." I did *not* sound like his teacher. Didn't feel like one, either. "What are you doing?"

"Making you come. Keep sucking, Greene."

I licked and sucked and got addicted to the sounds that left Jaime's mouth. I gave in and gave it my all. He kept on rubbing his toe against my swollen clit, and the feeling of an impending orgasm fired every nerve ending in my body. My knees shook with pleasure, and I greedily rubbed my pussy against his toe. I was sure my OB/GYN would have a lot to say about the hygiene of this act, but at that moment, none of that mattered.

Not even the nagging suspicion that he might've done this so he could brag to his friends and humiliate me in front of the whole school.

"I'm going to come in your mouth, and you're going to come on my toe."

He was so filthy.

It was beautiful.

Just when the warm liquid shot into my throat, I felt a sharp pain as my bra was torn from my body from behind. I gasped in horror, swallowing his salty hot cum and opening my eyes at once, shocked.

He fucking tore my favorite bra. *On purpose.*

Jaime used his toe to nudge me to a reclining position on the floor, and I collapsed, rubbing the pink skin where he'd pulled off my bra.

"What the hell!" I screamed but was silenced by a kiss. A dazzling kiss that was followed by the two strong fingers he shoved into my pussy. I clenched around him, watching him move his head south and graze my hard nipples with his teeth.

"That's for keeping me waiting. I don't take well to tardiness."

The fucker was late to 90 percent of the classes I taught him!

"Well, I don't take well to assholeness," I muttered.

"I'll make it up to you. I'm a master at oral sex," Jaime's perfect, skillful mouth said, his serene blues scanning me earnestly.

"How so?" I raised an eyebrow as he inched closer to my pussy, still pumping his fingers to the rhythm of my thudding heartbeat.

He gave a light shrug. "Spent summer camp last year eating pussy at Park City, Utah's most exclusive teen retreat. Campers, counselors, even a fucking park ranger. Twenty-six of 'em."

That was probably one of the most disgusting things I'd ever heard, but I was having too much fun to care.

"Not all women like the same things in bed," I croaked when his face was level with my pussy.

"True, but all women like *me* in bed." Jaime punctuated his cocky grin with a wink, reached for his jeans, pulled out something small, ripped it open—was it a condom?—and tossed it into his mouth.

"I know what you want, Ms. Greene. You want to come undone. I'll make you come. And with me, you'll never be done."

He dove in.

Jaime's cold, minty mouth met my hot-as-sin flesh. My hips bucked, chasing his touch as he sucked hard on my clit before breathing the fresh bite of mint into my pussy, driving his tongue deep inside. I tried to wriggle free, the intensity of my pleasure so profound I felt like I'd combust into burnt marshmallow under his body. But he pinned me down, placing a flexed muscular arm over my stomach, insisting I see this through with him.

It was tantalizing, the wave of weakness and lust that crashed over my body, head to toe. I gripped his long blond hair—so soft and shiny—in my small fist and jerked him closer into me, letting out a desperate mewl. A violent orgasm ripped through me, my muscles tightening in pleasure.

Jaime pinned me to the floor and crawled on top of me, devouring my mouth with his. "Taste it," he growled like a beast, disposing of his gum in my mouth. His tongue was everywhere—my teeth, the walls of my mouth, on my chin, even my cheeks. "It tastes like you, *Teach*."

I chewed on his gum. He was right. It tasted like my pussy.

Thrill sliced through my veins when Jaime raised his body and fumbled for his jeans. I prayed he was actually searching for a condom this time. I wanted to fuck him more than I wanted to hit the lottery jackpot, but I was still too flushed, my nerves too sensitive after my mind-blowing orgasm.

He rolled on a condom and guided his cock between my folds until his balls hit my entrance.

"Missionary, huh? What kind of camp was it? 'Book of Mormon' Youth?" I egged him on.

He laughed, hissing a moan, his eyelids half-mast as he started thrusting, finding the tempo that made us both groan. He was the perfect size. Big and thick, but not scarily so.

"Baby, I'm just breaking you in for the future." He bit my earlobe, his damp chest sticking to mine. "Once I'm done, you'll be begging for missionary."

I believed him.

The sex lasted nearly fifteen minutes, a lot longer than I thought an eighteen-year-old, even one who'd just gotten off from a blow job, would be able to last. He came again, and after flipping him so I was on top, watching his gorgeous, Channing-Tatum-meets-Ryan-Gosling face as I clutched his cock, so did I.

When we were done, I rolled back and lay on the floor beside him. He had one hand tucked under his head and the other on his stomach. Everything about him was so perfect. Even his blond armpit hair was sexy. And that made me sad because I knew guys like Jaime grew up to find women who were just as put-together as they were.

And that type of women? I wasn't among them.

He stared at my popcorn ceiling in contented silence.

"Say something." I cleared my throat, glaring. I had my head propped on one arm behind my head, my chest still dancing up and down. We were both naked, and it was starting to get chilly on my floor. But I wanted him to speak. Needed him to, badly.

"I've just fulfilled a fantasy." He slanted his head so we were looking at each other. "I think I'm allowed a moment to regroup."

"I was your fantasy?" How could that be? He was perfect, rich, and handsome. Young and sexily dangerous. And I was...*his boring teacher*.

"Ms. Greene..." he started, cupping my cheek.

I leaned into his hand before I realized what I was doing. By the time I felt his warmth against my skin, it was too late to pull away. "Please, call me Mel when we're alone."

His lips twitched, but he fought his smile. "Mel," he corrected. "You're it. You're so. Fucking. It. Smart, sassy, witty, and unimpressed with all the wealth and bullshit drama around you. You have no idea how hot you are. Which makes you even hotter. This is fucking happening, baby. *We're* happening."

I nuzzled into his neck, knowing that I was fueling a delusion that was just waiting to explode into calamity but not giving a damn anymore. His words moved something inside me. Not gently, either. They shook me to the core.

"Just until school ends," I whispered into his warm muscular shoulder, trying to convince myself more than him. He brushed his thumb along my back, sending goose bumps to my arms and scalp.

"This ends the last day of school," he agreed.

We had a deadline.

We had a plan.

And for a moment there, our warm bodies on that cold floor, with the haze of sex and bliss clouding our minds, I believed we were going to keep our careless promise. There was a little earthquake—a literal one—that moved some of the boxes as we made this agreement. I thought it was a coincidence. It wasn't. It was the devil in hell down below, rattling the earth with his laughter. Laughing at *me*.

At how wrong I was.

CHAPTER FIVE

The next week at school was paradise. My classes were perfectly behaved. I didn't struggle to hold the students' attention because my new fuck buddy, an intimidating senior jock who made people fall in line with his stare alone, spread the word not to mess with Ms. Greene. No one was ballsy enough to ask why. Everyone naturally assumed my fucked-up car and his freshly painted Range Rover and its retreat to the student parking lot were the answer to that question. To them, Jaime wanted to keep me happy since he bumped into my car.

No one suspected we were bumping a few other things in our free time.

I taught all my classes and then sat with Jaime in detention. I used the time to work, while he used the time to text. On the last day, I kept glancing at my watch, tapping my Sharpie against my desk. I couldn't concentrate on anything with him in the room. There were no words spoken between us. When his time was up, we both picked up our belongings and walked out of the classroom. I went to my car, he went to his, but by the time I got home, he was waiting inside my building, his hands shoved into the pockets of his jeans.

"Would you like to come in?" I sloped my chin down, biting a smile. He, too, grinned at his shoes. We were giddy. I liked that. I liked that, and I hated that I liked that.

"Nah…I can't. Football practice for the exhibition. The Kings are going to kill those pussies playing next year for the Saints if we don't pull their shit together. Trent's pissed. A scout's coming to watch the game and look at his leg. They might reconsider his scholarship now that his rehab's done. Seven okay?"

"Seven's perfect."

He nodded. We stood there, staring at one another, before he shrugged and closed the space between us with a long step. "Screw this shit, I missed those lips."

Then came a hard, desperate kiss where his lips assaulted mine for a good minute.

Breathlessly, I unlocked my door and disappeared behind it, pressing my back against it with a sigh.

That didn't feel forbidden or bad. Just a boy and a girl liking each other.

He came back at ten after seven, and for every extra second I waited, anxiety and disappointment built in my gut. I opened the door, frowning. "You said seven. I hate tardiness."

"That makes two of us." He roughly pushed me into my apartment, oozing charged energy. "So, about that missionary position…" The quarterback giant stepped into my orbit.

His cut lip and new purple welt were even more prominent with the pink flush on his cheeks after a grueling workout and his hair still wet from the shower. Between football and Defy, there were a lot of injuries among the HotHoles. A broken ankle had ended Trent Rexroth's football career in the fall. That happened in a locker-room accident. But it was almost like Jaime *wanted* to fuck up that pretty face of his. The Saints practiced and scrimmaged even in the winter, but he was a senior. He and his friends wouldn't be part of the team next year.

"Flip your dress up."

I did, without even blinking. *He* should've been the teacher with that kind of authority. Exposing my baby-blue panties, I awaited further instructions.

"Turn around and bend down to touch your toes, Little Ballerina."

I had no fucking clue how he knew I was a dancer, and asking him about it would force me to deal with the truth.

That he was a crazy stalker.

And that I absolutely liked that about him.

So I just did as I was told, my ass in the air, presumably level with his groin. The throbbing ache between my thighs demanded release. I felt his fingers clutching my pussy from behind. He ripped my underwear off in one go and served them to me from behind.

"Still wet despite my tardiness." He rubbed them against my lips. "Not that mad, I see."

Shit. The wet spot was obvious, even now, when my panties were merely a string.

"Can you please stop tearing my stuff apart? Not everyone's under Mommy and Daddy's financial wing." Goodie. The cat was out of the bag now.

He laughed, his abs bouncing against my ass, and then thrust three fingers at once into my entrance, making me stumble forward. He caught me by the shoulder before I fell headfirst.

"This week was an introduction," he warned. "Today... Today, baby, I'm marking you as mine."

It sounded crazy. And hot. *Crazy hot* actually. I was immediately game. If I was going to fuck up my career, better enjoy the ride, right?

"Let's see your ballerina's balance as I fuck every other guy you've ever had out of you."

With that, I heard his zipper rolling down as he freed his cock from his pants. His bulging head found the lips of my pussy, and I quivered in anticipation, lifting up slightly to gain more balance.

"Hands. On. Toes." He bit the crook of my neck from behind and drew circles with his tip around my pussy, making me mad with need. He was also fucking bare.

"Jaime, wrap up and get in before I die." My voice trembled.

"Shh," my stalker said, ripping the condom wrapper with his teeth, still teasing my entrance from behind. "You just keep holding on to those toes, ballerina. I'll take care of the rest."

He went in slowly. Painfully slowly. Every inch of him took a second to go in and then slid back even slower. My legs quivered. I cried out in pleasure and frustration. This was torture of the highest level, but I was enjoying every minute.

"Faster," I begged under my breath.

He wouldn't listen. The next time he went in, it was even slower.

"Jaime." I bit my lower lip. "Fuck me like you mean it."

"Then act like you fucking want it," he growled, grazing my shoulder with his teeth. "Don't stand me up. Don't give me shit when I'm ten minutes late, and don't try to act like you don't want this."

Inch. Another inch. Another inch. It was a beautiful torture. I wanted to push him away and run to my bedroom to finish my business with my plastic boyfriend, Victor the Vibrator. But I wasn't strong enough to resist him, no matter what he did to me.

"Fine," I grunted. "Fine, I promise. Now fuck me."

"That's better," he murmured, thrusting himself all the way in and making me stumble. He gathered my hair into a ponytail and jerked my head upward, pulling my body close to him so I wouldn't crash. Then he fucked me so hard, I felt numb from the waist down before he was done with me.

That's what happens when you come seven times in one night, I thought as I wobbled toward my bed. By the time he went home, around midnight, I couldn't feel my clit. Or my legs. Hell, not even my feet.

But he'd made his point crystal clear. And me? I wanted him to make it all over again.

CHAPTER SIX

Days filled with chain orgasms and hurried kisses in hidden corners and deserted classes ticked by. A blur of bliss and danger, uninhibited lust. The trick was not to think about it. Any part of it. Not about my future—as a teacher and an adult—or about what I was doing. And *definitely* not about whom I was doing it with.

No longer in detention, Jaime found other creative ways to stick around after school and spend time with me. Mostly, we fell into a routine where he visited me at my apartment after his football drills with next year's team.

Three weeks into our affair, when another Saturday rolled around, I was glad he had other plans. I finally mustered enough fake bravado to collect my thoughts and try to make sense of it all. The Saints were playing an exhibition scrimmage against the Kings of Sacramento, and technically, I could've supported my local team and watched Jaime play but decided against it. Putting some space between us and reminding myself that this was just casual fun was in my best interest. His too.

Besides, I'd made my own plans to meet my parents at an Italian joint in downtown Todos Santos this evening.

I did pass by the game on my way to Target that afternoon, taking the long way just so I could catch a glimpse of the game. I tried to convince myself it wasn't about Jaime. Football was a big deal at All Saints High. But no matter how you looked at it, when I stopped at the red light and glanced across the road to the field, I was looking for number four. For Jaime Followhill. For the HotHole who always made my stomach dip like I'd just gotten on a roller coaster. For the boy who felt too much like a man. And sadly, for the guy who filled the void in me with more than just his arousal and hot flesh.

I found him standing on the sidelines, chewing on his mouthguard with his hands on his waist while nodding at something his coach said to him. He looked distracted, and if I had the courage, I'd want to believe it was me he was thinking about.

His body looked cut and perfect, even through his jersey.

It was worrisome. I should have known right there. The way I smiled to myself, like I owned him in some way. Like this perfect creature, who was now yelling to his friends from the sideline, looking animated, looking *perfect*, was under my spell.

I kept on staring until someone behind me honked and I had to speed away, hitting the gas pedal too hard. Just then Jaime twisted his head in my direction, as if he heard it too.

It was ridiculous. There was no way he could know I was watching him. The place was crowded as hell, and the parents and students of All Saints High were very vocal about their local team.

But that didn't soothe the blush that crept up my neck and spread through my cheeks.

Nothing did. For the remainder of the day.

My parents and I had dinner, during which they asked about when my contract with the school would be renewed (probably never?), when I might find a man (ditto, but hey, I found a hot boy who knows how to go down on a woman thirteen different ways), and why my cheeks were so flushed (see the answer to question number two).

It wasn't bad, per se. The food was great. The company…well, made me feel like the biggest letdown humanity had to face.

That was the thing about being Celia and Stewart Greene's daughter. The minute my dream of becoming a ballerina died, so did their pride in me. I was never quite good at anything else, and I guess they knew that.

They made sure I remembered it too.

It wasn't an excuse for why I was like this—unmotivated and sarcastic—but it definitely didn't help.

The three of us walked back to our cars and passed by the central fountain in downtown Todos Santos across from Liberty Park, the home to a semi-famous lake and alarmingly aggressive swans. Teenagers were always roaming there on weekends, playing loud, shitty music. (Guess that was one reason why the swans were prone to attacking.) Not that night, though. That night, it was worryingly quiet.

My parents and I were about to round a corner and head to the parking lot when I saw Vicious's silver Mercedes-Benz McLaren slicing past us. I couldn't miss the 500K vehicle because *he was driving on the fucking sidewalk* opposite from us.

The kid was honking his horn at people like his daddy owned this town. Unfortunately, his daddy *did* own this town. Vicious's father was so rich, he hit lists like *Forbes* and shit every single year.

Maybe that's why his son feels entitled to hit everything and everyone else, I thought bitterly.

Pedestrians made way and let him pass through, accepting his behavior with bent heads. Everybody knew who he was and, more importantly, who he was going to be—a powerful, lawless cretin and the heir to a huge portion of the business interests in Todos Santos.

My parents and I skidded to a halt, our mouths shaping into stunned O's. We stared as my student parked on the grass, got out of his car, and strode toward a row of kids on their knees near the lake.

Well, fuck me sideways scissor-style. The older jocks were standing above the teenagers on the ground, yelling animatedly and pushing each other, on the verge of breaking into a huge fight.

I saw Jaime there. My eyes were drawn to him immediately, on instinct, before my mind even processed what I was staring at. He was leaning against the gazebo, exchanging hushed words with Dean Cole and Trent Rexroth, the former captain of the football team, who had his leg in a fresh-looking cast. Shit. He'd broken it again? What happened at the game today?

Jaime, Trent, and Dean kept to themselves, furrowed brows and brooding expressions on their faces. I recognized some of the kids on their knees, their heads down in surrender and their arms behind their backs. All failed, aspiring, or younger football players at All Saints High.

The Four HotHoles were up to something, I knew. And it didn't look like this was a voluntary game, like Defy.

It looked serious.

Vicious unrolled the sleeve of his white tee and took his soft Camel pack out of it, lighting a cigarette and squatting down, blowing smoke into the face of one of the kids who sat on their knees, awaiting the verdict. The guy gasped and choked on a cough but didn't dare move an inch. It looked like an ISIS execution line, and I knew I had to do something. The police chief was a kiss-ass friend of Baron Spencer Senior, Vicious's father, so calling the cops would have gotten me nowhere. But I couldn't just stand there and watch this happen. Right?

Right?

Vicious walked slowly along the row of suspects, his arms behind his back. "Listen up, fuckers. I know the Kings weren't the dickbags who greased the floor under Trent's locker. That's twice someone targeted him. The captain of your fucking team, you sorry-ass bitches."

He was so mad, he spat as he spoke. I watched the saliva flying out of his mouth, illuminated by the Victorian-style lamppost.

"Last time I figured this was an attack from a rival team to keep him from playing. Eliminate the competition." Vicious took another drag and spat near one of the meatheads on the end with a red varsity jacket and a baseball cap turned backward. "But Trent's graduating. No reason for another team to take him out now."

Some of the teens were crying as they looked down to the dewy grass, and some were moaning in pain. They weren't bleeding; they didn't look beaten up. Well, not physically, anyway. But Jesus, this kid was as fucking intimidating as Satan himself.

"I. Will. Find the fucker who greased the floor!" he shouted.

The jocks on their feet behind him roared, pumping their fists in the air. Jaime, Dean, and Trent were still deep in conversation. Luckily, they weren't feeding the troll.

"I *will* punish the motherfucker," Vicious screamed maniacally, thumbing his chest and looking around for support.

"Fuck yeah!" The jocks raised their hands, slurring into the night.

"And by the time we're done with him, he will be sorry his whore of a mother ever gave birth to him!"

"Yes! Yes! Yes!"

I had chills up and down my arms. I hated Baron Spencer. According to Coach Rowland, he wasn't even a very good football player, and I doubted he cared about the team that much. No. This whole nightmare of a night was orchestrated because he was a sadistic, violent fuck.

My mother yanked my white blouse and gritted, "I know some of these kids. They go to All Saints High. They are your students, Melody. You can't let this happen."

"The screaming one in the skinny jeans is Baron Spencer," I whispered back. "His daddy owns this town."

"Doesn't matter." My father shook his head, resting his hand on my shoulder. It felt so much heavier than it actually was, and I knew why. "This is about your integrity, Mel."

Oh, fuck. That old thing.

I knew I had to step in. I also knew I was about to be royally humiliated in front of my parents. Vicious feared me just a little less than he feared a Chihuahua in a pink tutu. Meaning, he wouldn't give a damn about me butting into this mess.

I crossed the road on shaky legs. Vicious's ruthless voice was still booming in my ears, getting louder with each step I took. My spine crackled, but I moved forward.

"Rat out the asshole who's responsible, or each and every one of you fuckers goes back home with a permanent mark." He pointed his cigarette at his potential victims. A few ballers behind them hauled them up to their feet by their hair, and the captives cried in agony.

Vicious stopped in front of a heavy guy who had tried to make it onto the football team last year and inched the burning ember of his cigarette toward the guy's forehead.

They are your students, Melody. You can't let this happen.

My dad was right.

"Baron!" I hurried, lightly jogging from the crosswalk into Liberty Park. He was not going to hurt the kid. Not on my shift.

Vicious didn't even have the courtesy to turn around and check to see who called him. "Take all suspects to the gazebo behind the parking lot for interrogation." His voice was clipped and low.

That gazebo was isolated, a deserted, scary place where no one set foot at night. Bastard had a touch. No surprises there.

"Baron Spencer!" I raised my voice, only a few feet away from him now. Some of the students cleared out of the way for me, but the majority just snickered as I raced toward the teenager from hell. They were more scared of him than they were of me. I couldn't blame them. "Stop this immediately! Let these boys go!"

When I reached him, he finally turned around, his face painted with boredom and pity.

When I didn't back down, his expression darkened. Vicious might not be as beautiful as Jaime, Trent, and Dean, but he somehow had the most memorable face. He looked like a guy whose shit list you didn't want to be on. I swallowed hard, hating myself for feeling intimidated by him.

"I'm sorry, remind me who the fuck you are?"

Of course he knew who I was. I taught him Lit every day, which was what made everyone around us laugh, pointing their beer bottles and Solo cups at me. Even his fucking captives chuckled.

I'm doing this for you, assholes.

Heat spread up my neck, and my hand tightened around my anchor necklace, as it did every time anger washed over me. I did everything in my power not to look at Jaime because I was afraid to see what was written on his face. Was he laughing at me like all the rest?

"Do it now, or I'm calling the police." My voice barely shook.

Vicious took a step forward, his face so close to mine I saw the crazy dancing in his irises. His eyes, black like an abyss, threatened to pull me to the dark side. I dug my heels deeper into the grass and balled my hands into fists. My body hummed with adrenaline. This was happening. I was standing up to him.

"I fucking dare you, sweetheart. Go ahead, test me. Actually, I'd love for you to do that. It'll get you kicked out of your job, and I won't have to see your sour-ass face every day."

That was it. I was so pissed that I wasn't above punching his smug face. I stepped back, fishing out my cell phone from my bag. So what if they fired me? They weren't going to renew my contract anyway.

A warm, familiar hand stopped me before my fingers dialed 911. "Apologize," Jaime's voice commanded.

But the order wasn't aimed at me.

Vicious tipped his head back and snorted, his straight teeth on full display. "Tanked again, Followhill? Jesus. It's not even midnight yet."

"You better do it," Jaime singsonged, ignoring the jab, stepping into his BFF's face. Nose to nose now, their gazes dripped defiance. "Unless you want out of the HotHoles."

I was baffled, to say the least. Two bullets in less than a month this guy had taken for me. Vicious and Jaime were locked in a staredown. Vicious glowered under his devilish brows, begging Jaime to let it go—every muscle in his face quivering in anger—but Jaime wouldn't back down. Finally, after a whole minute at least, it came. Sweet and orgasm-worthy.

"My bad, Greene." Vicious's words were sharp and insincere as his shoulder brushed past Jaime's. He looked like it physically pained him to say them.

As much as his indifferent act sprinkled fear-dust on everyone's heads at school, he was still mortal. Capable of feeling the loss of his best friend. And Vicious knew the truth. People didn't like him, not really. They loved Jaime, Dean, and Trent. The handsome, funny, wholesome jocks he hung out with.

He needed them.

But something told me that they needed him too.

"Apology accepted. Now, break this thing up immediately." I smoothed my blouse, arching one eyebrow and slanting my head to his captives.

"No," Jaime said firmly, turning around to face me.

I allowed myself to drown in his face, even if for only a second. We were back to acting like a teacher and a student, playing our roles, but I knew those lips, which he now rolled inward, probably to suppress words he should never say to his educator. Knew how they tasted and what they were capable of doing under my thin, worn blanket.

"Sorry, Ms. Greene, but you'll have to sit this one out. This is a team matter. I give you my word, it won't rub off on you. Someone screwed Trent over." He shook his head, his lips pinching in annoyance. "We need answers."

"Mr. Followhill—"

"No," he said, cutting me off. "You lose." The last sentence came out soft, and what came after was even softer. "Next time I catch you stalking me from across the road," he whispered into my ear, close enough for it to look suspicious but not enough for people to talk about it afterward, "you better come say hi. Better yet, you better show me how much you miss me with your lips instead of stripping me with your eyes."

There wasn't anything I could do about Vicious and his dangerous tricks, and I knew it. The HotHoles always took care of their own. Trent was injured again, and someone had to pay. I had very little power over the students of All Saints, but I very much doubted anyone else, including Principal Followhill herself, would be able to stop them from seeking retaliation.

Slowly, without breaking eye contact with him, I backed down, until I finally turned around and walked back to my parents, who were still waiting on the other side of the road.

"Well?" My mother elbowed me, her eyes shimmering with the same healthy curiosity she had about almost every subject matter in the world.

"I took care of it." I avoided her gaze, pretending to look for something in my bag. Maybe it was my dignity I was looking for. Either way, Vicious had won.

And Jaime had helped him.

But not at my expense. And that was something.

That was a lot.

CHAPTER SEVEN

I spent the weekend wondering what happened to the poor bastards the Four HotHoles had interrogated at Liberty Park and whether my face-off with Jaime and Vicious would change the pact between my fuck buddy and me. My fingers tingled to text him and ask all those things, but I knew it was risky.

Was I angry at him? Was the incident a wake-up call, reminding me that we were so different? That he was still a teenager, taking tentative steps toward becoming a man? These were exactly the kinds of questions I didn't want to deal with. No. I was biding my days, clinging to the weekend in the hope distance and time would wash away the fog of lust between us, making room for logic and rationality.

Monday was the best day of my entire career. Everything ran smoothly, and when I reached the last class with Jaime and his friends, they all behaved.

Everyone…other than Jaime.

He was messing with his phone as usual. Since he wasn't looking at me, I let it slide. I wanted to teach this class without feeling my nipples puckering under his scorching gaze.

My phone on my desk buzzed. I resisted the urge to check it, focusing on Millie, who was standing up, reading a poem she'd written. She was good. A creative spirit, with an artistic flair that poured through every cell in her body. Did she want to write? Maybe paint? Her textbooks and hands were always decorated with doodles, her nose always buried in a book. With the right guidance and nurturing, she could do great things.

I knew without a shadow of a doubt that I wasn't the person to bring them out of her. I lacked motivation, compassion, and authority, the three qualities that made a great teacher.

As I stared at her, I realized that even Vicious was quiet when she spoke. She had the kind of quirky charm a girl couldn't fake. Everyone's eyes were on her, which allowed me to sneak a peek at my phone. In the words of Julia Roberts in *Pretty Woman*: Big mistake. Big. Huge.

> Jaime: I missed you this weekend. Thought your ungrateful ass would text me a thank you for saving you from the wrath of Vicious. Alas, I was wrong.

Wow. Did he have any idea how much trouble he could get us into if someone saw this text? Students and teachers had each other's numbers for professional purposes only. I ignored him and continued nodding at Millie, smiling tightly. *Bzzz*, another text came.

> Jaime: It's cute how you pretend to listen to Millie when I know your just waiting for the clock to hit 3 so I can bend you over that desk and fuck you so hard the windows will rattle.

Of course, I didn't grace that message with an actual answer. Although I was itching to correct "your" with "you're." The Lit teacher in me hated when people misspelled shit. Apparently, even during sexting.

My cheeks darkened, and I played with my anchor necklace,

brushing it against my lower lip. I coughed, clearing my throat, and said, "Louder, Millie."

She looked around, anxious as I was, and reluctantly raised her voice with the next line. Her poem was pretty fascinating, actually. About life and death and the way the cherry blossom tree symbolizes both. Everybody was quiet and alert. Dean Cole had his elbows on his desk, leaning forward, absorbing her words like they were oxygen. And Vicious? He looked at her like she was his.

But there was no point. The only thing my ears were tuned into was what I secretly hoped to hear—the sound of my phone vibrating against the table as another message came through.

> Jaime: Your nipples are so tight I could cut fucking diamonds with them, baby. It's a turn-on when everyone can see what I do to you. In half an hour, I'm going to shove my hand into your pencil skirt and my fingers into that pussy. Digging into Ms. G's G-spot and hitting it again and again until you pass out from your orgasms.

I circled the table and leaned back against it facing the class, hoping they couldn't see the blush that was a daily challenge since the start of our affair. Jesus! *Affair?* That was a bit much. It wasn't an affair. I was fucking my student, and my future, all at the same time. Nonetheless, I couldn't stop. I scanned the classroom full of students, and his face was the only one that stood out in the sea of bland teenagers. I barely registered the other faces, lost in the fog of lust.

Another vibration. This time I waited a few seconds before I glanced his way and found him smirking at his phone. Asshole.

> Jaime: Then I'll take my hand out, let you lick my fingers one by one, suck on them hard, and beg for me to take you. But I won't. You'll have to go down on me first, and I'll

> make you choke on my cock until you can't breathe. How would you like that, Mel?

I was sweating. Sucking in short breaths. Millie finished reading her poem. She was still standing, expecting my feedback. All eyes were on me. She'd done a wonderful job from what I could decipher in my lust-induced haze, but the words wouldn't leave my mouth. I was truly afraid that I'd blurt out something about Jaime and his dick. It really was too fucking beautiful not to be celebrated by our fine nation.

"Millie," I started, clearing my throat when I realized my voice cracked. I heard Jaime softly chuckle in the back of the room. I was going to kill him when the class was dismissed. Her big, blue Bambi eyes followed my every movement as I spoke. "I thought it was brilliant. Your poem had a rhythm like heartbeats. It was…enchanting," I managed, my smile almost apologetic.

It wasn't the right thing to say. I needed to open this up for discussion, but I was having a hard time stringing together a coherent sentence while my panties were this wet. Damn Jaime and his texts.

Straightening my spine, I clapped my hands one time. "Let's hear your thoughts about Miss LeBlanc's poem. Anyone?"

Bzzz. Another vibration erupted. A handful of people raised their hands, and I chose Shelly, the girl who I knew wouldn't shut up, and therefore allowed myself time to read my incoming text.

> Jaime: So lost. So confused. So fucking mine. Owning someone has never felt this good.

His words hit me hard.

Was I really his? It didn't feel like it. Like it was real. Maybe for him, it was. But for me? I was too scared of the consequences of truly having him to even consider it an option.

Lost. Confused. I felt all those things. Not just in that moment but in general. Where was I going after this? I was a terrible teacher, and my students deserved better. What was more, I cared enough about them to acknowledge the fact that I needed to make room for someone more passionate. More caring. Someone who would take the Millies of the world and turn them into artists and not keep them here, in the gray classroom, reading poems they could barely understand.

After Shelly babbled something for the sake of talking and another student asked Millie a couple of questions, Vicious, who had his long legs crossed over the table, his boots nearly touching someone's back, held up his hand. My breath hitched. I didn't want him to shatter Millie's confidence. Actually, I wanted to talk to her about enrolling in a creative writing class I knew about across town. I liked to believe I saw some of me in Emilia. She was delicate, artistic, and unfazed by the privileged environment she wasn't a part of. I had a weird urge to protect her from Vicious, but no one else was lifting their hands.

I wanted to strangle the sulky bully as I ground out a weak permission for him to speak. "Yes, Baron?"

Vicious's hooded eyes were on Millie as he played with one of his rusty metal rings—a part of his iconic serial-killer attire. He bared his teeth, expecting her to shrink back into her chair like the rest of them, but Millie was still standing, eyeballing him like he was a punching bag she was about to swing her fist into.

I fucking like this girl.

"I thought it was spectacularly awful," he said, tugging at his full lower lip.

She raised one lone eyebrow, a smile on her pretty, round face.

"That's enough from you, Baron," I started, but Millie raised her hand.

"Please, Ms. Greene. Let him finish. What was so 'spectacularly awful' about my poem?" she asked him, and she sounded genuinely interested.

I cringed. Why was she doing this to herself?

Vicious slumped back in his chair, examining his rings. "Too wordy. Too many analogies. Some of them were corny. Ones we've heard a thousand times before. You've got talent, I'll give you that. Still…" He shrugged. "Your writing's sloppy. Stick to painting."

"And what would you know about writing?" I snapped. It was my turn to ask. It wasn't like me to lose my temper during class, but Vicious was literally being vicious. The fact that he'd won on Saturday night at the park didn't help either.

I think Jaime knew better than to continue sexting me because he tucked his phone into his jeans pocket and frowned at Vicious, his expression screaming *Shut the fuck up, man.*

"I know quite a fucking bit, actually," Vicious chirped, his face lighting up. Usually, his voice was like a straight line on a heart monitor, uncaring and flat. "Ass-kissing's never helped an author or a poet grow and develop. Constructive criticism does. Maybe you're in the wrong profession, Greene."

Fuck this shit. I was going to throw him into detention until he was seventy. I didn't even care that Jaime had just invited me to another sex fest after school and that all I could think about was his angry, swollen cock. I didn't want Vicious talking to me like this and, more importantly, to Millie. The girl didn't deserve it.

"Pack your stuff, Baron. You're coming with me to see Principal Followhill after class. I hope you don't have any plans for the upcoming month because you're going to spend it with your mediocre educator. In detention. Where you can explain to me all about good poetry and bad life choices. Like talking back to your teacher." I let loose a sugary smile and cracked open my notebook with the name list, looking for the next poor soul who had to share a poem with the class.

Trent groaned from his place on the other side of Vicious. "Good going, cunt. You just had to talk shit, didn't you? We've got team business to handle. Did you forget?"

"Language, Rexroth. Or you're up next."

I got ballsy. I had a back. It was Jaime. Who, by the way, looked just about ready to explode, staring down Vicious like he had just slaughtered a basket full of kittens. There was fire in his eyes, and it scorched everything it landed on. The bell rang, filling the class with laughter and noise, and people shoved their stuff into their backpacks.

"Mr. Linden, you'll be reading your poem next time. Class, I want you to read *The Rules of Poetry* by Michaela Steinberg and know it by heart for next class. There'll be a quiz," I barked into the chaos of teenage chatter.

Students poured into the hallway, but Jaime stayed put in his chair. His clenched jaw suggested someone in the room was about to get killed. Vicious was the only one still there other than us, and he took his time, stuffing his bag deliberately slowly with a grin so big, you'd think I was about to escort him to an exotic vacation on an island populated by strippers and international arms dealers.

I dropped Vicious at Principal Followhill's office and got back to class. I think she was both impressed and horrified with me calling Vicious on his bullshit. I had no idea how she was going to deal with him, but I didn't care either. I'd done my part.

The minute I walked back into my classroom, I heaved a sigh. "What did you do to those kids the other night?"

Jaime sprawled back in his chair. He was wearing navy Dickies, high-top sneakers, and a purple muscle shirt that showed off his corny tattoo of a stupid-ass quote he had inked on his ribs. I'd never bothered reading it but wouldn't be surprised if it was something from *SpongeBob SquarePants*.

Who cares? He was my own personal calorie-free dessert.

At least, that's what I tried to reduce him to in my mind.

Most of the time it worked.

But the more we spent time together, the more I needed to feed myself this lie.

"Come here." He crooked his index finger at me.

"Excuse me? I'm the teacher," I teased, happy to have him alone.

"And I'm the pissed-off guy who needs to put you in your place every now and again. Here." He patted his desktop and plopped back in this chair. I glanced at the closed door and back at him.

"Vicious could come back," I argued.

"Vicious would keep his mouth shut even if he walked in on me fucking Mr. Pattinson while the PTA president licks my asshole. I can do anything with anyone as long as it's not Millie. We're goddamned nearly blood brothers."

Millie, huh? Maybe the bastard did have a beating heart after all.

I took slow steps to Jaime and sat at the edge of his desk. He grabbed me by the waist and pulled me into his groin so that I straddled him, my legs curling around his waist.

"What did you do to them?" I whispered again, my hands buried in his golden hair as my arms circled his neck. Despite everything, I cared about those kids.

"Baby..." He brushed his knuckles against my lips, his eyes focused solely on them.

"Well?" I deliberately widened my eyes, questioning him.

He laughed like he thought my expression was cute. "Nothing yet. But we got a name. Toby Rowland."

"And?" Rowland was a junior, another douche who I taught. He was also Coach Rowland's son.

Jaime shrugged. "Dude's always hiding behind his daddy in practice. It'll be hard to pin him down, but neither one's getting away with what they did to Trent. Fuckers killed his ticket out."

Trent Rexroth, All Saints' stand-out football star, had slipped in the locker room before a big game this fall, breaking his ankle and ending his path to college and pro-football glory.

I opened my mouth, intending to convince Jaime to give up the retaliation, but he grabbed me by my ass and pulled me into his aching erection, sucking hard on one of my breasts through the fabric of my blouse and finishing on a teasing bite.

"Shit..." I muttered.

"How was your weekend?" He placed his lips on my neck and licked his way to my cleavage. I shivered into his body. "Did you miss me?"

"It was good." My hands ghosted over his broad chest greedily. "And no," I lied. "I thought we agreed this was just harmless fun."

"It is." He tipped his head back, staring at me seriously. "And it's fun being with you."

"I bet it's just as fun being with high school girls." My mouth went dry when I said it.

It was stupid and insecure, but it felt good to finally say what I'd been thinking about for weeks. Where Jaime went, girls followed. Bronze-skinned, shiny-haired cheerleaders with wide smiles and legs for miles. They caught up with his long steps in the hallways, leaned against his SUV after school, and laughed at everything he said...even when he didn't make jokes.

Jaime smirked, his right hand tracing my inner thigh, traveling upward and disappearing under my pencil skirt, which now rode all the way up, bunching over my stomach. "I beg to differ. High school girls are high maintenance. They're full of drama. They talk about fucking hair straighteners and parties for hours. The hot ones make you go to Jennifer Lopez movies. No. There's nothing fun about high school girls. You, on the other hand..."

His fingers found my soaking undies, and as usual, he cocked his head, smirking, letting me know that he was onto me. My body sang a tune only Jaime knew the words to, and my heart drummed so fast and loudly that I felt the pulse in my toes. Doing this was almost like begging to get caught.

A part of me was desperate to be seen.

"You talk back," he said. "You're cold and stubborn. Sad and snarky. I like your brand of weird. The whole package." He drew an imaginary circle with his finger around my face, leaning into me. "But most of all..." he breathed, placing a gentle kiss on the corner of my lips. "I like the chase. You make me sweat somewhere besides a football field. Turns out…that's the exercise I've been looking for."

Just as he said that, the door flung open, and Vicious pushed his way inside. Lucky for me, he was staring down at a piece of paper he held in one hand and the ripped-open envelope he had in the other. "Can't believe she says shit like this," he muttered.

That allowed me a minute to jump off Jaime's boner and rearrange my skirt, leaning back down and pretending to flip through one of the books he had on his table. "Here's the paragraph you were looking for." I cleared my throat and straightened.

Vicious finally looked up, but it wasn't at me. "Trent just texted me. Coach called a team meeting. Toby's been named as captain for next year."

"Whatever." Jaime's jaw twitched. The atmosphere in the room changed. No words were spoken, but plans were being made, right in front of my eyes.

Toby Rowland was in so much trouble, it physically hurt me to think what they'd do to him once they got him alone.

"Whatever sounds right," Vicious echoed, his voice flat. "Thanks a fucking ton for detention, Ms. G. Hope you know what *you're* doing." He shook his head with a sadistic smile. *A threat.*

"Vicious," Jaime gnashed. *A warning.*

Vicious strode to his chair and flopped down, waving his hand. "She's lucky you have a soft spot for her. Otherwise, I'd have reduced her to ashes at Liberty Park."

A hard spot, baby, I thought as I made my way back to my desk. *And you have no idea.*

CHAPTER EIGHT

That day changed everything because that day Jaime and I started texting. It made it so much easier to plan things. More hot dates at my partially packed apartment. More fucking in insane positions. More stealing kisses at school, getting off on the thrill of being caught.

At the end of the week, Jaime sent me a picture of himself flexing his guns in front of the mirror in their locker room. I almost didn't open the text message, fearing I'd see something horrific like someone else's junk, but then I remembered it was Jaime I was talking about. He was oddly responsible for someone his age and with his status. Out of the four of them, he was the quietest. The one with the working moral compass. If Vicious was the evil one and Dean was the stoner one and Trent was the lost, beautiful soul searching for its mate, Jaime was the cement that glued them together. He was the guy you could always count on. And I was starting to count on him too.

> Jaime: It's scientifically proven. You're riding the best stud in town. These guns could kill.
> Me: Jaime, you're an eighteen-year-old. Perspective, please.
> Jaime: This from someone who goes to sleep with my dick clutched in her hand. Pizza tonight?

Me: That happened once. By accident.
Me: And yes. But no onions.

I leaned back against a box filled with books and giggled, hugging my cell phone like an idiot. *A disaster*, I thought to myself. *What the fuck are you doing? Dating him now?*

Jaime: No onion? No condom then. I'm clean. Your on the pill.
Me: YOU'RE. YOU-apostrophe-RE.
Me: And deal.
Jaime: Nice doing business with you. x

Dear God, I needed to stop this. Stop this before I was going to get hurt. Already the way my heart squeezed every time I noticed him for the first time in class felt a little too hard. The pleasure of sleeping with him freckled with a dash of pain. He still filled me. Filled me with joy and laughter and amazing sex. But now he was sucking from me too.

Emotions, thoughts, logic.

That evening, Jaime got to my apartment and tackled me to the sofa, peppering my whole face with kisses. I laughed, throwing my fists at his sculpted abs. We rolled around, half making out, half fighting and laughing, before we both stopped to take a breath, examining each other's faces for the first time since he walked in. He was atop me, his eyes roaming my face, searching for answers to questions we were both too scared to ask aloud.

"How did you know I'm on the pill?" The silence rang so loud, I felt the urge to break it.

"Saw them on your bathroom counter. Duh."

"Well, let's get nekkid and do some dirty stuff then. I know it's Friday, and you probably want to hang out with your friends later." I grabbed the hem of my shirt and started getting undressed.

He stopped me, his palm on my hand. "Take it easy, missy. No rush. Let's watch a crappy nineties movie together while we wait for the pizza. I'm going to sleep here tonight."

I frowned. Vicious threw balls-out parties every weekend, and the HotHoles were always in full attendance. It was mandatory or some shit. I happened to know this because, at All Saints, getting invited to these things meant that you were one of the cool kids. I also happened to know there was a party tonight because yesterday the hallways were filled with hushed convos about which guys were going to be challenged to a fight in Defy and which girls were going to get inside Vicious's private media room where the HotHoles hung out.

"What about Vicious's party?" I asked. The last few weeks, the mere idea of having Jaime sitting there in the secluded room with young, willing women offering themselves to him made me lose my mind. I hated those parties and despised Vicious even more for throwing them.

"I'm planning an even bigger party between your legs tonight." He waggled his brows at me.

I rolled my eyes but couldn't help but smile. "I think I like you," I muttered, pressing my face to his muscled torso in a hug. I felt his heartbeat under my ear.

"I think I like you back."

My heart nearly exploded, and I found myself clutching the anchor on my necklace for dear life, knowing that this time, it couldn't save me from falling deeper into whatever the hell it was we were creating.

Actually, I knew exactly what it was.

Magic.

It's been psychologically proven—people lie to themselves in order to protect them from the things they do. From what they think and feel. I was in denial when it came to Jaime Followhill. In my head, I downplayed the whole thing. Reduced it to nothing but some fun. But the truth was, I was never so intrigued by a man.

Defy.

That's what I wondered about most. Why did he fight? He didn't look like the type who needed a violent outlet to unwind. Vicious, sure. But Jaime? No. He seemed like a laid-back guy.

So after the movie and pizza (no onions—he remembered), I asked him.

I prepped him beforehand. Knew that Jaime was not going to open up about things that had to do with his friends so easily. I got down on my knees and took him—all of him—deep in my mouth, covering most of his shaft, my fist doing the rest. He groaned and yanked my head back and forth, my hair in his fist.

"I'm going to come in your mouth," he announced. He stood, one foot lazily propped back against my fridge, in all his naked six-foot-three-inch glory.

I moaned into his hot flesh, lolling my head from side to side. I liked it. To feel admired and desired by a younger man. He was driving me crazy…but I was driving him wild.

My moan encouraged him, and he emptied himself inside my mouth. The warm, salty liquid shot straight into my throat, and I swallowed it instantly, desperate for every drop of him.

After his release, he glided down the front of my fridge, sinking into a sit-down position, his knees bent, as he slowly let go of my hair. We both grinned, the kind of private smile only we knew how to decode. I doubted I could give that smile to someone else even if I'd tried.

"What's up?" He grabbed my hand, offhand and confident, and jerked me to sit between his legs. I did, purring into his mouth as we shared a slow, seductive kiss. "Look at my Little Ballerina, learning how to give head like it's the eighties."

"What happened in the eighties?" I asked, feeling ridiculously stupid. You'd think I'd know more about the decade than he did. He shrugged.

"Nothing. People liked giving head, I guess."

I shook my head on a laugh. He was so ridiculous sometimes, but that's exactly what made it so easy to unwind with this guy. I flattened my palm against his chest. "I need to ask you something."

"Uh-oh. Am I in trouble, Ms. Greene? Have I been a bad boy? Do I need a spanking?" He wiggled his brows and laughed.

God, he was sexy. And God, it was creepy.

I shook my head, closing my eyes so I wouldn't see his reaction to my blush. "Tell me about Defy," I said.

None of the teachers knew much about Defy, other than the injuries we spotted on Monday mornings. Students got into bloody fights at Vicious's parties, and there was nothing we could do about it.

Jaime frowned. "What do you want to know?"

"I want to know everything." I cleared my throat. "Where, why, how, and most of all...why are *you* doing it?"

His eyes darkened, and he pulled his blond hair into a high bun. I watched him silently, swallowing hard while he examined me under his lashes. I was stepping deeper into a territory that wasn't mine. We both were. This was intimate and secretive, two lines we promised we wouldn't cross outside the bedroom.

Are we breaking the rules?

It occurred to me that I was the first one to step over the line that I had been so quick to paint in our relationship. But it also occurred to me that there wasn't one line. It was more like an abstract painting full of lines, circles, and triangles. It was a mess, and trying to maneuver your moves in this thing between us was hopeless.

"This doesn't leave this room," Jaime warned, dipping his chin down, his nose touching mine.

"Of course," I said as if that was obvious. We were still on the floor, my legs knotted with his. I wanted to toss aside my teacher hat at that moment. To burn it to ashes, more like. "This is between you and me. I'm just curious."

"Well..." He pulled me deeper between his legs, opening them wider to accommodate me. His eyes homed on an invisible spot on the wall. This was hard for him. Giving up a secret that wasn't wholly his. "Where? At Vicious's place. Every weekend. Guys know better than to come to his parties if they don't feel like fighting. And still… everyone does. Let's admit it. This town is fucking boring. We're all rich, privileged, and desperate to fill the void."

"What void?"

"*That* void. Whether it's sex or pressure or money. We fight on the tennis court. His father and stepmother never use it, so they never notice the bloodstains, which their handyman takes care of during the week."

That void was familiar. I didn't want to tell him that I had it too. The hole in my soul. And that I too found a way to fill it. *With him*.

Suddenly, he snaked one hand behind my back and lowered me along with him to the floor, doing it slowly so I wouldn't hit my head.

A wicked grin curved his lips. "Why? Because it's fun. Because men have become so fucking emasculated by society, we sometimes feel like having our balls back. Why do dudes love *Fight Club* so much? It's because behind every A&F boxers–wearing guy who smells like citrus aftershave and knows who Versace is and takes you out on a date to an Italian dinner and a foreign film, there's a savage who just wants to grab you by the hair and drag you to his cave."

His other hand moved between us, sliding down my belly, finding my soaking panties. I was wearing a knee-length dress, but it was flipped up, and Jaime didn't look like he was bothered by it too much. He rubbed my entrance through my panties furiously.

"How? Someone steps out to the pool with his sleeves rolled up. That's an invitation to fight. You can't challenge a specific guy. The other guy has to volunteer. Chicks dig it, even when you lose, so guys do it because pussy is nice, even when you have a bleeding lip. We use our fists. Kicks. Basic MMA shit. But we fight clean mostly. And if things get out of hand, which they usually don't unless Vicious is involved…" He bit my lip, tugging my underwear down roughly and pushing in two fingers. "Then one of the HotHoles breaks it off before shit goes to the ER."

I whimpered, tightening around him. He was rougher than usual, and I doubted it was a coincidence. He wanted to show me that he was a man, not a kid.

And he succeeded. In and out, in and out, he fingered me while I writhed on my kitchen floor underneath him.

So that was it. That was Defy. I had more questions I couldn't exactly articulate at that moment, but one thing was clear—Jaime wasn't afraid of getting hurt. Not physically, anyway.

But what about emotionally?

And what about me? Would I be able to take the hit when things between us went south?

All I knew was that *my* south liked him. So much so that I came on his fingers before he even had the chance to touch my clit.

"You feel pretty manly to me," I breathed out, all jelly-legged with half-mast eyes.

"And you feel like a woman worthy of a fight, Ms. Greene."

CHAPTER NINE

Six heavenly weeks ticked by before Jaime claimed not only my body but my heart. Unsurprisingly, it was the day I got my period (aka the time when my hormones were wreaking havoc with my body). It was also the day that I moved.

I'd found a place in a small beach town on the outskirts of Todos Santos, and I'd arranged for a substitute teacher to cover my classes that day. That didn't stop Principal Followhill from grunting that I had some nerve taking time off when my position was on the line and my classes were behind schedule on the required syllabus. She was back to her old ways now that she'd paid me off for Jaime's car accident.

Since I didn't want to spend much money on movers, I'd decided to do some of the heavy lifting myself. I spent my morning running from my old apartment to the new one, moving boxes up and down the stairs. I was sweaty and smelly, with my messy ponytail, PINK black sweatpants, and a yellow tank top that showed off my toned midriff. If there was a potential husband waiting for me in the dingy complex I was moving into, he was going to think that I was hot. And possibly homeless.

On my third run back to my old apartment, I saw Jaime waiting at my door. He was wearing a white sleeveless tank and khaki shorts. The kind that hugged his ass as if to say *You better believe I'm touching this all day, bitch.*

My heart fluttered in my chest, which made my soul lurch in pain. *Just until school ends, remember?*

"You're supposed to be at school." I slipped past him, marching into my apartment. Yes, I was cold to him because of his mother's behavior yesterday, and no, it was not fair, but I couldn't help it. I was on my period. He needed to cut me some slack here. Besides—he really was skipping school. I still cared about his education. A lot, actually.

"I thought you were sick." He hurried into my apartment before the door shut behind me, his hands tucked in his pockets. "You didn't even mention you were moving today when we saw each other yesterday."

"You saw the boxes."

"Yeah. They have been sitting around since the first time I was here. You never put anything in them. I thought you were moving in, not out. What kind of bullshit is this?"

"My landlord wants the place for himself, so I got a new one." I shrugged and refused to explain more because this thing with him was supposed to be fun. He didn't need to know my schedule, even though most days, we both knew exactly where the other person was. There was pain in his voice. I not only heard it, I felt it. Like a punch to my stomach. This was wrong. He needed to know we owed each other nothing.

With a sigh, Jaime dropped the subject. "Whatever. Let's hang out."

"You can't skip classes, Jaime. You'll fail. Even if you've already been accepted to college, it looks bad." I started gathering my clothes by their hangers. I was going to carry some more boxes to my car but didn't want him to see me melting into a sweaty pile of PMS rage.

"In other words, you don't wanna hang out with me?" He followed me, knocking over a stack of boxes with his huge body in the process.

"No. I don't have time to fuck around today." I kept walking back and forth, stuffing my hanging clothes into a pair of laundry baskets, hoping he'd get the hint.

Damn him. It was his fault I wasn't packed already in the first place.

Jaime grabbed my stiff shoulder, studying me. "You think that's why I came here? To fuck you?"

His raw gaze alone stripped off a layer of my shitty attitude, but I still needed him to leave. This had to stop. *We* had to stop.

Then why did I run out of breath every time I thought about my life without him?

I shrugged again. "No? Okay, no then. Still, I'm moving, as you can see, and I've got my hands full." I lifted up the heap of clothes in my hands for emphasis. "See you tomorrow."

"I'll help," Jaime announced, grabbing the biggest, heaviest box and throwing it up on one of his shoulders.

I wanted to protest, but, shit, that box was like a hundred pounds, easy. I was avoiding the thing like it was that drunk aunt at a wedding reception no one wanted to talk to. Scanning the prominent veins in his arms popping out, I knew I should decline his help. He should be in school. It could even raise suspicion, he and I not showing up on the same day. I remembered Vicious's veiled threat.

But…I really needed the help.

Also, I was helpless when it came to him.

"Right," I said after a pause. "I'll show you where I'm parked."

He tutted with a growl, reminding me who the boss around here was. "Makes more sense to use the Range Rover. More space. We can finish sooner. It'll leave us more time for ourselves."

I exhaled, climbing down the stairs. "Just to give you a heads-up—I'm on my period."

"You don't say. You hid it so well." He threw the box into the back of his SUV like it was featherlight. "Like I said, I'm here to hang out." He speared me with his scowl.

I guessed we were hanging out.

We finished moving (and unpacking) everything by seven that night, and Jaime made a quick run to the nearest Wendy's. He asked if he should pick up beer too, and after I said sure, I nearly bit off my tongue, realizing what I'd done. It was easy to forget he wasn't my age. Funny thing was, he *did* bring beer. When I asked him if he had a fake ID, he chuckled and mussed my hair like I was an adorable kid, explaining that the HotHoles never got carded in Todos Santos. I shook my head and cracked open my beer.

Jaime hooked up my TV and dragged the coffee table to the middle of the room. We watched a shitty game show from the eighties. His feet were on the table, while I curled up on the sofa. We looked like a couple. What's more—we acted like one.

It felt natural. And scary. For a moment, just a brief, crazy, I-obviously-need-help moment, I imagined that we were moving into this apartment together, he and I.

"How did we get to this point? Holy shit, I'm fucking my student," I mumbled out of nowhere, my eyes still glued to the TV.

"Well..." Jaime stretched, downing what was left of his beer in one swig and slamming it against the table. "I blackmailed you into it. That's how."

His sarcasm held a lie I wanted to believe. We both knew he hadn't forced me. I fucked him by choice. I put the beer to my lips, stalling.

"Okay." He licked his lips and turned off the TV, rubbing his thighs. "Let's play truth or dare."

I was tempted to remind him I wasn't twelve but didn't want to be even more of a grouch. So I batted my eyelashes innocently. "Are you going to milk my secrets out of me?"

"Might as well since you aren't going to milk the jizz out of me tonight." He got up from the couch, disappeared into my tiny new kitchen, and returned with a bottle of Jose Cuervo. Holding the bottle of tequila by its neck, he slouched back down beside me. Now we were both sitting cross-legged on the sofa, facing each other.

A fan hummed above us, and if we were really silent—which we were—we could hear the sound of the waves crashing against the shore, their rhythm systematic, like a sweet lullaby.

"This conversation needs booze, so a shot for every time we choose a truth over a dare." Jaime rested the bottle between us, his voice clipped. He was looking at me funny.

Jaime was normally impossible to read. A hot, carefree jock with darkness behind his light eyes, but the expression he wore…it was borderline pained.

"I don't want you drinking under my roof. You're under twenty-one."

"I'm eighteen. Any other place in the world—virtually all over Europe—I'd be allowed to get shit-faced wherever I want."

"We're not in Europe," I reminded him.

"We will be, one day. Together." His bizarre statement came out so confident, I almost doubled over.

Okay, then. Back to the subject, I guess. "I'm a daredevil." I cocked a brow, laughing mainly to hide my embarrassment at how nervous I was.

"Real daredevils choose the truth. It's always more challenging than a dare." His right eye twitched. "So…truth or dare?"

"Dare," I teased, hoping to lighten the tension. Wherever this conversation was leading, it was going to be a raw, dangerous place for the both of us.

Jaime dipped his chin down and ran his thumb over his lower lip, his playful self peeking from the wall of graveness he had built around him tonight. "I dare you to look me in the eye and tell me you don't have feelings for me."

His words were simple yet his request—impossible.

I blinked, realizing for the first time that the answer to his question was something I wasn't ready to face. "Truth," I said and swallowed painfully.

Jaime tipped his head back and laughed. It sounded gruff and unhappy.

I looked away, feeling my face whitening. "What? I'm allowed to change my mind."

"You're not." He reached for me, brushing his thumb over my cheek. "Tell me what you feel." His tone had changed to cushion-soft.

"Why?" I whispered, resisting the urge to close my eyes. If I did, a tear would escape. I never cried. Not since the accident in NY. I dealt. *Damn you, Jaime Followhill. I dealt.*

Jaime thumbed my chin, tilting my face to meet his gaze. Slowly, he brought his forehead to mine and closed his eyes, releasing a defeated breath. "Because I feel it too."

I wanted him to kiss me. To kiss me hard and soft all at once, a kiss that'd assure me that I wasn't crazy for discovering what I'd just discovered on this tattered sofa in this tiny apartment.

That I was in love with my student.

I'd tried to convince myself that it was just sex. It wasn't. It was pizza nights and laughing under my cheap, itchy blanket and nicknaming each other stupid names. I was Little Ballerina, while he was Giraffe Tongue, for reasons that gave me countless orgasms.

It was watching Tarantino movies and stealing breathless kisses at school, two thieves of pleasure, begging to confess their crime. I was spellbound, desperate, and possessed. And I knew with certainty that once he graduated and moved away for college, the blow would be just as hard as my subway accident.

Dancing *was* my life.

But Jaime? *Jaime is my life,* I realized.

He took a swig of the tequila, screwed the top back on, and jerked me into him, holding the back of my neck to bring my lips to his.

"Ask me." His alcohol-fumed breath oozed into my mouth.

"Truth or dare?"

"Truth. And it's gonna be ugly. Buckle up." He let me go, pushing away, his eyes fluttering shut. Frustration and hurt radiated from his face, and he slouched on the couch, looking almost defeated. This was not the Jaime I knew. The devil with the panty-dropping smile.

Worry gnawed at my gut.

"The first time I saw you," he began, "I wanted to slap my name on your ass, let everyone know that I was going to be the only guy to tap that shit. You looked like a princess, Mel. An insanely hot princess with perfect posture and unruly curls." He smirked. "Course, acting on it was out of the question. A fantasy. Then I came home that first day of my senior year, and Mom wouldn't shut up about you. *Melody this* and *Melody that*. How bad you were at your job, how you were gonna ruin Mr. Pitterman's legacy, blah blah bullshit blah. She hated your guts. Gave you the job only because he croaked so suddenly."

He was telling me things that I already knew, but it didn't make them any less painful. The previous Lit teacher had died of a heart attack two days before school started. Principal Followhill had needed to act fast.

"You became a favorite topic at our dinner table. She loathed your ass." Jaime took a sip, wincing from the bite of the tequila. "You were pretty and young and completely unimpressed by her power and the status and stinking money that runs our fucked-up little town." He spoke with his eyes squeezed shut. Embarrassed, probably for the first time in his life. "You were a good teacher. That's why I never gave you shit. It wasn't your fault we were a bunch of privileged assholes."

I placed my hand on his arm. He drank some more.

Your pain is mine, and I want to shoulder it because I can. Because that's what I do. I carry my pain all the time. Let me take away yours, my touch begged him.

"I told Mom to shut her trap numerous times. Not because I wanted to defend you but because gossiping about you was feeding a monster inside me. Talking about you only made it harder for me to ignore you. So fucking hot…" He nodded his head and bit his full lip, eyes still closed. "When I heard how you had to drop out of

Juilliard, I wanted to die for you. I had a feeling teaching wasn't your calling. I kept thinking about eighteen-year-old you. My age. Your heart broken by bad luck, shattered by an accident that'd left more than a physical scar."

I shifted on my small couch. It felt smaller with every word he said. My gaze traveled down to my hands. I was flattered. I was horrified. But most of all, I was confused. "You were thinking about me for the whole year?"

He snorted a sad laugh.

"More than thinking. Six weeks after school started, I had a huge fight with my mom. Coach Rowland was giving Trent shit about breaking his ankle. Like he planned to get hurt and fuck up his whole football future. We finally stood up for Trent against Coach, but Mom defended Rowland. My fight with her left me so frustrated, I gave in to my weakness for you. I followed you to your apartment, tried to steal a private peek through your bedroom window. I don't know why I did that. It was like drinking fucking Emergen-C. I just wanted to take the edge off."

Jaime opened his eyes, his blues challenging me. "You were the perfect sin to commit, Melody. Begging to be taken. Untouched by the rest of Todos Santos's posing and entitlement. I got hooked. From that day on, I followed you everywhere like an eager puppy. To the supermarket, the gas station…the fucking park every morning before practice, where I watched you doing yoga positions and tried not to rub a quick one out behind a tree. I followed you on blind dates, and when I realized you'd never met the idiots before, I also found your dating account and opened a profile under a fake name just so I could stalk you better."

My hand shook as I slapped it over my mouth. None of this sounded like the guy I'd dated. I mean screwed. No, wait, dated. Definitely dated. In the last ten minutes, this relationship had moved faster than a sprinter at an all-you-can-eat pasta buffet.

Another swig. Another deep breath. Another thorn in my heart.

Jaime was treading closer to shit-faced territory with every truth that rolled out of his mouth.

"I'm listening," I prompted, afraid that he'd clam up on me.

"Three months ago, I caught my mother cheating on my father with Coach Rowland. In my bed."

I wheezed. We were running barefoot in a minefield of emotions, and Jaime had just exploded an IED under my legs.

Jaime's dad had never bothered to hop on the gossip train traveling through Todos Santos. I didn't know much about him. Only that he was known as a philanthropist who worked with several big charities and that, despite his privileged lineage, he wasn't too interested in glitz and glamour.

"I don't know which part was worse. That she let Coach emotionally abuse Trent for years or that she was fucking the bastard in my bed. I'd like to believe the location was just convenient. My bed always smelled like sex anyway and was never made." His eyes glistened with pain.

I wrapped my arms around his neck.

Jaime spoke into my hair, his chin pressed to my shoulder. "Fucking someone who she hated sounded like good therapy. So I started planning, and you and I began talking more on that dating site. You opened up to me. Told me what you liked and disliked. Your taste in music. Favorite movies. Dream vacations, layer after layer peeled. And when it was time to strike—I set up a date. I was the loser guy who still lived with his mom at twenty-six."

Bastard.

I laughed. He laughed. Then I grew silent and started crying. Damn hormones. He wiped my cheeks and offered me the tequila. I snatched it from him and took a swig. Everything was a mess.

"You're a real asshole, Jaime."

Jaime rubbed his head, mussing his glorious man-bun. "The text message you got when you backed out of your parking space? Planned. The reason you bumped into me? I set you up, Mel. The text was a deliberate distraction. A trap. But you know what the worst part is?"

I shook my head, feeling my tears, hot and angry, running down my face.

He stared at me through red-rimmed eyes. He didn't shed tears, but I knew that he was holding them back. "Somewhere between the quest of wanting to fuck you and secretly rebelling against my mom, I fell in love with you. It wasn't a beautiful process. Hell…" He laughed, rubbing the back of his neck. "It wasn't even romantic. But it happened. Because you're strong but vulnerable. Witty as fuck but not bitter or deliberately mean. Because I had to chase your ass to nail you down and you still keep me on my toes. But if we're going to keep going on like this, where I have to convince you to give me the time of day while you look over your shoulder, constantly trying to shake me off, I need to bail out of this before I get hurt."

He took my cheeks and dragged my face to meet his. "Men with big cocks have fragile hearts. You know the saying: big cock, big heart. Well, I'm proof it's true."

I let out a breathless chuckle. Our noses brushed, and I sucked in a breath. A moment of silence ticked by.

"So…are you mine, Melody?"

Was I? Yeah. Without a shadow of a doubt, I was. God, were we really going to do this?

I nodded, sniffling with my runny nose. "No one else's." I pursed my lips, already tasting the saltiness of the grief that accompanied this statement.

Our lips crushed together, needy and demanding. I wasn't mad. I wasn't freaked out. For the first time in ages, I was just…content.

A foreign feeling I wanted more of. A drug I would later get addicted to.

"You need to go back to dancing," Jaime said through noisy, sloppy kisses. "Your leg's fine now."

"I'm twenty-six." I sniffed, more tears falling, but we were still kissing. "That's one hundred and eighty-two in dog years and, like, two hundred and two in ballerina years."

"Then settle for something outside of a ballet company, granny. *Teach.*"

Finally, I pulled away from his face, sucking in a breath. I tapped my lower lip. "The dance studio here is owned by a friend of your mother."

"So find a studio in San Diego. It's only a thirty-minute drive. You can fulfill your dream and still live close to me."

Whoa, what? This caught me off guard. My eyebrows knitted, and I searched his face. "Jaime, you're moving to Texas. You're going to college there. You have a great future planned."

He held my gaze, ignoring my words completely. "You could even teach ballet in LA. Vicious is going to college there. If he can get in, so can I."

I wondered if he was drunk or just crazy. He sounded like both. "Vicious isn't the greatest role model. He's just taking a little break until he burns this town down. You and I both know that."

Jaime shook his head, a sad smile on his face. "Even if he does, I'd help him light the match. The HotHoles stick together. That's who we are." He laced his fingers through mine.

"You're not staying here," I stated. Even though, selfishly, I didn't want him to move away. Moreover, the very thought of him living in Texas, far away from me, made my skin crawl.

"Bull. Shit. I'm staying where the only people I care about are. You. Vicious. Trent. Dean might even be staying if Vicious doesn't kill him…" He broke off.

"In Defy?" I prodded.

"Not that. It's more complicated."

I shook my head. As much as I liked having him around, it was in his best interest to leave. This place was hell. The city of saints was filled with nothing but sinners. He'd already been corrupted but not beyond repair.

"No." I made my voice firmer, trying to use that authoritative-teacher tone my parents were so good at. "You said you love me. If you do, then promise me you'll leave here before you get hurt. And no more Defy." *People have probably already been hurt,* I thought. "Go away, James."

"Can't." He brought my hands to his lips, kissing my knuckles one by one. "I'm not leaving you here or anywhere else. Hey, I never wanted to go to college in Texas anyway. You know how dangerous it is to look this good on a campus that big? I could get fucking roofied, Ms. G."

He winked. I laughed, but it died quickly.

"Then at least promise me you'll keep Vicious away from Millie?" I sighed. I wanted her safe, for the same reason I wanted me to be safe. She was my mini-me. Before I was broken, anyway.

"He'll never stay away from her." Jaime's expression grew tight. "For one, he wants to ruin her. And two? She lives too close. Her parents work for the Spencers."

I'd suspected she was the complication he mentioned, and now he'd confirmed it. She was a good distraction for us too. This wasn't the right time to talk about our plans as a couple. Jaime was too drunk. Too emotional to think clearly.

We both were.

But deep down, my truths were already starting to dig their way out of my layers of indifference. And they told me it wasn't about the alcohol or the late hour or the inconvenient talks about the future.

It was about us. It *was* us.

CHAPTER TEN

The next day, I woke up different.

I don't know how it happened, but it did, and it was all Jaime's fault. That emptiness that swirled in my gut like a storm, refusing to calm down despite my best efforts? It wasn't there the next day.

After the accident that ended my studying at Juilliard, I thought I'd never escape that empty feeling. Surely, when your future career and dreams consumed you, chased you around like bitter memories that nipped at your skin every time you saw a picture of a ballerina or heard about a traveling company in town, you couldn't come back from it and find something else to fill the void.

That void.

Logically, I'd assumed that I was probably going to meet a guy. Get married. Start a life. I still had things to do and accomplish, and some of them might even be fun. I thought that maybe I'd find my calling elsewhere. Not teaching high school Lit, but maybe with my kids? I could probably be a good mom. A soccer mom. Live through my children.

But the next morning, when I woke up in the arms of my student, he didn't feel like my student. He felt like my mentor. Like a man who knew the way to that slippery, elusive thing called happiness.

Not just physically. The way his hard muscles and long body enveloped me. The fact that he was so tall and wide made me feel protected and cherished. It was his warmth—not the one from his skin, the one from who he was—that filled me with something that wasn't emptiness.

"This is the part where you run away from this, Mel," he whispered into my ear, his morning voice gruff and his morning wood hard against my lower back.

We were spooning, and I couldn't smell his morning breath, but I bet it wasn't as bad as the average person's. The guy was just annoyingly perfect.

"Run, Ms. Greene. As fast as you'd like. I'm going to catch you, and I'm going to have fun showing you that there's no escape from this."

I rolled around to face him, the space between us warm from sleeping together in my new place. I grinned, a smile that wasn't controlled or calculated.

He yanked my hand from under the covers and pressed my fingers to his full lips. "Shit, Ms. Greene got brave."

"I'm about to get braver and offer you breakfast." I didn't know what I was saying or why I was saying it, but I knew I didn't want him gone. Not yet.

"You literally have nothing other than alcohol." Jaime laughed a throaty laugh, the type that left your mouth after you'd had a long night of sleep.

"I'll go out and get some groceries. You wait here." I gave him half a shrug.

"Or here's a better idea. I'll take you out to a local diner. Now what do you think?" He grabbed my waist and jerked me into his hot body, pressing his erection between my thighs.

I sighed, my teeth sinking into my bottom lip until I almost bled. How could I be so sexually frustrated every time he wasn't inside me? We'd obviously had a lot of sex.

"I think you're insane. People could spot us."

"We'll go somewhere outside of town. Maybe by the highway.

Stop being so paranoid. Todos Santos is full of old, rich white people. They don't venture farther than the city limits without a good reason. They're too scared of the unwashed masses in the outside world."

I let out a small chuckle. He was right, of course.

"We're playing a dangerous game here, Jaime," I warned.

"I don't know any other way to play it."

Another month ticked by. My relationship with Jaime became alarmingly intimate. He moved most of his stuff to my place and slept over 90 percent of the time. I couldn't tell him no after he'd confided in me about his mom and Coach Rowland. I didn't know many people who'd be eager to sleep on the same bed their mom used to cheat on her husband. But while we were enjoying more sex, more phone calls, more pizza nights, and more talks about our uncertain future—more, more, *more*—it was becoming evident that we were starting to raise people's eyebrows.

Vicious caught us red-handed, making out while hidden behind Jaime's SUV at Liberty Park after a midnight walk. (We only went out together when everyone else was fast asleep.) Vicious didn't look surprised. Just offered us his usual scowl, growling about how we grossed him out, and moved on, probably looking for a victim to murder that night. He kept his mouth shut.

But other people didn't. At school, girls were getting restless. Jaime wouldn't give them the time of day, and while he made up something about a girlfriend who lived in LA, nobody believed him. This HotHole in a steady relationship? A long-distance one too? *Pfft*. Yeah right.

One day, a cheerleader named Kadence went as far as following Jaime back to my apartment and reported back to the masses that he'd rented his own place. I was just glad that she didn't know the place was mine and that school was going to be over in few weeks.

But it was all too good to be true. The last week of school, I found that out.

It started with the innocent sound of a text message pinging in the dark, followed by an announcement.

"I'm going out," Jaime said.

It was half past midnight, and we were both snuggled up in bed. His mom thought he had moved in with Vicious, and Spencer confirmed the lie. Shockingly, his father and stepmother did too. This kid *did* rule everything around him, his parents included.

"Where to?" I breathed more of him into me, still clutching his waist. He got up, sat on the bed, and fired off a text message, avoiding eye contact.

"Don't." His voice was rough. Clipped.

I scooted up in bed, frowning. "Jaime, what's up?"

He groaned, pulling on a white tee over his bare chest. No matter how many times I'd seen him naked, it always made me feel a little sad when he covered those great abs. "Nothing's up. Last time I checked, it's not against the law to go hang out with your friends."

He had yet to look at me.

"Yeah." I grabbed his arm, prompting him to look at me. "But it is against the law to do half the shit Vicious makes you guys do. So it is my business."

"Actually"—he shook out of my touch, turning around and smiling tightly—"that's exactly why you aren't going to get shit from me. It'd only drag you into a pile of crap I'm not willing to pull you into. I'll be back later." He kissed my temple. "If you need anything, text."

"You've been Defied," I said dryly.

He ignored me, squatting down and tying his shoelaces.

"Vicious wants you to do something for him, huh?"

"Don't worry."

Like hell. "I'm nothing *but* worried," I gritted.

Petrified would be a better word to describe my feelings in that moment. Vicious always came up with stupid shit, and the HotHoles always played his dangerous games.

Watching him walk away stirred something in me I thought didn't exist anymore. Anger. Rage. Curiosity. I was tired of being led. Into relationships. Into situations. Tired of accepting everything that was handed to me—my broken dream, my broken leg, my half-assed career, and the job I hated.

I sat in bed, alert. I heard the quiet engine of the Range Rover purring outside, and that was my cue.

I threw some clothes on, slipped into my dented Ford and followed his vehicle all the way to the beach.

CHAPTER ELEVEN

There was no way I would be able to hide my car in the deserted parking area overlooking the marina, so I parked at a gas station on Main Street, near the water, and bolted straight into a convenience store. Its windows faced where Jaime had parked his Range Rover. A bell chimed above my head as I entered the deserted store, and faint Indian music greeted me from a staticky radio. A beautiful girl with long, black hair smiled from behind the cash register, her gaze returning to her book. Hiding inside the convenience store allowed me to watch Jaime without being caught. Considering Jaime was no stranger to stalking, I tried to downplay my actions, internally justifying myself.

My boyfriend left in the middle of the night without any explanation. I deserve answers.

I watched Jaime's large body through the glass door, jogging across the parking lot, as he approached Trent and Dean on the edge of the piers at the marina. Both men slapped each other's backs, talking animatedly before Jaime broke the circle. Then they strode up the wooden piers, where all the famous yachts of Todos Santos were docked.

The penny dropped and with it my heart. It wasn't a Defy fight. It was retaliation. It was cooking up revenge and making bad people pay.

Rowland.

The Rowlands had a restaurant on a big-ass boat, one of the most luxurious in SoCal, docked along one of the piers. It was their pride, joy, and main source of income. Hence, it was the sweet spot the HotHoles probably wanted to crush and eliminate from the earth.

Storming out of the convenience store, I ran toward the marina fast enough to leave a trail of smoke behind.

I wasn't completely opposed to Jaime staying in Todos Santos. The selfish (aka the biggest) part of my personality wanted him to stick around. I loved him and wanted to make gorgeous babies with him. (I wasn't crazy enough to utter this aloud. Then again, he was my stalker, so crazy was a language we were both fluent in.) But this was a whole different ball game—letting him do something insane that could permanently screw up his life. Even Baron Spencer and his peeps weren't above the law when it came to serious crimes.

And Vicious took his revenge very. Fucking. Seriously.

I ran across the skaters' ramp overlooking the marina and crept up the pier between two giant yachts. One of them belonged to the Spencers—*Marie*, after Vicious's late mother—and the other belonged to a Saudi tycoon who had a summer house in Todos Santos but never actually bothered to drop by, or so the rumor said. It allowed me a good angle on the boys, who, just as I suspected, stopped in front of *La Belle*, the Rowlands' boat and exclusive restaurant.

Trent fisted a five-gallon gasoline can while Dean spoke on the phone, his voice inaudible to me. Jaime produced his cell and looked to be typing up a text. A few moments later, my cell vibrated in my pocket. Luckily, I'd silenced it before I got here.

Jaime: Crashing @ Vic's 2nite. Don't wait up.

Fury flowed through my veins, sizzling and consuming. I knew why they were doing it. Jaime hated Coach Rowland for fucking his mom. Trent hated Coach Rowland for riding his ass when he broke his ankle during football season and his son for breaking it a second time. Vicious…he just hated everyone in general. And Dean? Dean looked like he loved everything and everyone in life, the player with the big, genuine smile, but I saw him. Saw below the perfect, shiny exterior. And what I saw wasn't pretty. Not by a long shot.

Regardless of how each of them viewed the retaliation, the HotHoles were like brothers. The reinjury to Trent's ankle—like my fall in the subway—was the final kiss of death to his football career. Someone had to pay for greasing the locker-room floor.

The Rowlands' money was the price.

The HotHoles waited on the pier beside *La Belle* until Vicious appeared at the top of the stairs leading down from the parking lot to the marina.

He wasn't alone.

Toby Rowland—gagged, bound by the wrists, and sweating like Danny Masterson in a confession booth—was standing next to him. There was a kidney-shaped urine stain over his groin. He didn't struggle, just glared at the ground, weeping silently.

Vicious was in full asshole mode that night. He descended the stairs behind Toby, pushing him one stair at a time, beaming like a groom on his wedding day. The marina was well lit, so it wasn't hard to catch him cracking his neck, his biceps flexing in anticipation.

"Look who's decided to join us." His voice was low, taunting. It sent chills down my spine. I sometimes wondered if Vicious's parents conceived him on Hitler's tombstone or if his mom had a freak accident involving poison and voodoo while she was pregnant. He was too scary for a teenager. Too dangerous for someone who grew up in pretentious luxury. *Too dead for a living human.*

Toby and Vicious stopped at the last stair, where Vicious pushed him headfirst to fall to the pier. Toby winced into the gag in his mouth, coughing. Jaime and Dean picked him up and tore the cloth from his face.

"Oh, man, your mouth is bleeding. Here, let me help." Jaime's hand reached toward Toby's face before he swung his arm back, throwing a punch from hell right into his nose.

Toby's head flew backward, landing against Vicious's chest.

Vicious clasped Toby's arms, hissing into his ear almost erotically, "Don't worry, I got you. I won't let them hurt you. No. I'm planning to do all the hurting myself."

Trent stepped forward and blocked my view with his broad back. All I saw were the three HotHoles' backs. Vicious and Toby were well hidden behind the other guys.

I heard Toby crying and whimpering, clomping his feet, begging, wailing, trying to break free. Then Dean stepped aside, allowing me a first glimpse at Toby's new face.

Bloated.

Bleeding.

Destroyed.

Seeing the welts—smelling the blood—in person felt so much worse than looking at them on a Monday morning. The four HotHoles were so troubled. Each had their own reason to be. I knew what ate at Jaime, but I didn't know why the others were so hell-bent on feeding and consuming so much pain.

Jaime was now grasping Toby's hair, pushing him down to his knees. Vicious slouched down to sit on a step, lighting a cigarette nonchalantly and pointing his Zippo at *La Belle*. His knuckles dripped blood, and his pale cheeks were flushed pink. Yet when he opened his mouth, calmness flowed out with every word.

"Nice boat your parents have. How many years have they put into that floating banquet room? Mom used to say your pasta tasted like stale balls."

Toby sighed in defeat, barely shaking his head, while Dean and Trent laughed.

"Okay, you're right. She didn't really say that. She wouldn't have known what stale balls taste like. But your mom does, right? Rowland is a nasty piece of fuck."

I was sure I saw Jaime's face twitch, but maybe it was because I was privy to his secret.

"Last words before we burn this beauty down?" Vicious puffed smoke, toying with his lighter.

"Please," Toby sniffed and coughed. "Just…please."

"You ruined my career," Trent said through a clenched jaw, fists tightening. "And didn't give me the option to beg for my leg before you greased the locker-room floor. Was it your dad's idea? Or did he just look the other way?"

"So s-s-s-sorry." Toby's words were drenched with red saliva.

Vicious stood up, slapping Trent's shoulder. "The kid says that he's sorry. Does that cut it?"

Trent shook his head slowly, eyes trained on Toby. Vicious swiveled to Toby and shrugged. "Apparently, sorry isn't gonna do it. Guess we're back to plan A."

Trent took a long stride toward *La Belle*, unscrewed the cap on the five-gallon can, and climbed the steps leading up to the yacht and the restaurant inside. The stench of gasoline filled the air. Vicious still played with his Zippo, thumbing it teasingly.

Light.

Out.

Light.

Out.

Light…

Normally the marina was patrolled regularly. I had no doubt the HotHoles had something to do with the absence of security. Trent poured gasoline from the restaurant's entry door along the wooden deck and back down the steps to the marina in a fuse-like line. After he threw the empty gas can into the water, he walked to Vicious's side and planted a hand on his shoulder with a little nod. This was Baron Spencer's cue.

"Goodbye, *La Belle*. You'll be missed…but not by us." Vicious chuckled darkly, flipping the lit Zippo toward the trail of gasoline.

A whoosh of flames erupted. Fire raced up the steps and across the deck to the restaurant door.

"Let's go!"

The boys turned around, holding Toby like a prisoner in both arms, and dragged him back to the parking lot. They made sure his face was toward the marina so he could see the destruction of his family's most precious possession. Flames leaped high, and black smoke engulfed the yacht in a choking hug.

I had to escape. To turn around and run away.

Why didn't you stop them, Mel? I knew the answer to that one. The retaliation was justified. The Rowlands deserved the HotHoles' wrath.

Running up the stairs, hysteria taking over my body as the heat of the fire licked at my legs, I heard the *clank* of something dropping behind me. I didn't have time to pick it up. Not even to turn around and check what it was. I fled the scene and bolted back to my apartment.

I locked the door. Twice. Took inventory: keys, phone, purse.

They were all there.

I sighed in relief and dragged my body down, my back against the door.

Safe. For now.

But then it occurred to me that I didn't care about my safety. Not as much as I cared about his.

I wasn't supposed to know where he was that night, but I couldn't help but text him, just to check that he's okay.

Me: Are you guys having fun?

Jaime: You bet we are. But I can't stop thinking about you.
Me: Is that why you left without explaining?
Jaime: Yes, Mel. That's exactly why I left without explaining. Because I think about you before I think about myself. Always remember that, Little Ballerina. Always.

CHAPTER TWELVE

"Ms. Greene. My office. Now."

Principal Followhill's face was thunder about to crack, and I knew she'd be unleashing a shitstorm on me the minute I stepped into her office. It didn't matter. It was only yesterday that I'd witnessed her son—my boyfriend—committing a serious crime. This was the last week of school, and I'd already started applying for positions at nearby schools for next year. She had no power over me anymore.

Or so I thought.

I walked into her office and closed the door, silently taking a seat.

"Straight to the point?" She leaned over her table, legs crossed. "Give me one good reason why I shouldn't call the cops and have you arrested right here on the premises."

My heart stopped, just like that. *What?*

"Excuse me?" My eyebrows shot up. My pulse vibrated between my ears.

Followhill tapped her shiny fingernail on her desk and shot me an insincere smile. "Let me refresh your memory—big fire. Burnt yacht. A devastated family. All happened yesterday. Now, again, Ms. Greene…" She leaned closer to me, whispering, "Give me one good reason not to call our beloved police chief?"

I took a deep breath, closing my eyes to gain strength. "Reason number one? Because I didn't do shit."

"Mr. Rowland and his son, Toby, don't seem to think so. They say you set fire to *La Belle* last night. Wanting to get back at the school's staff before you leave here. The family's restaurant is ruined." She cocked her head sideways, a smug smile spreading on her face.

Panic exploded in my veins, and my head became a jumbled mess of incoherent thoughts. I had so much to say and nothing at all to utter all at the same time, so I settled for "Huh?"

"I was skeptical too, at first. I said why would she? But then there was evidence." She slid her drawer open, producing a necklace. *My necklace*. Shit. That's what I dropped when I ran away last night. The silver anchor glittered between her fingers.

She tossed it to me, shaking her head. "And a motive too. I suppose you've heard Coach Rowland's sister, Chelsea, is going to take your position next year."

Actually, I had no idea, and I can't say I cared much either. At this point, I wouldn't have stayed in the job even if she'd offered me a seven-digit salary.

"Is that all you got?" I murmured, folding my arms over my chest. "People are still allowed to take a stroll in your town's precious marina. Doesn't make them guilty of burning down random yachts."

"Toby gave it to me this morning. He swears he saw you doing it."

I'd had it. I bolted up out of my chair and stared her down. "You know *exactly* who did it." Rage consumed every inch of my body, and I banged my fist against her desk. "And I get the feeling you know why too. This is blackmail." My lips twitched. "Twice in one semester," I added.

Principal Followhill stood up slowly, staring me in the eye. "You think I don't know you're sleeping with my son? Eyeing his fortune, his money, *his future*?" Her tone was low, and her intent was clear. "You're delusional if you think I'm letting you anywhere near my house and my money. Let him go to college, you little slut. Set him free."

Our chests were so close I could hear her breaths. The room was warm, but I was cold. Nothing felt right. Nothing.

"He is free," I sneered, shaking my head. "He chose me."

"Then don't give him the option," she gritted, fury making the muscles on her face twitch.

"Why? Because you said so?" Our faces were almost touching, too close for my liking, but I didn't back down. Our chests brushed, and I hated the scent of her Chanel No. 5 and expensive cosmetics in my nostrils.

"Because I have a lot of power in this town. Because what you're doing is wrong," she bit out, finishing on a whisper, "because no one can know this ever happened. Not to a family like the Followhills."

I was tempted to say she should remind herself of their reputation next time she jumped into bed with one of her staff, but that was Jaime's secret to tell, not mine. I would never out what he knew.

"Not scared of you or of getting kicked out of town," I retorted, only half doing it to push back at her. "Jaime was eighteen. This isn't illegal."

"But it's still forbidden," she yelled, throwing her hands in the air. I turned and moved for the door. She jerked me by the arm, making me slam to a halt. "Your teaching career will be over, and I'll make certain the *La Belle* arson sticks to you."

Her eyes ran over my face, mouth downturned in disgust. "My deal is off the table the minute you step out of this office. I'll call the police, Melody, and we all know who they work for."

Yes. The Spencers, who would stop at nothing to cover their son's ass. Just like Principal Followhill.

"You do that." I shook her away, fake smile and bravado plastered on my face. "See how it turns out."

I pivoted again, bolting to the door, but Jaime's mom—*my boyfriend's mom*—yanked me back into her office and shut it with a bang I was sure was audible to everyone in the hallway.

"Christ, what the hell is wrong with you? I'm giving you a

way out. Just leave my son alone, and I'll take care of the *La Belle* mess."

"I don't care what you do about that boat," I hissed into her face. My lips were trembling, and my nose stung. There was nothing I wanted more than to scream and tear her office apart. I had to stay collected for Jaime's sake and the future of my career outside All Saints High. "It's not *my* mess. Jaime courted me. Hell, Jaime manipulated me. Maybe he does have a bit of his mom in him after all. But the bottom line is we're together, and there's nothing you can do about it."

Those were the last words I told her before I managed to free myself from her grasp and get the hell out of there.

And those words would bite me in the ass later that day.

CHAPTER THIRTEEN

"Fuck," Jaime muttered, his arm extended above my shoulder, propped on the wall I was leaning against. He ran his other hand through his hair, frustrated.

I nodded, trying to regulate my breaths. He didn't have time to be mad, and he knew it. Rubbing his face and shaking his head, his gaze moved between me and the school building. We were tucked behind the concession stand at the football field, near the student parking lot.

"What the fuck, man? You *followed* me?"

"Hey, you knew where I live, where I work out, what I eat for breakfast, and my insurance carrier, all before we even kissed." I arched an eyebrow, reminding him that we were as bad as each other. At least when it came to one another. "She's got my necklace, and Toby says it was me."

"Of course he does." Jaime jerked me to him, squeezing me into a painful hug. "He'd never rat us out. The ball-less little dick. Your necklace was convenient. If he knew what you meant to me, he would've found another sorry ass to blame."

"Your mother doesn't make idle threats. She's got connections everywhere. And the Rowlands are powerful too. I'm a no one."

"Not true. You're my someone." He brushed his knuckles against my temple.

"I'm not going to jail," I stressed.

He shook his head. "Over my dead body, Little Ballerina. Let me talk to my mom."

"I'm not sure that's a good idea."

"I'm not sure I fucking care."

He left me, heading to his mother's office. At first, I stayed rooted in place, watching his broad back disappear behind the double doors of the school building. My fingers traveled to my naked collarbone, looking for my anchor, but it wasn't there.

Jaime was my anchor now. I had no one to trust but him.

A few minutes after he left, I walked to the teacher's lot and waited by my car, chewing on my nails. I was supposed to teach a class but had been excused for the rest of the day. I hated waiting for the verdict, for Jaime to try to persuade his mom not to frame me for something we all knew I didn't do.

Ten minutes after he walked into her office, my cell phone buzzed.

"Join us," he commanded in a tone I couldn't decode.

I did.

My knees wobbled and my breath sputtered as I walked the hallways of All Saints for what I had a feeling would be the last time. I knocked on Followhill's door and marched in.

"Come." Jaime patted a spot on the burgundy-leather sofa beside him, his eyes hard on his mom. He was sitting in front of her, and it looked like her desk was the only thing keeping them from pouncing at each other. The air was thick with revulsion.

Jaime's expression made my heart miss a beat. He looked about ready to commit capital murder. When I tried to read his mother's face, I didn't see love or compassion either. Just disappointment… and urgency. Urgency to keep a legacy, to protect her family name. To keep the pride, the money, and a lot of other tasteless shit in order.

My insides lurched, and for the first time, I realized I wasn't the only one who'd suffered destiny's wounds.

Just because Jaime didn't act like he'd been ripped to shreds didn't mean he was any happier than I was. No. We were both defective, chipped, and programmed to fight back. Sculpted by our fate. Scarred by who we were.

I was a dancer trapped in a teacher's life.

He was a free man imprisoned in his parents' ridiculous demands and great expectations.

I slouched next to Jaime, blinking away some of my shock. Fuck my life. Principal Miranda Followhill was the one in the wrong. But I did feel shame for caving into this affair with her son.

Shame over whom I fell in love with.

Because that was the problem with society. It cared too much about *whom* you fell in love with but never about the *why*. The why matters. The who is irrelevant (but the band was great, so there's that).

"We've reached an agreement." Mrs. Followhill's face tightened into a thin-lipped smile.

This didn't sound good. I nodded. Barely.

"And I think everyone shall benefit from this little arrangement."

Another beat of silence.

"Are you planning on announcing it at the LA Coliseum? Spit it out." I was no longer able to hide my true feelings for the woman.

Jaime snickered beside me, grabbing my hand and squeezing, his warmth seeping into me.

Mrs. Followhill scowled, unimpressed by my sass. "Jaime is going to move to Texas for college. In fact, he reconfirmed his attendance minutes ago on the phone with his dean. You will be let go after this school year. Your contract will not be renewed. You will not see each other anymore. In exchange, I will overlook the necklace found at the marina."

Her grin was victorious.

Yet all I saw was black.

My hand slid from Jaime's. Determined not to say anything, I fought the feeling of humiliation. He'd basically refused to fight for us, accepting her demand to go to Texas as he'd always planned. I simply shrugged. Whether he had shitty negotiation skills or he simply didn't care about me and was just using me didn't matter. His endgame was the same. And guess who was the loser? Yup, *me*.

Jaime could have easily told his mother the truth. His mother protected him. From anything. I wasn't naive enough to believe it was out of love. It was out of prestige and other meaningless things she cared about. Sure, she would give him hell, but she would also give him a way out.

He compromised me.

After he told me he wanted to protect me.

"Are you—have you spoken to the dean?" I jerked my head to look him in the eye.

He sucked his cheeks in with a heavy sigh, nodding. "Yeah. I'm moving to Austin."

"Sounds good to me."

"It does, huh?" Mrs. Followhill looked skeptical. Maybe even a little disappointed with my calmness. Her eyes glinted with ire, her lips thin and pressed together.

You can't win if I don't let you, I thought bitterly. *And I'm not. I'm not letting you see me break.*

"Yup. I mean, school's almost over. It was a nice fling." My lips curved into a smile, and I felt Jaime tensing beside me. I had a feeling there was a lot he wanted to explain. I wouldn't give him the chance though.

I hated him.

I hated *me*.

We deserved this heartache.

I felt his fingers trying to reconnect with mine and folded my arms over my chest, leaning back. I'd suffered enough whiplash from his mother. I was not going to be humiliated twice by getting dumped by her teenage son, listening to some "it's not you, it's me" bullshit.

"Guess it's time to say goodbye. I won't miss All Saints very much. And I definitely won't miss you, Mrs. Followhill. For a wealthy woman, your social skills are actually quite poor."

Translation: You're a bitch from hell, and I can't believe I actually thought your son would grow up to be any different. He obviously takes after you, even if he made me believe that he was anything but.

With that, I stood up. Jaime's gaze followed me, but I didn't risk looking at him. The confusion on his face was obvious, even if our eyes hadn't met. For the first time, I'd hurt a Followhill instead of having a Followhill hurt me. It made me feel lighter somehow, and that made me feel guilty.

Did I want Jaime to feel bad? *Why?*

"Melody." Jaime's voice was thick and dark.

I shook my head.

"Let her leave, sweetheart," Principal Followhill instructed, resting her palm on his back.

He stood abruptly from the sofa.

I needed to get out of there. "Yeah." I threw my bag over my shoulder. "We're done here."

I made my way out, leaving the boy-man who broke my heart and his bitchy mother behind me. He was moving to Texas. I shouldn't have been so disappointed. I pushed him in this direction. And his mom didn't leave us much choice. But I was hurt, so I'd stabbed him back with my words.

Jaime didn't follow me.

We'd both fucked up and had nothing to say to each other.

That day, I cried for all the years I hadn't cried. Buckets of tears. They were salty and sad and desperate.

They all tasted weird.

They all tasted like him.

CHAPTER FOURTEEN

Jaime didn't come to our apartment that day. He didn't call. Not surprising, considering I'd reduced him to a short fling. After continuously pushing him away. After telling him he should move to Texas. After bitching about his best friend.

I wasn't a good girlfriend.

Nurturing wasn't my nature. I was sewn together with tattered patches of consuming ambition and shattered dreams. Up until now, I had been stupidly proud of that. Proud that I didn't let mundane things like love or a man consume me.

But now, when my heart hurt like it was butchered into miniscule pieces, I realized what I was missing out on. Even the pain felt sweeter under the haze of love.

The next day, I showed up to teach Lit, and I was considering suicide halfway into my third class of the day. The warning had been lifted by Jaime, and my students no longer played nice with me. They laughed, screamed, and talked back. Even more than before, it seemed. My last hour was the worst. Dean and Millie were silent, but Trent Rexroth went the extra mile and fingered Charlize, who sat next to him, under his desk, all while keeping a straight face and talking about the future of the Raiders with Vicious extra-loudly.

Asking Trent to put his hands where I could see them only drew more attention to him and the chick he was making out with, and

I heard snickers when I turned my back to produce a book from my bag, probably because he shoved his tongue into her throat the minute he left my line of sight.

It was hell, and it was exactly where I deserved to be.

Jaime wasn't in class, even though it was the last time I would have taught him. It only confirmed what I already knew: Trent did what he did on purpose and on Jaime's behalf.

They all hated me.

My heart sank in disappointment. I tried to concentrate on teaching, but my mind kept drifting to him.

I'd fucked up.

I didn't even give him the chance to explain after the meeting with his mom. Just naturally assumed he'd betrayed me. But it was Jaime. Jaime never betrayed anyone. He stood by those he cared about. Even by Vicious…

Vicious.

When the bell rang, I rose from my seat, piercing Jaime's BFF with my eyes.

"Baron." I signaled him to come closer.

He snorted but did as I asked. The classroom had already emptied, leaving just the two of us sizing each other up suspiciously.

"Where's Jaime?" I asked, rubbing my tired eyes. I hadn't slept much the previous night.

"The fuck do you care?" He tucked a cigarette in his mouth, lighting it in class casually. "You keep tabs on all your *flings*?" he mumbled, the cigarette between his lips.

Someone was bitter.

"I need to talk to him," I said, ignoring the jab.

"Am I stopping you?"

"Tell me where he is."

He shrugged. "I'm not his goddamned secretary. Call him."

"He won't pick up," I cried in annoyance.

Vicious slid his thumb across his cheek with the hand that held his cigarette, deep in thought. "Yeah, he won't." His voice was chillingly flat. "He's at my house. Sulking like a little bitch. I'd invite you over to cheer him up, but I'm not sure if you wanna give him a lippy rant for saving your ass or a blow job for fucking up."

"I need to talk to him." The urgency in my voice scared me. The need to make this right was overwhelming. I just wanted us to work this out.

"I'm not him." Vicious's lifeless eyes held mine, sucking me in. "I don't do forgiveness, so if you hurt him again, the outcome will be devastating. To you."

Gulp. "I just want to fix this, Baron."

"My name is Vicious," he growled.

Goddammit. *This kid.*

"Let me see him. I promise, my intentions are good."

The HotHoles' brotherhood was almost touching, if it weren't for the fact that these boys had way too much power. Over me. Over this town. Over everyone.

Vicious tilted his head to the door, and I followed him to his brooding stone-and-brick mansion, my Ford stalking his Mercedes.

It was the longest journey I ever had to take, other than my flight back home from New York and Juilliard.

But it was the shortest trip to insanity. My love was madness.

And I was ready to fight for it.

CHAPTER FIFTEEN

He was in the pool. In the goddamn fucking pool. Doing laps. His long, lean sculpted body shooting like an arrow from one end to the other. I stood over the edge, not sure if I wanted to jump his bones, apologize, or yell at him. When he raised his head from the azure waterline, dark-blond locks raining water drops over his perfect face, my thighs clenched.

"You look heartbroken," I assessed sarcastically.

He rested his arms on the tiles and flashed me his straight teeth. But this wasn't a smile, it was a warning. "And you look like an animal out of its natural habitat. Missed me that much, Ms. G?"

"You didn't come to school today." My voice was grave.

"So? School year is practically over, and it's not like you give a shit. I'm just a fling, remember? Your words."

Touché.

When I arrived here, I hadn't been above begging. But now that I was in front of him, at Vicious's house, an overwhelming need to protect myself took over again. I couldn't ask him what his game was yesterday when we were at his mother's office.

"So you're all packed for Texas?" I changed the subject. *He's moving away to college*, I reminded myself. *This is over.*

He laughed, pushing himself upward and rising from the pool. His sculpted body shone under the sun, making him look like a

Calvin Klein ad. He stood next to me, so close the scent of chlorine wafted into my nostrils.

"Not yet." He took a step in my direction. I stumbled back. He took another step closer, ignoring me. "I need to buy another suitcase." His hand disappeared inside my curls. This time I leaned into his touch. *Such a loser. Already a goner again.*

"I thought men traveled light." I swallowed.

"We do, but I'm sure you'll be taking all kinds of girly shit with you when you move in with me."

Dumbfounded, I narrowed my eyes at him, fighting a grin.

"Jaime," I warned. From what, I wasn't sure. I didn't want it to be a prank. I realized as soon as he said the words that I wanted exactly what he'd just said. A lot. A new beginning. Away from All Saints High. With him.

It didn't make sense. It was wrong. It was going to lift a shit ton of eyebrows. A college kid moving to another state with his twenty-six-year-old teacher? It had disaster written all over it. But I wanted this disaster. I wanted to bathe in it and love it and *live* it. To make this disaster my chaotic reality.

"Mel," he answered, smiling. "Truth or dare?"

"Truth." I bit my lower lip, peeking at him from under my lashes. If Vicious saw this, he would have probably puked.

My breaths were coming in shallow pants. My heart was in my throat. I hadn't felt this alive since the last time I was onstage. I was going to say it, and fuck the world and what it'd think about me.

I placed my hands on top of his, still nestled in my hair, holding me still. "The truth is…I love you."

There was a hint of a satisfied smile, but it was quick. Like I was still in trouble. I felt like the scolded student.

He nodded, his wet hair dripping on my face as he hooked an arm around my neck and jerked me into his embrace. "See? Was that so hard? Still in one piece, aren't you, baby girl?" He raised an eyebrow at me in a smart-ass expression, and it was sexy as fuck. "I love you too, Mel. Fucking crazy about you, actually. Now pack up." He bit my lip playfully, smacking my ass at the exact same time.

"Excuse me?" I laughed. "What? Where? How? When? School's not even over yet."

There were four more days left of school. And I still hadn't said yes to moving to a whole other state with him.

"Yeah, but you have a job interview at a ballet academy in Austin tomorrow. Don't wanna be late, yeah? Bad first impression and all."

Jaime knew. He knew I had pocketed this dream in the back of my jeans but still danced every day in front of the mirror. That I carried it in my heart like a little souvenir and that I wanted the memory to become something real, now more than ever.

Just then, a horn honked in the distance, and I heard Vicious say behind his fancy Mercedes steering wheel, "Tell her to move her ass, or I'm sending you both to the airport in a cab."

These high school kids.

They had planned it all along.

They outsmarted Mrs. Followhill and me.

I laughed, collapsing into my boyfriend's arms. "Damn you."

EPILOGUE

TWO YEARS LATER

"You forgot the milk."

"You forgot your underwear."

I frown, pushing down my black tights. "I'm wearing underwear."

"Exactly." Jaime pushes me to the bed in one effortless movement.

I collapse onto our flimsy mattress. He follows, crushing on top of me, covering my face and neck with wet, hot kisses. Breathless giggles escape my mouth while his fingers push my tights away.

"I'll buy some on my way back from my shift," Jaime growls into my rib cage.

My shirt is already tossed aside, and he is sucking on my nipple so hard my skull prickles in pleasure. I sigh and rake my fingers through his tousled blond hair. He's been taking shifts at a local Starbucks after class. His parents cut him off after we announced we were moving in together. Tough luck. With my work at the ballet academy, his school and Starbucks job, and everything else on our plate, we have very little time to give two shits about what other people think or say.

"Can you get some fruit as well? We're out of bananas."

"There's one banana you can eat whenever you want, and it's right here." He takes my hand, guiding it to his cock.

I roll my eyes. Yup, still a typical twenty-year-old. I'm twenty-eight now, and you'd think I'd be obsessing over marriage and babies. But I'm not. All I think about is him. How it worked out so fabulously. It's our beautiful chaos, and we wouldn't have it any other way.

"I might take a bite later," I tease.

He winces. "Fine, I'll get you your stupid fruit, woman."

His tongue travels down from my stomach to my now-bare pussy, and he halts, his nose rubbing circles against my clit. "Oh, I think you have something here. Like a scratch or a spot or something." His hand dives between my legs, and when it rises back up, there's a small black velvet box in his hand.

I stop breathing altogether.

He licks his lips, offering a lazy smile. "I probably should warn you, it's not an engagement ring. I'm waiting to turn twenty-one so the trust fund my grandparents have under my name will kick in. I'll be richer and Starbucks-free. You deserve something incredible. But in the meantime, here's something to make you remember your high school fling from two years ago."

With shaky fingers, I open the velvet box, and inside rests a necklace. With a charm. A golden anchor. This anchor symbolizing so many things.

The burnt yacht that ripped us apart.

The necklace that brought us back together.

The missing piece I left behind.

My eyes glide up, piercing him with uncontained love. I'm so in love. So completely out-of-my-mind crazy about this boy who grew up to be a man and has given up so many things to be with me. Inheritance. College party life. Things that were his very essence of being two years ago.

"Help me?" I motion with the necklace between my fingers.

He grunts at my request for him to unglue his tongue from my inner thigh but rises to face me. Taking the necklace from my hand, he brushes my hair aside.

"Truth or dare?" he asks out of nowhere.

"Truth. Brave people always choose the truth." I grin.

"Is it true that you'll always be mine?" He lowers his mouth to my ear, his warm breath tickling my skin.

"It's a truth. And sometimes, when you piss me off, it's a dare. But it's my life, and you're a part of it. Always and forever," I say.

"Always and forever," he repeats, and I hold on to my anchor, squeezing it—and my real-life anchor—hard.

The angst. The fear. The part where I let myself go and fell in love with who should've been the wrong person but who turned out to be right, so right…it's all behind us now.

In the end, it was worth it. Every small piece of which made us who we are today.

Stronger.

Happier.

More whole.

JAIME

SIX YEARS LATER

"Why the anchor?"

I probably should have asked that eight years ago, when we first met, but I just couldn't bring myself to do it. I considered it pillow talk, and I was feeling pretty fucking frightened as it was about stalking my Lit teacher.

I'm watching my wife, Melody Followhill, intently as she rests her feet on top of the coffee table while leaning back on our new couch. The sofa and the table are the only pieces of furniture in our new Kensington apartment—or "flat," as they call it here in London. I said I'd take her to Europe, and I did. The fact I knocked her up here is just a bonus.

You're welcome, Mel.

"Why the anchor?" she parrots me, grinning as she rubs her thirty-six-week belly, staring at it lovingly as if she can already see our newborn daughter. "Because sometimes, it's nice to feel like there's someone who can save you."

"Who gave you that necklace?" I shoot. The urgency of my questions startles me. I've lasted eight years without asking her that, and suddenly, that's all I want to know about. Melody leans into me, placing her head on my chest. I brush her brown hair from her face and kiss her temple. When she talks, warmth fills my chest.

"I bought it for myself. I was at JFK Airport, just about to board the plane back to California after breaking my leg. I wanted something to believe in. More like *someone* to believe in. I had no one. My parents were supportive and sad for me, but they didn't understand. Not really. My friends were scattered all around the country, chasing their own college dreams, creating new, sweet memories. And there I was. Alone. I needed something. I saw this necklace at a store. I don't even remember the name. It sold hoodies saying 'I Heart New York' for ridiculous prices. It cost me a lot, but I remember thinking to myself, *I need this. I'm going to get this.*"

I look down, staring at her eyes, and I'm amazed. Amazed that this woman is mine. After all we've been through—and maybe precisely because of that.

She is funny and strong. So fucking talented, sarcastic, and smart. But at the same time, she is real. And vulnerable. And mine. God, so fucking mine.

"You don't need it anymore." I finger the anchor necklace I gave her when I was in college. "You have me."

"I need both." She smiles, kissing my pecs through my shirt.

She is wrong.

She doesn't need anybody.

She can conquer the world, in her sensible shoes and knee-length dresses, not giving a damn about what anyone thinks.

I take her hand, kiss her palm, and guide it to my raging erection. I'm always hard for this woman. Always.

"You mean the three of us?" I grin into her lips, and she clutches my jeans, a little too hard for my liking.

"You know what I need?" she asks, and for some reason, there's sweat coating her beautiful forehead.

I cock one eyebrow.

"I need you to drive me to the hospital. My water just broke."

"I knew you were wet for me." I lick her neck, and she punches my arm. Hard.

"Jaime!"

"Okay, okay, I'll grab your bag."

Fifteen hours later, Melody and I welcome our first daughter, Daria Sophia Followhill. My parents are boarding a plane from San Diego to see her. They're excited. Mel's parents are coming too, at the end of the month.

My father still doesn't know about Mom and Coach Rowland. I never told him. There was never much point.

He doesn't love her, and she doesn't love him.

They have so much money. So much means. And here I am, with a wife and a new baby, still cut off from their fortune because of the choices I took.

And I'm happy because I don't need money. I have my girls, and that's enough.

It. Is. Everything.

READ ON FOR A SNEAK PEEK OF THE SECOND BOOK IN THE SINNERS OF SAINT SERIES

PROLOGUE
ROSIE

I should probably get one thing out of the way before we begin. My story? It doesn't have a happy ending. It won't. It can't. No matter how tall or handsome or rich and captivating my Prince Charming might be.

And my Prince Charming was all those things. Oh, he was all those things and more.

Only problem was he wasn't really mine. He was my sister's. But there is something you should know before you judge me.

I saw him first. I craved him first. I *loved* him first.

All that didn't matter when Dean "Ruckus" Cole had his lips on my sister's in front of my eyes the day Vicious broke into her locker.

The thing about these moments is you never quite know whether they are the beginning or the end. The fluidity of life stops, and you're forced to examine your reality. Reality sucks. Trust me, I know firsthand just how hard it does.

Life ain't fair.

Daddy said it right when I hit sixteen and wanted to start dating. His answer was resolute. "Good Lord, no."

"Why not?" My eyelid ticked with annoyance. "Millie dated when she was sixteen." It was true. She went on four dates with our mailman's son, Eric, back in Virginia. Daddy snorted and wagged his index finger at me. *Nice try.*

"You're not your sister."

"What does that mean?"

"You know what it means."

"No, I don't." *I did know.*

"It means you have something she doesn't. It's not fair, but life ain't fair."

Another fact I couldn't argue with. Daddy said I was a magnet for the wrong kind of boys, but that was like sugarcoating a ball of dirt and rusty nails. I understood the underlying concern he had made, I did, especially as I'd always been his little princess. *Rosie-bug.* The apple of his eye.

I was racy. It wasn't intentional. It was even, at times, an inconvenient liability. With thick lashes, cascading caramel hair, long milky legs, and downy lips so full they took over most of my face. Everything else about me was small and ripe—wrapped in a red-satin bow with a siren expression that seemed to have been permanently inked on my face, no matter how hard I tried to wipe it off.

I attracted attention. The best kind. The worst kind. Hell, every kind.

There were going to be other boys, I tried to convince myself when Dean's and Emilia's lips touched and my heart shriveled in my chest. But there was always going to be one Millie.

Besides, my sister deserved it. Deserved *him*. I had Mama and Daddy's attention, all day, every day. I had plenty of friends at school and admirers lining up outside our door. All eyes were on me, while no one spared my sister a second glance.

It wasn't my fault, but that didn't make me feel any less guilty. My older sister had become the product of both my illness and popularity. A solitary teenager hiding behind a canvas, obscured behind paint. Quiet all the time, sending her message through her weird, eccentric clothes.

When I think about it, it was really for the best. The first day I noticed Dean Cole in the hallway between trig and English period, I knew that he was more than just a high school crush. If I had him, I wouldn't let go. And that in itself was a dangerous concept I couldn't afford toying with.

See, my clock was ticking faster. I wasn't born like the rest.

I had an illness.

Sometimes I conquered it.

Sometimes it conquered me.

Everyone's favorite Rose was wilting, but no flower wants to die in front of an audience.

It was better that way, I decided when her lips were on his and his eyes were on mine and reality became a complex, agonizing thing I was desperate to run away from.

And so I watched as my sister and the only guy who made my heart beat faster fall in love from my front-row seat.

My petals falling one by one.

Because even though I knew my story wouldn't end with a happily ever after, I couldn't help but wonder…could it have a happy ending, even if just momentarily?

DEAN

The summer when I turned seventeen was bad, but nothing prepared me for its fucking grand finale.

All arrows pointed to calamity. I couldn't isolate what path would lead me to it, but knowing my life, I braced myself for a sucker punch that'd send me straight to hell.

In the end, it all boiled down to one, reckless, movie-cliché moment. A few Bud Lights and sloppily rolled blunts weeks before our junior year was over.

We were lying by Vicious's kidney-shaped pool, drinking his dad's flat beer, knowing we could get away with it—Christ, with fucking everything—under Baron Spencer Senior's roof. There were girls. They were high. There weren't many things to do in Todos Santos, California, on the verge of summer break. Everything was scorching hot. The air heavy, the sun bloated, the grass yellow, and the youth bored with their problem-less, meaningless existence. We were too lazy to chase cheap thrills, so we looked for them while we were leisurely sprawled on pool floats the shape of donuts and flamingos and Italian-imported sunbathing chair lounges.

Vicious's parents weren't home—were they ever?—and everyone was counting on me to supply. Never one to disappoint, I brought over sweet hash and some Molly, which they greedily inhaled without even thanking me, let alone paying me back. They figured I was a rich, stoner bastard who needed more money like Pamela Anderson needed more tits, which was partially true. And I never sweated the small stuff anyway, so I let it slide.

One of the girls, a blondie named Georgia, flaunted her new Polaroid camera, which her dad had given her on their latest Palm Springs vacation. She took pictures of us boys—Jaime, Vicious, Trent, and myself—flaunting her assets in a little red bikini and clasping the freshly printed pictures between her teeth, handing them to us, mouth to mouth. Her tits spilled out of her small bikini top like overflowing toothpaste from a tube. I wanted to rub my dick between them and knew with certainty that I would by the end of that day.

"My, my, this one's going to be gooood." Georgia used an indefinite number of O's in the last word for emphasis. "Looking ubersexy, Cole," she purred when she caught me on camera pounding the remainder of the beer with a blunt clasped between my fingers and slamming the can on my hard thigh.

Click.

The evidence of my wrongdoing slid out of her camera with a provocative hiss, and she plucked it with her glossy lips, bending down and handing it to me. I bit it and shoved it into my swim trunks. Her eyes followed my hand as I nudged the elastic downward, revealing a straight line of light hair below my naval that invited her to the rest of the party. She swallowed. Visibly. Our eyes met, silently agreeing on a time and a place. Then someone cannonballed into the pool and splashed her, and she shook her head, chuckling breathlessly before skipping to her next art project, my best friend, Trent Rexroth.

Destroying the picture before I got home was always the plan. I blame the fucking Molly for forgetting. In the end, my mother found the photo. In the end, my father gave me one of his low-tone lectures that always seemed to eat my insides like arsenic. And in the very, very end? They made me spend my summer vacation with my fucking uncle, the one I really couldn't stand.

I knew better than to fight them about it. The last thing I needed was to stir shit and jeopardize my Harvard stint a year before I graduated. I'd worked hard for this future, for this life. It was splayed before me, in all of its rich, entitled, fucked-up, private-jets, timeshare, annual-Hamptons-vacation glory. That's the thing about life. When something good falls into your hands, you don't only hang on to the fucker, you clutch it so hard it almost breaks.

Just another lesson that I learned way too late into life.

Anyway, that's how I ended up flying to Alabama, burning two months on a fucking farm prior to my senior year.

Trent, Jaime, and Vicious spent their summer drinking, smoking, and fucking girls on their home field. Me, I came back with a shiner, generously gifted to me by Mr. Donald Whittaker, aka Owl, after the night that had changed who I was forever.

"Life is like justice," Eli Cole, my lawyer-slash-dad, had said to me before I boarded the plane to Birmingham. "It's not always fair."

Wasn't that the fucking truth.

That summer, I was forced to read the Bible cover to cover. Owl told my parents he was a born-again Christian and big on Bible studies. He backed it up by making me read it with him during our lunch breaks. Ham on rye and the Old Testament were his version of not being a dickface because he was pretty much horrible to me the rest of the time.

Whittaker was a farmhand. When he was sober enough to be anything, that was. He made me his barn boy. I agreed, mainly because I got to finger his neighbor's daughter at the end of every day.

The neighbor's daughter thought I was some kind of a celebrity just because I didn't have a Southern accent and owned a car. I wasn't one to crush her fantasy, especially as she was eager to be my sex ed student.

I humored Owl when he taught me the Bible because the alternative was brawling with him in the hay until one of us passed out. I think my folks wanted me to remember that life wasn't all about expensive cars and ski vacations. Owl and his wife were like *Low-Income Life 101*, so every morning I woke up asking myself what's two months in comparison to my whole fucking life?

There were a lot of crazy-ass stories in the Bible: incest, foreskin collection, Jacob wrestling an angel—I swear this book jumped the shark by the second chapter or so—but one story really stuck with me, even before I'd met Rosie LeBlanc.

Genesis 27. Jacob came to live with Laban, his uncle, and fell in love with Rachel, the younger of Laban's two daughters. Rachel was hot as fuck, fierce, graceful, and pretty much sex on a stick (as indicated in the Bible, though not in so many words).

Laban and Jacob struck a deal. Jacob was to work for Laban for seven years—then he could marry his daughter.

Jacob did as he was told—busting his ass under the sun, day in and day out. After those seven years, Laban finally came to Jacob and told him he could marry his daughter.

But here was the catch: it was not Rachel's hand he had given him. It was her older sister, Leah's.

Leah was a good woman. Jacob knew that.

She was nice. Sensible. Charitable. Cute ass and soft eyes. (Again, paraphrasing here. Other than the eyes part. That shit was actually in the Bible.)

She was no Rachel, though.

She was no Rachel, and he wanted Rachel. It was. Always. Fucking. Rachel.

Jacob argued, fought, and tried to talk some sense into his uncle, but in the end, he lost. Life was like justice, even back then. It was anything but fair.

"Seven more years of work," Laban promised. "And I'd let you marry Rachel, too."

So Jacob waited.

And lurked.

And *yearned*.

Which anyone with half a brain should know only gratifies your desperation for your subject of obsession.

Years ticked by. Slowly. Painfully. Numbly.

In the meantime, he was with Leah.

He didn't suffer. Not per se. Leah was good to him. A safe bet. She could bear his children—something Rachel, he would later find out, had difficulty doing.

He knew what he wanted, and it may have looked like her and may have smelled like her and, fuck—maybe even *felt* like her—but it was not her.

It took him fourteen years, but in the end, Jacob won Rachel fair and square.

Rachel might not have been blessed by God. Leah was. But here was the thing.

Rachel didn't need to be blessed.

She was loved.

And unlike justice and life, love *is* fair.

What's more? Eventually, love was enough.

Eventually, it was fucking everything.

Seven weeks into my senior year, another looming calamity had decided to blow up in my face in spectacular fashion. Her name was Rosie LeBlanc, and she had eyes like two frosted-over lakes in an Alaskan winter. *That* kind of blue.

The what-the-fuck moment grabbed me by the balls and twisted hard the second she opened the door to the servants' house on Vicious's lot. Because she wasn't Millie. She looked like Millie—kind of—only smaller, shorter, with fuller lips, higher cheekbones, and the little pointy ears of a mischievous pixie. But she didn't wear anything overtly weird like Millie. A pair of sea-starred flip-flops on her feet, black skinny jeans cut wide at the knees, and a tattered black hoodie with a name of a band I didn't know plastered in white. Designed to blend in, but, as I'd later find out, destined to shine like a motherfucking lighthouse.

Inferno-red hit her cheeks and crawled down the edge of her collar when our eyes tangled, and that told me everything I needed to know. She was new to me, but *I* was a familiar face. A face she studied, knew, and stared at. All the fucking time.

"Are we engaged in a secret staring competition?" Her recovery was immediate. There was something in the rasp of her voice that almost sounded unnatural. Too small. Too hoarse. Too uniquely her. "Because it's been twenty-three seconds since I opened the door and you haven't introduced yourself yet. Also, you blinked twice."

I had originally come there to ask Emilia LeBlanc on a date. She wouldn't give me her phone number. A hunter by nature, I was adequately patient to wait until she was close enough for me to pounce on, but it didn't hurt to check on my prey every once in a while. If we were being honest, though, pursuing Emilia wasn't really about Emilia. The thrill of the chase always made my balls tingle, and to me, she provided a challenge other chicks hadn't supplied. She was new meat, and I was an insatiable carnivore. But I wasn't expecting to find *this*.

This changed fucking everything.

I stood there like a mute and flashed my come-hither smirk,

taunting the shit out of Rosie, because on some level, she taunted the shit out of *me*. And it occurred to me that at that particular moment, maybe I wasn't the hunter. Maybe, for a split, flashing second, I was Elmer Fudd with an out-of-bullets gun in the woods who'd just spotted an angry tigress.

"Can it even talk?" The tigress's light eyebrows pulled together, and she leaned forward, poking me in the chest with her little claw. She'd called me *it*.

Ridiculing me. Undermining me. Fucking with me.

Wearing my best innocent expression (that shit was hard to begin with—I forgot what innocence was before my umbilical cord was thrown into the trash), I clamped my teeth beneath my lips and shook my head no.

"You can't talk?" She folded her arms and leaned against her doorframe, arching a skeptical brow.

I nodded yes, biting down a huge smile.

"That's bullshit. I saw you at school. Dean Cole. They call you Ruckus. Not only can you talk, but most of the time, you can't seem to shut up."

Fuck yeah, little pixie. Bottle that rage and save it for when I roll you between my sheets.

To understand my level of surprise, you first have to know that no girl had ever talked to me like this before. Not even Millie, and Millie seemed to be the only female student who was immune to my all-American, hot-jock, tear-your-panties-with-my-teeth charm. Hell, that's why I noticed her in the first place.

But as I said, plans change. It's not like we'd dated yet. I'd sniffed Millie's tail around school for a few weeks, debating whether she was worth pursuing, but now that I saw what I'd missed—this little firecracker—it was time to find warmth in her crazy flames.

I unleashed another dirty smirk. This particular one had landed me the nickname Ruckus in All Saints's hallways two years ago. Because I was. I was fucking chaos, brewing anarchy everywhere I went. Everyone knew that. Teachers, students, Principal Followhill, and even the local sheriff.

When you needed drugs—you came to me. When you needed a good party—you came to me. When you needed an amazing fuck, you came to me—and *on* me. And this was what my smirk—the one I'd been practicing since I was fucking five—said to the world.

If it's corrupted and dirty and fun—I'm all over it.

And this girl? She looked like a whole lotta fun to corrupt.

Her eyes traced my lips. Heavy. Wanting. Drunk. It was easy to read them. High school girls. Though this particular one didn't smile as wide as the rest. She didn't offer a silent invitation for flirtation either.

"You speak." She coughed her words accusingly. I sucked my lower lip and released it. Slow. Calculated. Teasing.

"Maybe I do know a few words after all." I got in her face on a hiss. "Wanna hear the interesting ones?" My eyes begged for me to slide down her body, but my brain told me to wait it out. I decided to listen to the latter.

I was relaxed.

I was cunning.

But for the first time in years, I had no idea what the fuck I was doing.

She gave me a lopsided grin that rendered me speechless. Shoving so many words into one single expression. Telling me that my attempt to butter her up left her sorely unimpressed. That she liked me—yes—and noticed me—sure—but that I was going to have to do better than casual, half-assed flirting to get there. Wherever it was, I was ready for the journey.

"Do I really?" She dallied, not even noticing as she did. I dipped my chin down, leaning forward. I was big, commanding, and confident. And I was trouble. She'd probably heard all about it, but if not, she was about to find that out.

"I think you do," I said.

Two minutes ago, I was determined to ask her sister out—older sister, I bet, this chick looked younger and, besides, I would have known if she was a senior—and lookie here, fate made her open the door and change my plans.

Baby LeBlanc sent me an odd look, challenging me to continue. Just as I opened my mouth, Millie galloped into my vision, sprinting toward the door from the small, stuffy living room like she was fleeing a war zone. She was clutching a textbook to her chest, her eyes puffy and red. She was staring straight at me, and for a second, I thought she was going to smack me across the face with the five-pound textbook.

In retrospect, I wish she had. It would have been far better than what she actually did.

Millie pushed the little pixie aside without even realizing that she was there, threw herself onto my chest—uncharacteristically affectionately—and pressed her lips to mine like a possessed demon.

Fuck.

This was bad.

Not the kiss. The kiss was fine, I guess. I didn't have time to process it because my eyes widened, darting to the spear-eared elf who looked horrified, her cornflower blues staring, processing, and boxing the three of us into something I wasn't ready to accept.

What the hell was Millie doing? A few hours ago she was still pretending not to notice me in the hallway, buying time, seeking space, faking indifference. Now she was all over me like a rash after a dodgy one-night stand.

Gently, I pulled away from Millie and cupped her cheeks so she wouldn't feel rejected, still making sure we had enough space to fit the little pixie between us. Emilia's proximity was unwelcome, and that was a fucking first when it came to a hot chick.

"Hey," I said. The body of my voice lost its usual playful tilt, even to my own ears. This wasn't like Millie. Something had happened, and I had a general idea who'd caused this little scene. My blood boiled. I breathed through my nostrils, determined not to lose my shit. "What's up, Mil?"

The emptiness in her eyes made me nauseous. I could almost hear the sound of her heart cracking inside her fucking chest. I chanced another glance at Baby LeBlanc, wondering how the hell I was supposed to walk out of this one. She took a step back, her eyes lingering on the hot mess express that was still trying to hug me. Millie was distraught. I couldn't deny her. Not then.

"Vicious," the older sister said through a loud sniff. "Vicious happened."

Then she pointed at the calculus textbook like it was evidence.

Reluctantly, my gaze drifted back to Emilia "Millie" LeBlanc.

"What'd the asswipe do?" I snatched the book from her hand and thumbed through the pages, looking for nasty comments or offensive drawings.

"He broke into my locker and stole it," she snuffled again. "Before stuffing said locker with condom wrappers and garbage." She wiped her nose with the back of her sleeve.

Jesus fucking Christ with this idiot. That was the other reason why I wanted to date Millie. The need to protect the strays had burned in me from a young age. A soft spot and all that bullshit. I wasn't *all* bad, like Vicious; neither was I *all* good, like Jaime. I had my own moral code, and bullying was a long, red line, drawn in blood.

See, as far as strays go, Millie was the perfect, shivering-in-the-rain fleabag in need of shelter. Terrorized at school and haunted by one of my best friends. I needed to do the right thing. I *needed* to, but fuck if I *wanted* to.

"I'll take care of him." I tried not to snap. "Go back inside."

And leave me with your sister.

"You don't need to, really. I'm just glad you're here."

I stole a glimpse at the girl who was destined to be the Rachel to my Jacob, this time longingly, because I knew I stood no chance with her the minute her sister kissed me to get back at fucking Vicious.

"I thought about it." Millie blinked fast, too caught up in her own mess to realize I had barely spared her a glance since she appeared at the door. Too busy to notice her sister was right fucking there beside us. "And I decided—why not? I'd love to date you, actually."

No, she wouldn't. What she wanted was for me to be her shield. Millie needed saving.

And I needed to smoke a fucking blunt.

I sighed, pulling the older sister into a hug, cupping the back of her head, the light-brown wisps of hair entwining between my fingers. My eyes still zoomed at Baby LeBlanc. At my little Rachel.

I'm going to make it right, my gaze promised her. It was clearly more optimistic than I was.

"You don't have to date me. I can make life easier for you, as your friend. Say the word and I'll kick his ass," I whispered into Millie's perfectly curved ear, my pupils honing in on her sister.

She shook her head, burying it deeper into my shoulder. "No, Dean. I want to date you. You're nice and fun and compassionate."

And completely in awe of your sister.

"Doubt it, Millie. You've been shutting me down for weeks. This is about Vic, and we both know it. Drink a glass of water. Rethink. I'll talk to him tomorrow morning at practice."

"Please, Dean." Her wobbly voice steadied as she balled the fabric of my designer tee in her fists, pulling me closer to her and away from my new, shiny fantasy at the same time. "I'm a big girl. I know what I'm doing. Let's go right now."

"Yeah. Go." I heard Baby LeBlanc rasp, waving her hand in our direction. "I need to study anyway, and you guys are a distraction. I'll drown Vicious's ass if I see him in the pool, Millie," she joked, pretending to flex her skinny arms.

Baby LeBlanc was a shitty student, with C minuses for miles, but I didn't know it back then. She didn't want to study. She wanted her sister to be saved.

I took Millie for an ice cream, this time not looking back.

I took Millie when I should have taken Rosie.

I took Millie, and I was going to kill Vicious.

ACKNOWLEDGMENTS

This book never would have happened if it wasn't for so many people. This is the part where I forget 40 percent of them, but I'm still going to do my best to cover the majority of strong, sassy, talented ladies who helped me every step of the way.

Sunny Borek. Seriously. This chick. One of my best friends and the only person who has the ability to drive me crazy and keep me sane at the very same time. Thank you for beta-reading *Vicious* time and time again. Thank you for loving him. For always being there when I needed you. But most of all, for being you.

My beta readers: Amy. Thank you for reading the story again and again, providing legal advice and making me laugh when I went through major meltdowns. Lilian, Paige, Josephine, Ilanit, Sabrina, Rebecca Graham, Ava Harrison, and Ella Fox. You're amazing. I appreciate your time, patience, and efforts so, so much. Each and every one of you brought something into this book that made it better in my opinion.

My street team members, to name a few: Julia Lis, Lin Tahel Cohen, Kristina Lindsey (who also took on managing my release and organized my release party because she's badass like that. Thank you for spending long, grueling hours on my marketing, fabulous woman!), Sonal, Jessica, Brittany, Sher, Tamar, Avivit, Tanaka, Oriana, and so many more. No matter where I go, you're there to support me. I'm the luckiest girl in the world to have you by my side.

Big thanks my professional team. (It was fun working on it, huh?)

(This is the part where I was about to thank my husband and my son, but then I remembered they were the very people who repeatedly begged for me to leave my office so I could fix them dinner/snack/watch TV/go out shopping with them. You don't deserve a thank-you, guys, but I still love you more than anything in the world.)

Huge-ass thank-you to all the bloggers who shared, pimped, promoted, and reviewed this book and my books in general. I don't know what I did right to deserve your attention. I just hope I'll always keep doing it, because you're gold. Each and every one of you—amazing. To my readers. Thank you for making my dream come true by purchasing my books. I wake up every day with a big smile on my face knowing that I make a living doing what I love and what I'm passionate about, and you make it happen.

Most of all, though, I'd like to thank anyone who's made it this far in the book. Whether you liked it or not, your review is always appreciated. Please consider leaving one before you move on to your next book adventure.

Love, hugs, and inappropriate glares,

L.J.

xoxo

ALSO BY L.J. SHEN

Sinners of Saint
Vicious
Ruckus
Scandalous
Bane

Forbidden Love
Truly Madly Deeply
Wildest Dreams